THE DESERTER'S DAUGHTER

by

Susanna Bavin

Magna Large Print Books
Long Preston, North Yorkshire,
BD23 4ND, England.

British Library Cataloguing in Publication Data.

A catalogue record of this book is
available from the British Library

ISBN   978-0-7505-4571-6

First published in Great Britain by Allison & Busby in 2017

Copyright © 2017 by Susanna Bavin

Cover design © Christina Griffiths
Cover illustration © iStock/Fotolia by arrangement with
Allison & Busby Ltd.

Published in Large Print 2018 by arrangement with
Allison & Busby Ltd.

Magna Large Print is an imprint of Library Magna Books Ltd.

Printed and bound in Great Britain by
T.J. (International) Ltd., Cornwall, PL28 8RW

THE DESERTER'S DAUGHTER

1920, Chorlton, Manchester. As her wedding day draws near, Carrie Jenkins is trying on her dress and eagerly anticipating becoming Mrs Billy Shipton. But all too soon she is reeling from the news that her beloved father was shot for desertion during the Great War. When Carrie is jilted and the close-knit community turns its back on her as well as her mother and her half-sister, Evadne, the plans Carrie nurtured are in disarray.

THE DESERTER'S DAUGHTER

*To the memory of Ronald Shires (1893–1976),
who in 1914 took a taxi to the docks
so as not to be late for the War.*

*And to Jen Gilroy, whose encouragement
and understanding kept me afloat.*

Chapter One

June 1920

'Carrie Jenkins! What in heaven's name is that you're wearing? Oh my goodness!'

Heat flared in Carrie's cheeks. She folded her plain shop dress in half longways and draped it over the footboard of the mahogany bedstead, trying to make it look as if her heart wasn't clattering like the holiday express to Southport. She forced a smile.

'Don't tek on, Mam. It's only a corset. It's the new fashion.'

'The new fashion for trollops!'

A sharp breath chilled her gullet. 'Mam! How could you?'

Mam clapped a hand over her mouth, work-worn fingers splaying across lined lips. Carrie tore her gaze away. She was outraged, of course she was, but she felt a thrill of fear too. With the curtains drawn for modesty's sake, the air in the bedroom the two of them shared was dense with heat, but was it the heat or her conscience making her flesh squeeze her bones?

'I'm sorry, Carrie. What a thing to say.'

The mattress dipped as Mam sank onto the pale-lemon candlewick bedspread as if her legs had given out with shock. Her face was slack with disappointment and Carrie felt an urge to plump

11

down beside her and wrap an arm round her, but Mam wouldn't want comfort from someone who looked like a trollop. Besides, standing on the other side of the bedstead, Carrie felt sheltered, half-hidden. To move around the bed to Mam would be like opening herself to public scrutiny.

Mam shook her head. 'I'm sorry, love. I shouldn't have called you that.'

Oh, not an apology. That made it worse. Not that she was a trollop, never that, but she wasn't a nice girl any more and hadn't been for some time. If Mam should guess, if just seeing the new corset Mam should guess, she would chase Carrie down Wilton Lane with the broom. No, she wouldn't. She would lock her in the cellar and not let her out till Saturday.

Saturday.

Her wedding day. And after that it wouldn't matter if she had been a nice girl or not, because she would be Mrs Billy Shipton. A floaty feeling permeated Carrie's limbs. Mrs Billy Shipton. She had known Billy was the boy for her ever since she first clocked him back when she was a lass of twelve, and now they were getting wed the day after tomorrow.

'How could you, Carrie? What was you thinking?'

'It's only a corset.'

'It's more than that. It's your reputation.'

'No one's going to know. No one's going to see.'

'They won't need to. They'll see summat else. A proper corset, a decent corset, one that comes up right under the bust where it's meant to, with all but the very top of your camisole tucked inside it, holds your cami in place and gives you some support. That – that thing you're wearing doesn't hold owt in place. You'll ... *jiggle*.'

'Oh, Mam, I've worn it all day and I haven't ... jiggled.'

At least she fervently hoped not. She had spent a self-conscious morning feeling hopelessly unfettered as she weighed sugar and currants and constructed a pyramid of Drummer Dyes boxes, all the while trying not to make unnecessary movements. But come the afternoon, when Trimble's was sweltering hot even with the door propped open, and the air was thick with the smell of wooden floorboards and tea leaves and lamp oil, and the customers were making shifty little movements that indicated they were trying to peel corsets from sweaty torsos, she had known herself to be the most comfortable person in the shop. More than comfortable: vindicated. Her new waist-high corset wasn't pure vanity after all. It was common sense too.

The mattress springs squealed as Mam bounced to her feet, her spine as straight as a poker. Her eyes were bright and she fizzed with energy, just like she used to before Pa died.

'We can't have Evadne seeing you like this, half-naked. She's a lady. You'd do well to tek a leaf out of her book, our Carrie.'

'*Mam,* will you stop it? There's nowt wrong with this corset. It's one of a range and Elizabeth's wouldn't stock a range if there wasn't a demand.'

'Elizabeth's? You bought that thing at the

knicker elastic shop?'

'You tell me and Letty off for calling it that. Anyroad, you know they sell undergarments.'

'Not like that, I didn't. Those two old biddies were born the same year as Queen Victoria, and they dress like it an' all.'

'Aye, but you don't know what they're wearing underneath, do you?'

'Carrie Jenkins! Fancy saying say that about your elders.' But Mam laughed and couldn't pretend she hadn't.

'I didn't buy it to be tarty.'

'I know, chick, and I'm sorry about the word I used. That were the shock speaking. But I still don't like it. It's not decent.'

'I got it because...' Carrie injected brightness into her tone. She refused to sound apologetic. 'You know the hours I spent embroidering my wedding camisole, and what a swine that sparkly thread was to work with. Well, I don't want to hide my cami under my old corset. I know no one's going to see it, but I want to feel special. I'm not a beauty like Evadne, but I want to feel special.'

'Oh, Carrie.'

Mam's face fell. Was she remembering all the times she had called Evadne the beauty of the family? That time Evadne stood in their kitchen looking demure in the smart brown tunic with the sashed waist that her posh Baxter grandparents bought for her when she started at the high school, and Pa said, 'Eh, you look reet bonny, lass,' and Mam, looking all swelled up, said, 'Evadne is the beauty of the family.' And the time new people moved in up the road and Mam had introduced them as, 'My lasses, Evadne and Carrie. Evadne is the beauty of the family.' Not, 'Evadne is the big one ... the older one,' even though, goodness knows, there was a whole eight years between them. Or even 'Evadne is the darker one,' because her hair was a wonderful reddy-brown like a conker, aye, and as glossy as a conker an' all, while Carrie's was fair, and not even proper fair at that. Dirty fair, Letty's mam called it.

'It's because Evadne was born a Baxter,' Mam had explained to the world and his wife, and that was all the explanation that was needed. As a child, Carrie had thought of them as the Beautiful Baxters, even though she had met Grandfather and Grandmother Baxter and they weren't raving beauties. Evadne's dad must have been a right bobby-dazzler.

In fairness to Mam, it wasn't just her. In those days, folks were falling over themselves to admire Evadne, and whenever they did, Mam would do that swelling-up thing and say, 'Evadne is the beauty of the family.' And no one had ever looked at Carrie and said, 'The little 'un is beautiful too.'

Not that she had noticed at the time. Back then, she had been the luckiest little lass in the whole world because all the other girls had only hopscotch and hoops and French skipping, while she had all those *and* she had Evadne to look at.

'I just don't want to hide my lovely new cami underneath my old corset – and if you aren't going to say summat kind, Mam, I'd rather you didn't say owt.'

Mam fluttered her hands. 'It's a nice colour. Pale pink.'

'Orchid.'

'You what?'

'Orchid. It said orchid on the box. The others said pink or cream. I thought orchid sounded a cut above.' She pulled a face. 'Turns out orchid means pale pink.'

All at once they were laughing, both of them, closeness restored, and things slid back to normal. Carrie hated being out of sorts with anyone. It wasn't her way. She wished she could get on better with Evadne, but she was long past being impressed by the Beautiful Baxter. Mind you, Evadne had asked to see her in her wedding dress today and that counted for a lot.

'Let's get you dressed,' said Mam.

Anticipation snaked through Carrie. The drawer glided open beneath her eager fingers and her hand hovered over her brand-new white stockings. The suspenders on her corset were made of pale pink (orchid!) satin ribbon with dainty satin rosettes. She glanced at Mam.

'Save the stockings for Saturday, chick. It's the dress Evadne's coming to see.'

Carrie pattered across the polished wooden floor. Her heart was pattering too. She was about to put on the wedding dress that she, Mam, Letty and Mrs Hardacre had slaved over, two best mates and their mothers working together. She opened the hanging cupboard and the nasal-cleansing aroma of eucalyptus came streaming out. Bloody hell! Yes, bloody hell, and that was swearing, and that was a sin, but she didn't care.

'Mam, did you have to? The cupboard reeks.'

'It's the only thing that gets a grease stain out

of serge. I can't present myself at Mrs Randall's with a grease stain.'

Why not? It was doing Mrs Randall's cleaning that had caused the stain in the first place. Carrie sucked in an anxious breath but stopped midway before the eucalyptus could scrub her lungs. Honest to God, if she was doomed to walk up the aisle whiffing of eucalyptus, she would put Mam twice through the mangle.

Taking her dress out, she snapped the cupboard shut and sniffed like a hungry dog. It took her nose a moment to stop tingling and confirm that her beautiful dress was unsullied. A smile tugged at her lips. One day she would tell her children. 'There I was, all excited, about to try on my wedding dress for Auntie Evadne, and when I opened the cupboard, what did I smell?' and the children would cry 'Eucalyptus!' in gleeful voices, because they would have heard the story a hundred times before. It would be one of their favourites.

And one day – goodness, she had always pictured her children as youngsters, but one day, when her oldest daughter was getting married, they would share the special family joke as they took Letitia's dress out of the cupboard. She and Letty had vowed years ago to name their oldest girls after one another. After today and the eucalyptus, Letitia's dress would smell of roses, because Carrie would make heaps of muslin sachets and fill them with rose petals to fragrance the cupboard.

The fine cotton streamed through her reverent fingers, flowing as elegantly as silk. Heart engorged with emotion, she let Mam help her into the dress, standing still, elbow raised, as Mam bent to fasten the tiny pearly buttons that ran from hip to underarm. The bedroom was hot as soup, but Carrie felt cool and lovely.

'There,' said Mam. 'Wait while I move the looking-glass.'

Lifting it from the marble-topped washstand, she placed it on the chest of drawers, angling it on its hinges. It was shaped like a shield from the olden days and Carrie had always considered it stylish, but now she would have given anything for a square or oblong with more glass. She stood on her toes, caught tantalising glimpses of rounded neckline and elbow-length sleeves, then dropped back again.

She pressed her lips together, longing to see herself properly. Then she felt a thrill of pride. Billy had shelled out for a photographer, so she would be able to see herself in her dress for ever afterwards. Anyroad, she would see herself head to foot on Saturday morning, because Mr Clancy was giving her away and they had a full-length mirror. Carrie dearly hoped Mr Clancy thought he was having the honour because of living next door and having known her since she was a nipper.

'Here. Use this.' Mam picked up the hand mirror.

Carrie turned to her, feeling the movement of the flared skirt around her legs – just a gentle flare, nothing showy. She had always been warned against anything fussy, as if having a sister out of a higher social drawer might have given her unsuitable ideas. But she had never hankered after minute pencil pleats or lacy cuffs. Fuss was for ladies, for beauties. Fuss was for Evadne – though, let's face it, she could wear a potato sack and still turn heads.

Holding the mirror in front of her at waist level like a bouquet, Carrie beamed at Mam. 'I'm so glad Evadne asked to see me in my dress.'

Mam's gaze shifted. 'She didn't actually ask, not as such.' She fiddled with the brush and comb that matched the hand mirror, lining them up as if they weren't perfectly tidy already. 'But I know she'll want to see it.'

Carrie's spirits deflated. She should have known. Mam did this now and again, tried to bring them close. It never worked, even though she was mother to both of them. It was Pa who had held them together. He had worshipped the ground Evadne's smartly shod feet walked on; he had fostered Carrie's childhood adoration.

'I asked her to bring the veil,' said Mam, 'and why shouldn't she see your dress? She's your sister.'

Carrie gave her a kiss. 'It was naughty of you to pretend, but I'm glad you did, because I get to wear my dress.'

'And the veil,' said Mam.

And the veil. Perfect.

Chapter Two

The air stilled in Evadne's throat. For a moment she couldn't breathe. Great Scott. As if she wasn't humiliated enough. Were they deliberately rubbing her nose in it? No, they weren't like that. Certainly not Carrie; she hadn't a malicious bone in her body. And Mother admired Evadne too much to imagine this might be difficult for her. And Evadne had never confided.

Something tingled in the pit of her stomach. Confide? Share her shame? Never! No one must ever know. Hadn't she just walked here from Oaklawn, golden fingers of evening sunshine failing to thaw the icicles in her chest, her head held high, a smile nailed to her lips and a cheery 'Good evening' for everyone she passed, whether she knew them or not? And she had managed that in spite of carrying this wretched box, tied with a double-knot to make extra sure it couldn't burst open en route.

It hadn't felt like carrying a box. It had felt like wearing heavy sandwich boards proclaiming MOTHER'S WEDDING VEIL TO BE WORN BY YOUNGER SISTER.

If only she hadn't taken the veil with her when she moved out. But, oh, how natural it had felt at the time. Mother had added it to her belongings and they had shared a smile, both of them knowing – or thinking they knew – that her new job didn't really matter, because she wouldn't need it for long.

'Look at Carrie,' said Mother.

Evadne smiled, then smiled more widely to look like she meant it. 'Pretty dress. It suits you. Here.' She dropped the box onto the bed. She couldn't bear to hold it a moment longer.

Mother pounced. 'Blimey, you tied it tight enough. I'll need to cut it.' Don't say it's a waste of string. 'What a waste of string, Evadne.'

The lid eased off with a sigh. With exquisite care that tore Evadne's heart straight across from side to side, Mother lifted out her twice-worn veil. Evadne removed her green felt toque and fussed with her hair. Hats were hell in this weather, though her natural waves never suffered. Not like some girls, whose hair ended up hat-shaped.

When she looked again, Mother was standing in front of Carrie. Fine silk tulle cascaded down Carrie's back. Mother's arms were raised, her brows drawn together in concentration as she settled the simple headdress of wax flowers and leaves in position. Evadne's scalp prickled, yearning for the headdress's gentle scrape.

It wasn't right; Carrie was only a kid. Mother was irresponsible to let her marry so young. Evadne had tried telling her when Carrie had insisted on getting engaged at sixteen. Sixteen!

'I trust Billy appreciates he's in for a five-year wait,' she had said.

'Five years! We can't wait that long,' Carrie had cried. 'Tell her, Mam.'

And she had obviously worn Mother down because here she was, a bride at eighteen.

21

Eighteen.

Evadne's hand brushed her pocket, flinching away as if it had been burnt. In her pocket were her clip-on bows for shoes. She should produce them now. Carrie would love them. Something borrowed. Evadne's hand fisted, neatly manicured nails needling her palm. Her fingers uncurled and her hand dropped away.

Her heart dropped too. When had she become such a meanie?

A sharp rat-tat on the knocker had her at the bedroom door in an instant.

'I'll get it.'

She ran partway downstairs, then stopped to gather herself, straightening her shoulders inside her cotton blouse, embellished today with a shawl collar. She had a stash of detachable collars. It was important to look crisp and smart, important to look a cut above her fellow teachers, though there was no need to make any special effort where Wilton Lane was concerned. Her natural superiority here was precisely that – natural, and always had been.

After the drawn curtains upstairs and the always-dim light on the stairs and in the hall, the evening sunshine flooded her eyes as she opened the front door. She expected to see a neighbour but found herself face-to-face with Father Kelly, and face-to-face was exactly the right expression. He stood right in front of her, as if he had been trying to meld with the door. Even before she opened it fully, he was inside the house, and down the hall before she could close it.

'Do come in,' she murmured, following him to

the kitchen.

He swung round to face her. 'Where's your mammy?' His pudgy cheeks were flushed, his voice loud. It was a demand, not a civil enquiry.

Evadne's heart pattered. What was going on? 'Upstairs.'

'Well, fetch her down.'

She quelled her heart and looked levelly at him. Wilton Lane might kowtow to this man, but she wasn't Wilton Lane and never had been, even when she lived here. She knew how to make the most of her social superiority. She was tall and slender. All she had to do was lift her chin a fraction and, so long as the other person didn't tower over her, it gave the impression of her looking down on them.

'Is something wrong?' she asked, lifting one eyebrow.

'Oh aye, very wrong, and has been for a long time – but you'd know all about that, wouldn't you?'

'I don't know what you're talking about.' She felt a flutter of unease.

His face changed. The pudginess hardened and his eyes glinted. 'Don't you? Well now, we'll see. Fetch your mammy down.'

She felt a powerful urge to protect Mother from this, to demand an explanation and deal with it, whatever it was; but Father Kelly produced his black rosary beads and shut his eyes. What a cop-out.

She nodded curtly. 'I'll see if my mother is available.'

She stalked along the narrow hall and up the

stairs. There were times when she was heartily pleased not to be Catholic any more. Mother had turned RC when she married Pa and she had made Evadne turn too, much to the horror of Grandfather and Grandmother Baxter. Foolish child that she had been, Evadne had enjoyed feeling that the grown-ups were fighting over her. Looking back, she could see how that would have been the perfect moment for her grandparents to insist upon adopting her, but all Grandmother had done was make her swear to say the extra words at the end of the Our Father, even if she only did it inside her head. Evadne had shed Catholicism the moment she was old enough, for which Father Kelly had never forgiven her, but she didn't give a fig about that. She could look forward to a better class of husband if she was C of E.

She opened the bedroom door. Mother had drawn the veil over Carrie's face and was gazing at her as though she were a priceless work of art. Carrie was gazing at herself in the looking-glass in much the same way. A little corner of Evadne's heart chipped off.

'Who was it?' Mother asked, but her attention was locked on Carrie.

'Father Kelly. He's in the kitchen.'

Mother's face swung round, her mouth and eyes circles of shock. 'You put Father Kelly in the kitchen? Evadne! You don't put priests in the kitchen.'

'I didn't put him anywhere. He put himself.'

Carrie was still looking in the mirror. 'Has he come about the wedding?'

The girl was becoming a prize bore. 'I don't

know what brought him here, but it seems serious. He insists upon seeing you, Mother.'

'I'll come down.'

'You too, Carrie,' said Evadne. Anything to stop that ridiculous preening.

'I'll get changed.'

'No time for that.' Mother patted her faded mousy hair and checked the position of the cameo she wore between the rounded corners of her Peter Pan collar. 'You can't keep a priest waiting. Just tek off the veil – here, let me.'

Evadne wanted to give her sister a clip round the ear. Honestly! Someone should tell her this dratted wedding wasn't the be-all and end-all.

She led the way down, aware of Mother fluttering behind, willing her to hurry, and Carrie bringing up the rear, presumably imagining herself as the Queen of Sheba descending the royal staircase. At the foot of the stairs, Mother nipped in front and hastened to the kitchen. She opened the door only to stop dead. Evadne cannoned into her and they stumbled forwards. Righting herself, Evadne stepped back, and if she had inadvertently trodden on the hem of Carrie's dress, which she couldn't because it was ankle-length, but if she had, it wouldn't have done Carrie any harm. It might have brought her down to earth.

Father Kelly stood sideways to them, little black beads dripping between meaty fingers. He was murmuring as they entered, but now he spoke clearly and, even though he gave no other indication of being aware of their presence, the volume itself was an order to spring to attention.

'...Holy Mary, Mother of God...'

He paused, the moment quivering around them. You had to hand it to him, he knew how to work his audience. Mother and Carrie bowed their heads and took up the chant in quiet, respectful voices that offered no competition to his practised rumble.

'...pray for us sinners...'

Evadne waited politely for the prayer to end. Please don't let there be another. She tried to see the beads. Was he going to drone his way through an entire decade?

He slipped the rosary into his pocket and turned to face them. Mother stepped forward.

'Good evening, Father. Sorry to keep you. We've been trying on Carrie's wedding dress.'

She moved aside, revealing Carrie behind her. Carrie gave a half-smile, modestly dropping her gaze. For someone who hadn't wanted to be seen in her finery, she had overcome her reservations pretty quickly.

But Father Kelly offered no compliments. He looked squarely at Mother.

'Won't you tek a seat, Father?' Having presented Carrie to him, Mother now presented the armchairs that snuggled beside the blue-and-white-tiled hearth.

'No, thank you. I'll not sit and be cosy in this house of sin.'

'House of – what?' Evadne exclaimed. 'What are you talking about?'

Mother froze like a terrified animal.

'You never told them, then?' he said. 'You never told your girls the sordid truth?'

'Told us what?' Evadne demanded. Her voice

sounded strong but her mouth had gone dry. She told herself it was anger at his shilly-shallying, but it wasn't.

'So it's just yourself who's living the lie, is it, Mrs Jenkins?'

Evadne had never seen it before; she might not have believed it possible, but the colour vanished, simply vanished, from Mother's face. Her skin was white – no, not white. Grey.

'Mam?' Carrie whispered, but Mother didn't utter a sound.

'And I said a requiem Mass for you and I sat in your parlour, dispensing comfort, and you let me, and all along you knew.'

Mother swallowed. Her throat convulsed as though she was about to splutter, but no sound emerged. The creamy smooth surface of her cameo brooch shimmered as her rigid body vibrated with tension. What the hallelujah was going on?

Evadne tried to break in. 'Knew what?'

'The parish has a visitor, Mrs Jenkins, a fellow priest who served as an army chaplain in the war, the very priest who spent the night alongside your husband before he ... died.'

There was a delighted ripple of pretend silk. 'He met Pa?' said Carrie. 'Can we see him? It would mean so much.'

But Mother and Father Kelly didn't acknowledge her, and her little burst of pleasure faded into frowning confusion.

'What say you, Mrs Jenkins?' boomed Father Kelly. 'Do you want your daughters, poor innocent doves that they are, to meet the priest

27

who prayed for their daddy's immortal soul the night before–'

Mother erupted into life. 'I'm sorry, I'm sorry. Don't do this, Father, I beg you.'

'What's this? You're asking me to live the lie for you, to perpetuate your own sin? Because a sin is what it is, make no mistake about that. You preferred to sin against your heavenly Father sooner than speak the truth to your fellow man.'

'I couldn't say anything. I couldn't.'

'And all this time you've been receiving the Blessed Sacrament.'

'I know, I know.'

'You defied God himself rather than face the shame of your husband being shot at dawn for desertion.'

A wave of shock reverberated through Evadne's frame, turning her cold to the centre of her being. Her gaze flew to the priest. He was all puffed up and righteous.

'Mother–'

But Mother was silent. She stood there and let Father Kelly make this appalling accusation and didn't say a word. Evadne's insides liquefied.

In a flash of white, Carrie darted forwards. 'Get out!' Her hands were raised, crammed into fists as if she was going to batter the living daylights out of him. 'Get out, get out, get out!'

'Carrie!' Evadne wanted time to think, to understand, but here she was, having to reprimand her sister. 'Stop caterwauling. Do you want the neighbours to hear?' She glared at Father Kelly, hating him for the foul suggestion he had brought into their house. 'Please leave. If there's any more to be said, we'd prefer to hear it from our mother, not from you.'

'What I want to hear is her prayers as she falls to her knees and begs for forgiveness from God the Father, God the Son and God the Holy Ghost.'

He wasn't about to whip out his rosary beads again, was he? Evadne stood aside, clearing the path to the front door. He brushed past, radiating displeasure.

She followed him down the hall. He threw open the door and turned round.

'Behold your sins will find you out.'

Away he marched. A couple of neighbours, chatting in the street, stopped to watch him. Before they could ask questions, Evadne shut the door. She had to lean her back against it. Anguish welled up. The cords inside her neck were so taut she couldn't swallow. Placing the flats of her hands against the door, she pushed herself away and plodded along the hall. She didn't want to reach the kitchen, but her feet were taking her there, taking her towards a truth she couldn't bear to hear.

She halted in the doorway.

'Well, Mother?'

And Mother dropped like a stone. Had she fainted? No, she was still conscious, still upright, only down on her knees, sitting propped up on her heels.

'Oh my goodness ... oh my goodness...' she whispered, eyes wide and unfocused.

Carrie slumped down beside her, trying to pull her into her arms, but Mother didn't lean into her embrace. Her breathing was shallow and ragged.

Carrie looked up. 'Help me get her into the chair.'

Evadne grasped one of Mother's arms and together they pulled her to her feet, the three of them almost swooping down in a heap when she swayed heavily. It was on the tip of Evadne's tongue to say, 'Pull yourself together,' but she bit it back. They more or less dropped her into the chair. She sagged over the arm like a queasy passenger leaning over the side of a boat.

Evadne couldn't hold back any longer. 'Is it true? What Father Kelly said, is it true?'

'Leave her alone.' Carrie placed a protective hand on Mother's shoulder.

Evadne barely let her get the words out. 'I can't believe it. I simply can't believe it. And you've known all along.'

It felt as if her head was full of angry wasps. It couldn't possibly be true – yet Mother's response declared it was. This would destroy them. What would Grandfather say? And Pa – imagine Pa being ... that sort of person. Nausea rolled in her stomach and she tasted bile.

Mother moaned, a long, wavering sound; then she was in floods of tears, her mouth wide and drooping, candles of snot streaming from her nose. Evadne felt revolted, but Carrie, heedless of her precious dress, crouched in front of the chair, trying to draw Mother to her.

'She needs to lie down,' she said.

'She needs to tell us the truth.'

Carrie rose to her feet, holding Mother's limp hand in both her own. 'Come on, Mam. Let me tek you upstairs. Help me, Evadne. She's ill.'

'Whereas you and I are right as rain. Oh, very well.'

Each with an arm looped around Mother's waist, they struggled up the stairs with her wailing and shuddering all the way and Carrie crooning and encouraging. God, what a mess. This was no time to collapse in a heap. Mother had kept her secret for four whole years. Surely she could have hung on to her self-control for ten minutes more to tell them what they needed to know.

Carrie probably intended to assist Mother tenderly onto the bed, but Evadne was having none of that. She got Mother to the edge of the bed and let go. Mother slumped and Carrie followed her down. Flinging an accusing look over her shoulder, Carrie scooped Mother's legs onto the bed and generally played nursemaid.

Evadne left them to it. She moved away, feeling restless and unclean. All the neighbours in Wilton Lane, all the housewives at the shops. How had Mother done it? How had she lived her life in such an ordinary way, all the while knowing what she knew? Were she and Carrie now doomed to lead the same kind of life? She rubbed the back of her neck.

Parting the curtains, she glanced out, her heart beating rapidly, as though an angry crowd might have gathered outside. It was an ordinary evening. Two or three lads were kicking a football around and across the road a queue of girls awaited their turn at the chalked-up hopscotch grid. Windows were open – as though anything could make a house cooler on a day like today. Some front doors were open too. A few neighbours sat outside on wooden chairs, enjoying a chinwag. It was only a matter of time before someone knocked to ask if everything was all right, 'only we saw Father Kelly...'

How loud was Mother's sobbing? Evadne pulled down the sash, leaning forward as she did so because it was stiff, and saw Billy coming their way along Wilton Lane.

She turned to Carrie. 'Billy's coming. Send him away.'

'I can't go down like this, not in my dress. You go. Tell him I'll be down in a minute.'

Evadne shut her eyes and breathed in sharply through her nose. That girl. Their world was collapsing around them and all she could think about was her dress. On a wave of irritation, Evadne ran down and opened the door just as Billy knocked. He blinked at having it opened so promptly.

'It's not a good time, Billy,' she said, even before he touched the brim of his bowler to her.

He shoved a finger inside his collar, easing the tightness. It was an attached collar, which was fair enough, really. He was only a clerk. His studs and good collar were kept for work. At home he wore a collar-attached shirt. Carrie didn't mind, but then she was only a shop girl.

'I shan't stop a minute. Is Carrie in?'

'She can't come down. We've ... we've had a shock. Excuse me.' She backed away, about to shut the door.

'I know.'

She froze. Surely not.

'Father Kelly were in't pub earlier with another priest and–'

She sucked in a huge breath. It was the only thing that kept her upright. She stared at Billy. Her face felt prickly. Was she losing her colour the way Mother had earlier? Her mind went blank. It had been bad enough when she thought only the two priests knew, but if the revelation had happened in public...

'I say, are you all right?'

All right? Dolt! How could she ever be all right again? Some of the hatred she had felt for Father Kelly welled up and spilt over in Billy's direction. Carrie thought him the last word in good-looking, but he was nothing special. Just an ordinary boy who had clawed his way into a town hall job, but didn't have the good sense to spend years saving up before he got married.

'They were in the pub?'

'It wasn't Father Kelly's fault. This other priest started talking about it, knowing that this was where Mr Jenkins came from. He didn't know...' Billy's voice trailed off.

'He thought it was the talk of the wash house, I suppose?'

'Look, I must speak to Carrie.'

'Well, you can't. Go away, Billy.'

He nodded, closing his eyes for a moment. Was that relief? Evadne shot him a direct look, then shrugged inwardly. Not her problem.

He leant forward. 'Can you give her a message for me?'

Chapter Three

'I shall change my name back to Baxter forth-with,' Evadne declared. 'God forbid that anyone should mistake me for a Jenkins after this.'

From her perch beside the kitchen table, Carrie, watching in a distant kind of way, saw Evadne's slender fingers grasp the arms of the chair, saw her perfect almond-shaped nails dig into the homey chintz. She wanted to tell her to shut up and stop being so selfish, but she couldn't rouse herself. She was numb. There was so much to take in. Not just Pa, but Billy as well. She looked down. Her hands – square, capable little paws – lay fisted on the skirt of her wedding dress. Had Billy really and truly abandoned her? And Mam – imagine her keeping such a frightful secret all this time.

'*My* father was a hero,' said Evadne, as if he had relieved Mafeking single-handed.

Carrie stirred herself; she wasn't having that. 'Pa was your father.'

'Not my real father. My real father died doing his duty. A father to be proud of.'

A father to be proud of: that's what they had thought about Pa until today, she and Evadne, the neighbours, everyone who came in the shop, the parents of Evadne's pupils ... everyone. Not Mam, though. Mam had known different all along. No wonder she had fainted clean away at the end of the two-minute silence last November. She was upstairs now, refusing to see them, though the sobbing had stopped at last, thank heaven. Carrie's throat clogged with guilt: she hadn't shed a single tear. By rights she should be weeping buckets, yet here she was, sitting rigidly on a spindle-backed chair in the centre of a cold and frightening calm.

Her hands unclenched and rubbed up and down her thighs in time with the dull thump of her heart – then she stopped. She mustn't rumple her wedding dress.

But if Billy had jilted her–

Her mouth went dry, her pulse wild as panic poured through her veins. Her insides felt loose and trembly. She met Evadne's gaze. Evadne looked like the queen of winter, cheekbones high and sharp, her lips a tight line of fury. How could she be angry with Pa? Pa had thought the world of her, and never mind that she wasn't his own flesh and blood. Being dad to a Baxter had meant something to him. How dare she turn on him?

But looking into the depths of Evadne's clever hazel eyes, Carrie saw – she saw fear, and her breath caught. She was frightened too. Now that the terrible truth about Pa had been revealed, they would never be able to hold up their heads again.

Shame pulsated in the air around her, so strong she could inhale it. Beneath the usual warm scents of herbs and pastry, it smelt of ... vinegar. No, that was stupid. And yet there it was. Yes, of course – Mam had cleaned the windows that afternoon, one of her regular Thursday jobs, and the crisp aroma of diluted vinegar lingered in the air.

What was she doing, thinking about windows and vinegar at a time like this? A time like this? As if there had ever been such a time. The wedding was off – or so Evadne said – and Pa, dear Pa, such a devoted family man, Pa was ... he was–

He was a deserter. He hadn't copped it going over the top like hundreds of thousands of others, including four of their own men and boys from Wilton Lane. He had been shot by his own side. Blindfolded, he had stood in front of a firing squad and paid the penalty for his desertion. Pa – a deserter. Dear, lovely Pa. Was he still dear, lovely Pa now that they knew this shocking, shameful thing about him?

The door squeaked open and Carrie's heart twitched at the sight of Mam, looking fragile and – and old. How had that happened? In the space of – what? An hour? – the fine lines about her eyes and mouth had become deeply gouged. Sinking into a chair at the table, she doubled over as if in the grip of a violent bellyache and gave way to another bout of weeping. Carrie reached out a comforting hand, but Mam's shoulder heaved so violently it bounced straight off.

'Try not to cry. I'll put the kettle on.'

'Oh yes,' Evadne cut in, her voice thick with unspent tears. 'A pot of tea will solve all our problems.'

Mam reared up, smearing the heels of her hands over her face. 'I'm sorry. I never meant anybody to know. I've hoped and prayed every day for it to stay hidden. I wanted to protect you.'

'If you'd wanted to protect me,' Evadne flared,

'you should have told me the truth so I could have found a new job a hundred miles away.'

'Evadne!' Mam cried.

'There's precious little hope of that now. Teaching posts are being given to men who served their country.'

Silence rattled round the kitchen. Muscles jumped beneath Carrie's skin. Men who served. Not like Pa, who had betrayed king and country, his family, everything he stood for. She felt battered from all sides. She had loved Pa. Was she still allowed to love him? Did she still want to? And what about Billy? She clutched her elbows, shivering like a sick dog.

'How did you manage to keep it secret all this time?' Evadne sounded weary, disbelieving.

'I didn't know, not to start with.'

'Wait.'

Evadne got up and crossed the kitchen to close the window, as though listeners might have sneaked into their backyard. Mellow sunshine spilt through the sparkling panes, painting golden rectangles on the beech dresser and turning the red floor tiles to garnet.

Evadne resumed her seat. 'Go on.'

Mam's lip trembled. 'We got a telegram the same as everybody else. You saw it.'

'Saw it?' Evadne exclaimed. 'We stuck it in the family Bible opposite the letter about my father. All this time I thought they were the same, two men dying for their country. I felt sorry for you, a soldier's widow twice over.'

Carrie willed her to shut up. 'Tell us what happened.'

Mam sucked in a breath. 'Like I say, I never knew to start with. It were only when the pension stopped, about six months later. I thought it was a mistake and I was vexed. I thought: What a way to treat a soldier's widow. I never imagined...' Her voice trailed away, her eyes black with despair. 'Then a letter came, saying I weren't entitled to no pension. It wasn't like getting a letter, not really. It were just a report of what had happened – hardly even that, just the bare bones. I didn't even know it was desertion until Father Kelly said.'

'They didn't...' Carrie had to clear her throat. 'They didn't tell you why Pa was ... shot?' The word crept out on a whisper. Uttering it was a betrayal.

'No. Just that it'd happened. He'd been court-martialled and shot. Only they called it executed.'

'It must have said more than that,' said Evadne. 'Where's the letter now?' She looked round, as if it might be sticking out from behind the clock.

Something glinted deep in Mam's eyes.

'I burnt it. I knelt in the hearth and tore it into shreds, then I dropped the pieces one by one into the heart of the fire. I was so close I could smell my apron scorching. I stirred it up to a right old blaze and I kept on stirring until it felt like the skin was peeling off my face.'

'Oh, Mam...' Carrie whispered.

'I realised none of his mates would know. Pa was injured a while before he died – do you remember?'

'He shot himself in the thigh while he was cleaning his gun.' Nostalgia swamped Carrie.

Mam had said, 'Daft bugger,' and she and Letty had squealed with delighted laughter.

'Trying to give himself a Blighty wound, more like,' said Evadne.

Carrie surged to her feet so suddenly she nearly toppled. 'Stop it! It's bad enough without you going on like that.'

'Girls, girls!' Mam was on her feet too, flapping her hands.

Evadne shut her eyes, then opened them again. 'What does Pa's wound have to do with it?'

Mam sat down with a bump. Tears spilt over and trailed down her face. Carrie's heart ached for her. She sat down, pulling her chair closer to Mam's, its feet scraping the floor tiles.

Mam's voice shook. 'He were carted off to hospital, but it was bombed and they were evacuated. At the same time, his regiment went elsewhere. I don't know the details. I had a letter from him, but he couldn't say much because of the censor. When he returned to the front, he ended up with a different set of men; and they were the ones he was with when he ... when he died.'

'So you knew none of our local men would come home knowing the truth,' said Evadne.

'Aye.'

'Until now.'

Mam shuddered so hard her teeth clicked. 'Four years, four whole years. It's an actual weight, you know, so heavy, right inside here.' She pressed splayed fingers against her chest. 'I've been so ashamed and frightened.'

A spurt of tears and spittle showered Carrie in a fine mist, settling softly on her cheeks, then Mam was sobbing lustily. It lasted mere moments, halting as abruptly as it had started.

Carrie reached out to draw her close. She smelt of soap and starch. Carrie kissed her hair. 'You poor love.' No wonder her grief had intensified a few months after Pa's death.

'It teks some people that way, Carrie love,' Letty's mam had explained. 'It can tek a while for it to sink in. Your mam has just realised, I mean really realised, that your dad's not coming home, God love him.'

But it hadn't been that at all. It had been the truth that had knocked her flat.

'That's why you went to work in the munitions at Trafford Park,' said Evadne. 'They paid good wages, so you could pretend some of the money was pension. That's the truth, isn't it?'

Mam jerked upright and Carrie glared at her sister. Did she have to stick the knife in?

'Be reasonable, Evadne. Even if there had been a pension, Mam would still have needed to work. Widows do. I were just turned fourteen, so I wasn't bringing much home; and you'd moved out long before then.' She turned to Mam. 'You were lucky to get the position with Mrs Randall when the munitions closed.'

'Aye. Mrs Randall used to have two live-in staff and a daily before the war, but girls have got above themselves these days and she can't get anyone to live in. Mind you, she is a bit of a tartar. And her brother, he slips me the odd half-crown now and then for services rendered.'

Evadne shrieked. Carrie might have shrieked, too, only the breath had been sucked clean out of

40

her body.

'Not that kind of service,' Mam snapped. 'You should wash your mouths out with soap, the pair of you.'

'We never said a word,' Carrie protested.

'You didn't need to. For your information, I keep his stump clean and medicated. It still has him in bad ways after all this time.'

Carrie slumped back in her chair. She couldn't believe it. Pa was dead, a deserter, and here they were talking about Mrs Randall's brother's manky stump. Her heart contracted on a pang of yearning. Oh, Billy–

'I'm going out.' She was on her feet. She didn't remember standing up, but here she was, on her feet. The skirt of her wedding dress swished.

'You can't,' said Evadne.

'You mustn't,' said Mam.

Carrie blinked. 'I have to see Billy.'

'What for?' Evadne demanded. 'I told you. He's called it off.'

Answers flooded Carrie's mind. You're wrong, you're mistaken, you're lying. You were too shocked about Pa to listen properly. Billy would never leave me.

'He should have waited to see me. I were only upstairs, for pity's sake.'

'Tek your dress off, love,' said Mam. 'We'll have a cup of tea, eh?' Take her dress off. Yes. She mustn't spoil it. But ... but if Evadne was right about the wedding being called off – which she couldn't be, but supposing she was – then Carrie might never put her dress on again. Distress swelled inside her, bubbling up towards the rim

41

of her self-control. Her dress, stitched with love and hope in every seam.

'I'm going to see Billy.'

Mam came to her feet and grabbed her arm, yanking her round. Almost tipped off balance, Carrie snatched at the table, her hands slapping down. Her palms stung. Heat darted up her forearms.

'You can't,' Mam insisted. 'Word will have got round by now. We have to stop indoors.'

'We can't stay in for ever.'

'You're not going and that's flat.'

'That's what's happened to the china serving dish, isn't it?' said Evadne. 'You took it to the pawn.'

Carrie stared. What was she on about now?

'I told you.' Mam looked shifty. 'I broke it. I dropped it.'

'If you'd broken it, you'd have stuck it back together,' Evadne retorted. 'No, you pawned it.'

'I needed the money.'

'What else have you pawned? Only it wasn't pawning, was it? People who pawn things redeem them and you never had any intention of doing that, did you?'

'I always meant to get them back, but it were never possible.'

'Them? What else have you got rid of?'

'Just one or two bits, nowt special. The ashtray, the brass candlesticks. Nothing we needed.'

The brass candlesticks? Carrie remembered them disappearing, remembered Mam claiming, 'I've put them in Miss Reilly's room. We're lucky to have a nice lady lodger. We have to give her the

42

best we can so she stays.'

Evadne jumped up. 'My God! If you've dared...'

She swarmed from the kitchen and Carrie flinched as the parlour door banged open. The room was probably flinching too. Evadne came flying back into the kitchen, heat highlighting her fine cheekbones.

'That barometer wasn't yours to dispose of. It belonged to my father and that means it was mine.'

She confronted Mam across the table. Carrie saw Mam shrink. Was she subsiding back onto the chair? No, she was shrivelling beneath Evadne's wrath. Carrie made an instinctive move to put herself between them, but the table was in the way. Instead she gave Evadne a push, then had to stand her ground when Evadne's glare ensnared her.

'So Mam pawned the barometer – so what?' Carrie flared. 'She needed the money. What does it matter now?'

Evadne cracked her hard across the face. The breath rasped in Carrie's throat. Her hand flew to her cheek in disbelief. It felt as if she had been burnt. A whiff of the light flowery toilet water Evadne favoured hung in the air between them. Carrie stared at her sister and Evadne stared back, then she flung herself into the armchair, fingers pressed across her mouth.

She shook her head. 'I'm sorry – I'm sorry.'

Carrie spun round, yearning for the comfort of her mother's arms, but Mam shoved herself clear of the table, overturning the chair in her haste, and vanished before it stopped clattering.

Chapter Four

That afternoon the air had been as heavy as a sack of potatoes and even though it had now eased into the tranquil warmth of evening, the gate's wooden planks and the bricks in the back wall were still packed with the day's heat, and it bounced out at Carrie as she lifted the latch and slipped through to hasten along the entries. She often walked down the entries – there was nothing new in that – but it felt new, because she was consciously avoiding the streets. Was this how life would be lived in future, skulking through entries, never lifting her eyes beyond the tops of the yard walls in case someone was looking out of an upstairs window? Her vision narrowed, focused solely on the cinder path crackling underfoot and the walls to either side. Typical Manchester, Pa used to say of the distinctive red brick. Was it wrong to remember him as an ordinary person, living an ordinary life and saying ordinary things? Was it disrespectful to all those other soldiers?

It couldn't have taken long to reach Billy's road, but it felt like for ever. Emerging from the entry, she stumbled to a halt, feeling exposed and vulnerable as if a crowd should have been watching for her. She longed for Billy to hold her while she wept for Pa, aye, and for Mam, too, clutching her dark secret to her through four desperate years.

A woman was standing on her doorstep, chatting to a younger woman with a small child on her hip. They noticed her the same moment she saw them. Should she smile, nod, say hello? The women gave her a nod and her face heated as their conversation resumed, the way their heads tilted closer together telling her what their topic was. She could barely raise her eyes to fix them on Billy's front door. It wasn't more than a few yards, but it might as well have been miles. First she had to brave a couple of girls skipping in the road, one end of their tatty rope tied to a gas lamp.

Raspberry, gooseberry, apple, jam tart
Tell me the name of your sweetheart
With an A, B...

Then the girl turning the rope accelerated while her companion skipped pepper, both of them yelling the alphabet at top speed. On G, skipper and rope became hopelessly entangled.

'G!' the turner cried gleefully. 'You're gonna marry Gregory Wells!'

'Am not!'

'Are so!'

A ghost of a smile fluttered across Carrie's lips. She had skipped that rhyme herself many a time. You couldn't stop on B, not without looking like you'd done it on purpose, but, by heck, it had been impossible, trying to keep going all the way to W.

'Look, it's Carrie. Tek an end for us, Carrie.'

'Go on,' wheedled the other. 'The rope keeps

slipping down't lamp post.'

'Sorry, not today.'

'Eh, Carrie Jenkins, is it true?'

'Is what true?' What a pathetic thing to say.

'About your dad. Margaret Harrison's mam said Mrs Shipton said your dad never went over't top. He were shot running away. He was a coward.'

Anger, white-hot, scorched through Carrie. She stepped forward, a sharp movement that sent both girls scuttling backwards. 'My dad weren't a coward and don't you dare say he was.' She caught the scared looks on the pinched little faces and her heart froze in shame. 'Just ... don't say it, that's all.'

She carried on walking. It was like being in a dream, the sort where you walked and walked but never arrived, even though your destination was right there in front of you. Then, with a shiver of surprise, she reached the Shiptons' front gate. She rested her fingers on top of it. In Billy's road, each house had a 'front', a small area boxed in by a low brick wall with a gate. It was nobbut a couple of steps from gate to door, but even so, a front gate was a front gate. It swung open without a squeak. Carrie lifted the knocker and executed a smart rat-tat that sounded braver than she felt.

The door opened and Billy's mother planted herself in the doorway. Carrie offered a tentative smile; she had always done her best to please Mrs Shipton.

'Oh, it's you.'

'Good evening, Mrs Shipton. Can I speak to Billy, please?'

46

'There's nowt to be said. He's done his duty by coming round to tell you.'

'I didn't see him. He told Evadne.'

'Same difference.'

Carrie lifted her chin. 'I want to see him.'

'Well, he doesn't want to see you. Now clear off back where you came from.'

Her stomach bubbled. 'Not without seeing Billy. I have to. We're getting wed Saturday.'

'Not any more, you're not. Didn't that sister of yours pass on the message?'

'You can't leave something like that as a message.'

Mrs Shipton's jaw hardened. 'Don't take that tone with me, young lady.'

'I need to speak to him. We have to sort this out.' A movement behind Mrs Shipton caught her eye. 'Billy! We need to talk—'

Mrs Shipton landed a great jab in her chest and she almost went over backwards, her feet scrambling for purchase as Mrs Shipton surged towards her, forcing her through the gate onto the pavement. Mrs Shipton delivered a final jab, thrusting her face down into Carrie's, eyes snapping with contempt.

'You're not welcome here. I'm not having any lad of mine marrying the likes of you. He's a bright boy, our Billy. It's not everyone can pass town hall exams. He'll end up a senior clerk one day – but not if there's a scandal dragging him down. No wonder your mother kept her mouth shut all this time. Happen she's cursing that army chaplain for turning up today instead of this time next week. Happen you are too.'

47

'I never knew about Pa until today.'

'Maybe you did and maybe you didn't. The result's the same. Our Billy's not being held back by anything or anyone, least of all you and your family scandal, so get that through your thick skull, Carrie Jenkins.'

'Whatever happened to Pa, you can't punish me for it.' Carrie reached out her hand.

Mrs Shipton dashed it aside with a stinging swipe. 'Blood will out. Just look at you, coming round here half-naked. Where's your decency?'

Bewildered, she looked down at herself. She had ventured out without her shawl.

'Billy! Come out, love – please.'

Mrs Shipton loomed in front of her. 'Hark at you, bawling like a fishwife. And you wonder why our Billy doesn't want you any more.'

With a shove that sent Carrie tottering off the kerb, Mrs Shipton did a smart about-turn and marched indoors. The door slammed and Carrie flinched. Her knees wobbled. Another moment and they would collapse under her and she would plonk down in the road.

A hand touched her arm. She looked into a lined, compassionate face.

'It's Carrie, in't it? Best get thee home, lass. Your mam'll be fretting after you.'

'She doesn't know I'm here.'

'Oh aye, and aren't things bad enough for her without you mekking 'em worse?'

The woman looked round. Carrie glanced about too, saw figures on doorsteps, faces at open sashes, sharp-eyed women, grinning children.

'Show's over,' called the woman. 'There's nowt

48

more to see … unless you was planning on beating down the Shiptons' door?' she asked with a wry lift of her brows. 'Go home, love. Best thing.'

Feeling the eyes of the neighbourhood clamped on her, Carrie headed for home, forcing herself to walk, though she was desperate to take to her heels. Her hand twitched, an instinctive movement, the desire to protect. She grabbed her elbows and hung on to them for dear life. She mustn't, mustn't, mustn't put a hand on her belly.

Chapter Five

Evadne hovered in the narrow hallway, fingertips brushing the parlour doorknob. All she had to do was walk in and draw the curtains. Simple.

She closed her eyes, unshed tears burning in the darkness beneath her eyelids. It wasn't simple at all, but she had her standards and her pride and she would not shirk this duty, however painful, however humiliating.

A flame of anger ignited inside her chest. Heaven help her, she had believed Carrie's wedding represented the ultimate humiliation. For weeks, her skin had been crawling with dread at the thought of having to hold her head up while Wilton Lane, waiting for the bride, amused itself by trying to work out how old she had been when Pa brought her and Mother to live here. Whoever would have imagined that she – beautiful, poised, well-spoken Evadne – would be unwed at … well, never mind how old. It didn't matter.

Yes, it did. It mattered more than anything in the world.

Now there was another shame to be borne. How could Pa have deserted? How *could* he? He had always been a decent, straightforward fellow. Not educated or cultured like the Baxters, obviously, but solid and dependable in a flat cap and baccy kind of way. Respectable – that was Pa. Trustworthy.

Yet he had let them down in the most frightful way imaginable. How *could* he? They would never recover from it. What would it do to her chances? It had already put paid to Carrie's wedding.

That was another thing. That foolish little piece had sneaked out, no doubt to beg and plead with Billy. It was too bad. Going out gallivanting made her look brazen and even if she didn't care on her own account, she might at least care that her sister and mother would be tainted by association.

Well, Evadne knew the correct thing to do, even if Carrie didn't. Her hand closed around the smooth wooden curve of the doorknob and the door breathed open. The smells of beeswax and lemon nudged the edge of her consciousness. Were there neighbours in the street? Would the door's movement be noticed? She would wait them out. She couldn't put herself on show.

Oh, this was ridiculous. She was waiting for people who might not even be there. It went against the grain to hide – or did it? Hiding often seemed highly desirable. Every time she looked in her dressing-table mirror and beheld a spinster, she felt like crawling under the bed and not

50

coming out, but hiding was a luxury that had never been open to her.

She took a step. She was across the threshold but still behind the door. Fear bloomed on her flesh. Inside the parlour, the grandmother clock ticked softly and she tried to absorb its sound to regulate her heart. Another step took her past the door. She forced her head to turn, her neck almost creaking with the effort as she dragged her gaze from the piano to the mantelpiece with its array of coloured glass ornaments. Were they all there? It appeared so. Which pawnbroker had Mother used? Had anyone seen her? Oh, was there no end to the shame? Beneath the mantelpiece, the empty summer fireplace boasted a vase of dried flowers front and centre. Mother had copied that idea from Grandmother Baxter, though naturally Grandmother's flowers had always been fresh – rich red roses, plump and fragrant, or fuzzy-leaved stocks, filling the room with spicy sweetness.

At last she turned to the window. No one there. Relief swooped through her. Her knees went mushy, but she didn't sag. She ghosted around the room's perimeter. Not like that other time. Four years ago, she had entered the parlour with quiet dignity and drawn the curtains to signify theirs was a house of mourning.

This time – this time–

With a rattle of brass rings, she twitched one curtain closed, insinuating herself into its shelter to reach for the other one. She drew it across, narrowing the gap – a face appeared. She exclaimed; so did the face – Miss Reilly. Heart banging, Evadne pressed a hand to her throat. Of all the moments for Mother's lodger to come home. She would let her go upstairs before quitting the parlour. She heard the front door open, but the sound of voices sent her hurrying to the hall.

Miss Reilly was dithering on the doorstep. She stumbled inside, apparently propelled by a squat figure all in black – Mrs O'Something.

An overwhelming urge to slink away consumed Evadne, but this had to be faced, just like every other bally thing in her life.

'Miss Reilly, you evidently haven't heard–'

The squat figure elongated. 'We've heard all right. We saw you, Evadne Jenkins, closing your curtains in shame.'

The scorn and malice pinned her to the spot. 'My name is Baxter from now on.'

'As if that makes any odds.'

Evadne caught her breath so sharply her throat burnt. 'This isn't the time for visitors, Miss Reilly.'

'Mrs O'Malley isn't visiting,' whispered Miss Reilly.

'I'm here to help her pack. You can't expect her to stop in this house of ill repute.'

'Who is it? Who's there? Evadne, shut the door. Oh, Miss Reilly–'

Oh lord, just what she needed, Mother tear-ravaged and dishevelled, stumbling downstairs like a corpse risen from the tomb. Where was her pride? It wasn't as though Pa's desertion had taken her by surprise.

'Well, Gwen Jenkins,' said Mrs O'Malley, 'you always thought yourself a cut above–'

'There's no call for that, thank you,' said Evadne.

Just when had she started sounding so school-mistressy? 'Mother, Miss Reilly has decided to leave–'

Mother's legs gave way and she crumpled onto the stairs, fingers cobwebbed across her mouth, a low keening sound dribbling through the cracks.

'Mam – oh, Mam.'

And wouldn't you know it, here came Carrie to add to the fray, darting from the kitchen and swinging round the newel post onto the stairs, kneeling on the step below Mother to gather her into her arms.

'I know, I know,' she crooned and Mother buried her face in Carrie's neck and wailed.

Evadne felt like clobbering the pair of them. Was she the only member of this godforsaken family to comprehend the value of appearances?

'Carrie, take Mother to the kitchen – now, please. Miss Reilly needs to go upstairs.' She swung round, fixing her eyes on Mrs O'Malley. 'You may wait outside.'

'But–'

Evadne walked straight at her, as if intent upon collision, forcing her backwards out of the house through sheer resolve. She tapped the door, allowing it to swing shut in the woman's face. Bitch – where did that word spring from? Were her standards crumbling under pressure? That was no excuse.

And on the subject of standards–

She threw open the kitchen door. Mother sat slumped in Pa's armchair. They still called it Pa's chair, though often as not he had given way to Evadne. 'Don't want you straining your eyes,' he used to say. 'You and your book learning. You sit by the lamp, chick.' How proud he had been of her, though, of course, it was her grandparents' pride she had striven for.

Mother lolled in Pa's chair, leaning against Carrie, who balanced on the arm, cuddling her close. Carrie was always cuddling someone, usually small children, whenever she could get her hands on one.

A flash of memory. Eight years old, cuddling her new baby sister. That moment of knowing life in Wilton Lane couldn't be all bad, if she had a baby of her own to look after. Another memory. Tea at Grandfather and Grandmother's house, and Mother trying to hang on to little Carrie, and Carrie slipping free and staggering over to her big sister, arms confidently lifted to be picked up, and herself obliging, loving the feel of the child's warm, squirmy, snuggly body. Then Grandmother's voice: 'Really, Evadne, whatever happened to keeping your hands to yourself?' And putting Carrie down with a bump. The child's look of surprise.

'Carrie, can't you keep your hands to yourself for once? Honestly. And what did you mean by sneaking out behind our backs? Deplorable behaviour.'

'I had to see Billy.'

'And did it make one iota of difference?' She arched her eyebrows, a technique perfected in the classroom.

Angling her head, Carrie gave her a direct look, an unusual sharpness in her normally soft blue eyes. 'If going out is so deplorable, does that

54

mean you're stopping here tonight? With Miss Reilly upping sticks, you could have your old room back.'

Cheek! Evadne didn't dignify that with a reply. The less she had to do with Wilton Lane the better had been one of her guiding principles ever since she moved into the schoolhouse. It would be even more important now. Was Oaklawn School sufficiently far away for her to be safe from gossip? If Grandfather had had to find her a pupil-teacher place when she left school, why did it have to be in Chorlton? Why not near his gracious home in Parrs Wood? Then she could have lived with him. Moving into the schoolhouse as the headmistress's lodger had churned up despair so potent she had been able to hear it inside her head, like listening to a seashell.

She closed her eyes, shutting everything out. If only her life could have been lived the way it had been intended. She inhaled crisply and straightened her spine. She was a lady and a soldier's daughter and those attributes would carry her through.

She spent an interminable hour with Carrie and Mother. Disgrace seeped into the atmosphere until it was thick enough to swim in. At last, as the lingering light of midsummer gave way to twilight, she rose to leave. Front door or back? Everyone, namely Mother and the neighbours, would say she should slip out the back and creep away into the fading light, but she never used the entry. Back doors and entries were for the lower orders, not for Baxters.

'May I borrow your veil, Mother? I'll pop it

55

over my hat so that...'

No need to finish the sentence, but she couldn't have anyway. Her throat was too tight. Veil: beastly word. Even though she meant the funeral veil, it was the wedding veil that popped into her head. The veil she had watched Carrie try on. Her younger sister. Her significantly younger sister.

With the world in a darker, softer focus, she paced the mile back to school through twilight from which the heaviness of the day's heat had lifted. As she left Wilton Lane behind, the roads became wider, the houses larger. Privet hedges smelt green and fresh. As she crossed the road-bridge over the railway line, she raised a hand and, quicker than any conjurer, whisked away the veil. Not far now to the school with its shrubby garden, and the schoolhouse next door.

As she let herself into the wood-panelled hall, Miss Martindale called to her.

'Good: you're back. Come and help me with this jigsaw.'

'I'll be down in a minute.'

Upstairs, she stood in her bedroom, absorbing her surroundings, trying to be the way she was before she knew about Pa. The room was the same, the bed with its brass bedstead, the dressing table, the matching washstand with its pretty china set on top, her shelf of books, the hanging-cupboard. Everything was the same ... except herself. If she looked in the mirror, would she look the same or would she see a ghastly caricature, changed for ever by this calamity?

She hung up her jacket, stowed away her hat and went downstairs, pausing in the sitting-room

56

doorway. Her heart thumped. Miss Martindale looked round. She had a kind face. Well, her kindness was about to be tested.

Evadne said, 'I've got something to tell you.'

Chapter Six

Ralph flexed his shoulder muscles, appreciating the smooth feel of the motor as it bowled through the country lanes, the breeze cresting the top of the windscreen and streaming across his face beneath the brim of his homburg. The motor was a Crossley, a real beauty. He had driven one in France during the war, ferrying bigwigs about, aye, and loathing them too, all that yes sir, no sir, three bags full, sir. But he had loved the motor, had cared for it like a baby. You sometimes saw surplus military Crossleys about; a bloke in Chorlton used one as a taxi. The vehicle this evening was one of the newer 25/30 models. The higher bonnet gave it a modern look and he liked that. It spoke of money.

He had learnt about motor cars in the army. They had trained him as a mechanic, which hadn't impressed him to start with, not until he had crossed the Channel and seen the trenches for himself; the bones and rotting body parts that came poking out when part of the wall caved in; the rats, as big as terriers, some of them, and scared of nowt; the mud, the foul water, the foot rot; and the waiting, the endless waiting, that brain-churning mixture of boredom and dread that was enough to send the strongest bloke off his chump. After experiencing all that for himself, he had found it a bloody great relief to be put back on driving and repairs.

Not that driving had been a picnic, not with the Hun firing from the air, but it had its compensations. Never for one instant had it occurred to him when he had been chucking up his guts on the Channel crossing that it might actually be to his advantage to come to this hellhole of a country. But some of the meetings he had driven the bigwigs to had been held in fancy French chateaux crammed with treasures. His eyes had popped out on stalks, fingers itching to pick up a trinket box or a statuette so he could take a proper look. He soon realised that much of the best stuff was absent – stolen possibly, or packed away for safekeeping. He had kept his mouth shut and his hands to himself, but his gaze had roved everywhere, assessing and valuing, while his brain had turned somersaults keeping up with the calculations.

He glanced about. In the gathering dusk, the hedgerows made dense green walls, woven through with buttercups and masses of frothy white cow parsley. Queen Anne's lace his mother had called it, and he had too, until that day on the meadows years ago when two of his mates had laughed their stupid heads off at him for using such a fancy name. Cow parsley they had called it, and they had called him a sissy. It had felt like they were jeering at his mother and he had flattened the pair of them with his fists, breaking

Tom's nose for him and knocking Will's front teeth clean out of his head. He felt afterwards that he had wiped out the insult to his mother, but it hadn't wiped out that bloody cow parsley name from his memory.

A dog – bloody hell. He pulled hard on the wheel, swerving the motor behind the animal, his heart thudding. A girl – he yanked the wheel the other way, but it was too late. There was a thud. She was in front of him and then she was hurled into the air. It seemed she might fly clean over the windscreen and come tumbling into the seat beside him; then she was gone.

He jerked the car to a halt. Christ Almighty, what had he done? He stumbled from the motor, caught his heel on the running board, steadied himself by grabbing the spare attached to the driver's side. He pulled back his shoulders before walking round the vehicle, aware that another chap might have run, but not him, not Ralph Armstrong. Stay calm. Assess the situation. That was something he had learnt in the army. Let others dash about like headless chickens, but make sure you stay in control.

In an overgrown gap in the hedgerow, beneath arching honeysuckle, was the stile she must have climbed over as she followed the dog. She lay crumpled on the grass, motionless, eyes closed, looking more asleep than damaged, but her proximity to the stile meant the back of her head must have fetched a nasty crack. No sign of any blood. Compared to some of the sights he had seen in France, she looked ... tidy.

The dog, a yappety little brute, came dancing

up, anxious and barking. He kicked it away, ignoring its terrified yelp. It kept its distance after that, torn between whimpering and growling. He squatted beside the girl – eighteen, nineteen years old. Simply dressed but clean. Alone? That brought him to his feet, eyes sharp, ears cocked.

They were alone in the lane. He stepped across her body, batting aside a couple of moths getting drunk on the honeysuckle. The rich fragrance poured into his senses, but he switched off his awareness of it, leaning over the stile to peer all round before, satisfied, he stepped back.

This time when he hunkered down, he lifted the girl's wrist. Her hand was work-worn, but the nails were clean. A pulse fluttered like a baby bird beneath the pads of his fingers. He waited to see if he felt anything, relief perhaps, but he felt nothing. Action first, feelings later. That was something else he had learnt in the army. Feelings later – by which time, what was the point?

The girl mumbled and uttered a soft groan. Bloody hell, that was all he needed. She gasped and her eyes squeezed tight. Don't open them, girlie. You mustn't see. Stupid bitch, stay unconscious.

He leant down, scooped a hand beneath her neck to lift her head. With his other hand, he walloped her good and hard so that her head snapped aside. He dropped her and stepped away. Job done.

He returned to the motor, quelling the urge to hurry. Act normal. Don't make yourself conspicuous. He cranked the starting handle, climbed in and drove away, heading back to Sale through the fading light, returning to the hotel from where he had helped himself to the Crossley. He drove round the side and jumped down for a quick recce before taking the motor into the stableyard, where a couple of vehicles were parked. He returned the Crossley and slid away, aware of being swallowed by the darkness.

He permitted himself a quick smoke, accompanied by the usual frisson of dread associated with smoking outdoors in the dark. Lighting up at night was the sure way to get your brains blown out. Even after all this time back in Blighty, that old fear could still put the wind up him. He took a final drag, then threw down the cigarette end, grinding it beneath his heel.

He kept a moderate pace all the way to The Bridge. It was tempting to forego his usual and head straight for home, but it was important to stick to routine, so he ducked inside for a pint, bought one for mad old Felix, passed the time of day with the landlord, behaved as normal even though he was primed and ready, alert for snipers.

When time was called, he nodded farewell. Others headed back up the lane into Sale, but he climbed the steps to the riverbank and Jackson's Boat. Presumably somewhere back in the mists of time there had been a boat and it had been rowed to and fro by a bloke called Jackson, but for as long as anyone could remember, Jackson's Boat had been a bridge. He strode across, listening to his boots striking the wooden planks in the still summer night, aware of the Mersey moving beneath.

On one side: Sale and Cheshire and a Crossley

with a cooling engine and a girl who might wake up in a few hours with a crashing headache or might not wake up at all. On the other: Chorlton and Lancashire and the promising future that had been his from the moment he first set foot inside a fancy French chateau.

Darkness brought a crackle of coolness. He set off at a triumphant jog across the meadows.

Job done.

Battling to prise open eyelids glued together by a night-time of tears, Carrie shifted on the mattress, seeking to ease the weight in her heart. The day stretched ahead and she didn't know what to expect. Instead of her precious plans, there was – nothing. By rights this would have been her last day in the shop, but the Trimbles had given her the day off as a wedding present. She had had it all mapped out. First she had intended to do the cleaning and nip to the shops while Mam was at Mrs Randall's, then pack her clothes and the contents of her bottom drawer into boxes lent by Mr Trimble. After that, instead of a dip in their tin tub, she had planned to take her home-made lavender bath salts to the public baths and luxuriate in a double session before collecting her flowers on the way home, and... Just thinking of it made anguish swell in her throat.

A streak of panic ripped through her, sending pulses jumping all over her body. She flipped over to cuddle up to Mam, only to find the other side of the bed creased and empty.

Picturing Mam forlorn and exhausted at the kitchen table, she swung her feet to the fuzzy latch-hooked rug and opened the bedroom door. She found herself looking straight across into the back bedroom. The door was open and Mam was standing beside the bed, looking jaded. Her hair, which had gone unplaited last night for possibly the first time in her life, straggled down her back.

Carrie was beside her in a heartbeat, drawing her into a hug. 'It'll be all right. Honest it will.'

'She's gone.' Mam sounded surprised. 'She's gone.'

'It's for the best. We'd rather be on us own just now, wouldn't we? It wouldn't feel comfortable having Miss Reilly in the house.'

'I suppose not, but it would have been respectable.'

Mam wasn't about to cry again, was she? Instead, a knock at the front door made her spring away. Tripping against the foot of the bed, she crumpled, but when Carrie reached to help her up, she tugged hard. Carrie's stomach gave a little whoop as she stumbled awkwardly into a heap beside her.

'Don't answer it,' Mam whispered. 'They'll go away.'

Carrie wriggled free. 'It might be Billy.' Had he lain awake all night, breaking his heart over how he had hurt her?

She hurtled across the square of landing into the front bedroom, lifting the corner of the curtain at the same moment as the visitor stepped away from the door and looked up. A rush of warmth engulfed her at the sight of Letty's face. At that moment, Letty was the only person she could forgive for not being Billy.

63

She waved, then hurried back to Mam, reaching to take her hands reassuringly.

'It's Letty.'

'Don't let her in.'

Mam tugged sharply and Carrie almost lost her balance, bending double to keep her footing, her face close to the urgency in Mam's eyes.

'It's Letty,' she repeated.

As Mam clambered to her feet, Carrie supported her, relieved that she seemed to be returning to normal, but then Mam snatched her arms, trying to hang on to her.

'Mam, let go! What's the matter? I don't understand.'

'Don't let them in.'

'There is no *them*. It's Letty. How many times have you said she's like another daughter to you? Get dressed and I'll put the kettle on.'

Disentangling herself, she hurried downstairs to open the door a crack for Letty to squeeze in.

'Oh, Carrie.'

They stared at one another, then moved into each other's arms.

'I'm that sorry,' Letty murmured.

'You've heard, then.'

Letty stepped back, her face crinkling. 'Course I've heard. Everyone has. I don't know what to say.'

'Don't try. Coming is enough.'

'Of course I came.'

'I'll put the kettle on.'

'Nay, I can't stop. I'm on my way to work.' Letty followed her to the kitchen. 'Sorry to barge in so early, but I wanted you to know that ... well...'

'I know.'

'He were always kind to me and polite to everyone. That's what I'll remember. I wanted to come yesterday evening, but Mam said best not. She said: Give 'em time to get used to it.'

Laughter erupted from Carrie's lips, a bitter sound. 'How are we meant to get used to this?'

She rubbed her hands up and down her arms. All at once she was fourteen again and the news about Pa had just arrived. Tears welled, scorching eyelids still tender from last night. Deep dry sobs cracked her ribs, just as they had when she was fourteen; and Letty's arms slid round her and held her, just as they had when she was fourteen. The sobs shuddered to a halt, leaving her feeling like an old dishcloth with every last drop wrung out of it.

Letty eased away.

'Sorry,' Carrie whispered.

'Don't be daft. It's what I'm here for.'

'Have you heard about Billy?' She absolutely would not ask if that too was common knowledge, but Letty's sympathetic nod left no room for doubt. 'I haven't spoken to him yet. I don't know what's happening until I've spoken to him.'

'But surely—?'

'I never saw him. He told Evadne. I went round, but Mrs Shipton wouldn't let me in, shoved me clean off her doorstep.'

'Eh, she never. What did she say?'

Carrie sank onto a chair. Letty sat too, pulling her seat close, bumping knees. Her eyes widened as Carrie explained.

'I can hardly believe it,' Carrie finished. 'I never

thought she'd tek against me.'

'She hasn't, not against you personal, like.'

'Is that supposed to make me feel better? I can't bear to think what's being said about Pa.'

'I know, love. Everyone's shocked at the minute. They need time to get used to it.'

'And we don't?' snapped Carrie; then she sighed. 'I shouldn't tek it out on you. Of course everyone's shocked.'

'Give her time. She'll calm down.'

Carrie's heart put on a spurt. 'There is no time. We're getting wed tomorrow. Oh, Letty, you should have heard what she said about holding Billy back in his job.'

'Bitch. It were that army chaplain, weren't it? The one what kept vigil with your dad the ... the night before?'

'Aye. Letty, what should I do?'

'Speak to Billy. Like you say, you can't do owt until you've seen him. And see Father Kelly. He'll have heard about the hoo-ha his friend has caused. The wedding isn't cancelled until you and Billy go to him and say so, and even then he'd want to know the reason why. Ask him to speak to Billy, aye, and to Mrs Shipton an' all, set her straight.'

'No. I'm not having it said Billy married me because Father Kelly made him. It's for him and me to sort out. I just need–'

'What?'

'Nothing.'

She couldn't say it. She could barely bring herself to think it. She needed to get Billy on his own, well away from Mrs Shipton. He should

66

have stood up for her yesterday, should have told his mam that she was his girl and always would be. As for skulking inside the house while Mrs Shipton made a holy show of her in the street...

He had never let her down before. Even jilting her didn't count, because that was the shock. She could accept that – just about. But not speaking up for her when she was right there on his doorstep ... that was ... it was – she flinched away. You didn't think things like that about your husband.

Chapter Seven

'You do realise, don't you, Doctor Armstrong, that the world and his wife think you're barking mad? A garden party, of all things!'

Walking down the wide, shallow steps of Brookburn's handsome main staircase, Adam glanced sideways at her. She was a good sort, Violet Wicks. She had been a top-notch nurse in France and would make an excellent sister here. Everything had to be the best at Brookburn. That mattered more than he could say. This hospital was his brainchild. More, it was his heart-child, if there was such a thing.

'I'm not going to hide these fellows away and pretend they don't exist,' he said. 'God knows, enough other people are pretending – including their own families, in some cases. As if these men's lives aren't wretched enough without their being cast adrift by their nearest and dearest.'

'Not all the families are like that, but how much more of a slog it's going to be for the men who lack that support as they recover.'

As they recovered. *If* they recovered – and that 'if' applied to the cherished men as well as those who had been abandoned.

Adam paused on the half-landing, where a large window overlooked attractive parkland and the gravel drive that swept down to the gates. What a place for a hospital! His critics muttered that a manor house was hardly the appropriate place, but he believed there was nowhere better for these men than spacious, peaceful surroundings; and heaven knew, after the horrors they had endured, they had earned the privilege.

Sister Wicks stopped beside him.

'And do you think I'm barking mad?' he asked.

'If I did, I wouldn't be here.'

Her dry tone of voice didn't fool him; he knew how deeply she cared about her work.

They continued down the stairs, Adam patting his pocket to make sure he had his tobacco pouch, and into the lofty dining room. One dining room for all the staff: he had insisted on that. Aside from the waste of space involved in separation, he and Todd wanted to get to know the staff. The work they were embarking on was pioneering and an atmosphere of trust was essential. He and Christopher Todd, ably assisted by Violet Wicks, had worked damned hard to turn their vision into a reality. The three of them knew one another of old, having served together in France.

All at once, his nasal passages, his throat, even

the backs of his eyes were coated with the sickly sweet stench of gangrene, the sharp tang of anti-septic and the bad-egg stink of pus. Only think: back in '14, he had taken a taxi to the docks so as not to be late for the war. He had spent the following years – God Almighty, the war had lasted years, not the few weeks it was meant to – patching up the wounds of those poor blighters who could be sent back to the bottomless pit of death and destruction, and amputating the pulped limbs of those that couldn't, and all done against a background filled with the ground-shuddering clump of heavy artillery.

The courage of those men beggared belief. Never once had he known a chap write or dictate a letter home that would give his folks any inkling of the extent of his injuries. *I am none the worse ... feeling bobbish ... doing well...* That was what they said, capital fellows the lot of them, from the lads so pitifully young their voices hadn't broken to the old 'uns who had lied about their ages the other way.

The men here at Brookburn weren't capable of writing letters. They were men who, after their wounds had been patched up and their bones were knitted together, simply didn't recover, men who had no physical reason to remain inert and yet who stayed silent and immobile.

'Mind-horror,' Doctor Nathaniel Brewer called it.

Men whose mental scars ran so deep that their physical bodies had shut down.

Brewer's experiences had provided the inspiration that led to the setting up of this hospital.

Before the war he had pursued his own dream of establishing a clinic in one of the poorest areas of Manchester.

Brewer and his wife, Mary, were to be among the guests today. Mary wrote a regular column in *Vera's Voice* and had promised to write an article.

'For all the good that'll do you,' Ralph had said scornfully the other evening when Adam called round. *'Vera's Voice* is for middle-aged women worried about getting stains out of chintz.'

'Middle-aged women who, between them, have lost an entire generation of sons. The perfect audience, I'd have thought.'

Not that Ralph's attitude had softened, but that had come as no surprise. There was nothing soft about Ralph, as the lads at school who had called him wet for knowing the difference between Wedgwood and Staffordshire had discovered to their cost. He had always had a tough streak.

Maybe if Molly—

Don't go down that road. Ancient history.

A swift bacon and eggs, then Adam started his morning rounds, accompanied by Sister Wicks. Some of the men were being bathed and shaved; the limbs of others were being put through a regime of bends and stretches to prevent muscle wastage. In each ward was a gramophone; soothing music was played softly during the night, jollier stuff in daytime. The staff were encouraged to talk cheerfully to the men, even to hum or sing as they worked, and it wasn't unusual to hear the strains of 'I'm Forever Blowing Bubbles' or 'Goodbye-ee' as you went about your business. Adam had set a bottle of champagne aside for the

70

day one of the chaps started mumbling along.

He sat beside a couple of beds and described to the men what was in store at the garden party tomorrow. He and Todd had described the arrangements to every patient over the past day or two. Could the men hear? To tell the truth, he didn't know, but it was essential to treat them as though they could.

'It should be a pleasant little shindig. Not too crowded. We've got some relatives coming – including your sister and nephews, if I'm not mistaken, Fletcher – and the local bigwigs.'

'And some of the men, Doctor,' one of the orderlies added with a grin. 'Don't forget them.'

'As if I would, Prosser. They're the most important attendees.' Getting the men outside was part of the treatment. He only wished they had more of the wheeled chairs with leg rests and sloping backs, in which the men could lie up when they were taken from their beds.

'You'll be rubbing shoulders with the toffs, Fletcher,' said Prosser. 'It'll be all right, won't it, Doctor? Wouldn't want Fletch and the others lying here stewing about it.'

'Nothing to worry about. Just staff, family, and locals who contributed to setting up this place, including my father, as it happens, getting together in pleasant surroundings on what is certain to be another fine day.'

'Hear that, Fletcher? Be grateful for good weather. Doc here 'ud have you outdoors in the rain if needs be.'

Adam laughed. Barking mad? Possibly. But if he was, then it was a top-hole thing to be.

Carrie went through the motions, sitting, standing, kneeling, the same as the rest of the con-
gregation at nine o'clock Mass, but her mind
wasn't on it. All she could think was that when
she was here last Sunday, she had been brimming
with excitement, knowing her next visit would be
as a bride. Instead, here she was, come to beg
Father Kelly not to cancel the wedding.

Her eyes prickled, but it was no use feeling
sorry for herself. She bowed her head, concentrating fiercely on the repose of Pa's soul. What
were the rules for the souls of executed soldiers?
The Church had a rule for everything else. Did
they have one for men like Pa?

At the end of Mass, she loitered in her pew,
heartbeats cramming her chest as she avoided the
stares coming her way from those filing out. Mrs
O'Malley leant over her, all beady black eyes and
stale breath.

'I noticed you didn't go to Communion. Can't
say I'm surprised.'

'I couldn't. I had breakfast with Mam to
encourage her to eat.'

'So much for repentance in the Jenkins household.' Mrs O'Malley sailed righteously on her
way.

'Well, Carrie Jenkins, you've come for a little
talk, have you?' Now Father Kelly was leaning
over her, vestments ballooning.

Her fingers curled around the edges of her
shawl. 'Do you know the trouble that friend of
yours caused?'

He straightened and stepped backwards, as if

72

making room for a thunderbolt to smite her.

Her hand scrambled across her mouth. 'I'm sorry. I didn't know I was going to say that.' She hadn't even known she was thinking it, but she was. It was roaring round in her head. Father Kelly's friend had blabbed in the pub.

'I don't expect you to point the finger, Carrie Jenkins.'

'I didn't mean it.' Yes, she did. 'I'm here about–'

She couldn't look him in the eye, but she mustn't drop her gaze because that would look like she was in the wrong. She fixed her eyes on the tiny red lines that gathered on either side of his nose, lines that said he never had to put his hand in his pocket in a pub.

'Mrs Shipton came to see me after seven o'clock Mass,' he said. 'Beside herself with fury, so she was, and I had to warn her to watch her tongue or else I'd be hearing the whole lot over again in confession.'

'You haven't cancelled the wedding, have you? Only I've yet to speak to Billy.'

'Do you want me to speak to him, child?'

'No – thank you. We just need to sort it out.'

'Wouldn't it be better to postpone things a wee while? You wouldn't want to make your mammy appear in public so soon, and her just revealed as a deserter's widow.'

Her muscles stiffened. 'You can't blame her for keeping it secret.'

'I'll expect to hear her confession before she sets foot inside God's house as the mother of the bride.'

Talk about pointing the finger. Carrie bolted

for the door. She didn't trust herself to speak. As for Mrs Shipton beating her to it by going to seven o'clock Mass, the thought took her breath away. Did Billy know? Of course not. He would never have let his mam go this far. Calling it off yesterday had been an aberration on his part. Mrs Shipton had lost her rag and he, shocked to the core about Pa, had got swept along by her outrage.

Oh, Billy. Carrie flung the message out to him from the depths of her heart. It'll come right, love. Don't fret. It'll come right.

It had to.

Ralph spent the morning sizing up pieces of furniture in a grand house off Palatine Road in West Didsbury. He already had a buyer in mind for that colossal mahogany display cabinet with the plate-glass doors, while that pair of rosewood whatnots and the Regency chiffonier would soon sell in the shop. Taking his leave, he strolled around Marie-Louise Gardens, taking swift drags on a cigarette. Not that he was the type for poncing around admiring flower beds, but he enjoyed the feeling of being his own man. A spot of business, then a few minutes to himself. He wasn't some lackey who had to hotfoot it back to the shop.

Joseph Armstrong and Son. He wasn't keen on that 'and Son'. As a lad starting out in the business, he had longed for it and had swelled with pride the day the words were painted over the shop, but that was a good few years ago now. Armstrong and Armstrong would be better, though nowhere near as satisfying as plain Ralph Armstrong.

The old man's retirement couldn't come soon enough for Ralph. He had been banging on about it for long enough. Even before the war, he was saying he didn't intend to die in harness like his father and grandfather; and during the war, on the couple of occasions Ralph had been home on leave, he had seemed more determined.

'It meks you think, this blasted war does, dragging on like this, meks you realise what's important.'

That certainty – certainty! What a joke. But at the time, that certainty had freed Ralph to make promises he might not now be able to keep.

And if he didn't keep them...

He threw down the fag end on the gravel path and ground it beneath his heel. He felt like grinding his father underfoot too.

He headed back to Chorlton on the tram, jumped off at the terminus and cut along leafy High Lane and past the smart houses on York Road. Pausing on the corner of Wilbraham Road to let an ice-cream seller cycle past, he looked diagonally across the wide street to where Armstrong's enjoyed a corner plot, an excellent site. Times were when the mere sight of the family business had made him puff out his chest. Now he felt more like flinging his hat in the gutter and grabbing his hair in clumps.

The other shops in the parade had canvas awnings that were pulled down this morning to shield against the sun, but not Armstrong's. The others looked like they were batting their eyelashes, but Armstrong's stared straight out at the world, making Jos. ARMSTRONG & SON all the more obvious.

Joseph bloody Armstrong. He should be growing dahlias and brushing up his crown green bowling by now, preferably a hundred miles away so that he couldn't stick his nose in when Ralph set up the auction room.

The auction room.

He had expected to have it up and running by now. And his associates had expected it too.

He crossed the road. His stride, quick with vexation, ate the ground as he approached the shop. Not only was it double-fronted, it also had a large window round the far side. It was a bloody crime how useless Dad was at putting together window displays, but he was too stubborn to let Ralph or Weston take over.

The brass bell jingled as Ralph opened the door. In the middle of the impressive array of walnut and satinwood, Sheraton and Hepplewhite, fruit stands and candelabra, marble clocks and fine china, stood Adam, looking relaxed, his jacket unbuttoned, its front pieces pushed out of the way so he could stick his hands in his pockets, his trilby smothering the head and torso of a bronze figurine of Nelson. Ralph could cheerfully have stuck Lord Nelson where the sun didn't shine. He didn't like others muscling in on his patch, and he liked his brother least of all.

Adam was passing the time of day with Mr Weston. And that was another thing: he needed to get shot of Weston every bit as much as he had to get rid of Dad.

'What are you doing here?' he asked bluntly.

Adam looked round. 'Good morning to you too.'

To his horror, Ralph heard himself utter a gruff humph that made him sound like Dad. He shook hands. Had Adam noticed? Old Weston faded discreetly among the porcelain with his duster.

'So what are you doing here? Not like you to make social calls in working hours. Left the waxworks to rot, have you?'

Adam's brown eyes hardened, an expression Ralph liked to provoke.

'They're men, just like we are.'

'Not like me!'

The palms of his hands went clammy at the mention of his brother's patients, though calling them patients was stretching a point, made them sound like they were human and they certainly didn't qualify for that description any more. Better to shoot them and put them out of their misery.

'I dropped in to see if Dad was free to join me for a bite to eat,' said Adam, 'and to make sure he's still coming to the garden party.'

Garden party? Freak show, more like. Waxworks on parade. And if Dad thought it so ruddy marvellous that 'our lads' were receiving what Adam called groundbreaking treatment, why didn't he pack in the shop and go to Brookburn as one of Adam's volunteer lackeys? Then they would all be happy.

'And is he free?' Ralph asked.

'Haven't seen him. He's gone out.'

Ralph drummed the top of a pedestal table

77

with his fingertips. 'It must be important for him to abandon ship while I'm out doing a valuation. What's he doing? Chasing a bargain?'

'In a manner of speaking.'

Ralph's senses sharpened. 'What d'you mean?'

'You won't know yet. Dad didn't hear about it until after you'd gone. Mr Weston has been telling me.'

'Heard what?'

'That woman he's interested in – Mrs Jenkins. It turns out her husband was executed for desertion. Dad's gone round to offer his condolences.'

'Pay his respects to a bloody deserter?'

'You know how he feels about Mrs Jenkins. This will be a difficult time for her. Put yourself in her position.'

'I'd rather not, especially with the old man sniffing round.'

'It could be what tips the balance in Dad's favour.'

'Are you suggesting she might marry him?'

'I'm pretty sure that's what he had in mind when he brushed his bowler and trimmed his moustache. The old man setting up in happy retirement with the new Mrs Armstrong, leaving the business in your capable hands – that would suit you, wouldn't it?'

Ralph pushed back his shoulders. Damn right it would. Damn right. Him – and his associates.

Chapter Eight

'More money than sense, some folk,' Mam had said about Mrs Randall's crazy paving; and Carrie, pausing with one hand on the garden gate as she checked the number on the front door, could see what she meant. She had never seen crazy paving before and she wasn't impressed. Useless for teaching your daughters hopscotch.

She hurried up the path between clumps of marigolds and snow-in-summer, drawn like a magnet to the good-looking front door with its gleaming brass numbers and circular stained-glass window, but at the last moment she veered round the side of the house in search of the kitchen door, where she knocked and waited.

No one came. Try again or walk right in? She tried the knob. The door was unlocked, so she stepped into Mrs Randall's kitchen, famous the length of Wilton Lane for its electric cooker, an item Carrie had vaguely imagined as being surrounded by a golden glow. It looked pretty much the same as a gas cooker, though there was barely time to feel surprised as the kitchen door was thrown open and a well-dressed lady planted herself in the doorway.

'What time do you call this?– Oh! Who are you? How dare you enter my house?'

'I'm Carrie Jenkins, ma'am, Mrs Jenkins' lass.' She spoke quickly before Mrs Randall could send for the police. With a bosom that size, she probably had the lung capacity to summon them all the way from Beech Road with a single bellow. 'My mam's poorly, so I've come instead.'

She held her breath. Had word of Pa penetrated as far as the dignified houses on Edge Lane? Would Mrs Randall sling her out on her ear?

'This is highly irregular.' Mrs Randall touched a hand to her old-fashioned pompadour. 'But I suppose it'll have to do. You may hang your shawl on that hook.'

'Thank you.' If she could keep the job open for Mam, it would be one less thing to worry about.

'You'll find everything you need in the broom cupboard. You may start in here.'

Mrs Randall walked into the hallway, which was as big as a room, with a vast hallstand with hat pegs and a mirror on top and cupboards underneath; a smaller cupboard bearing a rubbery-leaved plant; a dinner gong; and an umbrella-stand containing more sticks and brollies than Mrs Randall, her husband and brother could possibly use, even if they all took one of each.

There was wood everywhere – doors, floor, staircase panelling, furniture – and all of it shone. Carrie felt a burst of pride. Mam couldn't have signed her name more clearly if she had carved it into the skirting board.

Pride soon dissolved, however, replaced by bubbling frustration. Mam had often talked about Mrs Randall's attractive house with its ornaments and paintings, but Carrie found no pleasure working here. Mrs Randall followed her round, criticising everything she did and making her do things again even though she knew there was nothing wrong with her cleaning. It took longer than Mam's normal hours too, not least because Mrs Randall made her get out the library brush and dust the books, which she knew for a fact was one of Mam's Tuesday jobs, and why the blessed things wanted dusting anyway was anybody's guess when they were kept in bookcases with glass doors, but she didn't object for fear of losing Mam her place.

At last she was finished. She washed her hands in the scullery, cupping water into her palm and splashing the back of her neck, which afforded her a moment's refreshment. Taking her shawl from the peg, she went to present herself for payment, snatching a glance in the hallstand mirror and twitching a couple of strands of hair into place. Her face was flushed and she felt sticky after all that polishing and rug-beating in this heat. She had never realised how demanding Mam's job was. She had thought that, because of the long hours she put in at the shop, Mam had it easy, but that wasn't the case at all.

To cap it all, Mrs Randall announced that today would be docked from Mam's wages.

'But that's why I'm here,' Carrie spluttered. 'To do the work for her.'

Mrs Randall uttered a condescending laugh. 'I don't think a slip of a girl can offer the same standard of work as a grown woman with years of experience.'

She opened her mouth, then stopped. Was Mrs

Randall within her rights? 'Well, dock some of the money if you must, but not all of it. That's not fair.'

'Life, as you will discover, isn't fair. Why, for example, am I being harangued by the likes of you? I suggest you leave my house immediately – before I call a constable.'

Carrie's concern for Mam's job vanished in a puff of smoke. Bugger Mrs Randall. If this was how she treated her staff, Mam was better off out of it.

She bunched her fists on her hips. 'Go on, then. Let's see what the law says.'

Mrs Randall's eyes popped wide open. 'Now see here–'

'I've worked hard and I'm entitled to be paid. Does the bobby pass this way on his beat? I'll nip next door and ask.'

Mrs Randall made a gobbling sound. 'Oh, very well, then.'

Carrie made a point of counting the money Mrs Randall practically flung at her; she wouldn't put it past the woman to try to diddle her. Though she fought to keep her expression stony, inside she was boggling. Fancy her, who had been brought up to be polite and respectful, squaring up to Mrs Randall like a fishwife. Something must have got into her, because instead of meekly leaving via the kitchen door as befitted her station, she made a lunge for the front door and darted out, turning to find Mrs Randall gasping on the doorstep.

'And you needn't think you'll see my mam again,' she said. 'I wouldn't let her come back here, not if you paid her a hundred pounds.'

She skipped away before Mrs Randall could slam the door. It was a good job the Randalls had crazy paving or she might have hopscotched down to the gate.

Buoyed up by her triumph, Carrie headed for home with a spring in her step. Bright sunshine was bouncing off the flagstones, but merely being outside made her feel cooler after slogging away for that disagreeable woman. Further along the road, Mrs Jackson and Mrs Tilbury were coming towards her.

She started to smile but they crossed the road. She jerked her head back. They had crossed over on purpose. Look at them now, gazing into one another's eyes like a courting couple, anything to keep their attention away from her.

Was this how it would be from now on? People pretending not to see, crossing over to avoid her. Jesus, Mary and Joseph, it would kill Mam if it happened to her. Carrie glared over her shoulder at the women. If there was any justice, one of them would walk into a lamp post.

She felt a thrill of fear. Her children – would they be scorned at school? Kids could be cruel. The baby inside her, her precious first child – would he or she be made to suffer because of Pa? She felt sick at the thought.

'Don't trouble trouble till trouble troubles you.'

That was what Pa used to say. Not that he had been irresponsible or lax, but he hadn't taken his worries to heart. Yet he had acted in the most irresponsible way imaginable, leaving his family to face a lifetime of worry and shame. That wasn't the Pa she knew; and yet it was what he had done. She couldn't take it in, couldn't accept it.

But everyone else would accept it. They would hold him in contempt and his family would live their lives knowing the name of Jenkins was for ever tainted. Would her encounter with Mrs Randall turn out to be the last time in her whole life that she was with someone who didn't know?

Her shoulders curled. She pulled herself upright, but her heart beat faster and faster, out of control. It was going to explode. Was this how Mam felt? No wonder she was holed up indoors. Carrie longed to be home, safe, hidden. She put on a spurt, head down.

Outside the house, she gathered her resources before going in. She had to be strong for Mam.

Mam was sitting in the kitchen, elbows on the table, hands cupped over her nose and mouth. She stirred. Her hands fell away as she sat up.

Carrie glanced into the scullery. The breakfast pots were still on the wooden draining board, and that wasn't like Mam. They should have been put away long since. Likewise – she looked at the clock on the mantelpiece – Mam should have prepared something to eat.

Mam's gaze followed hers. 'Is it that time already? You've been gone ages.'

'Mrs Randall kept me. And I should tell you at once, she probably won't want you back.'

Mam let out a juddery breath. 'She's heard about Pa.' She clasped her elbows, pulling her arms to her body.

Carrie was beside her in an instant, bending so

84

their faces were close, but Mam wouldn't look at her.

'I should have said it first – it were me. I was rude to her.'

Mam leant away to look at her. Her eyes were fat with tears. 'You? You were rude to Mrs Randall? I never fetched you up to cheek your betters.'

'She deserved it.'

'No one deserves it, and now you've lost me my job.'

Was that a good sign? 'Perhaps if you went and talked to her–'

'No! I keep telling you. I can't go out.'

Mrs Jackson and Mrs Tilbury crossing the road. 'No, Mam, I know. Not yet. Let's not fret about that now. Let's have summat to eat. Shall I help?'

But Mam stayed put. 'You do it.'

The meat safe was empty. Carrie assembled plates of bread and butter with tomatoes and chutney, and a pot of tea. Yesterday she had commented on the flavour of the tomatoes, but now she couldn't taste them. Yesterday, she had washed her hands twice after tea because of trying on her wedding dress.

'Did anyone come round while I were out?'

'No – yes. No.'

'No yes no?' She spoke lightly, trying to encourage Mam into conversation. 'What does that mean?'

'Someone knocked but I never answered.'

'You didn't answer the door?'

'Two or three times.'

'It could have been Mrs Clancy or Mrs Hard-

85

acre, come to see how you are.'

'Or come to give me a mouthful for keeping it secret all this time.'

'They wouldn't do that. They're your friends.'

'Friends I've kept a terrible secret from.'

'Go round and see them, try to explain.'

'How many times must I tell you? I'm not going out.'

Carrie pushed her chair back. 'Then I can pop next door and fetch Mrs Clancy.'

'You'll do no such thing.' Mam's eyes were bright with anger, or possibly panic. She fetched a deep sigh. 'Leave it, love. Honestly, just ... leave it.' She closed her eyes.

Fine. Carrie looked at the plate in front of her. She had been brought up to think of the starving children in India, but she had done little more than pick at her meal and what she had forced down sat heavily in her stomach.

'Aren't you going to touch yours, Mam?'

'No, thank you.'

'You need to keep your strength up.'

'So do you.'

Carrie got up. 'I'll clear away, then I need a strip-wash.'

Right now, right this minute, she should be setting off for the public baths, armed with her towel and her lavender bath salts. A fist squeezed her heart.

Upstairs, she sprinkled some salts into the flowery china bowl on the washstand. It was only right. It was like saying she knew things would get sorted with Billy.

Afterwards, she washed her hair, though

without Mam to help with jugs of clean water, it took ages. She kept her hair long because that was how Billy liked it, and she did too. If only she could have proper fair hair, it would improve her looks no end. A couple of years ago she had tried rinsing it in vinegar to lighten it, but all that had achieved was to make her smell like a chip shop. Now she used rosemary to make it shine and told herself she was content, but she wasn't really.

She towel-dried it and put it in rags.

'Why are you getting all primped up?' Mam wanted to know.

'I'm seeing Billy later.' How calm she could sound, almost as if the two of them had agreed on it. 'He likes me to look my best.' It was important for a town hall clerk's wife to look the part.

Mam disintegrated into tears. She patted her skirt, searching for the pocket, and pulled out a sodden little scrap trimmed with lace. Carrie went upstairs and opened Mam's drawer. They hadn't kept Pa's clothes, but they had kept his handkerchiefs because Mam said they would be useful if one of them had a bad cold.

She shook out the hanky and offered it to Mam.

'This has ruined all our lives,' Mam mourned.

Carrie badly wanted to discuss the Billy situation. In particular, she would have appreciated sharing a jolly good gripe about Mrs Shipton, but with Mam focused solely on their disgrace, what hope was there of that?

The afternoon dragged by. Carrie kept one eye on the clock. At last it was time to take out her rags. Her hair was still damp and she wanted to give it a good brush, but if she did that, the waves would drop out. She fastened it up in a loose knot. The looser it was, the longer the waves would last. Evadne never had to worry about such things. Her hair had a natural crinkle that looked very modern.

There. She was ready to meet Billy on his way home from the office. She stood up straight, feeling tall – Billy's job always made her feel tall. He was a town hall clerk, and that counted for something. They might be starting out their married lives in a modest way, being so young, but one day they would have a house with a garden and Mam could live with them and help with the children.

As she went downstairs, the front door opened to admit Evadne.

'How is she?' Evadne asked without preamble.

'The same. She hasn't been out.'

Evadne's mouth went thin. 'Some of us didn't have a choice. Where are you going?' she asked as Carrie reached for her shawl.

'To meet Billy.'

'Not again. I didn't realise you were such a glutton for punishment.'

Carrie was stung, but she hid it. Evadne didn't understand. She had never been engaged. She didn't grasp how it bound you together. And Carrie and Billy had the baby an' all.

She went to say goodbye to Mam, standing behind her chair to drop a kiss on her cheek so she couldn't grab her and try to make her stay. As she walked down the hall, the letter box flap opened. The teatime post was early. But it wasn't

88

a letter. Carrie frowned as something floated to the floor. A piece of ribbon? No, a feather.

She opened the door in time to see children running away. She picked up the feather from the mat. It was grey – from a pigeon? Her first thought was that it might contain any amount of miniature wildlife and she held it out in front of her in between her fingertips to drop it outside.

Then the second thought struck.

A grey feather doing the job of a white one.

Chapter Nine

Carrie hovered at the tram stop near the corner of Sandy Lane, bouncing on her toes as she gazed along Barlow Moor Road, willing the tram to clank into view. Would Billy take one look and sweep her into his arms? Her heart put on a spurt. He was so handsome in his suit and bowler. His stiff white work collar always made her want to loosen the knot in his tie and unfasten his collar studs and top button, then pull him down by his lapels to kiss him.

The tram appeared. Nerves boiled up inside her, knotting her muscles. She threw her energy into relaxing them, striving to regain her calm. Calm! Try telling that to her tummy, which was rolling around like a drunken sailor.

She stepped back for passengers to alight. Her eager gaze caught Billy before he saw her and her heart turned to putty.

'Billy!'

He gawped. 'Carrie – what are you doing here?'

'I've come to meet you.'

His face changed. He flushed a dull red and his expression was... She recalled a term from the war: neutral territory. That was Billy's expression: neutral, not giving anything away.

'This is a surprise, Carrie.'

'Didn't you expect it? It wasn't decent what you did yesterday, speaking to Evadne instead of waiting for me. Heaven knows, I were only upstairs.'

'Aye, well, I'm sorry about that.'

'I'm not holding it against you. Everyone was upset, but we've calmed down now.' She waited for him to take up the cue, but all he did was shift awkwardly from foot to foot, so she had to say it herself. 'We need to talk. Can we go to the park?'

'My mam's expecting me home.'

'My mam's expecting me home an' all, but I'm making time for this. And my mam needs me right now a lot more than yours needs you.'

'How is she?'

Mam worn out with grief and shame. Mrs Tilbury and Mrs Jackson crossing the road. Once she got things sorted out with Billy, she could concentrate on looking after Mam.

'Let's go to the park, eh, Billy?'

They walked in silence. She wished Billy would offer his arm, but maybe he felt he couldn't after breaking off their engagement. Only – how could you break an engagement by telling your fiancée's sister? As far as she was concerned, she was still very much engaged. Lifting her head, she took Billy's arm, but he didn't bend his elbow to receive her hand, just let his arm hang. Shame slickened her skin. She couldn't wait for the park's green railings to come into view.

They walked through the open gates, where the brook bubbled along in the dip to one side, and veered off the main path across the grass. As they approached a bench, Billy all but shook her off.

'You never said how your mam is.'

'Very upset. I'm that worried. She says she can't face anyone ever again.'

'Perhaps you should get back to her.'

'Evadne's there. What about us, Billy?' She forced herself to remain steady when he wouldn't meet her eyes. 'Yesterday was horrible, but let's put that behind us and think about the future.' She waited, but still he said nothing. 'I understand about yesterday. You were shocked rigid, your mam blew her stack, and things happened that shouldn't. I'm not holding it against you. Billy – please look at me.'

And he did. His colour was high, his eyes desperate. 'I'm sorry, Carrie.'

'I know, love. It's all right. I know your mam saw Father Kelly this morning and called off the wedding, but we can go and see him tonight.'

'She's cancelled the registrar.'

'You what?'

'You can't have a Catholic wedding without the registrar. My mam went to town this morning and cancelled him.'

The air froze in Carrie's lungs. She couldn't breathe and she couldn't think. Somehow she managed to get to her feet and walk away. There was a breeze. She knew there was, because she could see the leaves moving in the trees, but she couldn't feel it on her skin. Down in the dip, Chorlton Brook must be chuckling along, but she couldn't hear that either. Somehow, even though she couldn't hear him, she knew Billy was coming after her. She swung round to face him, slicing through whatever he was saying.

'Not now, Billy. Meet me here–'

'I can't come tomorrow.'

Tomorrow. Saturday, June the 19th. Their wedding day. The world – this bizarre world she had somehow ended up in, after Father Kelly's friend had blabbed about Pa – swam around her.

'Sunday, four o'clock.'

'I don't know. My mam–'

Carrie walked away. She got through the gates before hot tears blurred her vision.

'God, not you again,' Ralph said as Adam appeared in the sitting-room doorway, looking like a society swell from the last century in his frock coat, carrying his glossy silk topper. 'What do you want now?'

'Evening,' Adam replied, unperturbed.

He placed the top hat on the art-nouveau side table and walked right in as if he had every right to, which he didn't, blast him. He didn't live here any more and the moment Dad retired, that would be the end of Adam's dropping in for cosy chats. Ralph would change the locks if needs be.

They shook hands.

'I brought this for Dad,' said Adam.

Ralph didn't look. What did he care?

'Give it here. Dad's in the office.'

'I'll pop down.'

Oh no you won't, me laddo. Ralph loathed Dad's habit of finding something to finish off in the office after he had gone upstairs to the flat when the shop shut, just like he had when Ralph was fifteen. Why the hell couldn't the old sod let go?

'No need,' he said. 'He'll be up in a minute.'

'You're looking handsome this evening, Doctor Armstrong. Are you stopping for your tea?'

Bloody hell, that was all he needed, the hired help putting her two penn'orth in. She was their daily cook, for Pete's sake. It wasn't up to her to hand out invitations. But what could you expect? She had been with them for donkey's years and that gave her certain privileges, or it made her think it did.

Adam smiled at her. 'Evening, Mrs English. No, I'm not staying, though I'm sure I'll be sorry when you tell me what you've prepared.'

'It was pork and rabbit pudding for dinner, so I kept back a bit of pork for pig-a-leekie.'

'Sounds delicious.'

'Next time, perhaps. You're always welcome, Doctor Armstrong.'

That was another thing. Dad was Mr Armstrong while Ralph, as – Christ Almighty, there must be a better word for it – the junior mister was Mr Ralph; but Adam, instead of being Mr Adam, was Doctor Armstrong. It was ruddy irritating.

Why wouldn't the old man retire? Then Ralph could get rid of Mr Weston toot sweet and set up his auction room. He would give Mrs English her marching orders too. It was like the Ghost of Christmas Past doing the cooking. Dad had hired her during Mother's illness and she would have been gone seven years ago if Molly–

His thoughts snapped shut.

Except they didn't quite. A few squeezed out and trickled across his consciousness.

He would never forgive Adam. It hadn't been Adam's fault, but that wasn't the point. In fact, that made it worse. More damaging.

Mrs English said, 'I'll serve up and leave the plates in the oven, Mr Ralph, and I'll tek the rabbit skin and get the thre'penny deposit back from the butcher on my way in tomorrow.'

'Yes, fine.' As if he cared.

'Thank you, Mrs English,' said Adam. Quite the lord of the manor.

The woman withdrew and Ralph eyed his brother. Why doctors had to deck themselves out in clobber like that, he had no idea. Mind you, the frock coat sat well on Adam's slim, muscular frame – not that he would ever tell him so. Truth to tell – and Ralph made a point of telling himself the truth, no matter what bilge he fed to others – he had always rather fancied himself in a frock coat and top hat. Imagine striding round the streets and people pointing him out with an admiring, 'There goes Mr Armstrong. Dresses old-fashioned like, but doesn't he cut a fine figure? Knows everything there is to know about old things, so they say.' And not just in Chorlton-cum-Hardy either, but in town too. Imagine walking past those high-class antiques places on Deansgate and being recognised as the antiques

94

expert from Chorlton.

Except that, being thicker-set, he wouldn't cut such a fine figure as Adam did. Besides, what if locals got them mixed up? And they would. People were stupid. He and Adam shared their mother's brown eyes and mid-brown hair, and Dad's aquiline nose, but that didn't make them twins.

'Where are you off to, all togged up?' he asked as they sat, he in an armchair, Adam on the bentwood rocker. 'Fancy-dress party?'

'Very witty.' Adam pushed the rocker to and fro. 'I'm going to visit a patient.'

'Oh yes, one of your charity cases. You can't possibly do that in a lounge suit.'

The chair stopped. Adam touched one of his silk-faced lapels. 'It's a uniform. People expect it.'

A uniform? Soldiers wore uniforms. They lived and died in bloody uniform. They lit a fag and got their brains blown out by a sniper or they went over the top and died after half a dozen paces – in uniform. They dived for cover into a crater and got eaten alive by the mud, or they died hanging off the barbed wire, a piece of target practice for the Hun – in uniform.

Or, in spite of horrific injuries, they lived and were sewn back together by the likes of his dear brother so they could be packed off back to the front to face it all over again. His bloody brother was so certain of his life-saving skills that he even thought he could bring back the dead – because that's what those waxworks were, to all intents and purposes: dead. And not content with treating the waxworks at Brookburn, he had to get out and about in the community, bringing hope

95

where none was due.

'You might as well paint your face and call yourself a witch doctor.'

'I beg your pardon?'

'It's not my pardon you want. It's the pardon of all those poor saps you've kidded into believing their soldier boys have a hope in hell of recovery.'

'The treatment we're using is groundbreaking.'

'So you keep saying. Break the ground open and bury 'em, I say. That's all they're fit for.'

'I see you two are getting on well as usual.' Dad walked in, blue eyes narrowed in vexation, but that was nothing new. It didn't take much to irritate Joseph Armstrong. 'I don't know what your mother would say.'

Now there was an interesting thought. If Mother were still here, Adam would be part of the business. It was Mother's lingering and painful illness that had prompted his highfaluting ambition to become a doctor and save the world. Ralph wasn't glad Mother was gone, but he was bloody delighted he would never have to share the business with his brother.

Adam rose to shake hands. 'Evening, Dad. Here's the book I promised.'

He resumed his seat and Dad lowered himself into the other armchair.

'Oof. I'm glad to get the weight off my feet. Come to ask after Mrs Jenkins, have you?'

'No.' Adam grinned. 'Well, maybe. How is she?'

'Don't know. Didn't see her. If she was in, she wasn't answering. I'll try again tomorrow.' He pursed his lips. He had a craggy face that lent itself to wry chuckles as much as it did to crusty vexation. 'The young lass is meant to be getting wed tomorrow. Sweet girl.'

'Mrs Jenkins won't have time for you if she's busy being the mother of the bride.'

'Surely they'll have postponed it after what's happened?'

'Damn right,' said Ralph. Who in his right mind would shackle himself to a deserter's daughter?

'We'll see,' said Dad. 'Off to see a patient, are you?'

'The techniques we use at Brookburn are worth trying on people who have suffered strokes,' said Adam. 'Of course, it falls to the families to do all the exercises. I hope we'll help some people.'

'Got many patients round and about?'

'Two at present. The boys at Brookburn must come first.' He looked at the time. 'I'd better be off.'

Good riddance.

Ralph pondered on his father's interest in the Widow Jenkins. Maybe Adam was right and this calamity would tip the balance in Dad's favour. A sour taste rose in Ralph's mouth. Would the old man really lower himself to wed a deserter's widow? But if that was the price he had to pay for his father's retirement, pay it he would.

Then at long last he would have the business, just as he should have when he returned from France. Just as he had assured his associates he would. When the war ended, they had agreed to bide their time while Ralph set up his auction room and established it as a legitimate business concern. The summer of '21 was the date fixed for their enterprise to start, and here they were in the middle of 1920 and the auction room was still nothing more than an ambition.

But if the old man married his hapless widow, all that would change. Goodbye, Dad. Goodbye, Weston. How do you do, independence and wealth.

Chapter Ten

Carrie blew out a breath. It had to be done. That was one thing she had learnt when Pa died. No matter what happened, you still had to clean your step. And Mam wasn't up to doing it, which meant she must. Would folk think her brazen for doing it? One thing was certain: they'd think her a slattern if she didn't.

And after that she would go and get her job back. Mrs Trimble had said they weren't going to start looking for a new girl until next week. Carrie had worked ten-hour days six days a week since she was thirteen, except for half-day closing on Wednesdays. That must count for something.

'You won't work once you're married to me,' Billy had said, and how proud she had been to think he could support a wife immediately. Most girls she knew went on working until the first baby was ready to drop.

Wrapping her pinny round her, she half-filled the bucket in the scullery and walked down the hallway to the front door, not permitting herself to pause, just opening the door and stepping

98

outside. She put down the bucket and pulled the doormat onto the pavement. Kneeling on the mat was uncomfortable, but the prickling in her knees and shins was a good thing because it took her mind off the possibility of being watched. Not that any housewives were stoning their steps this early. Was she cowardly to do it before six?

Briskly she wet the cloth and washed the step, then set to with the donkey stone, scrubbing the light cream colour all over. Mam took pride in creating a swirly pattern, but all Carrie wanted was to get back indoors. Besides, might a pattern look frivolous?

The moment the step was finished, she gathered up her bits and darted back inside, her heart racing. Why the panic? She had more to worry about than being seen in the street. If she could get her job back, that would be a start. She wasn't letting Mam go back to Mrs Randall, no matter what, so she needed to bring in a few bob to tide them over until Mam found somewhere else and she and Billy got wed. Would Father Kelly be able to marry them next Saturday? Would the banns still count? She and Billy loved one another, and anyroad, there was the baby.

After coaxing Mam to eat some eggy bread, she hurried through the waking streets. The shop opened its doors at six, though her starting time had always been eight. She crossed Chorlton Green, where the dew sparkling in the early sunshine took her by surprise. Things could still be pretty – she hadn't realised that.

On the Green, she paused beside the makeshift memorial. There were going to be memorials all

99

over the country, proper memorials made of stone with lists of names engraved on them so that no one would ever forget the great sacrifice that had been made. That would be grand and fitting, of course, but she did love this impromptu memorial with its simple vases and jam jars of flowers, several of them discreetly labelled with the name of a husband, a son, a sweetheart who hadn't returned.

She looked for Pa's jar. She had gone onto the meadows on Tuesday evening with Billy to pick wildflowers, though of course Billy had wanted to do a lot more than that and she hadn't exactly protested. On their way home, she had picked some scabious, remembering how Pa had called them pin-cushion flowers, and placed them in his jam jar. Wildflowers were beautiful, but they didn't last long once they were picked.

Where was Pa's jar? Surely no one had moved it. No one interfered with other people's flowers. But it wasn't in its rightful place and there were no purply-blue flowers to be seen. Had someone thrown away Pa's flowers? She went all wishy-washy inside.

'Oh, Pa,' she whispered.

Aware of someone close by, she went rigid. She glanced round, then checked herself, frightened of who it might be. Someone who knew about Pa? The person – oh, goodness, the person responsible for chucking away his flowers? She scurried off, her feet automatically carrying her alongside the graveyard wall and into Hawthorn Road, a long street of red-brick terraces, giving off on to similar streets, and several corners boasting a shop.

She had always been proud to work at Trimble's. She loved the hard-working couple and their open-all-hours, we-sell-everything shop. She had never received anything but approval from them, so as she entered the shop, with its Brasso, Cherry Blossom and tonics for brain-fag and anaemia near the door, and food behind the counter, she expected at least a kindly smile, if not an exclamation of surprise. There was surprise all right in Mr Trimble's eyes, but he looked away.

She tried telling herself he was simply paying attention to his customer, Mrs Bradshaw from round the corner, but she didn't believe it. Mrs Bradshaw left, not without a quick glance at her, but Carrie had to walk right up to the counter before Mr Trimble would look up and acknowledge her.

He cleared his throat. 'Well, lass, we weren't expecting thee.' Turning to the bead curtain through which lay the living quarters, he shouted, 'Mother! Carrie's here. We're reet sorry to hear of your family troubles, lass,' he added as his wife appeared, her lined face showing surprise and concern – and was that wariness?

'Thank you. I was hoping I could have my job back, being as the wedding's postponed.'

'Postponed?' questioned Mrs Trimble. 'That's not what I heard.'

She held her head up. 'I hope to get wed next Saturday instead. You said you wouldn't be looking for a new girl just yet, so I thought maybe I could come back for another week.'

'Aye, well,' said Mr Trimble, 'thing is, we're already fixed up.'

'You are?' said Carrie.

'We are?' His wife looked at him.

'We are. That is, we've decided who we want and we're asking her later today.'

'Oh,' said Carrie. 'Well, if she's working, she'll need to give notice, so if I come back, you'll have help until she starts.'

'You don't want to do that, lass,' said Mr Trimble. 'Think how folks'll stare.'

'Whisper an' all,' added his wife.

'I can't afford to mind. So can I come back? Just for the week.' The answer was there in the way they glanced at one another. She bit down on a pang of humiliation.

'Thing is,' said Mr Trimble, awkward but resolute, 'we can't have your family troubles in't shop. Not good for trade.'

'There's many a war widow and orphan round this way,' added Mrs Trimble. 'Folks might take their custom elsewhere and we can't have that.'

'I'd best go.' Carrie turned away, then turned back. They were sagging with relief, but she had to pretend not to see. 'Who are you offering the job to? Anyone I know?'

'Letty Hardacre.'

'Letty? My Letty?'

'A good lass is Letty, an' you're always saying as how she hates that laundry. It'll be a good job for her and they need the money in that house. Letty and her mam and their Joanie have it all to do, what with poor Ernie Hardacre leaving his legs behind in Flanders. He's a real war hero, if you ask me. Unlike some, no names mentioned.'

'Shall I tell you what's happened? You and your secrets.' Evadne's voice was cold. It was the only way she could cope. Dear heaven, what had happened to her life? 'Thanks to you, I've lost my job and my home. All you had to do was tell me the truth when first you knew it, then I could have moved away. The school governors informed me this morning that my services won't be required next term; and Miss Martindale has advised me to seek accommodation elsewhere. You may well look stricken, Mother. It's all very well, you slouching here at home, but you aren't the only one affected.' Her conscience prickled, but she couldn't afford to soften. 'At least you have a roof over your head and a job to go to. Why aren't you at Mrs Randall's?'

Mother flinched. 'I can't. I just can't.'

'Don't be ridiculous. You've the rent to pay. Where's Carrie?'

'Gone to get her job back.'

'I'm glad one of you has a sense of responsibility.'

'What will you do?' Mother whispered.

Evadne didn't reply. The truth was that this could turn out to her advantage, but she couldn't say so after she had just ranted about how vile things were and how it was all Mother's fault. She couldn't say so, even if she hadn't ranted. This was her secret. The hot anxious hope that had nourished and tormented her through the years was her secret.

It was inconceivable that Grandfather Baxter, with his proud military bearing, would permit her to suffer like this. He had never approved of his

103

daughter-in-law's second marriage. Evadne could remember living with her grandparents in their smart Victorian villa in Parrs Wood after Daddy died and before Mother threw herself away on a nobody from Chorlton. After Mother married Pa, there had been monthly visits to the Victorian villa for Sunday tea. Proper afternoon tea, too, all dainty and formal, not the hearty high tea that filled lower-class bellies. She remembered butter knives and snowy linen and dishes of preserves – or jam as she, infected by plebian ways, had once called it, only to receive a look of such shocked disdain from Grandmother that she nearly died of embarrassment.

Grandmother passed away when Evadne was twelve and she had fantasised about Grandfather taking her to live with him, but he didn't. He paid for her to stay at school until she was fifteen, then paid for the inoculations she needed to be a pupil-teacher and found her a place in Oaklawn School, where she had been ever since. Not that she had anticipated such a long-term arrangement; no one had. She had regarded it merely as a stopgap to be tolerated until she married.

Not that that had happened.

Yet.

She closed her eyes. Her lashes brushed her high, elegant cheekbones. She willed the fear away.

Yet.

Oh, please let this scandal be the catalyst that would prompt Grandfather to take her under his wing, and more to the point under his roof. She imagined him escorting her to his solicitor to see about changing her name back to Baxter, and took heart.

A brisk rat-tat at the front door had Mother's hands snaking out to grab Evadne's best skirt, which she had spent hours on, taking in the seams to give herself an up-to-date silhouette, and worn today in honour of visiting Grandfather. With a small cry, she prised the fingers away.

'Leave it. Don't answer it,' Mother begged.

'Pull yourself together,' Evadne ordered, going to the door.

She was expecting a neighbour, but instead it was an older man, his appearance crisp and pressed but somehow not perfect. Her swift eye went to his shoes. You could tell a lot about a person from their shoes, and this fellow wore short boots. Pre-war. The width of his trouser legs said the same. Yet nothing about him suggested hard times. He was thin, though by no means underfed, and the set of his shoulders spoke of confidence.

This must be the antique shop fellow whose eye Mother had caught these past few months.

He raised his bowler. 'Good morning. Joseph Armstrong, here to pay my respects to Mrs Jenkins.'

'My mother is indisposed.'

'I heard about her trouble. I came yesterday, but there was no answer. I hoped she might see me today.'

She was about to dismiss him, then changed her mind. Dealing with her unwanted suitor might provide the jolt Mother needed to resume her responsibilities.

'My mother will be available at half past one. Good morning.'

She closed the door on his response.

Chapter Eleven

Ralph was particular about the customers for whom he opened the door as they left. Never for a gentleman: he wasn't a butler. Not for a couple, either: that was the man's job. But for a lady he would, especially when, as now, the lady had just coughed up nearly seventy pounds for an ebony and ivory chess set and a variety of china and cut-glass knick-knacks.

As he saw her out, Dad crossed the road, raising his bowler to her as she departed.

'The widow still barricading herself in?' Ralph spoke off-handedly. Don't look keen. Don't look as if it matters.

'One of the daughters was there – the older one. Didn't take to her, I must say. The young one's a sweetheart – I've met her a couple of times – but this one's a stuck-up crow. Looked straight down her nose at me, she did. Still, she's letting me in to see her ma, and that's what counts.'

'When?'

'This afternoon, my boy.' He twirled his bowler. 'Half-one sharp.'

'You can't. Weston's not here,' Ralph objected, 'and I'm off out at two to do an evaluation.'

'So shut up shop. Who knows, today could be

the day. She's a lady in need of protection and when she sees what I can offer...'

And there it was. At the very moment when he should be all fired up with anticipation because his father was going to swan off into genteel retirement with the new Mrs Armstrong, at the very moment his plans for the auction room should be dancing before his eyes – there it was, that sudden unease.

Just like when Dad knew about Molly.

The old bitterness came surging back. There was something going on here and it was just like last time.

Last time.

It had been Dad who had unwittingly alerted him. Dad had suspected, had seen something, had guessed. Ralph had had no idea. Why would he? He had loved Molly. He had trusted her. And she had loved him too.

Or she said she did. Afterwards – a long time afterwards – he had wondered about that. Had she truly loved him? If she did, how come she had looked at another man? How come she had looked at his bloody brother?

And he hadn't realised – until something in Dad's manner prompted a gut reaction, an unthinking certainty that something was wrong.

Molly loved Adam.

If Adam had seduced her, if he had tempted her away, that would have been bad enough, but nothing like as bad as the excruciating truth that she didn't want him any more. She wanted his brother.

And here it was again, that same gut reaction,

that instinctive knowledge that danger lay in wait.

What the hell was going on? Instinct screamed at him not to trust the old bugger.

The morning passed. Ralph sold a musical mechanical piece of a monkey artist painting a landscape, and a set of gilt-bowled fruit spoons in a velvet-lined case, but all the while his senses were on the alert.

At midday, he turned the sign to CLOSED and locked the door. Upstairs, Mrs English served fish-and-spinach pie, and almond tart. Ralph ate automatically. Food was fuel and fuel kept you on top form.

'What's going on, Dad? You've got something up your sleeve.'

'Wait and see.'

Just before one o'clock, as Ralph was about to head downstairs to reopen, Dad stopped him beside the hallstand on the landing near the top of the stairs that went down to the rear of the shop.

'Do my back for me, will you?'

Ralph took the clothes brush and dealt with his back and shoulders.

'When will you be back?' he asked.

'After I've called on Mrs Jenkins, I'm going straight to Adam's do at Brookburn, so you'll have to hang on to your curiosity till then.' He chuckled. 'All will be revealed.'

Ralph felt like swiping him round the back of the head with the clothes brush, something Dad had done more than once to him for cheek years ago. He dropped the brush on the shelf and ran downstairs, leaving the old man faffing with his cuffs.

He flicked the sign to OPEN and unlocked the

door. He was behind the counter looking at paperwork when his father appeared; but once Dad had clapped his bowler on his head and gone whistling out of the door, he moved swiftly to one of the windows to watch him swagger down Wilbraham Road. The sight of that swagger made his hands clench. Should he, shouldn't he? Damn right he should.

Seizing his homburg, he locked up and set off after him, keeping a careful distance, ready to duck into a doorway should the old man glance back. Senses sharp, he kept pace behind his father, footsteps light, nerves raw, muscles ready to respond.

Presently he was hanging back from the corner of Wilton Lane, watching as, along the line of two-up two-downs, Dad stopped, shifting his wiry shoulders inside his jacket before he knocked. The door opened. Not the widow; a young woman, tall and thin, and even the merest glimpse took in the haughty demeanour. Stuck-up, Dad had said, and he wasn't wrong. She allowed him to enter and a minute later the door opened again and she re-appeared in a hat and jacket and walked briskly up the road. Ralph turned away, hunching over the lighting of a cigarette, and her footsteps tap-tapped past him.

He walked down Wilton Lane, glancing at the number on the Jenkins' front door, then cut down the entry to find the back gate. No stopping, no pausing, he kept walking, took himself off to Chorltonville to do the evaluation. It was a good piece, a handsome table with an inlay of tortoiseshell, and he could think of a couple of customers who would be interested. Oh, for an auction room! Never mind any other use it would have, it would also be an asset to the legitimate side of the business. He agreed a price and said he would arrange collection, cursing Dad in his heart at the thought of the horse and cart when what a modern business cried out for was a motor van.

Business concluded, he slipped back to Mrs Jenkins' house.

Now to find out what the old bugger was up to.

'Jenkins *what?*' roared Grandfather Baxter and Evadne lowered her chin and looked down at the petersham bow trim and pointed toes on her shoes to conceal her gratification. Her feet were placed neatly side by side, one slightly forward of the other, on the wine-red carpet in Grandfather's sitting room, soon to be her sitting room too.

Raising her eyes to meet, and silently celebrate, Grandfather's fury, she repeated what she had said about the desertion and execution, and how Mother had kept the shameful secret, with Grandfather's complexion all the while going purple and mottled in a most satisfactory way. She allowed an interval for him to bluster and harrumph and exclaim 'Good gad!' a few times, then she got down to business.

'There's been all manner of repercussions.' She spoke mildly. That would rile him more than vexation. 'Miss Reilly left, and Carrie's young man has jilted her.'

'Good job you don't live there. Best keep your distance.'

She dropped her glance to hide the triumph in

her eyes. The distance would be all the way to Parrs Wood if she succeeded.

'The school governors don't want me to return in September and Miss Martindale feels she can no longer offer me a home.'

'If the lodger's gone, there's room for you back at your mother's.'

'Well – until the end of term, maybe. But after that...'

Her words of acceptance were ready on her lips, but instead of inviting her into his home, Grandfather went off on a different tack.

'Good gad! And to think I've been sending her ten shillings a week. She must have known I'd never have dreamt of subbing her had I known the truth.' He slapped his hands down on the carved mahogany arms of the chair. 'Ten shillings a week for four years! Fetch me a pen and paper, Evadne. What does that add up to?'

'Are you saying you've been helping Mother with money?'

'Ten bob a week! She's had a small fortune off me. I thought I was doing the decent thing, helping out with the rent and coal and whatnot, and all along she's been taking me for a fool.'

'I had no idea.' Heat flushed through her body. 'She never told me you gave her money.' If there had been money being handed out, it should have been given to her. She was Grandfather's flesh and blood, while Mother was merely his daughter-in-law. Not even that. His former daughter-in-law.

'I did it out of duty to Philip – your father. Never could understand what he saw in her and now I've been proved right. She should have stayed a widow but, oh no, she had to go and shackle herself to a bally coward. A deserter! My God! A deserter – and I've been helping support his widow. If the members of my club hear about this, I'll be blackballed.'

He snatched the silk handkerchief from his top pocket and dabbed his forehead.

'Grandfather.' She raised her voice. 'I'm reverting to the Baxter name.'

'Don't blame you. Just watch out when people ask why. Don't mention that Jenkins scoundrel, whatever you do. Ten shillings a week for four years!'

Shoving the handkerchief into his pocket, he came to his feet, headed for the door, threw it open. Evadne blinked in surprise. 'Where are you going?'

'Where do you think? To see my solicitor, of course, and cancel his instruction concerning your mother's weekly postal order.'

'It's Saturday afternoon. He won't be in his office.' Panic fluttered. She had to keep him here, had to make him concentrate on her predicament.

'You think I'd take this to the office, where it might be overheard? No, I'll catch him in the privacy of his own home. Best way – safest.'

He gave a jerky wave of the arm, which might have been in farewell or could have signified furious frustration, and then he was gone. She heard him banging about in the hall, shouting for his hat and his cane; she heard the housekeeper's scurrying footsteps – the very housekeeper whom she had intended to supplant when she became mistress of this gracious house.

The front door slammed and the air around her vibrated with frustration.

Chapter Twelve

Ralph ghosted his way down the back entries until he stood outside the Jenkins' house. The wooden gate might be in need of a lick of paint, but someone had kept the hinges oiled and it opened quietly on to a tidy yard – mangle in the corner, tin bath hanging on the wall next to the rainwater butt, a pot of herbs on top of the coal-hole. Ducking beneath the washing line, he cracked open the back door on to the scullery. Brooms and pail, clothes horse, roller towel, the copper, two sinks – not bad. This might be a simple two-up two-down, but if it had separate sinks for dishes and clothes, it was a better place than he had thought. His opinion of the widow went up a notch.

The door to the kitchen was ajar. Good.

Dad's voice. 'I'll tell thee straight, Mrs Jenkins. You need protecting from your husband's actions.'

'Mr Armstrong, please–'

'Nay, madam, let me finish. I can offer that protection. I'm prepared to buy a house. Buy, mind, not rent.'

Buy? Where was the money to come from?

'Somewhere with indoor plumbing and a garden, electrics too, maybe, and right away from here. By the sea, if that suits you. Southport's reet grand, or Lytham St Anne's. Young Carrie can come too, and welcome.'

Southport, Lytham. As far away as you damn well please.

Mrs Jenkins whispered, 'What would your lads say? Aren't they expecting to have the shop one day?'

'Not Adam. I paid for him to get a fancy education and he's a doctor. As for Ralph – well, yes, in different circumstances he would get the business; but he can get a job in one of them posh antiques places in town. He's even mentioned us having an auction room – as if we have time for that! But if auctioning is what he's set his heart on, working in a posh place on Deansgate would be a good move. He might even see if there's an opening at that auction place in Chester – Foster and Whatsits. Don't fret, I'll see him all right for money.'

Ralph's heart caught between his ribs. So this was it. The old bastard wanted to wrench the business away from him. He planned to sell the whole bloody concern to the highest bidder so he could piss off and grow roses in Southport. All Ralph's years of work counted for nothing. All the years he, Dad and Adam had assumed – more than assumed, had known, dammit, *known* – that the business would one day be his were to be dashed aside. Bung him a few hundred and send him to Deansgate – did Dad really think that was enough?

Did he really think Ralph would permit it?

And it wouldn't be just Ralph's inheritance he was selling. It would be the highly lucrative

114

future that he and the others had bided their time and waited for. His associates wouldn't tolerate being let down. Just see what had happened to Jonty Fellowes when he pulled out.

He wouldn't let it happen, by Christ he wouldn't, and he would deal with it now, here, in this house, in this kitchen. Contain the damage. Before she could accept the escape route on offer. Before Dad could march off to Brookburn with the glad tidings. Before anyone else could know what had been suggested. Kill it now. Kill it before it could grow.

How could Dad do this to him? How could he show him such lack of concern, such disrespect?

Heat pumped round his body, preparing him. His brain surged with small explosions of argument, persuasion, anger. He barged through the door, seeing everything at once; the war had taught him that. Two faces turned to him, eyes wide, mouths slack. They were sitting facing one another across the kitchen table.

'What the hell d'you think you're playing at? Sell everything and fob me off with a job on Deansgate? Not on your life. That's bloody outrageous.'

'Watch your language in front of a lady.'

'My language is the least of your problems. You want to retire – fine. Off you go, and about time too. But you don't need to sell the business and you don't need to buy a house.'

'I'll do as I please.' Dad came to his feet, the chair screeching on the tiled floor.

'You damn well won't.' Ralph strode forward. He squared his shoulders and expanded his chest. 'I've worked in that shop my whole life. I was running errands and doing small deliveries when I was eight years old. Every minute I wasn't at school, I was in the shop, watching, learning, listening to you and Weston discussing pieces, pricing them. Adam never did that, even before he got his high-and-mighty calling. But I did, because I knew what I wanted – and you're not taking it away.'

'Nay, your ideas for the shop are pie in the sky. Adding an auction room – have you lost your senses? If you keep the shop, you'll end up losing everything because of your fancy ideas. You want a better class of customer – go to Deansgate. You want auctions – go to Chester. But don't kid yourself I'm going to let you run my business into the ground. I'm doing you a favour.'

'A favour?' He took another step forward, crowding the old fool. He planted his feet apart, jutting his chin, but kept his voice low. 'Destroying my inheritance – a favour? You think I can't manage the business? You're the one that can't cope. You're stuck in the past. Who needs a delivery van when there's a perfectly good horse and cart? Who needs elegant displays when you can cram the windows full to bursting? Who needs modern ideas when you can carry on as if Victoria is still on the throne? Your time is over. You're holding me back; you're holding back the business. I don't care what you do as long as you do it somewhere else and leave me to build up the shop as it deserves – as I deserve. I worked hard for this. I've fought in a war, for God's sake; and I did it in the expectation of getting the business when I came home. This is my time, old man. Your time is over, finished.'

A potent mixture of resolve and triumph poured through his veins. He took a step closer, forcing his father to step away, step backwards; old man giving way to young, old ways and old values submitting before the inevitable might of the new, the enterprising, the ambitious.

'You come barging in here–' Dad blustered.

'When were you going to tell me? Were you going to tell Adam first? Was I to be the last to know?'

Another step; a corresponding step back. The school bully all over again. The strutting step, the probing glare, the gratifying contempt in the thrust-out chest.

'You think you can take away what is rightfully mine?' He delivered a sharp jab to his father's breastbone; Dad stumbled back a step. 'I've earned that business. You can't manage without me.'

Dad's chin flew up. 'I managed well enough during the war. You've got above yourself since you came back, thinking you know better'un I do. Why d'you think I've stopped on so long? To save the business from you, that's why, you and your "modern ideas" – modern claptrap, more like. I'm not letting you have that business for you to overreach yourself. No one's ever going to say Armstrong's went downhill.'

Another step forward. This time Dad held his ground. They were chest to chest. From his superior height, Ralph regarded his father, his lip curling as he took in the deep lines that ran from nose to mouth, the puffiness under his eyes, the

117

slackness in his cheeks, the stringy neck above his collar. Joseph Armstrong was old. A has-been. A stupid old duffer clinging to the past because he had lost the ability to look to the future. And he thought he could stand up to his son. Pathetic.

Ralph spoke in a murmur, the words almost a caress. 'You're not selling up. You're retiring and I'm having the shop.'

'You can't stop me. Tek your modern ideas and see how they fare on Deansgate, or if you're that fixed on auctions, go to Chester, but you're never having auctions at Armstrong's.'

The man was a joke. He wasn't listening. Didn't he know what a mistake it was not to listen to Ralph Armstrong? Didn't he realise Ralph was going to win? Ralph Armstrong always won.

Power flooded Ralph's hands: his gloves felt tight; his muscles were hot and ready. He grasped his father's lapels and in a fluid movement hoisted him onto his toes.

'Armstrong's is going to have an auction room.'

And he threw the old codger from him, casting him away as he deserved. Dad's arms flailed; his feet caught and stumbled and he went over backwards, right down to the floor. There was a crack of bone as the back of his skull struck the corner of the hearth. A dark stain slid from beneath his head.

A strangled exclamation and the sound of chair legs scuffing the floor made Ralph look at the widow. Her face was pasty and beaded with sweat, her mouth hanging open. She breathed in small hiccoughing gasps.

God preserve us from hysterical females.

118

Peeling off a glove, Ralph dropped his fingers to his father's neck. Nothing. Dead, then. And his vile, treacherous plan dead with him. Ralph felt the muscles in his face shift and settle into a mask of resolution. He pulled on his glove.

'Is he ... is he...?' she spluttered.

'Dead? Yes.'

With one hand pressed to her throat, she extended the other and pointed a quivering finger.

'You killed him ... you murdered him...'

Stupid bitch. He moved swiftly to her. She stood transfixed. The pointing finger fluttered and dropped. The other hand trailed from her throat and down her bosom.

Before he could speak, something in her changed. Something in her face. A slackening of the mouth, a strange drooping of an eyelid. One arm fell to her side as though it was too heavy to hold up. Her mouth worked, but not properly. A ragged gurgle struggled out. Then she crumpled.

Well, that was unexpected.

And lucky.

The last thing he needed was to be linked to his father's death. Bad for business. Catastrophic for his associates' plans. And if Ma Jenkins had taken it into her thick skull to think he had killed the old man on purpose, that would stir things up horribly. His word against hers. Messy.

He had come here to deal with a problem; and he had dealt with it, albeit in a way he hadn't foreseen. No point in leaving a potentially dangerous detail behind. She had accused him of murder. If she woke up, she would scream it from the rooftops. Can't have that.

She had called him a murderer. It was only polite to let a lady have the last word.

Plucking the cushion from the armchair, he dropped to his knees beside her. Holding the cushion in both hands, he positioned it over–

The front door opened, a small sound but his heightened senses caught it. The snooty bitch was back. He tossed the cushion onto the chair and dived into the scullery, leaving the door open a trifle to watch through a crack.

The kitchen door opened, but instead of the tall, thin female, there stood the loveliest girl he had ever seen. A fist seemed to close around his heart and when it relaxed, a great surge of heat and desire scorched through him. She was shorter than the snooty bitch, and with more flesh on her. Not plump, in fact you could see she needed feeding up, but there were some decent curves that a red-blooded man would relish the feel and the taste of. A gentle face, fairish hair, a clear complexion and, in that first instant of entering the room, the sunniest smile he had ever seen. God, she was captivating. Had Dad ever mentioned her name? Why hadn't he listened? How could he not have listened when she was mentioned?

How could he ever have imagined he loved Molly Slater?

Her smile froze and faded as she took in what was before her. His heart ached. A cry was wrenched from her and it was all he could do to prevent himself from leaping across the room and dragging her into his arms. That was where she needed to be: in his protective embrace – for ever.

Chapter Thirteen

Carrie's sigh came from so deep inside that it almost dragged her bones to the surface. She still felt numb after yesterday's horrifying events, yet now she must wrench her mind away and meet Billy. Before yesterday afternoon, he had been all she could think about. Now, it felt as if that part of her life lay at the far end of a long tunnel.

She gazed at Mam's slackened features. Would it help her, would it make her come back to them, if Carrie told her she was going to be a grandmother? Or would she be appalled to learn that her lass wasn't a nice girl any more?

Not that Carrie could have whispered any such confidence anyway, not with Letty sitting on the other side of the bed, holding Mam's other hand. Letty might be her best friend, and ten times the sister to her that Evadne was, but she didn't know about the baby. Carrie had planned to tell her after the wedding, when Letty was helping her out of her veil. She had planned to whisper, 'Now that Billy's made an honest woman of me, I'll let you into our secret. You're going to be an auntie.' She had imagined Letty's squeal of joy a hundred times; but if she told Letty now, Letty would say, 'No wonder you couldn't let him go,' and even if she didn't say it, she would be thinking it.

Carrie squeezed Mam's hand. It was a stroke, according to the doctor.

121

'Best if she just slipped away,' he had said.

At first it had looked like an accident, Mr Armstrong having tripped and fallen, striking his head on the hearth, and Mam then collapsing, unable to bear this calamity on top of her other troubles. But last night the police had suggested something else. If Mr Armstrong had tripped – and what was there for him to fall over? – he would have fallen forwards or sideways, not straight over backwards. Could someone have entered their house and attacked him? But then, wouldn't there be signs of a struggle, some other injury, a bruise on his face perhaps? And who could it have been? Surely not someone infuriated about Pa, barging in to give Mam a piece of his mind? Had Mr Armstrong paid the ultimate price for protecting her?

None of the neighbours had seen or heard anything. The lone witness was Mam and she couldn't speak, didn't respond in any way, maybe never would again.

Best if she just slipped away.

Carrie dipped her face to the pillow to whisper in Mam's ear. 'I have to see Billy. You'd wake up, wouldn't you, to be the mother of the bride? I couldn't bear it if you weren't at my wedding.' A tear burnt its way down her cheek.

'Oh, Carrie.'

She raised her head to see Letty smearing tears away. Carrie managed a flimsy smile.

'Look at us, Mrs Jenkins,' said Letty. 'What a pair. You'd best go, Carrie, before we cry enough for your mam to float away.'

She went downstairs. The neighbours who had

left them alone after their bad news had been clucking round ever since she had stumbled into the street yesterday, banging on doors and crying out for help. Food had appeared: bubble-and-squeak, calf's foot jelly, a dish of dripping. Sheets had been lent – 'If your man's bedfast, you'll need these,' – and the hearth had been scrubbed clean.

Mrs Clancy from next door sat in the kitchen, working on Mam's darning. 'How is she?'

'No change.'

Mrs Clancy snipped off her thread. 'I'll pop up and keep her comp'ny with Letty.' She heaved her bulk out of the chair.

As soon as she was gone, Carrie grabbed her shawl and slipped out, grateful not to have to explain herself to anyone, especially Evadne. The two of them had sat up with Mam last night. At breakfast time, Letty and Mrs Hardacre and their Joanie had piled into the house, complete with a basket of bread, eggs and jam. Mrs Hardacre set about scrambling eggs, then ordered Carrie to bed in Miss Reilly's old room, soon to regain its former status as Evadne's bedroom when she quitted the schoolhouse. Carrie had been sure she wouldn't so much as snooze, but had fallen deeply asleep.

Evadne had already left. Had she gone to see her grandfather? She would want to tell him the news, but surely it could have waited ... or was Carrie a hypocrite to think so, given that she was creeping out?

She hurried to the park, forcing herself to slow her steps as she approached, not wanting to look flushed and breathless. Billy wasn't there and she felt a lurch of disappointment. No use telling herself she was early. No use remembering how, at sixteen, she had all but swooned with pleasure when Billy said, 'It's the sign of a gent to be a few minutes early so you never keep your young lady waiting.'

Arriving at the bench where they had sat on Friday, she struggled to pull her thoughts together. Mam lying immobile in bed and Mr Armstrong struck down dead. Carrie hadn't really known him, other than to find him agreeable company.

'Mind you don't leave me on my own with him,' Mam used to say. 'I don't want him getting any daft ideas.'

Now he was dead and no one knew how it had happened. 'Hello, Carrie.'

'Billy.' Her heart gave a little leap and then plummeted. How awkward he looked. 'Aren't you going to sit down?'

He perched on the edge of the bench, tilting forward, elbows on knees, hands clasped. She hadn't expected that. She had expected him to look at her. Normally he loved to look at her and she basked in his admiration. She wanted to shake him, to make him look, but that wasn't keeping your hands to yourself. Billy hadn't exactly kept his hands to himself whenever he had managed to get her on her own. And now he wouldn't even look her way.

'Have you heard about my mam?'

He looked up. 'Yes. I'm sorry. What a shock.'

'I thought perhaps you hadn't heard. I thought you'd come round if you knew.'

124

His gaze fell away. 'Don't go on, eh, Carrie.'

He might as well have slapped her. She came to her feet.

'Let's go over to the trees. This bench feels too public.'

Billy sighed, but he got up and slouched along beside her. How many times had they disappeared behind a tree for a quick cuddle?

Now he was behaving like an oaf.

In the shelter of the trees, she launched into what needed saying.

'Billy, the last thing I want is for anything done by my family to hold you back, but what's done is done and we have to get on with our lives. You, me and the baby. I know you were shocked when I told you I were expecting, but you got used to it and said you didn't mind.'

'I know what I said.'

'We can't leave it to get wed. I'll start showing. We need to get fixed up for next Saturday and you have to book the registrar.'

'Who says it's mine anyroad?'

'What?'

'The baby. How do I know it's mine?'

Carrie's heart shrivelled. 'Of course it's yours. There's never been anyone but you.'

'I don't know that, though, do I? I mean, you went with me willingly enough–'

'Billy Shipton, you know fine well this baby's yours.' Fear ribboned through her.

'Aye, well, that were before. You know what they say. Blood will out.'

'What's that supposed to mean?'

'Knowing about your dad, well, who's to say

125

what kind of person you really are?'

'Are you saying you don't trust me any more because of Pa?'

'Well ... who's to say?'

'I am, for one! And you for another. How long have we known each other? And we've been courting from the moment my mam said I were old enough.'

'There's my job to think of, and my future.'

'And mine, and the baby's – our baby's.'

'Like I say, I don't know it's mine.' At last he looked her full in the face, his eyes resentful, mouth sullen. 'I mean, if you'll do it with me...'

'We're engaged. And I'll remind you we'd been engaged a whole year before I let you go all the way.' Dropping her voice, she hissed, 'There's never been anyone else. Why are you doing this? You know the baby's yours.'

He shifted from foot to foot. 'There's nowt more to be said. I'm sorry you've got yourself into trouble, but I've got myself to think of. I've got a good job; I've got prospects. Do you know how hard it is for someone like me, who left school at thirteen, to get a clerking job in the town hall? It's bad enough being surrounded by bloody grammar school types – and you want to lumber me with a father-in-law that was executed. Have you any idea what that could do to me?' He walked away, tossing words over his shoulder. 'Leave me be, Carrie. It's over. I've got enough to worry about without you.'

Ralph stood motionless behind the tree. Sharp as a knife, his glance flicked after the cowardly lying bastard scurrying away as fast as his feet could carry him. Billy, she had called him, Billy Shipton. Well, he was going to follow Billy Shipton, but he mustn't let Carrie glimpse him. God, but it was hard, when all he wanted was to scoop her up in his arms and crush her to him, breathing in her scent, learning it, learning her, discovering how she felt in his arms, beneath his hands.

This afternoon he had been on his way to call on her when he saw her leaving the house. He had followed her instead, and a bloody good thing too, given what he had just witnessed. The muscle flexed beneath his black armband, worn for convention but worn also to wrench at the heart of the delectable Carrie Jenkins. He had used many different approaches with women, cocky lines for brassy females, heartless flirting for eager maidens, smooth seduction for married women, but this was the ultimate. 'How do you do? My father died in your kitchen.' It made one hell of an introduction.

He had gone to Wilton Lane to make polite enquiries after the mother. The police had informed him that she had taken bad ways. Still breathing but immobile and unable to speak – like one of Adam's dummies. She would be better off dead, poor bitch. Pity he hadn't had time yesterday to finish her off. With luck, she would have snuffed it in the past few hours. That would be good, another reason for Carrie to learn to lean on him.

Instead, he had found himself following her. She had entered the park, and he was indulging in a hectic fantasy about what he could do to her in the bushes once he got her trained in his ways when he realised she was here for an assignation. He bunched his fists. He wasn't going to stand for this. He slid among the trees as Carrie and the young man came over. If they were after some privacy for a spot of canoodling, he would break the bloke's arms. No one got a feel of his girl. But it turned out they had sought seclusion for a different reason. She was pregnant – and now she was jilted.

She was still standing there. Ralph could see the side of her face, the curve of her cheek. Her pallor shocked him. He burnt with protectiveness – and anger. He longed to tell her that being abandoned by the faithless Shipton was immaterial because she had Ralph Armstrong looking after her interests now.

He moved stealthily away, then lengthened his stride as he set off after Billy sodding Shipton.

'There you are, Carrie! Where've you been?' Mrs Dunnett bustled across the road. 'Father Kelly's come to give your mam the last rites.' She sketched a quick sign of the cross.

The last–? No – absolutely not. Wrenching herself out of the shock of her meeting with Billy, Carrie dashed indoors and upstairs at such a lick she tripped over her feet, but she hardly had time to bark her shins before she was up again. She flew into the bedroom, where the sweet aroma of incense enveloped her. There was Father Kelly, and Mrs Clancy, Mrs Hardacre and Letty were all on their knees round the bed. Four faces turned her way, but not the fifth, not Mam's.

'You're just in time,' said Father.

'She isn't–?'

'Nay, love,' said Mrs Clancy.

Carrie squared her shoulders. 'Then there's no call for this.' She looked straight at Father Kelly, aware of a flutter at her waist-level as the kneeling women caught their breath.

'There's every need,' he said. 'Didn't I call on Doctor Cumming and ask him the likely outcome? And didn't he say she'd be better off–?'

'She isn't going to die,' Carrie insisted through clenched teeth. Her shoulders were clenched too, and the muscles in her arms.

'That's in God's hands, child. And if she does, then her soul will be in a state of grace and what more could anyone ask? You wouldn't deny her that, surely, a loving daughter like you?'

She felt like hurling the chamber pot at him.

Mrs Clancy shuffled along. 'Come here by me.'

She did as she was told. What else could she do? But she refused to listen to her mam being given the last rites. She bowed her head and stuffed her mind full of other thoughts.

Carrie trailed home. She had been to the laundry and secured Letty's old job, though, because of Mam's condition, she had asked not to start until next week. She had made it sound as if that would make a difference. Would it? Her thoughts froze in fear.

Miss Hopkins, the overseer, had sniffed and pulled at her immaculate cuff. 'I'm not pleased, but I suppose, under the circumstances...'

'Thank you.' It was such a relief to have a job that she felt as though she were about to fall to the floor.

Even so, as she headed home, holding her shawl round her as loosely as she could so as not to die of the heat, it was hard to feel glad. Laundry work was back-breaking. She knew how tough Letty had found it and Letty was no slacker. She pictured Letty working at Trimble's and herself toiling in that steaming-hot laundry. Her shoulders shuddered and her shawl slipped.

She turned into Wilton Lane. Women stood in little clusters up and down the street. They all turned and looked at her – because of Pa or because she had been after Letty's old job? She didn't care. It didn't matter, compared to the worries she was dragging around with her.

Mrs Clancy came hurrying to meet her. 'Have you heard? Yon Billy Shipton–'

'He's been here?' Oh, if only–

'Nay, lass. He's been beat up that bad he's ended up in hospital.'

Carrie's chest tightened. Before she knew what she was doing, she had dodged past Mrs Clancy and started running. Then she swung round.

'Mrs O'Leary's in with Mam. Could you–?'

'Wait, Carrie. Are you sure–?'

She flew to the Shiptons' house, where her urgent knocking was answered by a neighbour. She slipped past and rushed into the kitchen. It was empty. There were voices in the parlour – the *parlour*. Her flesh went clammy. Was Billy dead?

She forced herself to open the door. Billy's mam, his auntie, both his nans and another neighbour turned startled eyes towards her. They looked upset, but gossipy-upset, not stricken-

130

upset. Carrie's throat swelled and tightened, then released, leaving a sharp-edged ache.

'I've just heard,' she cried. 'What happened?'

'You!' Mrs Shipton came to her feet. 'Get out of my house.'

'But Billy–'

'I said, out!'

'I only want–'

'I don't care what you want. You're nowt but trouble.'

'Come on, love.' Auntie Mabel took her arm.

Finding herself propelled to the front door, she twisted free. 'What happened? How is he?'

Auntie Mabel pushed her outside and took a step after her. 'He were beaten up yesterday teatime. Took a real hammering, he did.'

'Who did it?'

'Dunno. Some bugger what crept up from behind and shoved him up an entry. He never stood a chance.'

'Poor Billy. I can't believe it.'

'Mabel! Are you coming back in or what?' Mrs Shipton boomed from indoors. 'I hope you're not telling that girl owt. She's not entitled.'

'How bad is he?' Carrie whispered. 'Please!'

'Terrible bruising, eyes all swollen, nose broken, poor lad. His teeth are bad and they say some ribs are cracked.' Auntie Mabel wiped away a tear. 'Now, go.'

She disappeared, leaving Carrie to weave her way home, fighting waves of horror. As if things weren't bad enough already. Back in Wilton Lane, she went indoors, her feet taking her upstairs. Her mind felt fuzzy; she couldn't sort out her thoughts.

She was aware of voices as she went into the bedroom. Her throat was dry, but she wanted to talk. She wanted to pour out what had happened. She wanted sympathy, understanding. After being rejected at Billy's house, she wanted someone to treat her as if she was entitled to be upset.

'We've got to do summat about your mam,' Mrs O'Leary said immediately. 'Mrs Clancy and me had to change the sheets again while you was gone.'

'Lie her on newspapers,' said Mrs Clancy. 'That'll save the bedding.'

They looked at her. She had to shunt her thoughts around. 'But that's undignified.'

'Well, lovey, shitting herself like a babby in't exactly dignified neither.'

'And think on,' added Mrs O'Leary. 'Some of these sheets are on loan.'

'Aren't you going to ask about Billy?'

'Later, lovey. Your mam comes first.'

Carrie caved in and cadged old papers from up and down the road. Now, when she was exhausted and busy, everyone wanted to ask about Billy until she was sick of repeating herself. At last she was home again, helping the neighbours rearrange the bed, the newspapers crackling as they were laid in position and Mam was settled on them. Then there was silence.

'That's better,' said Mrs O'Leary. She sounded pleased and Carrie experienced a terrible urge to shout at her. How could it possibly be better, with Mam lying so still that there wasn't even the tiniest flicker of sound?

Chapter Fourteen

Hoping against hope, Carrie counted out a heap of silver and copper for the second time. A knock at the door made her heart jump. Scooping the cash into the pocket of her pinny, she went to answer it, bracing herself to tackle the rent man but finding instead a stranger. A good-looking one too, with keen brown eyes and broad shoulders. He was crisply turned out in a smart three-piece suit of dark grey with a black tie. When he raised his homburg, she noticed the black band on his sleeve.

'Good afternoon. Ralph Armstrong. My father–'

'I thought you were the rent man,' she blurted. 'I were going to fob you off with a few bob less until next week – I'm sorry. How rude of me.' Her cheeks burnt. 'Won't you come in?'

'Thank you.' He removed his homburg.

Mr Armstrong's son. Should she have expected him? She led him into the kitchen, then wondered if she should have offered him a seat in the parlour.

'This is where it happened.' He looked at the hearth.

'Yes. I suppose the police told you. I'm sorry for your loss.'

'Thank you.'

He looked at her expectantly and she sat,

waving him into an armchair, suddenly ashamed. He was tall and handsome and everything about him was smart: the silk handkerchief sticking up from his breast pocket, the wing collar and black silk tie, the sharp central crease down the trouser legs. He was too good for their kitchen.

'I'm Carrie Jenkins.'

'I know. I should extend my sympathies too. I understand your mother is in a grave condition.'

Somehow or other it all came tumbling out, not the really intimate horrid details, like the incontinence, but everything else, all about Mam's condition and what was being done for her.

'I'm sorry,' she finished at last. 'Here I am burdening you with my problems when you've your own sorrow.' She had shed some tears; she felt about in her pocket for her hanky. Her fingers clashed against the coins. 'Rent,' she murmured, mopping her cheeks.

'You said something about not having enough?'

Damn. Her and her big mouth. 'Things are tight at the minute. I left my job last week and I don't start my new one till next Monday. My sister is moving back in, but she hasn't tipped up yet.'

'What is this new job?'

'The laundry.'

'You can't go there.'

That made her look straight at him. 'Pardon?'

'I mean, you'll ruin your hands. You don't want to do that.'

'No choice – now that really is the rent man,' she added as someone knocked.

Spilling the money onto the table, she swept it

134

into one palm only to find her hand cupped inside Ralph Armstrong's. His hand was warm. He tipped the coins into his other hand, exerting pressure when she tried to pull away.

'Permit me. You shouldn't have to deal with this when you've so many worries.'

'Hang on,' she objected, but he had already taken the rent book and was out of the kitchen. Vexed at herself as well as him, she took a step to follow, then hesitated. A smartly-turned-out man would have more sway with the rent collector. Annoying but true.

She heard low voices, then he returned.

'Don't worry about this week's rent, Miss Jenkins. The collector knew about the tragedy and the landlord has given him leave to be lenient.'

'He'll wait till next week?'

'The landlord will accept less as a token of respect. It won't need to be made up.'

That didn't sound like Mr Dawson. Her skin prickled.

'I'd hate to think you'd paid the rest yourself, Mr Armstrong.'

'Do you think that's what I did?'

Did he have to be so direct? 'I wouldn't want to be beholden.' She tried to brush it aside. 'Of course, you didn't pay.' She didn't want it to be true, couldn't make room in her head for it to be true. 'I'm that tired, I can hardly think.'

'Then I'll leave you to get on.'

He shook her hand, looking into her face as they exchanged goodbyes. Carrie took a step backwards. He let go of her hand and put on his hat. She folded her arms across her stomach,

135

tucking her hands out of the way. He tipped his hat to her and strode off along the road.

She stood on the doorstep, watching him go. Mam said it was polite to see someone on their way and she had always done it. But when Ralph Armstrong turned and looked back, she felt hot and uncomfortable and wished she hadn't watched.

Carrie gazed at Mam, willing her to wake up. Doctor Cumming might have said that awful thing about her being better off dead, but he had also said, rather reluctantly, that sometimes people got better.

'Properly better?' she had asked, eagerness lifting her heart.

'It all depends.'

He hadn't stayed long. Did he see no point? She had been sitting here since he left. If she had been with Mam at the vital moment on Saturday afternoon, if she had fetched help sooner, would it have made a difference? She hadn't dared ask.

Mrs Clancy, puffing from the stairs, looked in. 'Eh, Carrie, there's a gent outside. Says he's a doctor, but he's not dressed like one.'

With a strong sense of *What next?*, she went down. The front door stood open. She glimpsed a man, tall, well dressed. Ralph Armstrong: what did he want now? She looked again and realised her eyes were playing tricks. Not Ralph Armstrong. Good. This was the brother.

'I'm Carrie Jenkins. I'm sorry about your father.'

'Thank you.'

She looked at him.

'I may not look like it in this suit, but I am a doctor.'

'I know. Mam said one of Mr Armstrong's sons was.'

'I didn't want to turn up in my doctor's weeds in case it looked presumptuous, but I'd like to offer my help. May I come in? I'd like to talk about your mother.'

Carrie stood aside to let him by. 'The parlour is the door on the left.'

'The kitchen is fine by me.'

'Well, not by me,' she breathed. She had made that mistake yesterday. She darted past and opened the door. 'Here you are.'

The curtains were open. Evadne had drawn them in shame over Pa, but Mrs Clancy had opened them on Saturday evening. 'To show your mam is still with us.'

Doctor Armstrong waited for her to sit before he did.

'I gather your mother has suffered a stroke. That's linked to the kind of work I specialise in.'

Carrie pressed a hand to her chest. No words would come out.

'No charge,' he added, misinterpreting her silence.

'You can help?'

'Possibly.'

She clutched her elbows. Otherwise she might have grabbed his hands and rained kisses on them. 'Thank you. I can't tell you what this means.'

'Perhaps I could meet Mrs Jenkins?'

That pulled her up short. 'I haven't changed

the sheets.'

'Not to worry. This way, is it?' He was out of the room and halfway upstairs, Carrie bobbing behind. 'Front room?' He tapped softly and went in, saying to Mrs Clancy, 'Could I have a few minutes with Mrs and Miss Jenkins?'

He even held the door for her – fancy a doctor doing that! She and Mrs Clancy raised their eyebrows at one another.

'How do you do, Mrs Jenkins? I'm Doctor Adam Armstrong. You knew my father. I'm here to see if I can help you. May I move your arm? This way ... now that way.'

Carrie watched in fascination as he manipulated one arm, then the other, all the time speaking to Mam as if she could hear every word. Doctor Cumming hadn't done that. Her heart swelled. This man could be trusted. Some of her burden lifted.

Doctor Armstrong laid Mam's arm on the sheet. 'I'm going to speak to your daughter now, Mrs Jenkins.'

Carrie sat on the bed, reaching for Mam's hand, then realised what she had done. Fancy behaving so casually in front of a doctor! What must he think? But before she could slither from the bed, he smiled at her. His eyes crinkled and he looked friendly. She smiled back. It seemed a long time since she had smiled.

'I work at Brookburn House. Do you know what happens there?'

'It's a mansion. It belongs to the Kimber family.' And they had another mansion in grounds on the other side of the same road. All right for some.

'It used to be their dower house, I believe. It's a hospital now – a highly specialised hospital. The patients are former soldiers, incapacitated, like your mother. Not so many years ago, they'd have been left lying in their beds with no hope of improvement, let alone recovery; but we know more now and we're learning all the time. My great interest lies in helping these men.'

It sounded hopeless – and yet he spoke with conviction. Carrie leant forward. 'How?'

'Stimulation, both physical and mental. Talking to them – we treat all our patients as if they can hear.'

'Can they?' Could Mam?

'There's no knowing until they recover sufficiently to tell us; but we work on the basis that they can.'

All those things Mam could have heard: Doctor Cumming calling her better off dead, Father Kelly delivering the last rites.

'We try to make life interesting for them. We open the windows so they have fresh air and hear the birds; we read to them and play music; and they undergo a regime of physical exercise.'

'But if they're like Mam...'

'They can't move themselves, but someone can manipulate their limbs for them, get the blood flowing, exercise the muscles, give the brain something to think about.'

'And that would help Mam?'

'No promises, but she might improve. You must understand, the soldiers are incapacitated not for physical reasons but because they bear horrific mental scars. In your mother's case, the cause is physical. Nevertheless, the treatment could help her. At the very least, it will do no harm.'

'What must I do?'

'It will be hard work.'

Carrie was flooded by a sense of purpose. 'I wasn't here when she needed me most. I won't let her down now.'

He shot her an approving look. 'First, I need her doctor's permission in writing. If he agrees, then I'll work out a regime and train you to administer it.'

'I'll go and see him this minute.'

'Is there a man who could speak to him? He might listen more readily to a man.'

'There's just me and my sister. I suppose Evadne ought to do it. She's a teacher.'

'Very well. I'll also organise some assistance from the hospital, but it'll be limited, I'm afraid. Most of the work will be done by you. And we must get some food inside her or she'll waste away. It will involve a tube down her throat. Rather unpleasant, and I shan't permit you to be present.'

Carrie's stomach twitched in sympathy, but she lifted Mam's hand and kissed it. 'I'll be beside her, if she needs me.'

He addressed himself to Mam. 'The sooner you start your treatment the better, Mrs Jenkins. And you never know' – he looked at Carrie and his eyes were clouded with pain – 'if she recovers, she'll be able to tell us how my father came to have that fall.'

Ralph stopped dead at the sight of Adam emerging from Wilton Lane. What was he playing at? Ralph strode across the road and blocked his path, conscious of his own superior body weight.

'What are you doing here?' he demanded.

'I might ask you the same question. I've been visiting Mrs Jenkins in my capacity as a doctor.'

'Another waxwork for your display.'

Adam shot him a look of distaste. 'What brings you here?'

'Seeing how things are.'

'That's not like you.'

He smothered a flash of anger. 'Just a courtesy.'

'Then I'll leave you to be courteous.'

Adam walked away and Ralph headed straight for the Jenkins' door. When Carrie opened it, he saw the difference in her. She was brighter about the eyes. The improvement lifted his heart, but also made him want to give Adam a good kicking.

'Your brother's just been here.' Even her voice sounded less strained. She glanced along the street, but Adam had vanished.

'May I come in? If it's convenient.'

The flicker in her eyes told him it wasn't, but she let him in anyway, leading him to the kitchen, where, to his annoyance, a fat woman was sitting at the table, nursing a cup of tea. Carrie introduced her as Mrs Clancy from next door.

'I've just been telling Mrs Clancy what Doctor Armstrong said about Mam,' Carrie burbled happily.

It was odd how he could be enchanted and enraged at the same time. He longed to have Carrie to himself, but the neighbour didn't look like moving her fat arse any time soon.

He said flatly, 'I was hoping for a private word,

141

Miss Jenkins.' He gave the fat female a look.

'I'm sorry,' said Carrie, 'but Mrs Clancy has to go in a minute to start Mr Clancy's tea and she's going to help me change the bed first.'

He gritted his teeth. 'Then I'll say my piece and leave you to it. I came to invite you to my father's funeral.'

'But I barely knew him.'

'Perhaps you'd like to represent your mother, especially as my father carried a torch for her. Thursday, three o'clock at St Clement's, followed by the burial down the road in the old graveyard.'

'They stopped using that place years ago,' said the fat cow. 'Everyone goes to Southern Cemetery.'

'We have a family grave there with two spaces, so we've been given permission.' Plus, of course, every man had his price and the vicar's was the cost of retiling the lychgate tower.

He watched Carrie and waited.

'Well – I'll come,' she said, as he had known she must. How could she refuse?

'Nay, chuck, you can't go there. It's Protestant.' The fat bitch's interference made Ralph's hand itch to clout her. 'Father Kelly won't let you.'

Bloody Papists. 'Then don't tell him.' He smothered his impatience as they both stared. 'No one needs permission to attend a funeral, especially in these circumstances.'

Carrie looked helplessly at the fat bitch, then transferred her gaze to him and nodded.

Good. He wanted an obedient wife.

Chapter Fifteen

Was she being watched? Carrie's flesh prickled as she scuttled across the road. She couldn't have felt any more self-conscious had she been wearing a placard round her neck with her destination painted on it in bold black letters. As she came to the gate, her feet halted of their own accord. If she set foot on that land, it would mean – she wasn't sure what it would mean, except that it would be serious, maybe even a sin. Not one she would confess, though; Father Kelly would throw a fit. And not confessing would be another sin.

With a hasty glance to ensure no one she knew was in sight, she hurried up the path into the church, stopping beside a pew at the back, nearly making the person behind her fall over her as she paused to genuflect. She stumbled into the pew and scooted to the far end, hardly daring to raise her eyes.

She had barely known Mr Armstrong. Supposing someone enquired after her connection. She could hardly say, 'He died in our kitchen.' She could say her mam knew him, but then she might be asked where her mam was. Her mind buzzing with complications, she made herself as small as she could during the ceremony.

At the end, the coffin was loaded into the glass-sided hearse and the black-plumed horses set off at a sedate pace to lead the mourners down the road, past Chorlton Green to the old graveyard. Loitering at the back, Carrie considered slipping away, but that would be wrong – disrespectful. She went with everyone else to the graveside, hanging back, keeping her eyes down.

When it was over, she glanced round, choosing her escape route. Her heart sank as Ralph Armstrong came purposefully in her direction. She just knew he was going to insist she attend the gathering. A couple of gentlemen stepped into his path, wanting to shake hands.

'Good afternoon, Miss Jenkins.'

She turned and there was Doctor Armstrong, his face showing the strain of the occasion. He was better looking than his brother, because his eyes were kind.

'I didn't know you were coming,' he said. 'Thank you. It's good of you.'

She remembered his brother's words. 'Mam would want me to.'

That was obviously the right thing to say, because he nodded. But at the same time it was the wrong thing to say, because that wasn't why she was here. She was here because she had had her arm twisted. She wished she could take back the lie.

'I'm so sorry about Mr Armstrong. I lost my pa four years ago and I know how shocked and hurt I was for ages afterwards. You might not want your dad and mine spoken of in the same breath after what Pa did, but I do know how hard it is to lose your father. You remember so many things that are never going to happen again. I used to daydream, only it felt more real than that, about

144

Pa coming home from the war. He'd march up Wilton Lane with a rucksack slung off one shoulder and I'd race to meet him, even though in real life I'd have let Mam reach him first. I'm sorry to talk about him when we're all meant to be talking about Mr Armstrong, but I wanted you to know I feel for you.'

'Thank you.' He leant towards her, his face serious but his brown eyes soft. 'The mother of one of my patients told me she wouldn't let her youngest become a telegram boy in the war. She said everyone dreaded the sight of those boys, desperate for them to cycle past, and there was enormous relief when they did, but there was guilt as well for having wished death on another family. We had a garden party at Brookburn on Saturday. That's where I was when Dad visited your mother. I kept expecting him to arrive; and then I saw the police constable on his way up the drive and I knew just how those people had felt, seeing the telegram boy.'

Carrie's fingers reached instinctively, seeking contact, wanting to give comfort and reassurance – what was she doing? She snatched her hand away, cleared her throat, stepped back. 'Excuse me. You must have other people to...'

He took a step after her. 'Wait. I'm sorry if I embarrassed you.'

'You didn't.'

'I've heard a lot of platitudes in the past few days. You're the first person to speak to me openly and honestly. Thank you. It means a great deal. Now, if you'll excuse me...?'

She felt an odd wrench at losing him. It was just

145

the emotion of the moment. Had she truly helped him by sharing her feelings about Pa? She hoped so. When she thought of how Doctor Armstrong intended to help Mam, she hoped it even more.

From the corner of her eye, she saw Ralph Armstrong take his leave of the men he was with. She slid through the group of mourners and headed up the path to the lychgate. Was it mean of her? But she didn't feel comfortable with him the way she did with his brother.

Carrie woke up as she did automatically every two or three hours, even though her brain felt sore with tiredness and she fell asleep feeling as though she wouldn't surface for a week. She lay listening to the harsh edge of Mam's breathing. She was balanced on the edge of the bed; that was automatic too, because if Mam soiled herself, it might seep across and touch her. She was ashamed of herself for that, but she couldn't help it.

The room was stuffy and her skin was clammy inside her nightie. The air was tainted. She and the good-hearted neighbours worked hard to keep Mam clean and it was unfair that the bedroom now possessed a faint aroma of sourness. It was something else to be ashamed of. Did it give the impression Mam wasn't being properly looked after?

This night last week she had tossed and turned and wept because Billy had jilted her. And they had just found out about Pa. Now, on top of those calamities, Mam had been struck down.

Was it time to get up yet? Next week, when she

began at the laundry, she would have early starts, and how was she to cope with Mam on top of a job? She didn't want the neighbours feeling taken for granted. She really ought not to work at all, but could Evadne support them? Evadne was moving back in tomorrow and it was something they ought to discuss.

She would give Miss Reilly's room a good bottoming today to welcome Evadne home. As sisters, they might not be close, but it couldn't be easy for Evadne losing her room in the schoolhouse. And in another month she would lose her job as well. Had she started looking for something else? She was clever. She could work in an office.

After Mrs Clancy and Mrs Dunnett had been in to help give Mam a bed bath and put her in a fresh nightie, Carrie took the cleaning box upstairs; and there she was, sleeves rolled up, hair working loose, when someone knocked. On the doorstep stood Ralph Armstrong with, of all things, a bunch of pinks tied with ribbon.

She stared – at him, at the flowers. He must have come to the wrong house. Yet she knew he hadn't.

He smiled. His eyes didn't crinkle like his brother's. 'I brought you these.'

She swallowed. Then she practically dragged him indoors before the neighbours could see him and think – she didn't dare imagine what they might think.

'That was more of a welcome than I was expecting,' he said.

He sounded amused. She wanted to chuck him straight back into the street.

'I brought you these.'

147

'You can't give me flowers.'

'Why not? They'll cheer you up.' He laid them on the table and stepped away.

She rubbed the back of her neck. 'I can't tek them. People would think...'

'Think what?'

Her ears burnt. She wouldn't say it. She looked away.

'Give them to your mother.'

He said it in such a reasonable voice. Was it reasonable? She was too churned up to tell. But she would sound churlish if she refused. And it was kind of him.

'Thank you.'

Inside her head, another job clanged into place on the never-ending list. Remember to remove the flowers from the bedroom when she drew the curtains tonight. Everyone knew flowers sucked the oxygen out of the night air.

'Flowers for the invalid,' he added, 'though she's in no state to appreciate them.'

'She might smell them. Your brother said she might.'

'Did he now?'

She didn't know how to respond. 'Mrs Clancy will be here in a minute to sit with Mam while I nip to the shops.' It wasn't true, but she wanted rid of him.

Once she had seen him out, she arranged the pinks in a vase, but finishing Evadne's room and then washing and ironing kept her busy and the flowers were still on the kitchen table when Evadne arrived to see Mam. Too late to move them. Carrie stood in front of the table as Evadne opened the kitchen door.

She looked strained and brittle, but nothing could diminish her beauty. She pulled off her hat and gave her wonderful conker-brown hair a shake, making its waves ripple. She wore a soft green blouse with elbow-length sleeves that ended in a froth of lace. Carrie ran her hands down the front of her pinny. Evadne was lucky to have a job that permitted her to wear pretty things. But she wouldn't have the job much longer.

'Any change?' asked Evadne.

'Still the same.'

'I'll sit with her. Put the kettle on, will you?'

'Evadne, have you seen the housekeeping book? I can't find it.'

'I've got it.'

'Oh. Well, I need it. I can't work out how Mam managed now that I know there's no widow's pension.'

'My grandfather paid her ten shillings a week. That's how.'

'That was generous of him.' Wasn't it? Why did Evadne sound so sharp?

'More than generous, but it's finished now, thanks to Pa. I'll let you have the book tomorrow.'

'Why did you take it?'

'To see what happened to all those ten shillingses, to see if she'd saved anything; because if she had, and if she ... dies, that money would be mine.'

Carrie bridled. 'You're welcome to it.'

'There's none to be welcome to. She used it all keeping house.' Evadne frowned. 'Mind out of

149

the way.' Her eyes narrowed as she looked at the pinks. 'Not Billy, surely?'

Carrie shook her head.

Evadne groaned. 'You've not got another in tow already?'

'Of course not–'

'There's an old song about girls like you. Something about being off with the old love before you are on with the new. You'll get yourself a reputation.'

'They're for Mam. Ralph Armstrong brought them.'

'So he's the new admirer?'

'I told you. They're for Mam.'

'And I told you: you'll get yourself talked about.'

Adam was still fuming as he turned down Wilton Lane, but he wasn't sure which of them he was annoyed with, Ralph or himself. They weren't exactly the best of friends and, with Dad gone, it would be easy to let distance grow between them; but he was determined not to let that happen, so today he had set off early in order to take the long way round and go via the shop. When he rounded the corner onto Wilbraham Road, his eyes had nearly popped out of his head when he saw the signwriter at work up a ladder outside the front of the building. Ralph was already having the shop's name changed.

He had felt a spurt of anger, and yet why shouldn't Ralph do so? It was his shop now. Was he being childish to care? But he did care. It was as if Ralph was wiping Dad away. The funeral had taken place just yesterday, for pity's sake.

It had been decent of Carrie Jenkins to attend, the more so when you considered everything she had on her plate, poor girl. But she would cope, he felt sure. The first time he saw her, he had been ready to feel sorry for her, her dead father transformed from hero to coward in the twinkling of an eye, her mother rendered silent and immobile; but she had shown quiet determination in the matter of helping Mrs Jenkins and he was confident she would see it through. She might be a slip of a thing, and young to be carrying such a burden, but she had backbone.

She had heart too, as her words after the funeral had shown. She had pierced the layer of conventional sympathy that had surrounded him, speaking directly to his sense of loss. He wouldn't forget that in a hurry.

When he knocked at the Jenkins' door, a neighbour let him in.

'Carrie!' she called up the stairs. 'Doctor's here.'

He hung his trilby on one of the coat pegs, ran upstairs and was in time to catch her rolling down her sleeves and stowing a broom in the corner. The window was open and there was a vase of flowers on the chest of drawers. The room was spotless, with a snap of fresh linen in the air, but there was no disguising the faint sour smell of incontinence beneath the tang of carbolic. The aroma was unavoidable, but she would be mortified if he mentioned it.

'Good morning, ladies. I've drawn up an exercise regime for you, Mrs Jenkins.'

'Did you hear that, Mam? We're ready, aren't we?'

'May I?' Adam removed his tweed jacket. 'Here I am yet again minus my frock coat, but these clothes are more suitable for demonstrating exercises.'

She removed a hanger from the cupboard and hung the jacket off the front of the door.

'I'll show you what to do,' he said, 'and then watch while you do it.'

She drew a breath and nodded.

'You're a quick learner, Miss Jenkins,' he said a while later. 'There's one more to show you. This involves bending the knee and pushing it towards the chest. You have to keep it straight, so position yourself like this.' He demonstrated, then stood aside. 'Your turn. Wait, that's not quite right. Allow me.'

He took her hand to place it in the correct position. A warm, tingling sensation jumped from her fingers to his, flooding him with surprise edged with delight. Recollecting himself, he showed her what to do and stepped back, his heart clattering against his ribs. His mind split in half. He spoke and behaved as the doctor; and at the same time, his thoughts and senses ran riot.

'Is that right, Doctor?'

'Yes – splendid.' He cleared his throat.

She smiled at him and his heart turned over. That smile! It made her face light up, imbuing her clear skin with dewy radiance and making her cornflower-blue eyes shine. He folded his arms, trying to contain the emotion lest it burst out. He stepped back, tilted his head, acting the part of the careful observer.

'Go through the exercises once more to be sure

you know them.'

Damn! He regretted the words the instant they left his mouth. Spinning out the visit was unprofessional – and that was a word he had never thought to apply to himself.

He walked round to the other side of the bed, so there could be no possibility of physical contact, accidental or otherwise. Before she finished he put his jacket on, signalling the end of the visit.

Walking back to Brookburn, Adam couldn't tell which was swirling more, his thoughts or his feelings. He drew a deep breath, savouring the beautiful day, beautiful because Carrie made it so.

He had to be sensible. He wasn't allowed to form a relationship with a patient and while she wasn't the patient, she had placed her trust in him as a doctor. He mustn't take advantage, nor did he want to. His duty was to Mrs Jenkins and he would do his best for her. In doing so, he would also be doing his best for Carrie.

That would have to satisfy him for now.

Chapter Sixteen

The question was: would Carrie confess her condition and pray he wouldn't run a mile or would she keep it secret and hope to pass off the baby as his? Ralph turned the possibilities over in his mind, fascinated by the ramifications. Either way, she needed a husband, and quickly. If she intended to pretend he was the father, she would

153

have to lure him into bed: he didn't know how far gone she was but she couldn't afford to hang about. That suited him. He had no intention of waiting either.

It had been irritating when she didn't want to accept the flowers, but she hadn't been able to refuse when he turned them into a gift for her mother. Now he needed another gift. She would be forced to accept and it would pile on both the discomfort and the gratitude. But what the hell constituted a suitable gift for a dummy? A present for a girl – easy. But something for a corpse that had forgotten to stop breathing?

He took the question to the chemist's.

'Toilet water,' said the chemist's wife. 'They can sprinkle a few drops in the water they use to wash her and it'll make her skin smell nice.'

'What's the best you've got? Put it in a box and tie it with ribbon.' No point in making this even vaguely easy for Carrie.

Later, his stomach fluttered as he watched the gift tear her in two. She didn't want to accept it, yet how could she refuse something for her mother? Except it wasn't for Ma Jenkins and she knew it.

'Your brother sent round sheets from Brook-burn,' she ventured.

He wanted to kick Adam to hell and back for interfering with his girl, but he hid his anger behind a rueful smile.

'His interest is professional, whereas mine...'

She ducked her head, trying to conceal scarlet cheeks, and he felt a potent mixture of triumph and something strangely close to contempt.

Carrie stepped free of the laundry's steamy atmosphere, a weary sigh escaping her as the building's excessive heat and damp loosened its grip on her skin, leaving it slick and oddly chilled. Her clothes were sticking to her and her scalp prickled; her hair felt thin. She rolled her aching shoulders. Laundry work was punishing and the sweltering atmosphere sapped her strength. Or perhaps it was the baby telling her to ease up. She had been lucky so far; no morning sickness, no tiredness: the perfect pregnancy – apart from a certain something missing from her left hand.

What on earth was she going to do? Here she was, pregnant and alone, just like any common tart who would happily drop her knickers up against the entry wall for a port and lemon. She would be for ever marked as a slut and her baby would be a bastard, doomed to be pointed at and shunned by anyone with half a claim to decency; and that was before you took into account the difficulties of raising a child without a man's wage behind you.

A man's wage and, more importantly, a man's name.

Suddenly, Ralph Armstrong filled her head. She didn't want to think of him, but it was impossible not to. She didn't want his attention – and yet she had to consider her predicament, not just the baby but Mam as well. Once she started showing, folk might say that here was the real reason Billy had jilted her – because she had let another chap have his way with her.

She could turn to Father Kelly. He would sort

Billy out and have the pair of them up the aisle quick sharp, even if poor Billy had to be carried on a stretcher.

Her stomach gave a lurch of distaste. She would be ashamed if Billy had to be forced to marry her and part of that shame would be at marrying a man who was less than she had believed him to be. Her Billy, whom she had been so proud of, had shown a feeble streak. She had blamed it on the shock; she had blamed it on his mother; but in the end she had had to face the truth. Billy should have stood by her, and he should have done it all the more determinedly because of the baby.

Now there was a voice inside her, whispering that he wasn't good enough. Nevertheless, he was her baby's father. But how would their marriage fare if Pa's desertion spoilt his prospects? Would he resent his own child? The thought of her baby's not being wholeheartedly loved and wanted tore at her conscience. She placed a hand protectively over her stomach.

She wanted her baby with all her heart and she would do her best for it.

But it would be a poor sort of best if she were an unmarried mother. And so she was back where she started, her thoughts pounding the familiar route. From the depths of the dread swirling in her heart sprang a rush of fury. Her baby needed a father – and it ought to be Billy. Dammit, it ought to be Billy.

All at once, she found herself taller, shoulders back, chin up. Billy had made promises and she was entitled to have those promises honoured. 'Breach of promise' it was called when a man jilted you, and you could take him to court for it – well, you could if you had money. But she didn't need the law; Father Kelly was the law around here. He would bring Billy into line for her – aye, and Mrs Shipton an' all.

With a brisk step that belied her clattering heart, she set off to confess her condition.

Evadne scrutinised the pinks, seeking the smallest imperfection so she could declare them past their best and throw them out. Flowers for the invalid, indeed! Just like that expensive toilet water was supposed to be for Mother. Who did that wretched girl think she was fooling? And did Ralph Armstrong imagine he was being discreet? What did he see in Carrie, anyway? She was nothing special, just a shop girl, and another man's cast-off to boot. If Ralph Armstrong had any taste, any sort of cultivation, he would have centred his hopes on Evadne, unable to resist her beauty and refinement. Not that she wanted his admiration, but it was frightening to think that perhaps she was past her best.

It was all Mother's stupid fault for marrying Pa. But for that, Evadne would have grown up in middle-class comfort with middle-class expect-ations, leading to a comfortable marriage with two or three well-behaved children, a couple of charity committees and a monthly dinner party to advance her husband's career.

Instead, she had been dumped into a life where she was a cut above everyone else. She hadn't minded in the beginning, foolish child that she was. She had enjoyed it, befriending a group of

157

sycophantic girls and basking in Pa's admiration. He had thought it quite something for an ordinary fellow like himself to have such a well-spoken daughter.

It was only later that reality gripped her. Leaving school was the moment when Grandfather should have claimed her. Instead, he used contacts at his club to fix her up at Oaklawn School.

'It's just until I get married,' she had consoled herself.

How many times had she dreamt of visiting Grandfather and finding the handsome bachelor son of one of his cronies ... or his solicitor, there with papers for signing ... or an eligible gentleman, recently moved in next door? How many dreams had she dreamt over the years? And what an unutterable waste of time they had proved.

She closed her eyes. There were times when she felt as if she never wanted to open them again. But she was a soldier's daughter and no one could accuse her of cowardice. She opened her eyes – and there were the flowers.

They were flawless and something twisted inside her. Her gaze fell on the toilet water beside them. She might not be able to justify discarding the flowers, but she could do something about this. Raising her hand, she was about to swipe the bottle to the floor when an idea struck her. With a smile hardening her lips, she took the toilet water to her bedroom, feeling a small clutch of hurt and shame as she stood before the chest of drawers. At the schoolhouse, she had had a proper dressing table.

Picking up a pretty cut-glass bottle, Grandfather's coming-of-age gift, she undid the silver stopper. Carefully, she filled her bottle with toilet water. It was quite the best toilet water she had ever come across, its rose fragrance delicate but lasting. Wasted on Mother, and unsuitable for a chit like Carrie. Expensive and discreet: perfume for herself.

Returning to Mother's bedside, she replaced the half-empty bottle. There was no one else in the house. On Carrie's first day at the laundry, the neighbours had told Evadne to her face that they expected her to come home promptly from school and do her share. It suited her not to have them buzzing round when she was in the house. She had nothing to say to the likes of Mrs Clancy.

'I'll top up the vase,' she announced, glancing at Mother and then away. There was something about speaking to the invalid that made her go rigid inside, but Carrie had made such a song and dance about treating Mother as if she could hear that she had gone along with it to shut her up. Besides, what if Mother really could hear? The thought of a motionless body housing a conscious mind was too horrifying to contemplate.

She gave the toilet water a sharp push. It banged on the floor but didn't shatter. Retrieving it, she hurled it down, dancing away a couple of steps as it broke.

'Butterfingers! What a shame, your lovely toilet water. I'll clear it up.'

The scent of roses lifted into the air. Evadne bustled away to fetch a cloth. Halfway downstairs she had to stop and lean against the wall. When had she become so contemptible?

Chapter Seventeen

Carrie sat up straight. Inside she might be shrinking, but she wouldn't let it show. Her gaze skimmed round the room, landing on the small statues of the Sacred Heart and Our Lady on the shelf, before she made herself meet Father Kelly's eyes. He would be appalled when she told him. Her heartbeat quickened. It had been easy not to be ashamed when her wedding was imminent. Now – not so easy.

But when she stumbled into her explanation, he took her breath away with the words, 'I know you're in trouble, child. Didn't Billy tell me so himself?'

'Then he said it's his?' If he had, it would help heal things between them ... wouldn't it?

'He said you'd say that.' Father Kelly's bland features stayed the same, but there was a glint in his eyes. 'He also said he has no way of knowing.'

'That's not true! He's the only boy I've ever– Father, you have to believe me.'

'Ah, the word of a girl who has fallen from grace. You see my difficulty?'

'I'm not lying!'

'There's been a girl in confession recently, seeking absolution for sins of the flesh. Would that have been you, Carrie Jenkins?'

'Certainly not.'

'If it wasn't you, then it should have been. You,

an unwed girl, and now paying the price.'

That put her back up. She might have apologised for not confessing to her and Billy doing it, but the suggestion that her baby was included in the sin sent fire shooting through her veins.

Silence rolled round the room. Father Kelly sighed.

'I went to see Billy in his sickbed and took the opportunity to have a word with him about letting you down. But after hearing what he had to say, I'm wondering just who did the letting down.'

'Well, I didn't. So you'll not help? I hoped you'd talk sense into him.'

'Did you now? And here's me thinking I could talk sense into you. If you've a babby on the way, and don't know who to call the father—'

'But I do—'

He sat back in his chair, pressing his lips into a crinkly line. He steepled his pudgy fingers and patted the tips together. 'Carrie Jenkins, what are we to do? You say the child is Billy's and he says he doesn't know. The sad truth is you need help. You and your babby need help. Will you let me help the both of you?'

She pressed the flat of her hand to her chest. She nodded.

He uttered a throaty chuckle. 'That's a relief. You're a good girl at heart and I knew you'd be sensible, so I've already written to the sisters.'

A frown tugged at her brow. Evadne?

'So it must be the good Lord himself who brought you here in time to hear the news. They'll take care of you.'

'Wait a minute.' The hair lifted on her arms.

161

'Are you talking about–?'

'Adoption. Of course. And when you come home, you can make a good confession and start again with a clean slate like the decent girl you really are.'

How kind he sounded, but his kindness was a trap. His voice faded in and out of her hearing as her ears filled with the desperate beating of her heart. Springing up, she made a dash for the door, wrenching it open so hard she stumbled backwards. Sick with terror, she ran through the streets. Could he send her to the sisters? Could they force her to part with her baby?

Swinging round the corner of Wilton Lane, she stopped short at the sight of Ralph Armstrong approaching her front door. He liked her – more than liked her. She thought of the presents she hadn't wanted from him. She thought of pretending they were for Mam; she felt the chilly squeeze that pretending gave her. But Ralph Armstrong was persistent and maybe he was hers for the asking.

Her heart slammed, locking Billy out for ever, a feeling that was followed by a whoosh of relief that made her skin tingle all over. She would never have been able to trust him again. He was weak and she was strong. She had a baby and an invalid mother to provide for, and provide for them she would.

'Mr Armstrong!'

Forcing a smile, Carrie walked towards him. She would give the orchid corset to Letty. She would give herself to this man because she had to, for her baby's sake, and she would let him

162

think she was doing it willingly, because that was how it had to be if she was going to ensnare him.

But she drew the line at handing herself to him on an orchid-coloured plate.

Once Carrie had accepted his advances, it amused Ralph to watch her agonise. Would she confide her shameful secret? He wasn't bothered either way. He would accept the child as his own and that would bind her to him all the more, out of gratitude if she had told him, out of guilt if she hadn't; so he would win, whichever decision she made. He smiled to himself.

He brought muslin sachets of lavender.

'To go between your mother's sheets after they've been washed.'

'Perhaps I'll put one on her pillow at night,' said Carrie. 'Lavender is soothing.'

'You could pop one in your clothes drawer.'

She hesitated, before making the correct response. 'I will. Thank you.'

'Shall I call round tomorrow to ask after Mrs Jenkins?' he offered, his insides lurching with desire at the way her teeth grazed her lower lip. 'Half-seven?'

Sure enough, when he got there the next day, there wasn't a neighbour in sight.

'Are we alone?'

'Well, there's Mam, of course, and my sister's in the parlour. She calls it her sitting room. She's used to nice things.'

Stuck-up bitch. Ralph clamped his mouth shut to prevent the words growling out. Soon it would be Carrie who had the best of everything and the snooty sister needn't come crawling to him for handouts.

'Doesn't she want to play chaperone?'

'Evadne says she's got enough to worry about and what I do is my lookout.'

'She ought to look after you.'

'Are you and your brother close?'

Now there was a question he hadn't expected. He briefly considered melting her heart with a touching description of brotherly devotion but, even though he wasn't generally fussed about the truth, that was one lie he wasn't prepared to tell.

'No,' he said bluntly, 'so that's something we have in common.'

'Oh, but I like Doctor Armstrong,' Carrie exclaimed.

Heat scorched through him, but he spoke calmly. 'I mean, we each have a sibling we're not close to.'

'Oh.' She accepted the rebuke with a quick lowering of the eyes and he gulped as her lashes caressed her cheeks.

Later, rising to leave, he touched her arm, gently but firmly drawing her to him. Her eyes clouded with alarm and confusion. Such beautiful eyes. He held her gaze, making her wait. He bent his head towards hers, saw the fleeting expression of determination as she accepted that she must kiss him, then he drew back, gave her a load of claptrap about not taking advantage, and left.

Two days later, after she had time to grow more scared about her situation, there was a glimmer of desperation in those lovely eyes as his lips

164

closed over hers. Forcing down the powerful urge to plunder her mouth, he kept the kiss tender, though his insides damn near exploded with the effort of reining himself in.

When the kiss ended, he looked down at her, sensing she was expecting him to apologise so she could murmur something like, 'Don't be sorry – I'm not.'

He asked candidly, 'Was that what you wanted?' and when she blushed and looked away, he thought he would burn up with desire.

He listened as she admitted to her previous engagement, careful to show no emotion as she told her tale of being jilted because of her father, even though his muscles were so tense his whole body felt sore.

'The thing is, if you and I are...' Her voice trailed away.

'Courting,' he prompted. 'I know I don't take you out, but that's because you've got your mother ill upstairs. But make no mistake, we're courting strong. I don't care what your father did and I don't care that you were engaged before. What I want to know is, do you still have feelings for this Shipton bloke?'

'No,' she whispered.

'Look at me when you say that.'

She raised her eyes. There was defiance in them. 'I don't love Billy any more, not after what he did to me.'

He nodded. 'Fair enough. And what about me? Are you on the rebound? You must know that for me this is the real thing.'

Her eyes flickered. 'For me an' all. With Billy–'

'Enough!' he barked, making her flinch. The vehemence took him by surprise too. It hurt like hell to hear her speak of another man, another engagement. He wished he had pounded the life out of Billy Shipton. Maybe he still would. 'That's the last time you speak his name, do you understand?'

And so he drew her along, wrong-footing her, saying the unexpected, forcing responses from her. The cleverness of it added an edge to his pleasure that made him anticipate even more keenly his eventual triumphant possession of her, the mere thought of which made him groan aloud in the darkness of his thoughts.

Carrie might have been stupid enough to open her legs to that cowardly Shipton bastard, but she had done it in good faith and Ralph had confidence in her status as a decent girl who would find it immeasurably difficult to go through with it when it came to the point of surrendering to him. Even so, he wasn't having her pulling away at the vital moment. The best thing all round would be to get her relaxed and willing with some booze.

By unspoken consent, Saturday afternoon was the appointed time. According to Carrie, the posh bitch was going to see her rich grandfather in Parrs Wood.

There was some polite conversational pussy-footing around to start with. His breathing had been rushed all day and his throat was dry. Carrie looked terrified, poor little bitch, the colour gone from her face, eyes huge. Christ, he wanted to tear her clothes off and have her there and then.

'You're nervous,' he observed frankly. 'Here, have some.'

She looked uneasy as he withdrew a silver hip flask from his pocket and unscrewed the top, tipped up the flask and swallowed. He took less than a mouthful, though he gave the impression of knocking back more. He rolled the Scotch around in his mouth, though not because he was savouring it. He prided himself on his fastidiousness and one thing he couldn't abide was the stench of alcohol on a woman's breath; but a few fumes of his own might make him less aware of hers.

He poured three fingers into a glass and handed it to her. Her eyes were troubled: she didn't want to drink, but couldn't afford not to.

'Knock it back.' He spoke softly, but it was an order.

She lifted it. The smell made her grimace. Then she visibly made a huge effort and did as she was told. She coughed, but he barely gave her time to recover before he pressed another few fingers on her, and another. It didn't take long to get her drunk. She was soon swaying on her feet, her eyes struggling to focus, words slurring. His lips curled in disgust.

'That's enough,' he said. 'Don't want you passing out.'

Pulling her to him, he gave her a few rough kisses, tugging a response from her. His muscles quivered and heat poured through his body. He kissed her long and deeply, grinding her mouth all the harder when she tried to breathe. When she was half-senseless from alcohol and desire, he kissed his way down her throat. Kissing wasn't enough. He wanted to bite her as well, had to restrain himself. His fingers twitched open the buttons on her blouse. Underneath, the top of a camisole bunched over the rim of her corset. The small hook-and-bar fasteners melted away under his fingertips and he slid his hand inside, groaning as her breast rolled beneath his palm.

When she caught her breath in a loud gasp, all his nerve ends jangled. With his free hand, he cupped the back of her head, tangling his fingers in her hair, and plunged his mouth down over hers before throwing her hard across the kitchen table, swiftly lifting her skirt and petticoat and, with one deft flick, ripping apart the legs of her camiknickers. Shoving her thighs apart, he set his tongue to work. He felt her try to writhe but, flat out on the table, legs spread and dangling, all she could manage was a helpless wriggle that sent desire pumping through him. She was powerless and he couldn't wait any longer.

He leant over her to drag kisses across her mouth and face, smearing her skin with her own juices, then he unfastened his trousers and rammed his way inside her as hard as he could, jarring a cry from her. His body had craved this from that first instant of seeing her and it was all he could do not to explode inside her. He made it last as long as he could, dragging her hips towards him and pounding into her until release overcame him with such vividness that his legs crumpled.

He slumped on top of her, his breathing ragged. He felt magnificent and he couldn't wait to do it again. Carrie belonged to him now.

When his pulse had subsided, he adjusted his trousers and went upstairs. The dummy was in the front bedroom. Walking round the bed, he knelt beside her and murmured in her ear.

'Remember me? I was here the afternoon Joseph Armstrong came a-courting. Mine was the last face you saw. Are you listening? Carrie thinks you can hear. Did you hear the sounds she was making a few minutes since? I've just had her across your kitchen table. Christ, like a bitch on heat she was. Does she get that from you? I'm going to go down now and enjoy her delectable body all over again. Goodbye ... mother-in-law.'

Chapter Eighteen

February 1921

Carrie caught the eye of another pregnant young woman as they queued in the butcher's. When the other girl said, 'Eh, I'll be glad when it's over,' she smiled, feigning agreement, though the truth was that this pregnancy couldn't last long enough for her liking. She had been two months along in June when she was supposed to marry Billy. It was now February and she reckoned she was a fortnight overdue. Having supposedly got pregnant by Ralph in June, with the baby due in March, her relief and gratitude at having carried into February knew no bounds.

In any case, she adored being pregnant. She felt

169

radiantly healthy and marvelled at the sensation of the new life growing inside her, being nurtured by her own body. What could be more wonderful?

She had certainly provided her baby with a good home and that was something to be grateful for; proud of, too. There was no scrimping in the Armstrong household. She still experienced the remnants of astonishment when she remembered the lavishness of their Christmas fare. It was easy to call it the best Christmas ever: it had certainly been the strangest, finding herself married to Ralph after years of looking forward to being Billy's wife, and with Mam still bedfast and helpless. Adam had been right about that: there was no possibility of swift improvement, though the feeding tube had soon been discarded, thank God. After the first week or so, Mam had emerged from her unresponsive state, much to Carrie's joy, but her joy had fizzled out when it became clear that Mam wasn't on the verge of recovery. She seemed to drift in and out of consciousness, but when she was awake, if you could call it that, she didn't respond – couldn't, according to Adam. But at least she had the swallowing reflex, so she was able to mumble spoonfuls of food as long as it was mushed up like a baby's.

'Good practice for you,' said Ralph, which was unkind, but Carrie didn't say anything.

She was determined to keep the promise she had made to herself the day she accepted Ralph's proposal: concentrate on the good things. And there had been many good things. Ralph had seen to that.

'I'll always look after you,' he had promised back in Wilton Lane the day after she had gone through with it. 'You'll never want for anything. We can get married immediately by special licence.'

'Oh, but I want a church wedding.'

'That would mean waiting for the banns. Do you want to wait that long?' He had looked at her so intently that it was as if he could see inside her head.

'No.' She had eased away, terrified that the banging of her heart would reverberate through her body and into his. 'Let's get married as soon as we can.'

Within days, having stayed up till all hours during the nights in between unpicking every lovingly embroidered S on the linen in her bottom drawer and replacing each one with an A, she was married and installed in the spacious flat above the shop on Wilbraham Road.

Saying goodbye to her old neighbours had been hard. They were shocked that she was marrying a man she barely knew and made no bones about saying so until she felt bruised all over.

They weren't alone in making their opinions clear. On her first morning in the flat, Father Kelly came knocking. To her eternal relief, he didn't enter the shop, but had found the flat's front door, tucked between Armstrong's and the next shop. Carrie led him up the enclosed staircase.

'So it's living in sin now, is it, Carrie Jenkins?'

'I'm Carrie Armstrong now, Father.'

'Not in the eyes of the church. And this Armstrong fellow, he's the father of your babby, I take it?'

'Father!'

'And him not Catholic. Is there no end to it, child? What would your mammy say?'

She lifted her chin. 'She'd say: Thank you for marrying a man who can take such good care of us.'

'And is your poor innocent babby to be a heathen brought up outside God's Holy Family? If you care about your child's eternal soul, Carrie Jenkins, not to mention your own, you'll get yourself properly married in the eyes of God. Shall I speak to Mr Armstrong on the subject?'

'No, don't.' She might have only just found out how many sugars Ralph took, but she knew as certainly as if she had been born with the knowledge that he wouldn't take kindly to being bossed about by anyone, not even a priest.

Nevertheless, it played on her mind, but when she introduced the idea of a church ceremony, Ralph cut her off sharply.

'I hope you aren't about to use the words "really married".'

'No.' How had he known?

'Good, because I wouldn't want you in any doubt as to your position.'

And that was that.

There was a lot of *that was that*. As Mrs Billy Shipton, she would, in true Wilton Lane style, have managed Billy, all the while letting him think he was boss. It wasn't like that with Ralph. He was the master and she had to fall into line. She wanted to be the wife his position required, but it

172

didn't always come easily. As Billy's wife, she would have known precisely what was expected, but Mrs Ralph Armstrong was a different person, and more than once in the early days she came up against a flash of annoyance that had her kicking herself for not knowing the ropes.

The morning Ralph found her stoning the doorstep, he hauled her unceremoniously up to the flat.

'If you shame me like that again, so help me, I'll belt you one.'

She stared. 'I were only doing the step. Any decent housewife does that.'

'Not – women – with – chars.' He spread out the words as if she were stupid. 'My wife doesn't demean herself or shame me by cleaning the doorstep.'

And that was that.

There used to be a daily cook called Mrs English, who had seen to the needs of Ralph and his father, but Carrie wanted to do her own cooking and Mrs English had been happy to retire.

'Doing your own cooking is all right for now,' said Ralph, 'but we won't always live over the shop. When I get us a house, we'll use hired help for everything.'

'But I like cooking.'

'Then you'd better make the most of it while we're still in the flat, hadn't you?'

And that was that.

Mrs Porter, the char, was a wisp of a creature, but she possessed an unexpected wiry strength and was a big help in taking care of Mam. Remembering how Mrs Randall had treated her,

Carrie treated Mrs Porter as well as she could. It was amazing to find herself in such an elevated position. To send a servant home with a slice of cold pie in her basket made her feel like a real lady.

Mam had been installed in one of the bedrooms in the flat. Carrie talked to her about anything and everything: the shop, the weather, the price of meat, what she could see from the window, housewives going by with shopping baskets, the comings and goings at the Lloyds on the corner opposite, where the auctions were held in a spacious function room. She had even, in a dark sort of way, got used to receiving no reply.

It was strange what you could get used to. Look how she had got used to living with Ralph. Her life bore no resemblance to the one she had spent years daydreaming about, yet here she was, getting on with it. That was how to cope: keep busy, don't think about it, just do it.

She told Mam about their comfortable home, wanting her to know they had fallen on their feet.

'We've got a real inside bathroom with a bath that has feet like a lion's paws, and a gas geyser, and an indoor privy in its own little room. Let me put your hand on this so you can feel it. Ralph has given me a tablecloth of real linen. It's snowy white and there are scoops of lace all round the edges – can you feel them? This goes on the table for meals and there's a dark-red chenille cloth to cover it the rest of the time. Ralph gives me plenty of housekeeping money and on top of that he gives me spends every week, though I'm supposed to call it pin money.'

As for the food – she had heard of people who could buy a Sunday joint big enough to last, cold or curried, hashed or minced, until Thursday, and now she was one of them. Anxious for Ralph not to mind being served fish every Friday, she picked the fishmonger's brains for tasty ideas and, after weeks of frantic stirring, had mastered the tricky business of making sauces without lumps.

'D'you think if you slather it in gooseberry sauce, I won't know it's fish?' he had enquired. Then he grinned. 'Bake it in cider. My ma used to do that.'

It sounded vaguely sinful to cook Friday fish in alcohol; but then she recalled the beery fumes that informed midnight Mass every Christmas Eve, so why not? If it pleased Ralph, that was reason enough. She wanted him to be glad he had married her, wanted to make up for not loving him. That he was in love with her – passionately – she had no doubt. Look at the way he had wooed her so determinedly and swept her off her feet – or so he thought.

She still went cold when she thought how she had hurled herself at him. Not that she could remember it as such, thanks to the alcohol. She was ashamed of getting drunk, but could she have gone through with it had she been sober?

She had awoken the following morning to an empty memory, a cracking headache, tender thighs and a tongue like an old doormat. Pleading illness, she had skipped Mass, spending the morning slumped over the teapot, not daring to probe her memory. By midday she had revived sufficiently to start panicking. Suppose her forwardness had disgusted Ralph and she never saw him again. She had never behaved that way with Billy, wouldn't have dreamt of it, and Billy would have been appalled.

Ralph hadn't seemed appalled, though, when he came knocking that afternoon. She had been dreading seeing him, but he surprised her with a hug and the words, 'You're mine now,' and relief had swamped her. How quickly could she announce her pregnancy and trust him to do the right thing? But even that worry was taken out of her hands. Within days they were man and wife.

Just over a fortnight into the marriage, not daring to leave it any longer, her face and neck had burnt as she murmured that it was early days and she couldn't be sure, but it should have been her monthly this week, so maybe...

'It was that time on the kitchen table,' he said. 'I told you that made you mine.'

It was a good job she was sitting down or her legs would have crumpled beneath her. She had got away with it. As payment to Ralph for marrying her and providing her, Mam and the baby with a secure existence, she vowed to be the best wife she could.

When Ralph wanted her to have her hair cut into the new shorter style, she was quick to obey, even though she didn't want to. She didn't want to look like she was aping Evadne, especially when the style looked as though it had been designed with Evadne in mind. The bob made her self-conscious, not quite herself any more, not that she said so to Ralph. He never seemed to notice that she was forever hooking her hair behind her ears

176

every time it fell forwards.

Adam noticed, though.

'Why do you do that? Your hair frames your face nicely when you let it hang.'

She gave him a smile. His goodness to Mam was never far from her thoughts. 'It's a nuisance. It gets in the way.'

'What made you have it cut? Silly question. It's the fashion nowadays.'

'I've never bothered with fashion.'

'You don't appear keen on this one, anyway. Will you let your hair grow long again?'

'Oh no! Ralph likes it. He's the one who wanted it cut.'

Adam looked at her. 'I prefer it long, myself.'

'So do I,' she said in a pretend whisper, 'but don't tell Ralph.'

'Don't tell Ralph what?' And there was Ralph glowering in the doorway, mouth hard with anger.

'We were discussing Carrie's preferences in hair-styles,' Adam answered easily, though Carrie's heart was thumping.

'If you want to have a personal conversation with a woman about her appearance, I suggest you get a wife of your own and leave mine alone,' Ralph retorted and Carrie went cold at such rudeness. 'Was there anything else or have you finished?'

'I'll be on my way.' Adam stood up.

'But I've asked him to eat with us,' she said. 'There's plenty.'

'Perhaps not today,' said Adam.

'Perhaps not,' Ralph agreed and she winced at

177

the sarcasm.

She didn't say another word. She constantly reminded herself of the security and comfort Ralph provided. It was her job to keep things smooth for him so he didn't get annoyed.

She was delighted to find one area in which she did please him. When she took an interest in the shop, he approved, and she was thrilled to find a niche for herself in doing the window displays, a skill that blossomed after Ralph complained about the overcrowded displays still there from his father's time.

'The old man wouldn't let anyone else do the windows.' Knowing how busy he was, now the auction room was up and running, she offered to lend a hand.

'I did displays at Trimble's.' She tried not to mind when he laughed out loud.

'This is hardly the same. Still, if you want to have a go, why not? I like the idea of having you here close to me.'

'I'd be happy to provide any assistance you require,' said Mr Weston.

She beamed at him. Mr Weston had a quiet way of moving about that made you feel the shop's precious stock was in capable hands and his grey hair made him look distinguished. Immaculately turned out, he always wore a silk handkerchief in his top pocket. He had worked here for years and seemed to Carrie to know everything there was to know about fine things.

She spent ages on her task, selecting items, re-arranging them, nipping outside to examine the effect from the passer-by's point of view. When she had everything just so, she showed Ralph.

'The trouble is,' he observed and Carrie felt her skin prickle in anticipation of criticism, 'that this is so good, it makes the other windows look even worse. You've got yourself a job, Mrs Armstrong.'

Displays had been her responsibility ever since, until a sudden increase in her girth made Ralph decide it wasn't seemly for her to be seen working. Much as she loved being pregnant, it wasn't easy pretending to be eight months gone when really she was overdue.

'Hold on a little longer,' she whispered to her baby. 'Every extra day helps.'

Chapter Nineteen

'Oh – you've come,' said Carrie, startled. 'I never expected you on a day like today.'

Adam walked into Mrs Jenkins' bedroom. She had the room at the front, which had once been his. He had hoped that by this time she would be sitting propped up in a chair, watching the world go by, but after all these months, she was still bedbound and immobile.

Not that there was any view today, what with the world wrapped in a dense fog that muffled and distorted sounds, and made it impossible to see even the length of your arm.

He smiled at Carrie – he couldn't help it. Her smile of welcome was irresistible. She was always pleased to see him. Pleased. Not thrilled or delighted. Her heart didn't leap at the sight of him, as his did when he saw her. She was pleased. That was all.

He put down his hat and unwound his scarf. 'It was a harder journey than I expected, I must admit. I bumped into someone and said sorry, then realised I'd apologised to a pillar box.'

Carrie laughed. 'Me and my friend Letty once blundered round Chorlton Park for two hours before we found the way out.'

'It's a proper pea-souper today.'

'Grandpa used to call them phlegm fogs and Nana threatened to bash him with the saucepan for being disgusting.' The memory brought a pretty smile to her lips. 'Let me put your coat by the fire, mek it warm for you to put on.'

He shrugged his wool overcoat into her waiting hands. She had no qualms about standing close to him, no idea what her proximity did to his emotions. She popped a wooden chair in front of the bedroom fire and draped his coat over it.

He moved away. It wasn't appropriate to be near her. She might not suspect anything, but he would never take advantage in any way.

Or was just being here taking advantage? Should he hand over the case to Todd? Would that be the honourable thing to do?

Possibly. But there was also the professional question. Mrs Jenkins was a puzzle. She had made no progress to speak of and that made him all the more determined to help her. He knew it wasn't for the want of trying on Carrie's part. She nursed her mother devotedly, working at her exercises every day without fail, and even though it must be uncomfortable for her now that she was nearing her time, she was the most devoted of the various family members who were supervised by Brookburn nurses on twice-weekly visits. If she ever got disheartened by her mother's lack of progress, she never let it drag her down. You had to admire her pluck.

Adam went through his usual routine of examining Mrs Jenkins, then moved aside while Carrie straightened the bedclothes. Over the winter she had made a jolly patchwork quilt, using scraps with all kinds of textures to stimulate her mother's sense of touch.

'You're a born looker-afterer,' he told her. 'You'll be a wonderful mother.'

'Mam's always been a wonderful mother to me. I'm happy to take care of her. You hear that, Mam? You're never to think you're any trouble.'

She spoke lightly, but she looked pleased at his compliment. Pleased. Pleased to see him and pleased by his praise. Pleased.

Did Ralph pay her compliments? And what business was it of his, anyway?

He was hopelessly in love with his brother's wife, and Ralph didn't deserve her. He wasn't the cherishing sort, and Carrie ought to be cherished.

'Would you like a cup of tea before you go?' she offered.

He would love it, would love the chance to enjoy her company. It would feed his soul until next time.

'I mustn't, I'm afraid. It took me ages to get here and I ought to make tracks.'

'Thank you for coming through the fog to see

us. We're always pleased to see you – aren't we, Mam?'

Pleased. Of course.

Bugger.

Ralph turned up the gas lamps in the shop, but it didn't make much difference, not with that impenetrable yellow-grey mush pressing against the windows. Normally, Armstrong's was bright, even on the dullest days, having those two splendid windows at the front and a third on the side, but the blasted fog put paid to that. It also put paid to a day's custom.

It was funny how fog cut you off from everything. The rest of the world was out there in that clotted atmosphere, but so what? Fog made you feel separate and alone, something that disturbed him not in the least. He always felt separate, trusting no one, relying on no one. It would take more than a few socking great lumps of fog to make him feel uneasy about that.

And now he thought about it, was there someone he trusted? Did he trust Carrie? He supposed he did. For all that she thought she had got away with landing another man's bastard on him, she was a decent girl with principles and a good heart. Her deception made it even more important to her to do right by him. She was beholden to him and that was how he liked it.

He wound his way between items on display to stand in the middle of the shop. The place was far more attractive than in his father's day: gone was the clutter; the window displays were elegant and enticing; the shop floor pleasantly laid out with ample room to move. He felt at ease, in control, fulfilled. This was what he had always wanted and Dad's death had been a reasonable price to pay.

Adam appeared from the back of the shop. Who'd be a doctor, eh, turning out on a day like this to see an old dummy?

'How is she?'

'No change.'

Good. That was how he liked it. Well, obviously, if she were to die, that would be perfect, but failing that, continued dummyhood would do.

As usual, Adam attempted conversation. Ralph wasn't interested in small talk and he certainly wasn't interested in cosying up to his brother. Fortunately, Adam, with one eye on the murk caking the windows, didn't hang about. He opened the door, the bell's tinkle almost swallowed by the curdled grot trying to ooze its way in. Adam vanished into the sludge.

Good riddance.

When it was time to close for dinner, he gave Weston the rest of the day off, glad to lock up behind him. Maybe he would get run over and killed in the fog.

With the fog holding the world at bay, Ralph's whole world was here, everything that mattered – his business and Carrie, his two most precious possessions. His world.

And the waxwork.

He went upstairs. Carrie was in the kitchen.

'I'm about to dish up,' she called. 'Shan't be a minute.'

He walked along the landing to the front bedroom. It had amused him to suggest Adam's old

183

room for the dummy. He didn't often come in here. Just sometimes, when Carrie was busy or out. Or asleep.

She had drawn the curtains against the fog. As if her mother could possibly appreciate it, but that was Carrie for you. He looked at the figure in the bed, the shell that used to be Carrie's mother, the object of Dad's affection. 'Object' was the right word. Not a person any more, not by any stretch.

People thought him good for taking her in, his mother-in-law – dummy-in-law – but the fact was, he hadn't had a choice. Since she hadn't had the common decency to snuff it, he needed her here to keep an eye on her.

He had thought in the early days, and still pondered on it from time to time, about helping her on her way. He'd be doing her a favour, really. Not that that was of any moment. He didn't care about her in the slightest, other than to find her continued existence a nuisance.

He had come close to killing her. He had stood over her with the edges of the pillow bunched in his fists. She thought he had killed his father. Well, he had, and he wasn't sorry, but it had been an accident. He had grabbed Dad's jacket and shoved and Dad had cracked his idiotic head open on the hearth. An accident with a highly agreeable outcome.

But her last words, the dummy's last words, the stupid bitch's last words, had accused him of murder. Deliberate. Premeditated. Malice aforethought. Black cloth over the judge's wig.

Her word against his. Hers, of course, would

carry less weight. She was female. She had been married to a deserter. And who could say how much the stroke had mashed up her brain? Even so.

Her blabbing would do untold damage to his reputation, even if no one believed her. He couldn't risk that. She had to die.

But he couldn't risk that either. Adam had been in and out every few days to start with, and since then a Brookburn nurse had come twice a week. Adam talked about recovery, never the possibility of death. If she were to snuff it unexpectedly, would he be able to tell she had been smothered?

So he had held off; and the improvement had never happened. If it ever did, he would review the situation, but for now...

Sometimes he talked to her. Not that he believed she could hear, or if she could, she couldn't understand. Adam's waxworks had nothing to speak of between their ears.

He opened the curtains. Fog was plastered against the window.

'Pea-souper today,' he remarked.

Just like the inside of her head.

Chapter Twenty

The front door snapped shut behind Evadne and she stamped down the front steps, heels tapping resentfully on the path. She routinely quitted Grandfather's house frothing with frustration and today she could feel the blood sizzling in her veins.

Her wool coat flapping against her shins brought a long-standing grudge to the fore. It was beastly of Grandfather not to let her have her pick of Grandmother's clothes. She was positive the attics must be groaning with trunks crammed with Grandmother's things, and she, the only descendant, was entitled, especially in this weather. She remembered a vast ermine stole and matching muff, and that three-quarter-length fur with all those tails dangling from the gorgeous deep collar. Instead, she was doomed to wear this overcoat she had had for donkey's years: a good coat, of course, since she always bought the best she could afford, but a plain garment compared to Grandmother's fabulous furs – and doubly plain when she saw herself through the eyes of Grandfather's visitor.

Grandfather's visitor. She had made a point of coming here today, and never mind how Grandfather had tried to put her off. Ever since catastrophe had descended upon her last summer, she had been visiting him more frequently, desperate for him to recognise his obligation and offer her a home. But his sense of obligation, not for the first time, seemed assuaged by the provision of a job – and what a job! Of all the places he could have found, of all the cronies he had at that wretched club, he couldn't possibly have chosen her a less desirable position.

Last time she had come to Parrs Wood, she had as always announced when her following visit would be. 'I'll see you next Saturday, Grandfather.' Times were when it had made her feel important to invite herself to this gracious address, quite as if she belonged here; but these days, doing so occasioned a dark fluttering beneath her ribcage.

'Not convenient, I'm afraid. I've someone coming. An old crony has written, don't y'know.'

The thought of two old codgers rehashing long-ago campaigns made her purse her lips. Then her ears pricked up. Not the old crony, but his grandson. Her fantasies of meeting an eligible man under Grandfather's roof came stampeding back.

She had arrived today at her usual time.

'Wasn't expecting you,' Grandfather said, bluntly.

'I always come at this time on a Saturday.'

'Told you not to. Told you I had a visitor.'

Impossible to keep the heat from her cheeks. 'I'm sure you didn't. I'm so sorry if I'm intruding, Mr...?'

Which obliged Grandfather to remember his manners. 'This is the Honourable—'

Honourable! She would have bought a new dress had she known. She was too dazzled to catch the rest of the introduction, but fortunately Grandfather called him Larter once or twice afterwards, so at least she knew his surname. She studied him covertly. A few years her senior, he was tall – she liked that; she was tall herself – with a narrow, bony face, his hairline interrupted by a scar that puckered his left temple. There was another scar, the faintest of lines down his left cheek. Everything about him spoke of breeding: the cut of his clothes, his polish and confidence. He had called on Grandfather as a courtesy to his own grandfather, but there was none of the deferential younger man about him. This was a man who had been in the war and had been a leader of men, as befitted one of his class.

'What brings you to these parts?' Grandfather enquired.

'Business. My family expected me to stay in the army, younger son and all that, but...' He lifted one shoulder in a careless shrug, as if generations of tradition meant nothing. Evadne was thrilled: only someone who could trace his ancestry back to the Conquest could be so blasé. 'I have fingers in a few pies. I have an interest in a new auction room hereabouts. Chorlton-cum-Hardy.'

'Humph. Not the most select area.'

'Up-and-coming.'

'Humph.'

'Perhaps my connection will help it to be up-and-coming.'

Evadne could scarcely believe it. 'Are you – you can't be connected to Ralph Armstrong?'

Keen grey eyes sliced the air between them. 'Yes, as it happens. Do you know him?'

Indeed she did, and that was another reason she was now bubbling with bitterness as she marched through the slush to the tram stop. After months of virtually ignoring her cheap tart of a sister, it turned out that Carrie's husband could be the means of furthering her acquaintance with the Honourable Mr Larter.

She felt sour towards Carrie. With Pa's disgrace hanging over her and Billy jilting her, instead of keeping herself to herself, the girl had hurled herself at the next man to walk past their front door, leaving Evadne barely able to hold up her

188

head. To cap it all, little Carrie from the corner shop had bagged herself a well-to-do husband. Did she possess more brains than Evadne had given her credit for? She had certainly escaped the immediate disgrace of living surrounded by people who knew about Pa. How Evadne resented that. It was she, the innocent stepdaughter, who should have been spirited away into a better situation – instead of which, Grandfather had produced a job, courtesy of one of his cronies.

Her heart quaked with indignation at the thought of returning to that place. She had deliberately not attempted to find herself a new position last summer because she had had no intention of making it easy for Grandfather to ignore his responsibilities. Hence she had ended up with no alternative but to accept the post at Brookburn when Carrie upped and married, thereby rendering her homeless since Mr Dawson wouldn't rent a house to a single lady. Not that she had had any desire to remain in Wilton Lane; the only place she wanted to live in was a certain address in Parrs Wood.

She stepped in a puddle and gasped as icy water sloshed over her shoe and soaked her stocking. The raw air bit her face, leaving her cheeks smarting and her nose numb and no doubt bright red. It was hateful having to turn out on a day like this, worse knowing what lay at the end of her journey.

Brookburn. She loathed everything about the place. No, that wasn't entirely true. The administrative work suited her; she was proud of her methodical mind. Sometimes when she was in her office with the door closed, she could almost

189

convince herself that this horrid situation wasn't so bad after all.

Sometimes.

Almost.

Who did she think she was fooling?

She had nothing to do with the patients – well, virtually. Sometimes she couldn't avoid seeing them, like when she needed a doctor to sign something and had to search for him in the wards – a creepy experience, with all those figures silent and motionless beneath the sheets. And not just in beds: there was a rota for getting them out of bed and wheeling them about. They were taken outside whenever the weather was even halfway decent. The grounds had been littered with them until the end of September.

'We have reason to think this helps,' Doctor Armstrong had said, coming upon her curling her lip at the sight.

That was another thing she detested about Brookburn – Doctor Armstrong. But for him, she could have introduced herself as the fiancée of a soldier killed in the war. Better a bereaved fiancée than an old maid. But having Carrie's brother-in-law here had put paid to that. There was also the constant discomfort of knowing that someone at Brookburn knew what had happened to Pa.

'I trust you won't mention my stepfather to anyone,' she had said to him. 'My name is Baxter. There's no need for anyone to know the connection.'

'Of course.' He looked at her with what might have been pity, something that made her stomach muscles clench with hurt pride, anyway. 'But I think you'll find that our patients and their families have other things on their minds.'

Evadne trudged up the drive, tired and chilled. Through the sleety murk of the winter teatime, Brookburn's lights glowed. Soon the staff meals would start. Not that she cared; she made a point of having a tray sent upstairs. A stiff breeze swept across the grounds and stung her face. To her left lay the park, while on her right, down in a dip of five or six feet, was Chorlton Brook.

As she drew closer to the house, she realised someone was down there in the dip, standing at the edge of the water, facing the bank; just standing there, staring. She felt a flutter of alarm before she recognised Ted Geeson, the grounds-man. Geeson was a former soldier, and you only had to see how he swung his right leg when he walked to know he had an artificial limb.

She was going to walk past, but something tugged at her conscience and she halted with a disgruntled sigh, squeezing her frozen toes inside her wet shoes.

'Geeson! What are you doing? Are you all right?'

He looked up at her, raising gloved fingers to his cap. 'Evening, miss. I'm fine, thank you.'

She turned to walk on, vexed as she realised he was blundering up the bank to the drive. She didn't stop. People could say what they liked about social barriers starting to come down, but she was perfectly happy with the old ways, and small talk with the groundsman was definitely not on her agenda.

He was nippier on his feet than she had thought,

however, and in a moment he was swinging along beside her.

'Sharp evening, miss.'

'Indeed.'

'And a cold night to follow.'

She didn't bother answering.

'You were wondering what I was about down there.'

'I'm not interested, Geeson.'

'Truth is, I was feeling ... well, quiet, I suppose. Sort of peaceful, you might say.'

She couldn't help looking at him, a thickset figure bundled up in a greatcoat and scarf. 'Whatever for?'

'It's when the riverbank gets all slick with rain, you see. I've been here four years now, miss. Times were when the sight of that bank all wet and muddy would make me want to dig into it with my bare hands. Did it once or twice an' all; couldn't help myself. But now – well, now I don't need to no more, and that's something to be grateful for. It's sad too, in a way, sobering like, though that's something I never thought I'd hear myself say. Sad to think mebbe I don't need to help them no more.'

'Help whom?'

'Fallen comrades, miss. Digging 'em out.'

She stopped, swung round on him. 'You're mad.'

Even in the darkness, she could see how his eyes clouded in his lined face. 'Sorry, miss.' He touched his cap to her and loped away at surprising speed.

'That was cruel, Miss Baxter,' said a voice beside the front door, and she turned in annoyance to see Doctor Armstrong leaning against the porch, smoking his pipe.

'It's none of your business.'

'It's everyone's business, what happened in the war. The more who know about it the better, for all our sakes. It's rare that a man says a word about it. You should feel honoured.'

'It depends on the man,' she retorted. She imagined the Honourable Mr Larter telling her about his war; she would listen to that for hours, though she rather thought a gentleman wouldn't trouble a lady with such unpleasantness.

Doctor Armstrong knocked the bowl of his pipe against the side of his hand to eject the ash. 'Knowing more might help people understand what happened to your father.'

She whipped round, eyes narrowed in fury. 'He wasn't my father.'

He opened the door for her. 'Good evening, Miss Baxter.'

Evadne swept inside.

Chapter Twenty-One

Carrie was careful not to show it, but she didn't like Ralph's new assistant. Saying goodbye to Mr Weston had been hard. The poor man was deeply shocked; she could tell by the hitch in his voice, even though he remained his usual courteous self.

'I need someone young and fit who can do some toing and froing between the shop and the auction room,' Ralph told her. 'And no, I'm not keeping Weston on as well. He's lucky to have worked here as long as he has.'

She had been dreading going downstairs to say goodbye on his last day; but, dear man that he was, he came up to the flat to bid her farewell.

'It's been a pleasure knowing you, Mrs Armstrong.'

'Likewise. What will you do?'

'I hope to be taken on by one of the antiques houses in town.'

'They'll be lucky to have you.'

'Mr Joseph Armstrong always said Armstrong's was lucky to have me,' Mr Weston said sadly.

His replacement was Arthur Renton, a thin-faced ferret of a man with a permanent five o'clock shadow. He couldn't be faulted for his efficiency, but Carrie thought he lacked the proper deference for working in this class of shop, and he didn't seem the sort to dust the stock every day like dear Mr Weston used to.

Adam dropped in one morning, as he did now and again. Carrie had realised that, without these informal visits, there would be no contact between the brothers. They didn't even go to the pub together. She was in the back room, dusting some small items, and could hear their conversation.

'Where's Weston?' Adam asked.

'Gone. Sacked.'

'Why? He devoted his life to this place and there was nothing he didn't know about fine things. Dad always said so.'

'Do I tell you how to do your job? Then don't tell me how to do mine.'

'Even so—'

'The business belongs to me and you have no say in it.'

'I'm aware of that.' Adam's voice sounded stiff. 'I simply wanted–'

'Wanted what?'

'To be on good terms. It's what Dad would have wanted.'

'Dad isn't here to want anything.'

Carrie gasped. Evadne had put her in her place more times than she could count, but even she had never been this brusque.

Later, she said to Ralph, 'What you said to Adam...' She saw the displeasure in his eyes and the warning as well. 'Nothing.'

'Nothing? Are you sure, Carrie?'

'Yes,' she whispered.

'Only I wouldn't want to think you were entertaining disloyal thoughts.'

'It was nothing, Ralph. Honest to God.'

The next time Adam called, it was in his professional capacity. He checked Mam's pulse, listened to her chest and manoeuvred her arms, testing the muscles. Then he asked the usual questions before looping his stethoscope and dropping it inside his topper, then made some notes.

'I went to see Weston,' he told her.

'How is he? I was so sorry he lost his job.'

'He's been taken on by a place on Deansgate, but only for a day a week as they're fully staffed, so he's at rather a loose end. He's going after a job in the bookshop on Beech Road as well. I've asked him to come to Brookburn to read to the lads. I can't pay him, but at least it'll get him out of the house.'

She felt a stab of guilt. 'Would you like me to read to the patients an' all?' Not that she could imagine how she would fit it in, but she would if she had to.

Adam's smile touched his eyes, turning the brown deeper and warmer. She had never seen Ralph's eyes soften like that.

'You've more than enough to do, though I appreciate the offer. I've just finished a book that you might care to share with Mrs Jenkins. It would make a change from newspapers and magazine articles. It's by a new lady author called Agatha Christie. I'll drop it round.'

She had to look away. It had never occurred to her to read to Mam. She talked to her, told her all kinds of things, but she had never been a great reader. Pa used to say that reading was for the likes of Evadne. Yet here was Adam, whose good opinion she treasured, taking it for granted that she read to Mam. Well, in future she would. It would give her something to use her spends – sorry, her pin money – for, with an easy conscience. She would buy *Vera's Voice* and give the old copies to Letty.

She decided to call on Mr Weston every week – yes, and she would take him a batch of scones or a slab of cake. After the first visit, what she really wanted to take was some slices of beef or half a dozen eggs. She was sure he wasn't eating as well as he used to. But while cake was a gift, meat would be charity, so she couldn't.

Carrie came downstairs to do some dusting. She had loved helping Mr Weston with this. She had seen things she never knew existed, like a spoon warmer – fancy warming spoons! – and a mug with two handles that Mr Weston said was called a loving cup.

At the foot of the stairs, she opened the door, pausing to ensure there were no customers. Ralph and Arthur had their backs to her, their heads bent over something.

She heard the words, '...solid silver. What a beauty,' before they looked round.

She came forward, smiling, expecting Ralph to invite her to take a look, but he said nothing. Both men looked at her and she felt uncomfortable, which made her say with artificial brightness, 'What is it? Oh, a tray – though I should call it a salver, shouldn't I, with it being solid silver? Why rich folk can't have trays like the rest of us, I don't know.'

'It's not solid silver,' said Arthur.

'I thought I heard–'

'You heard wrong,' said Ralph. 'It's just plated.' He pushed it into Arthur's hands. 'Put it in the back. What do you want, Carrie?'

'I thought I'd do some dusting.'

'I'll bring some things through.' He didn't like her being seen in the shop now she was so heavily pregnant.

She slipped into the room beside Ralph's office. The office door was open and she could see Arthur putting the salver – or was it a tray if it was simply plated? – into a cupboard. Ralph came through and placed two or three items on the table.

'You'll like this one. It's a musical box.' He gave

197

her one of his direct looks. 'What you heard was a spot of wishful thinking, Carrie. We were just saying what a shame it's not solid silver or it would be worth a pretty penny.'

She didn't know what to say, so she just said, 'Oh.'

'That's what comes of listening in.'

'I'm sorry, Ralph.'

'Mind you don't do it again.'

Pleading a headache at work, Evadne sneaked off and caught the tram to town. She had seen an advertisement for the new department in Affleck and Brown's, where the 'modern lady' could purchase an almost-finished garment, which the in-house seamstress would then fit and finish for her.

'For that personally tailored look,' the soberly dressed assistant assured her. 'May I show madam some of our styles?'

Evadne enjoyed being addressed in the third person. She chose a slightly drop-waisted wool dress the colour of caramel that would show off her colouring to perfection.

'And could your seamstress sew bands of brown velvet around the cuffs and neckline for me?'

That would give just the right finishing touch, especially to the boat neck, which revealed a tantalising glimpse of the dip between her collar bones at the base of her throat.

First the dress, next the man – which meant making up to Carrie, something she loathed the thought of, but the moment she had achieved her purpose, she would drop her like a hot potato.

The shopkeeping Armstrongs – because that was what Ralph was, after all, a shopkeeper, even if he did sell expensive goods – would have no place in the refined world of the Honourable Mr and Mrs Larter.

Evadne had visited Carrie's new home every fortnight. She wouldn't have been there at all if it hadn't been for Mother. Not that there seemed much point in sitting at the bedside of an invalid who had made no progress whatsoever, no matter how much Carrie rattled on about exercise regimes and stimulation.

'It doesn't appear to be doing her any good,' Evadne had said last time.

'Adam says it's important not to give up. And you must have seen it work at Brookburn – haven't you?' Carrie's eyes were anxious.

'My work is purely administrative,' she replied repressively, but Carrie's words had made her think. Only a couple of days previously, she had seen a young man – well, she assumed he was young; his face was such a mess that it was difficult to tell – taking a few shuffling steps in the corridor, leaning heavily on two sticks, while staff stood around him, far enough away to allow him space but close enough to leap to the rescue.

'A few months ago, he was flat on his back, couldn't move, couldn't speak,' an orderly had murmured to Evadne. 'Look at him now.'

The man's progress was excruciatingly slow; how much longer before she could get by? She lost patience, retraced her steps, went downstairs to the floor below, walked along the landing and back up the far staircase, emerging beyond the shuffling man and his entourage.

She hadn't bothered telling Carrie about it at the time, but maybe she would mention it today. She needed Carrie on her side.

'I'm sorry not to come more often,' she remarked, sitting with Carrie at Mother's bedside. 'I'm aware Ralph doesn't like me.'

Carrie's silence confirmed it and Evadne waited, knowing that eventually Carrie would feel obliged to say something.

'Well ... he doesn't really know you, does he?'

'Doesn't really want to,' she said, keeping her tone light, 'which is a shame because I could be of assistance in the auction room. It must generate a great deal of paperwork.'

'There is a lot of work – Ralph's always saying so – but not enough to need another person, and then there would be the cost.'

'Exactly. I'm not looking for another position. I'm simply offering my services on an ad hoc basis. I could handle the paperwork and that would leave Ralph free to do other things.'

'That's generous, Evadne.'

'It wouldn't do Ralph any harm to have someone of my social calibre associated with his auction room.' She left the tiniest pause, as if a new thought had occurred to her. 'I could rearrange my working hours so that I work evenings at Brookburn in order to be available on auction days. There is just the one auction each month, isn't there?'

'At the moment. Ralph hopes to increase it to fortnightly.'

'I could offer assistance on auction day; or if ...

I don't know, if Ralph had an important visitor – a colleague, say, or an investor – I could be at hand to act in a secretarial capacity. That would show him in a favourable light, you must agree.' She glanced at her sister. 'And it couldn't do us any harm as a family, could it?'

Carrie's gentle eyes misted over. 'I'll ask Ralph tonight.'

Evadne said no more. She couldn't imagine what she would do if Ralph refused. She had to have the chance to meet the Honourable Mr Larter accidentally on purpose in the auction room, she simply had to.

Chapter Twenty-Two

Carrie heaved herself downstairs to the shop. She had had a few twinges during the night that had made her wonder whether the baby was starting. She felt elated, but she couldn't breathe a word because she wasn't supposed to be due. She had to keep going as normal, so had gone out shopping that morning, anxious in case her waters broke in the greengrocer's.

Now she ought to do a spot of dusting. She didn't feel like it. All she wanted to do was take the weight off her feet, but being told off by Ralph over the silver-plated tray had left her with the odd feeling that she ought to go back to the shop to show she wasn't scared.

When she peeped in, she was disconcerted to

see Arthur on his own. She felt like heading back upstairs, but that was silly. Anyroad, he had seen her.

'Afternoon, Mrs Armstrong. What can I do for you?'

'Are you on your own?'

'Looks like it.' He gave her a grin, and she couldn't tell if he was being impertinent. 'Mr Armstrong is out doing a valuation.'

'Of course. I'd forgotten.' Carrie shook her head. Her memory had faltered a few times recently, presumably something to do with her condition, though there was no one she could ask. She had lost not only her dear mam's wisdom and support, but also that of all the women in Wilton Lane. She hadn't been back even once. Ralph had forbidden it.

'You're a cut above that now,' he had said on their way home from the registry office, and Carrie, instead of feeling proud of doing so well for herself, Mam and the baby, had felt uncomfortable – guilty, too – when she remembered all the kindness and assistance that had been lavished on Mam.

'He'll be an hour or so yet,' said Arthur.

'I came down to do some dusting.'

'I'll bring some bits through.'

She settled in her usual place and Arthur brought a canteen of cutlery and a set of small ornamental bowls in lacquered brass.

'I'll fetch the Brasso,' he said.

She glanced up in surprise. Hadn't Mr Weston said you shouldn't use brass polish on lacquered brass? Yet here was Ralph's assistant apparently happy to make that very mistake. She opened her mouth, then shut it again, not liking to correct him. He must know his stuff or Ralph wouldn't have employed him.

As she worked, she heard the shop door open and the bell ring, then male voices. Arthur popped his head round the door.

'Sorry, Mrs A, but could you keep an eye on the shop for five minutes? A dining suite we're auctioning has arrived early and I need to sort it out.'

They were lucky to have the use of some rooms at the hotel over the road, though Ralph hadn't been pleased when Carrie said so.

'It isn't luck. It's a sound business arrangement. It makes sense for me to have my auction room nearby and, as well as my rent, the Lloyds makes extra by serving refreshments to the punters.'

Arthur left the door open so she could see into the shop. He was gone rather longer than five minutes. Was he sneaking a crafty cigarette? He would never dare try it on with Ralph.

The bell over the door tinkled and she looked up in dismay. Ralph wouldn't be amused to know his hugely pregnant wife had been in the shop, but at least the customer was a woman, and an elderly one at that.

She pushed herself to her feet, trying not to waddle. 'Good afternoon. Can I help you?'

The old lady turned to her. Feathery grey hair wisped out from beneath her old-fashioned large-brimmed hat. 'I hope so. I'd like a silver tray – plated, of course, not solid silver.'

Carrie smiled. This was one request she could

cope with. 'We had one a few days ago. Let me see if it's still here.'

As she picked her way carefully through the pieces of furniture on display, feeling thoroughly ungainly, the old lady began to chat.

'We had one when I was a girl. It was my mother's pride and joy, but she had to sell it after my father died and I've always promised myself I'd buy one if I could afford it. Now my dear brother has left me a legacy and here I am.'

'I'm sorry. It's been sold.' How disappointing. It had given her such a rush of pleasure to help a customer again. She had forgotten how much she had enjoyed working at Trimble's.

'What a pity.' The old lady looked crestfallen.

'We have another tray in the back. If you don't mind waiting...'

She retrieved the silver-plated tray, the one she had mistakenly thought was solid silver. A minute later, she was smiling at the customer's delight.

'It's charming. One moment while I put my spectacles on.' She fished in her bag and hooked her glasses over her ears. 'There. Oh, it's even prettier than the one my mother had. Look at that fancywork. How much is it?'

Carrie was ready for this. She remembered the price tag on the tray that had been sold. That tray had been bigger but this one's scalloped edging suggested that more work had gone into it, so it seemed fair to ask for the same price. She looked anxiously into the old lady's face, badly wanting her to be able to afford it.

'Well, it's more than I was hoping to pay, but

it's worth it.'

She beamed. 'I'm sure it'll give you a lot of pleasure. May I have your name and address?' She wrote down the details and accepted payment. 'I'll wrap your tray and have it sent round, Miss Deacon.' That was something else Mr Weston had told her, always use the customer's name. Not that either of them had ever expected her to be in the position of selling anything. She felt a glow of pleasure. 'Much obliged,' she added, the way Mr Trimble had taught her to say to customers who paid upfront.

'Well, Armstrong, how are you? You must be relieved you've got your auction room sorted out at last. I was starting to lose patience, thought we might be parting company.'

Ralph gritted his teeth but kept his expression neutral as he shook hands with Alex Larter. Meeting in his office should give him the advantage, dammit. Larter's words rankled in so many ways and he was entirely aware of it, the smooth bastard. Calling him Armstrong, for one thing, when Ralph had to address him as Mr Larter, thanks to their relative social positions. Alex Larter's father was some sort of lord and Larter was an honourable. He had been Ralph's superior in the army too, like so many of the nobs who were given rank just because of who they were. Not that Larter had been bad at it, not like some of them.

'There was never any doubt I'd get sorted,' he said, stiffly.

'Wasn't there?' Larter spoke lightly, his tone not quite an open taunt. 'I can think of a number of fellows who would disagree. But never mind that now.' His shoulders didn't move inside his costly double-breasted jacket, but his voice suggested a dismissive shrug. 'I met an acquaintance of yours the other day.'

Ralph expected him to name someone from their army days even as he acknowledged that Larter was the last man to indulge in a spot of auld lang syne. Or maybe the last but one. He, himself, would be last.

'Miss Evadne Baxter. Your wife's sister, I believe.'

Ralph felt the skin around his eyes stretch as they widened. He hated being taken by surprise, because it was a sign of weakness, but he couldn't hide it.

Larter regarded him with amusement. 'Yes, that's approximately how pleased she looked as well. Turns out her grandfather and mine took a pop at the French together back when Egypt became a colony. I want you to offer her a job.'

'You what?' He couldn't believe his ears. Just the other day, Carrie had told him that Evadne had offered her services and he had turned the suggestion down flat. It was his proud boast that he would do anything to please his Carrie, but nothing would induce him to cosy up to her stuck-up bitch of a sister. And now here was Alex flaming Larter suggesting–

'Not bloody likely! I'm not employing her.'

'Oh, but you are. I have plans for the lady.'

'Like what?'

Larter's grey eyes were flinty and Ralph could have sworn the flesh twitched beneath the scar down his cheek. 'Are you questioning me?'

The moment was rock hard with tension and instinctively Ralph raised his guard. He wouldn't back down, though, not for anyone. Instead, he sidestepped. 'You must admit, it's unexpected.'

'Old man Baxter told me about her. The beautiful Evadne has pretensions, apparently, which he isn't inclined to fulfil, thanks to the mother having made an unfortunate second marriage that dragged Evadne down in the world. That would be your mother-in-law, I think I'm right in saying? Miss Baxter has been endeavouring to claw her way back up again ever since, but the old boy won't soil his hands. He that toucheth pitch, and all that. Once the stepfather was revealed as a deserter, that was proof to old Baxter that he'd been right all along to keep Evadne at arm's length. Meanwhile, the lady is doing everything she can to worm her way into his good graces, but to no avail. I feel sorry for her, poor bitch.'

'Really?'

'No. But she'll be useful to our venture; and so you, her beloved brother-in-law, will offer her a position.'

Over his rotting corpse. He hated the power Larter had over him. One wrong word and it really would be over his dead body.

They both knew he had no choice, but he couldn't bring himself to utter the words. Instead he asked, 'What have you got in mind?'

'I have the impression you're not keen on her.'

'I'm not.'

'Then you won't care what becomes of her, will you?'

Chapter Twenty-Three

As three o'clock approached, Carrie made tea. Before she got so huge, she used to take the tray downstairs into the back of the shop; now, Arthur fetched it. She had the tray ready as the clock struck: Ralph didn't like to be kept waiting. She listened for Arthur's tap on the door, but it didn't come.

At ten past, she ventured down. She didn't want it to be her fault the tea was late. She glanced into the shop. It was empty so she opened the office door, aware as she did so of a loud voice, yet rejecting the sound because it was out of place. The next moment, her fingers slipped from the knob and the door swung wide while she stood there, gawping.

Ralph had got Arthur shoved against the wall and was bellowing into his face. Ralph's left hand was clenched around a fistful of collar and tie, his forearm and elbow digging into Arthur's front, holding him pinned while his right fist hovered menacingly below Arthur's chin. Carrie glimpsed Arthur's face, the skin shiny with sweat, blotchy too. Blood was streaming from one nostril.

'You bloody thieving bastard!' Ralph roared right into Arthur's face, jamming him harder against the wall as if he wanted to shove him straight through it. 'I'll teach you to steal from me. Tell me what you've done with it or I'll bust your kneecaps with the hammer.'

'I never touched it. I don't know where it is...'

'Then see if this jogs your memory.' Ralph delivered a series of heavy slaps across Arthur's face, and Carrie flinched as his head snapped this way and that. 'Remember the salver now, do you?'

She went hot and cold. Plunging across the room, she pulled at Ralph's arm. Without slackening his grip, he looked down at her over his shoulder.

'Get upstairs, Carrie. This isn't for you to see.'

'No – Ralph – please. I know what happened.'

The room fell still. The hairs lifted on the nape of her neck. Both men were looking at her now. Arthur, still fastened against the wall and trying to sniff the blood back up his nose, screwed his face round to see her.

Her mouth was dry. All that emerged was a croaky whisper: 'I sold it.'

'You what?'

'I sold it.'

She gazed at Ralph, willing him to relax his hold on Arthur and smile and say in a relieved voice, 'That's all right, then.' But he didn't. His eyes were cold and sharp. She licked her lips.

'Mr Renton had to go across to the Lloyds, and a lady came in. She wanted a silver-plated tray. I thought I was doing the right thing.'

Ralph released Arthur so abruptly he slumped to the floor. Ralph swung round to confront Carrie. Confront? Her heart swelled painfully and the baby kicked as if in protest. She placed her hands over her belly. Something stiffened inside her: she would fight to the death to protect

209

her child.

'Good afternoon. I trust I'm not interrupting.'

The smooth, cultured voice was so totally at odds with the charged atmosphere that she had to rearrange everything inside her head. A tall, well-dressed gentleman was standing in the doorway, surveying the scene through knowing grey eyes, though his expression was bland, broken only by the narrow thread of a scar down one cheek.

'Mr Larter!' Ralph said; and 'Mr Larter!' said Arthur a split second after, the blood in his mouth endowing the words with a thickened quality.

The gentleman stepped into the room. He looked at Carrie as if assessing her before raising his hat. Her gaze was drawn to the left side of his forehead, where the hairline was interrupted by the angry ridges of a scar that puckered his temple.

He said, 'Aren't you going to introduce me, Armstrong?'

'Carrie, this is the Honourable Mr Larter, a business associate. Mr Larter, this is my wife.'

'How do you do, Mrs Armstrong? A great pleasure.'

She found herself shaking hands with an honourable. Mr Larter's educated voice and polished manner were a powerful reminder that she was nobbut a girl from Wilton Lane. She felt as if she should curtsey. Worse, she felt as if Mr Larter thought so too.

'What did you want, Carrie?' Ralph asked.

She glanced at Arthur. 'I came to remind Mr Renton about the tea.' The men were ignoring

210

the blood, so she did too.

'Never mind that. Go back upstairs.'

It was dismissal, and blunt dismissal at that, but she didn't care. All she felt as she guided her massive bump from the room was waves of relief.

Approaching Adam Armstrong's office, a secret smile playing across her lips, Evadne was triumphant. It had been a bitter blow when Ralph had turned down her offer to work for him, but he had evidently thought better of it.

'I'm pleased you've seen sense,' she had told him with calculated condescension, determined to rub his nose in it. 'I'll make myself available immediately.'

'No need. Wait until the next auction.'

But she wasn't going to be put off. She had no way of knowing when the Honourable Mr Larter would call to see the auction room and that meant she must be there as often as possible.

'I must familiarise myself with the administrative processes, which I expect could stand some improvement. Perhaps an hour each morning. I can easily organise that.'

So she had made this appointment with Doctor Armstrong, certain of his agreement. After all, his own brother stood to gain.

'Time off to do another job?' he said. 'I don't like the sound of that.'

'I would naturally make up the time here by working in the evenings. After all, it can hardly be said to matter when administrative work gets done.'

'In that case, you can do Ralph's administrative

work in the evenings after you've fulfilled your obligations here.'

'My grandfather–'

'I'm aware that Major Baxter pulled strings to get you this position; but now you come under my authority, no one else's.' He eyed her thoughtfully. 'I do understand family loyalty, however, and I know how much this would mean to Carrie; so I'll come to an arrangement concerning the auction days, if your presence at them is so vital. I'll speak to Ralph.'

She forced herself to say, 'Thank you,' although the words nearly choked her.

She flounced out of the office, hating Doctor Armstrong for lording it over her. As if she cared tuppence for this stupid job! But she couldn't afford to jeopardise it. Not only did she need the income, it also provided a roof over her head, and a pleasingly elegant roof at that, even though it was marred by sheltering a hospital.

Just let him wait. She pictured herself sailing into Adam Armstrong's office to wave her resignation under his nose. She would make sure she did it with her left hand too.

Carrie flew to Mam's bedside, clutching Mam's hand in both her own and pressing herself as close as she could to the motionless body, wishing with all her heart that Mam could squeeze her hand or pat her arm, anything to give her comfort; but even had Mam been capable of such a gesture, Carrie couldn't possibly have told her what had happened downstairs. Not for anything would she worry her with that.

The afternoon was dark and sleety. When she got up to draw the curtains, each splatter of sleet seemed to land inside her heart.

When Ralph came upstairs, she fetched his slippers and hung up the waistcoat and jacket belonging to his suit, while he changed into the knitted pullover and comfortable tweed jacket he favoured in the evenings.

'Smells good,' he observed, taking his seat at the table.

'Hotpot, with jam roly-poly and custard for pudding.'

'Proper cold-weather food.'

'About what happened–'

'Not at the table, Carrie.'

Don't speak to me like that. I'm not a child.

Later, when she had finished clearing away and came to sit by the fire with her knitting, Ralph folded his newspaper and looked across at her from his armchair.

'You didn't tell me you'd sold something.'

She felt confusion bloom in her cheeks. She laid down her knitting, giving herself a moment even as she asked herself why she should need any such thing.

'I'm sorry. I should have said.'

'Aye, you should. Why didn't you?'

'I don't know. It weren't on purpose.'

'Who bought it?

She perked up. 'A dear old lady, a Miss Deacon. She'd wanted one for ever such a long time and her brother had left her some money.'

'You sent it round, of course.'

'Of course. It's all written up in the book. I'm

213

sure I did everything right.' She felt her pulse skitter. When had she become so jumpy?

'I'll check.' He unfolded the newspaper with a flick.

Her hand hesitated over her knitting. 'Ralph?'

'Mm?' He looked over the top of the newspaper.

'About this afternoon...'

'What of it? It's all cleared up now that you've admitted what you did.'

Admitted? As if she had done something wrong. She felt a spurt of resentment. She wasn't going to back down. 'What you did to poor Mr Renton–'

Ralph lowered the newspaper to his lap, his eyes boring into hers.

'I was ... shocked.'

'How do you expect me to react when I have reason to believe I've caught a thief?'

'Even so...'

'Even so – what, Carrie? What do you think I should have done?'

'Sent for a policeman, I suppose.'

'Good job I didn't or you'd have ended up looking an even bigger fool. It would have made a fool of me as well and I wouldn't have appreciated that.'

She flinched, but she wouldn't stop. 'You hit him.'

He laughed, a mirthless sound. 'Well, if he has ever entertained any idea of doing the dirty on me, he'll never think of it again.'

The shock and upset that she had been suppressing ballooned inside her chest. Lifting swimming eyes, she burst out, 'You frightened me,' and, to her disgust, she began to cry. She couldn't help it. She scrabbled in her pockets for a hanky and mopped at her face, but the tears wouldn't stop.

He sat on the arm of her chair and pulled her to him, which was what she had been aching for ever since she had fled to Mam's bedside, but now that it was happening, it felt wretchedly uncomfortable. She felt squashed and cramped. The baby was squashed too, squeezing her insides out of the way.

'Are you all right now? I don't know whether to tell you not to cry or to cry it all out. Which is best for the baby?'

She pulled herself together, trying hard to manage it without any inelegant sniffing, but that proved impossible, and he thrust his handkerchief into her hands. He continued to soothe her and as her tension released, her heart filled.

It was only later, lying awake in the middle of the night, too huge to sleep, that she realised that in amongst all the soothing things Ralph had said, not once had he said he was sorry for upsetting her.

Chapter Twenty-Four

Rocked by resentment, Ralph showed Alex Larter the premises he rented at the Lloyds. It didn't take long: a sizeable outbuilding for storage and an office off the big public room where the auctions were held. Larter was having a look only to emphasise his right to do so. That it was only what

Ralph himself would do, had their positions been reversed, was beside the point.

'You should have received the first consignment,' said Larter.

'It's here.'

'Good. The sooner we start selling these goods the better. And how is the lovely Miss Baxter shaping up?'

'Well enough.'

She was a bloody nuisance, if ever there was one. Her offer to be available in the mornings had come to nothing, and instead she was turning up in the evenings, which was a damn nuisance because it drew him away from his fireside. The sight of her made him want to skin Alex Larter alive. He still didn't know what Larter had in mind for her, and that rankled too. He had allowed Evadne into the auction office and showed her how it ran. Of course, she had immediately declared she could organise it better, but she wouldn't make that mistake again, not after he had told her in no uncertain terms that it was his way or not at all.

'My way, or bugger off back to Brookburn,' had been his exact words, and her face had paled at the language.

But she was tenacious, he had to give her that, and much as it galled him to admit it, she was proving useful. She had a knack for using the typewriter. He gave her letters to type and she was working her way through the next auction list, deciphering his notes. Typewritten catalogues for the punters would make the auction room look good, and the task kept her out of his hair.

'A quick one before we eat?' suggested Larter, leading the way into the bar. He had offered Ralph dinner this evening, though the invitation hadn't included Carrie. Not that Ralph would have permitted Carrie to be entertained in public when she was on the verge of dropping the baby, but the absence of an invitation hadn't gone unnoticed. Alex Larter wouldn't demean himself by socialising with a girl from Wilton Lane, even if she were now the wife of an associate.

An hour later, accommodated at the best table the dining room offered, Ralph was enjoying braised beef in onion sauce and a second glass of full-bodied red wine when there was a flutter close by and he glanced up to see – bloody hell, Evadne.

'Forgive me for disturbing you. Good evening, Mr Larter. What must you think of me? I do assure you, I wouldn't normally barge in un-announced.'

There was the tiniest fragment of silence and Ralph wondered whether Alex Larter might be about to cut her dead, but Larter courteously rose to his feet, prompting him to remember his own manners.

'I can't imagine a more pleasant interruption, Miss Baxter,' Larter said, the smooth bastard.

'What do you want?' Ralph demanded.

She held out a page of notes. 'I can't make out your writing here ... and here. I was on my way to see you in the flat, but I noticed you here. I thought you wouldn't mind.'

'Won't you join us?' Larter offered, to Ralph's surprise.

217

Another flutter. 'You're most kind, but I couldn't possibly.'

'At least sit down while Armstrong deciphers his scrawl.' Larter pulled out a chair and Evadne sank gracefully into it. When Ralph had read out a few words that seemed to him perfectly legible, Larter added to Evadne, 'Please join us for coffee in, shall we say, half an hour. I insist.'

And the hoity-toity Evadne, who by rights should have delivered a disdainful refusal, accepted in a voice that sounded a little breathless. The men rose as she left, then resumed their seats.

'My,' said Larter, 'she's eager.'

Had there been space in the glory-hole Ralph called his office, Evadne would have danced. She could hardly believe what had happened – and yet why not believe it? She had earned it, enduring those dreary evenings slogging away at the blasted typewriter, trying to eke out a job she could have polished off in half the time. Each evening, she had crept through to the public rooms in the increasingly desperate hope of seeing the Honourable Mr Larter; and now it had happened. And he had invited her to return for coffee. What could be better? All it needed to make it perfect would be for Ralph to be called away because Carrie had started the baby.

Although coffee didn't last as long as Evadne would have liked, she could tell by Mr Larter's friendly interest that she had made a favourable impression. Ralph sat back and let them get on with it, which just showed what a graceless oaf he was.

'You have an interest in fine things?' Mr Larter had enquired.

'I have a certain appreciation of them. As a child, I lived with my grandparents. You've seen my grandfather's house. He possesses some beautiful pieces.'

'You won't learn much, hidden away in Armstrong's office, clacking away on that infernal machine.' He turned to Ralph. 'What d'you say we take her on a valuation? I'll escort you myself, Miss Baxter, if you don't consider it improper.'

Her heart had felt ready to burst as she murmured demure acceptance. The coffee pot ran dry and, although Mr Larter politely offered to call for more, she sensed their tête-à-tête was over and gracefully took her leave.

'I'll be in touch,' Mr Larter promised, and she hurried away lest her blushes betrayed her.

Now, she slipped into her outdoor things and locked the office. She sighed, feeling lighter of heart than she had since she couldn't remember when. She could have skipped like a child. Goodness, how silly, she could actually feel a certain elasticity in her step—

'Evening, miss. It's going to be another sharp night.'

Oh, lord, not him again. Ted Geeson had taken to hanging about outside the Lloyds to see her back to Brookburn. The first time, he had declared stubbornly, 'A lady like yourself ought not to be out alone after dark.'

'I don't require your company, Geeson,' had been her unyielding response.

'Then happen I'll walk along behind, miss, just

219

to keep you in my sights, so to speak.'

'Nonsense,' she had snapped. 'I'm perfectly safe.'

'Aye, that's true, with me watching out for you.'

The third time he had waited for her, Ralph had been leaving at the same time and Evadne had pointed out Geeson to him. 'He's the Brookburn groundsman. Irritating fellow, he insists on watching me all the way back, so don't be alarmed if he seems to follow me.'

'I saw him follow you last time and managed to restrain my alarm.'

Ralph had stalked across the road, leaving her staring after him. He had seen Geeson, who was then unknown to him, follow her into the dark and he had simply let it happen. What kind of brute was he?

Chapter Twenty-Five

Ash Wednesday was early – it wasn't even the middle of February yet. Valentine's Day was this coming Sunday. Could the baby hold on until then? A Valentine's Day birth would be ideal. Everyone would be so busy crooning over a honeymoon baby being born on Valentine's Day, or else asking one another, 'D'you think she'll call it Valentine? Poor little bugger,' that they would clean forget the birth was 'premature'.

As much as her bulk and a dull backache would allow, Carrie hurried through her morning jobs so she could get to midday Mass. The Trimbles had always been good about letting her use her dinner time on holy days to attend Mass and they extended the same kindness to Letty. Since marrying Ralph, Carrie hadn't seen much of Letty and that grieved her. In the early days, she had done some of her shopping at Trimble's, but once Ralph found out, he forbade her to go there again.

'We Armstrongs have no need to use a cruddy little corner shop like that.'

'Trimble's is a good shop. I should know – I worked there long enough.'

'You don't live in the backstreets now, Carrie Armstrong, and you'll not do your shopping in that place.'

It had been difficult for her to see much of Letty after that. Letty was at work all day and Carrie's place was at home with her husband in the evening. Even if Ralph went out for a pint, he expected her to stop indoors, and the time he came home earlier than expected to find Letty keeping her company, the crisp way he spoke to Letty made it obvious to Carrie that he didn't expect to see her friend here again of an evening. Much to Carrie's embarrassment, Letty evidently realised it too, because she didn't suggest any more evenings together, though she still came loyally on alternate Wednesday afternoons to chat with Carrie while they sat facing one another across Mam's bed, each gently stroking a limp hand.

There had been more snow. Carrie slipped and had to catch her footing on the way to Mass. She was puffed out when she arrived.

'Eh, look who it is! The size of you, Carrie

Jenkins-as-was! You're as big as the eighty-two tram to Oldham.' And there was Mrs Clancy, fleshy cheeks ruddy with cold, eyes bright with pleasure. 'Eh, you look ready to drop at any minute, chuck.'

'It's this coat. It's bulky.'

A pudgy hand reached out to finger the lapels. 'Aye, that's reet good quality, is that. He's not short of a bob or two, yon chap. You've done well for yourself, lass.'

'Too well to bother coming back to see them what fettled for your mam in her hour of need,' said another voice, sounding chillier than the breath-steamed air.

Fortunately, Letty came hurrying along and Carrie was grateful to go inside. As always on holy days, she and Letty slipped out after the priest's communion. Today, with those unwelcome words still stinging her ears, she was glad to get out early.

'There's summat I need to ask you,' said Letty as they trod carefully on the slippery pavement. 'Would you mind if I walked out with Billy?'

'You what?' Carrie stopped dead. One of her heels caught a slippery patch, but it wasn't that which caused the swooping sensation.

Letty stopped too. Her cheeks, which had been rosy with cold, turned a dull red.

'You heard.'

'Billy? My Billy?'

'No, not your Billy. He's not been your Billy in a long while.'

'He's asked you to walk out with him?' Carrie didn't know what to think. Her best friend and her former fiancé; her best friend and the man

222

who had jilted her.

'There's not that many chaps left. There's been a war, in case you hadn't noticed.'

'When? How?' *And why didn't you say summat before?* That was what she really wanted to ask. She thought of Letty and Billy getting friendly behind her back and her skin went all prickly.

'Well, we got talking one day.'

'Talking?'

'Aye, that's right. You open your mouth and words come out. It were a while back. I hadn't seen him in ages. It were the first time I'd seen him since he took that beating. Poor chap. He took a heck of a pounding.'

Carrie bit her lip. She had assumed Billy would go down in Wilton Lane history as a jilt. She had never thought of that beating turning him into a sympathetic character.

'Anyroad,' said Letty, 'we fell to talking, and then we bumped into one another again.'

'And one thing led to another.'

'It happened gradual, like.'

'You never said.'

'I'm saying now. I know Billy let you down, but there's a lot of good in him; and it's not as though you didn't find consolation elsewhere.' She didn't say: *and right quick an' all,* but she was undoubtedly thinking it. 'Look at you: married, your own home, a baby on the way. You're never going to begrudge me this chance, are you?'

'Of course not. It's a surprise, that's all.' And that was an understatement, if ever there was one.

'I didn't want you hearing it from anyone else.

Look, I'd best get back.'

'Are you coming round after?'

'Sorry, not today. I promised Mam I'd give her a hand. She wants to turn the sheets sides to middle. It's a lot of sewing ... well, you don't need me to tell you...'

Carrie was dismayed to see her dearest friend prattling in such an embarrassed fashion. Was this how it was going to be in future? She seized Letty's hand.

'I'm sorry if I didn't sound pleased, only I were that surprised. But I am glad for you, and I don't want it to come between us.'

'Thanks. Look, I really must go. I'll see you soon.'

Carrie watched her hurry away before walking back to the shop. Letty and Billy: how was she going to get used to that? Then she pulled herself together. She would be home in five minutes and Ralph would expect her to be her usual cheerful self, so she had better get used to it pretty sharpish.

'You've got a smut on your face.' Ralph rubbed his thumb between Carrie's brows and she let him, not liking to say he was removing the ashes Father Kelly had smudged onto her forehead.

She set about dusting the pieces Ralph had brought through to the office. She couldn't stop thinking about Letty and Billy; she felt fluttery and unsettled. That was what had brought her downstairs. To stay upstairs might have seemed like she was hiding, as if she had something to be ashamed of, as if she were still harbouring feelings for Billy.

224

Would he tell Letty about the baby? And if he did, which story would he tell? The truth – but that would make him look a complete cad; or the tale he had told Father Kelly. Would Letty shun Carrie ever after – or would she refuse to believe her best friend capable of making free with a string of lads? Carrie closed her eyes and hoped with all her heart that Letty and Billy would both feel too awkward to breathe a word about her.

'Carrie? You all right?'

Her eyes flew open. 'The baby kicked. I swear my insides are black and blue.'

'You look peaky. Maybe you should put your feet up.'

'I'm fine.' She attempted a laugh. 'I've a while to go yet. I can't be resting all the time.'

'Is that friend of yours coming this afternoon?'

She wanted to say, 'She has a name,' but she had found herself being careful what she said since Arthur had been roughed up. 'Not today. She's busy.'

'Good.'

And what was that supposed to mean? Ralph was generous with housekeeping and pin money and since her marriage she had received more presents than in the whole of her life put to-gether, certainly more than she felt comfortable receiving. 'I'd give you anything you wanted,' he said time and again, yet somewhere along the line she had sensed he was capable of taking things away too – like Letty's friendship.

Well, perhaps he wouldn't need to separate her from Letty. Maybe Billy would do the job for him.

Running the duster over the hand mirror that

was the last piece in front of her, she decided to call it a day. Checking there was no one but Ralph and Arthur in the shop, she went to Ralph at the counter.

'I've finished.'

'Righto. Put everything back, Renton.'

As she turned away, something caught her eye on the shelf under the counter. Spectacles.

'Whose are those?'

'No idea; some customer or other. Lost property.'

The bell pinged as the door opened to admit a lady and gentleman. Ralph moved, shielding her from view, and she was quick to take the hint. She was halfway upstairs when she remembered Miss Deacon rummaging in her handbag to find her spectacles. Going back down, she peeped into the shop. Ralph was ushering the couple towards a splendid table on the far side. She retrieved the spectacles and hurried out.

Putting on her outdoor things, she smiled, her spirits lifting. She would enjoy returning Miss Deacon's glasses. The old dear must have been lost without them. She remembered the address. It wouldn't take her long to walk there.

A sharp wind had got up and sleet was whipping through the air, slapping bitterly as it landed. Miss Deacon lived a couple of minutes from where there was talk of public swimming baths being built. The terraced houses were tall and smart, with lacy nets and a small semicircular stained-glass window above each front door. Carrie lifted the gleaming brass knocker and executed a cheery rat-tat. When there was no reply, she tried again. Still no answer.

She was about to walk away when she hesitated, thinking of poor Miss Deacon in need of her spectacles, thinking too of her baby, more than a fortnight late and surely due at any minute. Much as she would like to come back another time and have the pleasure of finding Miss Deacon at home, it would be better if she left the glasses now. They would fit through the letter box, but what if they smashed on the hall floor? She delved in her coat pockets and produced an old shopping list. If she popped round the back and left the spectacles in a safe place, she could write a quick note and put it through the letter box for Miss Deacon to find when she came home.

Down the entry, Carrie pushed open Miss Deacon's back gate and found a small garden, a square of lawn, shallow beds against the fences and a sprawling twiggy mass that presumably would resolve itself into something pretty in the flowering season.

She walked up the path, deciding between the window ledge and the coal-hole roof as the safest place for the specs. The back door looked like it was ajar. Another step nearer and she saw it was indeed. She knocked, holding on to the door when it would have swung open.

'Miss Deacon? I tried the front, but you never heard me.'

No answer.

Gently, she pushed the door open on to the kitchen, seeing a pair of wooden cupboards, a shelf with saucepans, a table with a single chair, a door in the far corner, presumably to the cellar.

As the back door swung fully open, she saw the fireplace, empty and black, with not so much as a glowing ember, and all of a sudden she felt cold in a way that owed nothing to the weather.

She stepped inside. Above her head, dry washing hung from a pulley. Picturing the old lady lying injured at the foot of the stairs, she made straight for the far door, which was half-open. The hall was gloomy and no figure lay sprawled.

'Miss Deacon! It's Mrs Armstrong from the antiques shop.'

No reply. Perhaps she was ill in bed. Carrie didn't like to venture upstairs before checking downstairs. The door to the back room was shut. She opened it; no Miss Deacon. Imagining herself finding the old dear bedridden, she popped her head round the front-room door, expecting to withdraw it immediately, only to gasp in shock at the sight of furniture turned over and things on the floor. Then she saw the crumpled form on the rug and her breathing stopped.

She staggered forward a step or two, halting abruptly, a wordless exclamation bursting out of her chest all the way up her throat and out of her mouth, as she saw the eye blackened and swollen, the marks along the papery cheek, the dark dry stain spreading from the side of the open mouth, the same stain blotching the rug, a single tooth sitting in the middle of it.

Her gaze lingered on the tooth; it looked so incongruous. For a split second she was back in Wilton Lane and there was Joseph Armstrong on the kitchen floor, and Mam in a motionless heap. The next thing she knew, she was blundering from the room, clutching the walls for support, her eyes fixed on the front door. Her fingers scrabbled numbly for escape, tearing at the door chain. She threw the door open and stumbled forward, turning her ankle on the step. A sharp pain raced through her foot and shot up her calf, at the same moment as water gushed down her thighs.

She was aware of someone walking past and heard her own voice calling out. Her legs collapsed beneath her and she sank onto the slushy path. Her head was swimming and she thought she would faint clean away, only she didn't; she carried on feeling woozy and distant.

Someone came bustling beside her, then someone else; she heard voices without being able to catch what they were saying. They would think she had wet herself. They would think how disgraceful, and they wouldn't know what had happened to Miss Deacon.

A spasm of pain started in her spine and thrust into her abdomen. She thought she would pass out; instead, the pain brought her sharply awake.

'You need the police. There's a lady inside... And could someone please take me home *right now...*'

Chapter Twenty-Six

Ralph clamped his fists at his sides. It was the only way to stop himself raining blows on that bloody idiot Renton, who had returned without the doctor. Without the bloody doctor! He should have gone himself. He would have found out the address the doctor had been called to, gone round there and marched the quack here, with his arm twisted up his back if necessary.

'Is he coming?' The midwife appeared, wiping her hands.

'No, he sodding well isn't!' Ralph fixed Renton with a glare. Seeing the way Renton blanched, he took a threatening step towards him. When they're scared, make 'em more scared. Don't stop till they're shitting themselves.

'You'll need another doctor, then,' the woman said, as if he couldn't have worked this out for himself, 'or I'll not be responsible.'

'What's going on?'

He swung round. Jesus, trust Adam to turn up when he wasn't wanted.

'The door was open so I came up.' Adam looked from one to the other. 'I heard raised voices.'

'What, and you've come rushing to the rescue? I hope you left the door open. It'll make it quicker for you to leave.'

In the bedroom, Carrie cried out and Adam

looked round. 'Is Carrie in labour?'

'Yes.' Ralph shouldered his way across the room, intending to hustle Adam back through the door and straight down the stairs, preferably without benefit of gaining his footing first, but Adam held his ground, fixing his attention on the midwife, who was still standing there, stupid bitch, when she should have gone back to Carrie. What the hell did she think she was being paid for?

'Is everything all right?' Adam asked.

'It's fine,' Ralph butted in before the woman could answer. 'Get back to your job,' he ordered her, 'and leave me to deal with the other thing.'

'What other thing?' Adam wanted to know.

'We need a doctor,' the midwife said before Ralph could shut her up. 'Baby's a breech.'

'Have you sent for him?'

Ralph inhaled sharply. 'Of course I have. Now get gone, will you?'

'Doctor's out,' snapped the woman, giving Ralph a defiant look that made him want to deal her a bloody good crack across her self-righteous face.

'I'll find another.' His words snarled out between clenched teeth. 'Now will you do as you're told and get back to my wife?'

As the woman vanished, Adam said, 'I'll deliver the baby.'

He stared. It would never have occurred to him in a hundred years to turn to his brother for help. 'You – the waxworks man?'

'It might surprise you to know this won't be my first birth.'

'Not flaming likely. That's my wife in there.'

'Carrie needs a doctor and she needs one now.' He was actually shrugging off his jacket, damn him, the interfering bastard.

Ralph squared up to him, muscling close. 'If you think I'm letting you clap eyes on my Carrie in that position–'

'Good God, is that was this is about? Don't be a fool, man! I'm a doctor. Carrie's got nothing I haven't seen before.'

'Not on my wife you haven't.'

He could see that Adam almost laughed, but fortunately for him he didn't or the next medical procedure he performed would have been to extract a fist from a sodding great dent in the front of his face.

'Get out of here,' Ralph barked. 'I don't need you.'

'But Carrie does.' Adam didn't budge an inch, blast him. 'Are you prepared to deny her the help she needs because it's more important to keep me from seeing certain parts of her anatomy?' His voice rose. 'Do you have the first idea what a breech birth means?'

'I'll fetch another doctor,' he began.

'Fine! Do that. Meanwhile, I'll see to your wife and child.'

Before he could grab him, Adam was through the door and marching down the landing to the bedroom. Boiling with rage and hatred, Ralph caught up just in time to have the door slammed in his face.

Gazing tenderly on her baby's downy head,

Carrie was filled with wonderment. Here was perfect love. 'Joey,' she whispered over and over, cuddling her little boy close. It had been her idea to name him Joseph. She wanted to make this baby Ralph's in every way she could. When she suggested the name, she had trembled with hope and generosity; and his easy, offhand acceptance, 'Yes, if you like,' had surprised and hurt. But that was her own fault. Naturally, Ralph attached no significance to her choice; he probably took it for granted. It was her guilty conscience that lent it such meaning.

Ralph presented her with a pretty bedjacket and helped her into it.

'It's lovely,' she breathed, fingering the ribbon detail. 'But what an extravagance.'

'Nothing's too good for my wife.'

'I only meant, when will I ever wear it?'

'For the next ten days, at least. That's how long you're staying there.'

She couldn't believe her ears. 'You want me to stop in bed for ten days?' Back in Wilton Lane, a woman was lucky to get twenty-four hours, and then only if she had a daughter of an age to make herself useful.

'You're not in the backstreets now. You don't have to haul yourself out of bed to mop the front step for fear of setting tongues wagging. In the decent world, wives rest for ten days after giving birth.'

'But what am I supposed to do? I can't just lie about.'

'You'll rest and nurse our son and rock him and sing to him. You seem to be quite an expert at those things already.'

She laughed, seeing bed rest through different eyes. Ten whole days, just her and Joey.

'What about Mam?'

'She's in good hands. Mrs Porter is doing extra hours and I can eat over the road if I have to.'

Carrie settled back against the pillows. Not that she could have said so to Ralph, but she was sore where she had been stitched. How lucky she was to be able to heal properly before she had to be up and doing. It was another reason to be grateful.

The next day she swung herself gingerly out of bed, wincing as the stitches tugged, inflicting a burning sensation. Tenderly, heart swelling with love, she lifted Joey from the cradle she had insisted be placed next to her side of the bed instead of at its foot.

'Time to meet your nan,' she murmured, laying him gently against her shoulder and feeling a thrill of pleasure as his tiny face snuggled into her neck.

Padding along the landing, she paused at Mam's door and knocked politely because of the nurse. In she went – shock whooped through her. The bed was empty. More than empty – stripped. Her fingers spread out in a fan over her chest.

She stood staring; then, clutching Joey to her, she turned and blundered her way along the landing.

'Carrie!' Ralph was at the top of the stairs. 'What are you doing out of bed?'

'Where's Mam?'

'Here, let's get you back where you belong.' He

tried to guide her away.

She pulled free. 'Where's Mam? Tell me.' Had she died? Joey started to squawk and her body began an instinctive rocking motion.

'I'll take him,' said Ralph.

'No–'

'You're hysterical.'

Deftly, he removed the baby and swung away, heading for the bedroom. She flitted anxiously behind.

'Get into bed. I'll let you have him once you've calmed down.'

'Mam's vanished and you want me to calm down?'

His handsome face froze and she knew she had gone too far. 'That's no way to speak to me. I'll come back later.'

'Ralph – wait! I'm sorry.'

But he had gone, Joey with him. Stitches burning, Carrie flew after him, the need to reclaim her baby pounding through her. As she reached out her hand to grasp Ralph's arm, he turned, looking at her so coldly that her hand fell away.

'What did I tell you?' he said.

'Don't speak to me as if I'm a child.'

'I wouldn't have to if you conducted yourself like a good wife.'

'I've always been a good wife to you.'

'Good wives obey their husbands and they don't need telling twice. I won't have my son upset. Your outburst will unsettle him. You have to calm yourself. You don't want him to be unhappy, do you?'

'Of course not.'

'Then do as you're told. I'll bring him back to you when you're serene, as a new mother ought to be.'

How had she ended up in the wrong? She would never do anything to Joey's detriment. She had barely begun being his mother, the most important job of her life, and already she had gone wrong. She returned to bed. The sheets were rumpled and chilled. She was stunned at the speed with which her perfect world had tilted sideways. She felt lost without Joey and couldn't bear the thought of what must have become of her beloved mam. Had she been deemed too frail to be told Mam had died? Were new mothers to be protected from such things in Ralph's so-called decent world? If so, she wanted no part of it.

Presently the door opened. She perked up at once, but Ralph's arms were empty.

'Where's Joey?'

'Mrs Porter has him. About Mrs Jenkins–'

'Is she dead?'

'What?'

'When did it happen?' And had anyone told her she was grandmother to a beautiful little boy and Carrie was safe and well?

'What are you talking about? She's in hospital.'

'Hospital?' Her heart hammered. 'Another stroke?'

'Use your head. All along you've insisted on looking after her, but you can't while you're confined to bed, can you? So I sent her to hospital.'

'But I thought you'd got her a nurse. Here. In the flat.'

'I don't know why you should think so. I never

said anything of the kind.'

No, he hadn't. He had said everything was taken care of and she had just assumed. It was her own stupid fault.

'I want her at home.'

'She's fine where she is.'

'Please, Ralph. I'll worry myself to death otherwise.'

'You're in no state to look after her.'

'There's nowt wrong with me. All this stopping in bed is codswallop. I can tend to Mam, same as always, with Mrs Porter to help.'

'You're having your bed rest and that's all there is to it.'

'Then get in a nurse.' She reached out a hand to him. 'I never ask for owt, do I?' Should she remind him of the times he had declared he would do anything for her? But it seemed too much like a challenge.

She could see from the way the muscles rippled along his jaw that he wasn't pleased, but she saw too the moment when his features softened – no, not softened, but eased.

'Very well. If it will save you fretting.'

Relief washed through her and tears began to spill down her cheeks. The memory of that moment when she had seen the empty bed hit her and she glimpsed the grief she would suffer when she truly did lose her mam. All at once she was sobbing. The mattress dipped as Ralph sat and drew her into his arms.

'What's this for?'

'It was such a shock, seeing the empty bed.' Taking a huge breath, she stemmed the flow.

'Bring Joey back and I'll be fine.'

'Not while you're in this state. Pull yourself together and then we'll see.'

Chapter Twenty-Seven

Evadne sat behind her desk, pen in hand, supposedly working on next week's duty rota but really devising a way of achieving what Alex Larter had delicately hinted at – so delicately, in fact, that she couldn't be sure it had actually been a hint. He had taken her on a valuation that he had considerately organised for Saturday afternoon so as not to interfere with her commitments at Brookburn, driving her – they must have appeared quite the married couple – to the appointment.

On the way he entertained her with ghost stories about Barlow Hall, convincing her that that splendid establishment must be their destination. She was obliged to bite back severe disappointment when he took her instead to a place not unlike Grandfather's, where the widowed lady of the house, as Alex murmured on the doorstep, was struggling to fend off hard times.

He introduced her as 'my colleague, Miss Baxter', which she found most gratifying. She bestowed a small, professional smile upon the widow. Mrs Bentley was good-looking, though she would never see thirty again.

They stood in front of the mirror they had come to inspect.

'Rococo style.' Alex indicated the scoops and swirls adorning the frame and the fancy candle-branches protruding from either side. 'Middle of the last century, I'd say. Wouldn't you agree, Miss Baxter?'

'Quite,' she said, with a secret quiver.

'Is it worth much?' Mrs Bentley asked.

Alex turned to her. 'I'd be happy to pay forty.'

'Forty pounds?'

'Guineas.'

His cultured voice made it sound natural to deal in guineas instead of pounds. That extra shilling did so much more than turn the humble pound into an exotic guinea. It turned a straight-forward business transaction into an upper-crust affair. Evadne shivered in delight.

'You appear surprised, Mrs Bentley,' said Alex. 'May I enquire whether you have had the piece valued by someone else? What did they offer?'

'Twenty pounds.'

'Well, I can tell you this. Whichever dealer you choose to do business with will sell on your mirror for around fifty guineas; but whereas I am happy with a profit of ten guineas or so, others seek more. My hope is that you will invite me back, should you wish to part with other pieces. I'm involved in a new auction house and it's important to have a good supply of worthwhile items.'

'As a matter of fact,' Mrs Bentley started to say, with an eagerness that made Evadne glance away to conceal her disdain.

Alex held up a courteous hand. 'Permit me to stop you, madam. This isn't the moment to get carried away. Is there perhaps a trusted friend you can confide in? The family solicitor or a friend of your late husband? Today I'll purchase your mirror with pleasure. As to further items, I'll be happy to return on another occasion when you've had time to consider.'

'Do you think she'll invite you back, Mr Larter?' Evadne asked as they drove away.

'I expect so,' he answered easily, as if it didn't matter. 'What did you think of the mirror?'

She hedged. 'It wasn't to my taste, but—'

'Shame on you, Miss Baxter. There was I thinking we were on our way to becoming friends, but how can we be if you won't tell me the truth? The mirror was a monstrosity and if you say different, I'll stop the motor and you can walk home.'

'Well, yes, it was hideous.' She kicked herself for missing the opportunity to share a joke.

'Mrs Bentley might recommend me to her friends. That's always a good thing. I couldn't help admiring that bureau in Major Baxter's drawing room. I wonder if he has any friends or neighbours who find themselves in need of a bit of cash. All done discreetly, of course. Could I tempt you to stop at a tea shop, Miss Baxter, before heading for home?'

Evadne was delighted to accept. She expected him to refer again to the possibility of introductions to Grandfather's acquaintances, but he didn't. Well, naturally not. He wouldn't be so crass.

But the idea was inside her head. It was inside her belly too, fluttering about. Using Grandfather's connections to put more business Alex's way would guarantee they spent more time together.

'What's wrong, love? Why are you still in bed?' Letty came bustling across the room, not bothering to take off her hat or unbutton her coat as she hastened to Carrie's side. To Carrie's chagrin, she didn't even glance at the baby.

'There's nowt wrong,' she said in surprise.

'Then why aren't you up?'

Carrie's cheeks burnt. 'Bed rest.'

'You what?' Letty sounded incredulous. 'How swanky.'

'Don't say that. Ralph wants the best for me, that's all.'

'Aye, but ... bed rest,' grimaced Letty, and suddenly they were both spluttering with laughter.

'Here, say hello,' said Carrie. 'Joey, this is your Auntie Letty.'

'Eh, he's a little corker. Can I hold him?'

'Tek off your coat and have a proper cuddle.'

Letty was eager to know all about the birth. She clapped a hand over her mouth when Carrie told her who had delivered Joey.

'I'd never be able to look him in the face again, if it was me.'

'Trust me, when you've a baby coming, you won't care tuppence if a monkey delivers it, so long as it's been trained.'

'Have you seen him since?'

'Not yet.' She couldn't understand why Adam hadn't come to see her and the nephew he had brought into the world.

'And is Joey all right? Him being early, I mean.'

241

'He's perfect.'

'Bad enough that you had that appalling shock, without it affecting Joey an' all.'

'My goodness.' Carrie went hot and cold. 'I'd forgotten. Oh Letty, you should have seen her.'

The door opened and Ralph came in. 'What's the matter? Carrie?'

Letty looked at him. 'It's my fault, me and my big mouth. I reminded her about that poor lady what died.'

Seeing the sharp flare of Ralph's nostrils, Carrie went taut with anxiety.

'You stupid creature! Why the hell did you do that?'

'Ralph!' Carrie protested.

'Christ Almighty, I come upstairs to say goodbye to my wife and child before I go out and what do I find?' He glared at Letty.

'Ralph, please, she never meant owt by it,' said Carrie. 'It's my fault. I'd forgotten.'

'Quite right, too. I won't have my wife troubled by such things.'

'Perhaps I'd best go,' Letty murmured.

'There's no perhaps about it,' Ralph retorted.

Carrie wanted to curl up and die of shame. She wanted to set Ralph straight, but it would be disloyal in front of another person. Where was his loyalty to her? He had shown her up good and proper.

She made a point of clasping Letty's hand and pulling her down for a goodbye kiss, but Letty couldn't get away fast enough. Would she tell her mam about Ralph's outburst? Would she tell Billy?

Carrie made a tremendous effort to bring her

emotions under control, saying as mildly as she could, 'I wish you hadn't made her go.'

He sat on the bed and looked at her. 'And I wish she hadn't jolted your memory.'

'I can't believe I could have forgotten.'

'It's understandable. The shock, followed by the birth.'

'Poor Miss Deacon. Who'd do such a thing?'

He shrugged. 'Burglars. She lost various bits and pieces, apparently.'

Including her life. Poor lady.

'What were you doing there?' Ralph asked.

'Taking back her spectacles, the ones from under the counter. I remembered they were hers.'

'So you took it upon yourself to return them. Why didn't you tell me whose they were?'

'I didn't like to. You were so angry when you thought Mr Renton stole the silver-plated tray. I didn't want to remind you of the trouble I'd caused.'

'So instead you caused a great deal more.'

'Ralph, no–'

'Aside from the possible damage you could have done to yourself and the baby by collapsing in public, you've brought trouble on my head. The police have been asking questions, Carrie, about why you were there. I couldn't tell them. The old woman wasn't a friend. They asked if she was a customer, so I had to show them the delivery book. The silver-plated tray is one of the pieces missing from her house, as it turns out, and since the old biddy kept herself to herself and didn't have many visitors, no one can properly describe what else is gone, which leaves the police concentrating on the tray.'

'Is that bad?'

'It's hardly the kind of publicity I want for my business.'

'But it's better that I found her, surely? Otherwise she might have been lying there for who knows how long – especially if she didn't have visitors.' Had Miss Deacon been lonely?

'The police want to speak to you. I've said they must wait until you're up and about.'

'I can't tell them owt. I just went in and ... found her.'

'What did you think you were doing? Suppose the burglars had still been there. It was stupid of you.'

She crumpled inside, but raised her chin. 'Have they been caught?'

'No, but that's not your problem. I'll tell the police you have no recollection of what happened.'

'But I can remember.'

'Did you see the intruders? Can you describe them?'

'No, they were long gone.'

'Then you've nothing to say, have you? Be sensible, Carrie. If the police think you remember something, they'll never leave you alone. I won't have you hounded.'

He consulted his pocket watch, lifted her chin to plant a kiss firmly on her mouth, then stood up.

'Must be off.' At the door he looked back. 'Put it out of your mind. I won't have you upset over the gory details. A good mother is a serene mother. Don't forget what we had to do last time you got yourself in a state.'

Chapter Twenty-Eight

Evadne remained in the back of the taxi until the driver realised what was required and got out to open the door for her. She emerged elegantly, swinging her legs out neatly, trim ankles together, and glanced round as if she were sizing up a place she had been invited to for the weekend.

'Wait for me,' she instructed the cabbie over her shoulder, and if she caught anything of a muttered response along the lines of not being a bleedin' chauffeur, she ignored it. Alex had insisted upon the taxi and had given her the money for it in a courteously matter-of-fact way.

'It'd be unseemly for my colleague to arrive on foot from the tram stop. Besides, if Mrs Bentley parts with the painting, you can bring it back with you. You'd better take some sheeting from the auction room.'

It was disappointing, of course, that Alex wasn't with her. On the other hand, how gratifying it was to be depended on. They had visited Mrs Bentley together a second time and purchased a dainty-legged desk. They had also been asked to call upon Mrs Bentley's friend, Miss Kent.

'You'll accompany me, I hope, Miss Baxter?' Alex had requested. 'I'm sure it will make the experience easier for Miss Kent to have another lady present.'

It had sounded as if he were asking the most

enormous favour. That visit had seen the purchase of a sideboard with one cupboard fitted as a plate-warmer, and Alex, just like he had in front of Mrs Bentley, had fed Evadne little cues that made her look as if she knew about furniture.

Miss Kent had also shown them a small table. Previously, Evadne would have spared it little more than a cursory glance, but now she found herself studying the scalloped edging around the tabletop and the trio of feet curving out from the graceful pedestal. Not that she had the slightest idea what these features revealed as to age or value, but she felt interest stirring.

A couple of evenings later, Alex had found his way to the office next to the auction room and leant against the door frame, blowing smoke rings.

'Mrs Bentley telephoned, hoping for a third visit, but I had to turn her down as I'm going away for a few days.'

'But you are coming back?' Had she sounded too eager?

'Yes, though I'm not sure Mrs Bentley will wait. I have the impression the vultures are circling.' He blew a perfect smoke ring and watched it drift into the air and disperse. 'Unless, of course … but I couldn't ask.'

'Ask what, Mr Larter?'

'If you'd pay the call yourself.'

And here she was. There was a snap in the air and she wasn't pleased to be kept waiting on the step by the maid.

Mrs Bentley appeared. 'Miss … Baxter, isn't it? What can I do for you?'

She put on her professional smile. 'Good evening, Mrs Bentley. I believe you're expecting me.'

'Well ... no.'

'I understood Mr Larter was going to arrange this appointment.'

After the initial confusion, Mrs Bentley was happy to let her look round, though the door remained firmly shut on the sitting room, where Evadne suspected the lady of the house had been dining off a tray in front of the fire before her unexpected visitor arrived.

Evadne knew what to do.

'Have a look round to show willing,' Alex had advised, 'but there's only one piece left that's worth our while and that's the small painting at the foot of the stairs. Offer twenty.'

'Guineas?'

'Pounds.'

Within fifteen minutes, the painting was wrapped in sheeting. 'My driver will carry it out,' Evadne said graciously as she shook hands. 'Thank you for your custom, Mrs Bentley.'

A lesser person might have departed on an apology for the misunderstanding over the appointment; but the future Mrs Alex Larter had no need to make herself amenable to someone in financial straits.

Ralph looked round as the bell jingled, his expression turning to steel as Adam walked in. He had yet to forgive Adam for being the one to deliver the baby. Maybe he never would. Carrie was his property and he couldn't bear the idea of his bloody brother having cast eyes on her flat on her back with her legs splayed and her privates on show. No man should have to suffer that indignity at the hands of his own brother.

They exchanged a brief how do as they shook hands before Ralph demanded, 'What do you want?'

'From you, nothing. I've come to see Carrie and my nephew.'

'You can't. She's still in bed.'

'Surely–'

'You said you needed nothing from me, but you're wrong. You need my permission.' Ralph looked into his brother's eyes. 'Permission withheld.'

'In that case,' Adam said after a moment, 'I'm here in my professional capacity as Mrs Jenkins' doctor. I'll go through her exercise routine, since Carrie can't at present. Presumably you won't object to that?'

'No need. She's not here.'

'What are you talking about?'

'She's in hospital. As you say, Carrie's in no fit state, so I sent Mrs Jenkins to hospital.'

'Did Carrie agree?'

'I make the decisions in this house.'

'In other words, no.'

Ralph's fingers flexed and fisted. 'It's Carrie's duty to abide by my decisions.'

'She must be worried sick, poor girl. She's devoted to her mother. Mrs Jenkins won't get the correct treatment in hospital. They'll keep her clean and comfortable, nothing more. You should have asked me. I could have provided a suitable nurse.'

Flex and fist, flex and fist. Heat spread through

his fingers as his fist prepared for use. 'Who the hell d'you think you are, coming here laying down the law?'

'I'm Mrs Jenkins' doctor. I'm entitled to know what care she's receiving. And I want what's best for Carrie too.'

'And I don't?' He could feel a roar of rage building up, though his voice was soft.

'I don't know. You're always claiming you'd do anything for her, but is this what she wants? Her mother stranded in hospital?'

He bridled. 'Not that it's any of your business, but I'm bringing her home.'

'When?'

'When I get round to it. Now clear out before I throw you out.'

Opening the door, Adam looked back. 'You don't deserve her,' he said quietly and walked out.

That was too much. Ralph grabbed his shoulder and spun him about. 'What did you say?' He thrust his face forwards to fill Adam's vision.

'You heard. I pity that poor girl, married to you.'

Ralph glared. His fists were ready; the blood was in his fingers; his knuckles were like iron. For the space of a heartbeat, he stood ready, seeing the flicker of uncertainty in his brother's eyes, even as Adam squared his shoulders in response. Then he laughed in Adam's face.

He leant forward. 'You don't pity her,' he whispered. 'You want her for yourself. That's the truth, isn't it?'

Adam's face was unreadable, the eyes guarded in a way that was outside his character. 'Don't be

249

a fool.' He swung round and strode into the bitter wind.

It wasn't easy for Evadne to ask for Carrie's help. Still, better her than Ralph, who was the only other person she could think of. She didn't want to ask Alex. It would look like a blatant attempt to impress him and she recoiled from that. Besides, she wasn't doing it for his benefit: she wanted to do this for herself and that was a novel feeling. For years she had been trying to please Grandfather so he would invite her into his home. She had worked tirelessly to maintain her high standards to ensure the world saw her as the lady she was. But when had she ever done something purely for the pleasure of doing it?

She had to visit Carrie, anyway, to see the baby. Evadne had never been one for babies and didn't expect to be interested in this one, but when she took the chair beside the bed and looked at the tiny shawled form in Carrie's arms, something tender slid into place inside her. Before she could stop herself, she reached out to touch him, drawing in a breath of pure delight when a tiny starfish hand clamped around her finger.

In all those years when she had blithely taken it for granted that she would marry and have children, it was the getting married that had mattered. Children were just something that happened afterwards. She had had no idea that having children would matter too.

She almost spilt out her revelation to Carrie – almost – but she held back. How could she, when she was older by eight years, and still unmarried?

The dreaded words *on the shelf* would appear in Carrie's mind, if not on her lips.

She let Carrie prattle. The girl was thrilled about Joey, but upset because Ralph had sent Mother to hospital.

'A reasonable thing to do, I'd have thought,' said Evadne. 'Or were you expecting the char to see to her? I'll go and visit.'

'There's no need. Ralph's having her brought home.'

Well then, what was the fuss about? 'Has he mentioned that Mr Larter has invited me to accompany him on valuation visits? It is only right, now that I'm assisting with the auction work. I'd like to build up my knowledge and I wondered if Ralph has books I might borrow.'

'I'm not sure. He seems to carry his knowledge around in his head. I expect Mr Larter does too.'

Evadne concealed a sneer. There was a clear distinction between the shopkeeper's knowledge cobbled together tortuously by Ralph over the years and Alex's elegant mastery of the subject that had soaked into his bones during a lifetime of gracious living.

'If you're really interested,' Carrie said, sitting up straighter, 'speak to Mr Weston. He used to work here. Ralph's father had a high opinion of him and so does Adam, but Ralph wanted someone young and strong when he started the auction room.'

'Does he live surrounded by fine items he could use to teach me?'

'Well – no. He's rather hard up, actually. He works one day a week at a posh antiques place in

251

town and he does four mornings in the bookshop on Beech Road. You might know him. He goes to Brookburn to read to the patients.'

'I have nothing to do with the patients. I'm in the office.' And she made sure she stayed there. But it might be worth venturing forth if... 'I can learn at Brookburn. The wards are pure hospital, but other parts of the building have some of the original furnishings. That might do the trick. Thank you, Carrie.'

She dropped a kiss on Carrie's cheek. Drawing back, she saw the astonishment in her sister's expression and was sure Carrie's surprise was only a fraction of her own.

She adored Joey, but Carrie was sick to death of being stuck in bed. Yesterday she had ventured along the landing, but when Ralph had come across her snuggled with Joey in the armchair by the sitting-room fire, he had ordered her back to bed, plucking Joey from her arms to ensure she obeyed.

Back where she should be, she had held out her arms for her baby. 'I really don't need all this time in bed,' she said, careful to smile and not sound complaining.

'When you were growing up, did you imagine you'd marry a man who could afford to give you bed rest? You should be grateful.'

'I am. You've done so much for me, and for Mam. I know how lucky we are.'

Today, lying against the pillows with Joey slumbering on her chest, she stroked his head with her finger, murmuring to him when he snuffled and stirred. It was wretched of her to be fed up of bed rest, but she couldn't help it. Yes, she loved devoting herself to Joey and, yes, she was aware of her good fortune in having married so well. But how much luckier she would feel when she could take Joey out and show him off, when she could care for him alongside her daily tasks. That was what she longed for, to be up and doing, with Joey absorbed into her everyday life. Not being allowed to do so made her feel not lucky, but stifled.

She wanted Mam back too. Several days had passed since Ralph had agreed to bring her home, but nothing had happened and Carrie had had to bite her tongue. She didn't want to nag. Ralph was a busy man with a shop to run, auctions to set up, valuations to make. She wished she hadn't put Evadne off visiting the hospital.

'Daddy will bring your nan home as soon as he can,' she told Joey as he stirred. 'And you know what I think? I think that wanting to be a proper nan to you will be just the medicine she needs to set her on the path to recovery.'

When Joey started to cry, she fed him, marvelling at the feeling of his mouth sucking energetically. She laid him against her shoulder to wind him, praising him when he burped. When she laid him in his cot, he began to grizzle.

'You're getting too used to being cuddled, that's your trouble,' she told him ruefully, 'and I'm getting too used to doing the cuddling. That's another reason we have to stop this bed-rest lark. You're getting spoilt rotten. But you've got to settle now, my little love, because Mummy needs a wee.'

She crept across the room, glancing over her

shoulder at Joey as she turned the doorknob. The door didn't open. She was being too gentle because of not disturbing Joey, but it didn't open when she tried firmly either. About to knock and call for help, she remembered Mrs Porter was out shopping. She experienced a moment of panic before telling herself not to be silly. The door was stuck – so what? It was only a matter of waiting.

The keyhole was empty. None of the rooms in the flat was ever locked; the keys were left in the doors just for somewhere to keep them. But the bedroom key was missing. And the door wouldn't open. Surely Ralph wouldn't have...?

Chapter Twenty-Nine

'Are you sure we won't be interrupted?' Alex Larter asked as Ralph showed him into the flat.

'Positive. The woman who does for us is out shopping and the wife is having bed rest.'

'Bed rest?' Larter quirked an eyebrow. 'How ... refined.'

Ralph clamped his jaw so hard his teeth almost cracked. 'This way.'

He opened the door, intending to lead the way, but Larter marched in and stood looking round the sitting room, probably comparing it to the ancestral splendours he was used to. Ralph didn't want to care what the Honourable bloody Alexander sodding Larter thought of his home. Did Larter find it pretentious that the Armstrong sitting room contained a walnut bureau and matching whatnot, a longcase clock, and a music canterbury beside the piano? Did he think these items should be for sale downstairs and the Armstrongs should live like cottagers?

Ralph went to the chimney breast, where a small door in the side announced the presence of an airing cupboard. He unlatched the door and reached in. He had taken the key from its hiding place earlier. Now he opened the secret compartment, standing so as to block Larter's view.

'I've never seen a safe inside an airing cupboard before,' said Larter. 'How domesticated.'

Ralph ignored that. He retrieved a flat item wrapped in cloth. Folding back the fabric, he held out the silver salver.

Larter nodded. 'You're sure Mrs Armstrong knows nothing?'

'The old biddy had been dead for hours before Carrie got there. I've been using this bed-rest tripe to keep the police at bay. If they do speak to her, I've told her to keep her mouth shut.'

'And will she?'

'She does as she's told.'

Larter gazed at the salver. Ralph wanted to thrust it into his upper-class hands with a brusque 'Hold it yourself'. At last, Larter moved away, producing a gold cigarette case from an inside pocket. He extracted a cigarette but didn't bother offering Ralph one.

Ralph threw the covering back across the salver and placed it on the table. 'That's caused us a lot of trouble, that salver.'

Larter inhaled and lifted his chin to blow a

smoke ring. 'You say that as if it's the salver's fault. The trouble, in fact, has been caused by you and "the wife", as you so elegantly call her. You permitted her to see something she shouldn't have seen, which you then left lying around for her to sell–'

'It wasn't left lying around.'

'–and no sooner do you retrieve it than your wife blunders onto the scene, which in turn brings you to the attention of the police. Since you can suggest no connection between the dead woman and Mrs Armstrong, the police trawl through your records and, behold, the victim has made a purchase in your shop. Not only that, but Mrs Armstrong has helpfully written a description of the so-called silver-plated tray she bought. It's the only item the police know for certain was stolen, no matter how many other bits and pieces you removed. They have been suitably taken care of, I suppose?'

'Disposed of.'

'Which leaves the police searching for this,' Larter waved his cigarette at the wrapped salver, 'in connection with not merely a burglary but also the brutal killing of a defenceless old lady, who no doubt led a blameless life and was kind to animals.'

'I'm not a suspect.'

'Because of this fiasco, the operation has been compromised when it has barely begun. You have displeased a number of people, Armstrong. You're lucky not to be lying dead in the gutter, but interestingly the silver salver that could have been your downfall is also your guarantee of safety. We can't draw attention to you, you see. So,' he continued with a smile that twisted unpleasantly into the scar down his cheek, 'you're safe – unless, that is, the police ever suspect you of … anything.'

'What's that supposed to mean?'

'This is the second time in – how many months? – that you've been brought to the attention of the police; first as the son of a man whose death was never satisfactorily explained, now this. I don't care for it and I'm not the only one. If you'll be kind enough to wrap the salver, I'll take it with me.'

'Renton can wrap it,' Ralph snarled.

'I think not. He has so little experience. You're the real shopkeeper.'

When Larter left with a brown paper parcel tied with string tucked securely under his arm, Ralph banged about in the back of the shop, venting his anger on various packing cases. Renton peeped round the door but hastily withdrew, no doubt reckoning Ralph would have preferred to inflict damage on human flesh and bone. Ralph sneered after him. Bloody coward. He had been right to scarper.

The instant the door opened, Carrie pricked up her ears, but was too late to hear whether a key had turned in the lock first. Wondering made her feel disloyal, yet the fact remained that the key was missing and the door hadn't budged.

Anxious to ask, though without actually asking, she said, 'You had no trouble with the door. It wouldn't open for me earlier.'

'You're not supposed to be out of bed.'

'I needed to be excused. The key wasn't in the lock.'

'So what? The door's not locked.' Ralph bent down and when he stood up, the key was in his hand. 'Fallen on the floor, not that it matters.'

He stepped aside and she scuttled through. Indoor plumbing: yet another thing to be grateful for, though she still felt uncomfortable using it in case she could be heard through the door.

Returning to the bedroom, she found Ralph bent over the cot, his finger caught in Joey's eager clutches, and emptiness rocked her. How wrong it was, how unfair. If any man deserved to be loved by his wife, Ralph was that man. When she thought of everything he had done for her, including the all-important thing he didn't know about, she could have sunk to the floor and kissed his feet.

But she had learnt one painful lesson. No amount of gratitude could make you love someone. She had hoped that when the baby came, loving her child would spill over into feelings for Ralph; but all she felt, all she continued to feel, all she dreaded she would ever feel was – gratitude.

And it wasn't enough.

She was an ungrateful wretch. And that was a stupid thing to think, because ungrateful was the last thing she was. Wasn't her head stuffed full of lists of the many things she was grateful for? New shoes; her pantry groaning with provisions; the hairbrush backed with mother-of-pearl; a dressing table with a triple mirror. She felt like a princess standing in front of those mirrors and wished she were prettier, for Ralph's sake. And the bath, too, the sheer luxury of turning on taps and wallowing in scented water as regularly as she pleased.

If only she could love Ralph! A sharp longing invaded her hollowed-out heart. After everything he had given her, still she craved more. She yearned to feel bound to him in the truest, deepest sense, but it would never happen. Some animal part of her wanted to howl in desolation.

She climbed back into bed.

'Let me have him,' she whispered, not meeting Ralph's eyes.

'He's asleep.'

'Please.'

She thought he would refuse, but he lifted Joey into her waiting arms. She settled back with Joey on her chest, his head beneath her chin, her hands tenderly supporting his little body. It was her favourite way of holding him. Ralph bent down and she knew she must raise her lips to his. His tongue filled her mouth, huge and questing, tangling with her own.

He drew back slightly, his breath warm on her face, eyes gleaming. 'Can't wait for bed rest to be over.'

'Ralph,' she murmured, dismayed.

'I mean it literally, Carrie. I can't wait. Straight after the seven o'clock feed. We've got some catching up to do.'

Heat suffused her cheeks as he left her. That was another thing she had learnt: marital relations didn't make you love someone. He could help himself to her body as much as he liked, but he would never touch her heart.

A loud voice broke in on her thoughts. Ralph's voice, raised in anger, made her pulse flutter. There were some noises that she couldn't identify, then another voice, a man's, loud yet conveying an impression that he was endeavouring to keep his voice down. She wanted to get up and investigate, but Joey was snuggled on her chest, sleeping sweetly. She held him closer to protect him from the noise, dropping kisses on the soft fluff of his hair.

The bedroom door was thrown open and as her gaze flew to Ralph, she experienced a sensation of something igniting inside her chest as her heart reached out in unreserved response. She was utterly still, held captive in the moment. There was an instant of communication between the two of them, private and complete and deeply harmonious, as if their love had already been tested and found staunch and true. She felt safe and whole; she had the most wonderful sense of family. She and Joey and Ralph were bound together in the truest sense. She wanted to hold on to the moment and savour it for ever.

A sound on the landing, a movement. Then Ralph pushed his way in from behind, shoving Adam aside. Carrie blinked. Her eyes made the adjustment and her heart froze.

Adam.

The silence was sudden and deep. Ralph was staring at her. He wrenched his gaze away and challenged his brother.

'What the bloody hell d'you think you're doing? Get out of my wife's bedroom!'

'I thought she'd like to know I've brought Mrs

Jenkins home – since you couldn't be bothered.'

Ralph dragged him from the room. There were more sounds, louder than before. With her baby nestled on her chest, Carrie remained motionless, propped on her pile of pillows. Deep inside, her soul quaked.

Adam.

Chapter Thirty

Evadne had succeeded. She had managed, in the most sympathetic way possible, to get one of Grandfather's neighbours to agree to a valuation. It hadn't been easy. First she had had to butter up Grandfather's housekeeper, a woman she had never cultivated because it had long been her intention to oust her, but eventually, Mrs Hanbury had unbent sufficiently to chat about the neighbours over a pot of tea. Evadne learnt that old Mrs Warburton over the road had let go one of her maids, and she had had two maids for donkey's years, as Evadne could remember from those halcyon days when she and Mother had resided in Parrs Wood.

She had called on Mrs Warburton, ostensibly to pay her respects. Bringing the subject round to the servant problem that was the consuming issue these days in those circles she was so desperate to infiltrate, she murmured her shock and sympathy at the news that her hostess had let Maisie go.

'The trouble with girls today,' Evadne declared

as if she had personally lost half a dozen maids recently, 'is that they've had their heads turned by the munitions. They got more money during the war and it's made them forget their place.'

That was clever, blaming Maisie's greed instead of Mrs Warburton's depleted finances; and from there it had been but a few tactful steps to the possibility of a valuation, confidentiality assured.

She thought of Mrs Bentley and how that association had led to the introduction to Miss Kent, which had in turn spawned a meeting with the Howards, from whom Alex had purchased a ship's decanter, though he had sent Evadne alone the second time.

'Most men wouldn't choose to do business with a woman, but Howard's a different sort. It's difficult for him to let another man see his hardship, though a lady such as yourself is a different matter. You might murmur something admiring about how his selflessness in parting with that carriage clock on the dining-room mantelpiece would make his dear wife's life easier; I'm sure he'd lap it up.'

'And I'll suggest that it's not as though something valuable would be disappearing from the sitting room,' Evadne added, 'so Mrs Howard will save face with the neighbours.'

Alex had given her a broad smile, shaking his head slightly, apparently admiring her astuteness. She tried not to be disappointed when all he said was, 'Offer him fifteen.'

'Guineas?' He always offered guineas. It seemed a stylish and gentlemanly way to do business.

'Pounds.'

Mr Howard was pleased with his fifteen pounds and Alex was pleased with Evadne, complimenting her on her ability to handle meetings with clients.

'You have everything that is required: refinement, education and tact. You enable the client to sell without embarrassment and that is essential.'

She had modestly dropped her gaze. She would far rather Alex considered she had the qualities he needed in a wife, but if there was any justice in this world, that would follow.

Ralph dragged Adam along the landing, the pair of them grabbing and shoving, breathing hard.

'Stop it, man!' Adam hissed. 'Don't be so bloody stupid!'

In the tangle, Ralph almost lost his footing, found it again, felt Adam trying to pull free, snatched him closer, increased his grip. They were at the head of the staircase down to the shop. He swung Adam round to hurl him down, intending for him to snap a few bones en route. Adam staggered and Ralph shoved, but Adam held on, struggling for balance, and the pair of them toppled, clattering downwards, struggling and punching all the way, yelling and swearing as ribs and shins, backbones and skulls banged on steps and walls.

They hit the floor with Adam underneath. Ralph felt the breath whoosh out of his brother's body. He pushed himself up using one hand and one knee, pulling back the other arm, feeling the power flood into his fist as he prepared to slam it into Adam's face. Adam bucked, pitching him sideways. Ralph threw out his hands to save himself from losing his teeth against the stairs, felt the sharp twang singing through his wrists and up his arms as his fingers snapped back under the impact. With a curse, he lunged, but Adam scrambled to his feet, chest heaving, body bent forward, one arm wrapped protectively across his ribs.

'You're mad,' he rasped. 'You're bloody insane. What's got into you?'

Ralph came to his feet and surged forwards, grabbing handfuls of lapel. He kept moving, kept charging, and slammed Adam into the wall. The glass shade tinkled on the gas mantle close to their heads. Ralph got in one heavy blow to the stomach and a sharp uppercut to the chin, relishing the crunch of bone on bone, before Adam launched himself, throwing his weight behind a massive shove that sent Ralph stumbling backwards, fighting for balance.

There was space between them, hot and heavy with anger and confusion.

'Is this because I brought Mrs Jenkins home?' Adam demanded, the question scraping on his ragged breathing.

'You can't leave any sodding thing alone, can you? I told you I was going to bring her back.'

'The difference between us being that I actually did it.'

Ralph stepped forward. 'And what for, eh? Not for the old dummy's benefit. If all you wanted was those bloody exercises, you could have sent one of your precious nurses to the hospital. No, you haven't done this for your patient, have you?

You did it for Carrie.'

'I did what you were in no hurry to do.'

'And why the hell should I be when my wife's busy with her new baby?'

'It must have torn Carrie apart, knowing her mother had been sent away.'

'And you'd know, would you?' Ralph saw caution spring into his brother's eyes.

'I know Carrie is devoted to Mrs Jenkins.' Adam tugged lightly on his sleeves, moved his neck inside his collar, tidying his appearance, though it would take a lot more than that to remove the hectic red marks on chin and cheekbone.

He thought it was over. The bloody fool thought a bit of argy-bargy and it was over. 'And you'd do anything to ingratiate yourself with Carrie, wouldn't you?'

'I'd best go.'

Ralph blocked his path. 'I don't think so.' His blood raced and his heart gave a twist of excitement. 'I saw the way she looked at you.'

'I don't know what you mean.'

'Don't try it on with me. I know what I saw.'

Bloody hell, it was Molly all over again.

'Carrie's feelings for me are nothing more than gratitude. She endured a difficult birth. The horror of that, and the joy of motherhood – that's a powerful combination. Of course she feels warmth towards me, but it's only gratitude.'

'Gratitude, eh? And what is it called when the doctor gazes at his patient in a certain way?'

Adam stiffened, the implication leeching the colour from his face. 'She's my sister-in-law, of whom I'm very fond.'

'She's your brother's wife that you're panting over.'

He flung himself on Adam once more, employing such force that they were propelled across the floor and crashed into a table. Ralph threw several punches in quick succession, his aim tight and true, giving Adam no time for anything beyond instinctive defence. Adam managed to spin away, immediately turning and flinging himself bodily into Ralph.

They were pummelling and wrestling before they hit the floor, their breath bursting out in loud pants and grunts as they slogged away at one another. Adam was on top, but Ralph bucked and heaved him off, hanging on as Adam staggered up. Ralph yanked him back down, simultaneously flinging his leg across Adam's body. He threw himself into a sitting position across Adam's chest, fists ready to bombard him with blows.

Instead, he found himself being pulled in the other direction. Some interfering bastard had grasped him under his armpits and was hauling him clear of the struggle. Well, not for long. Ralph wheeled round, throwing the idiot off and sending him flying, ready to kill him barehanded if it was Arthur bloody Renton daring to intervene.

But it wasn't; it was one of the ambulance men who had brought back that damn waxwork; and his colleague was hanging on to Adam, an altogether easier job as Adam was obviously happy for the fight to be over. More fool him. Courtesy of the man drawing Adam away, Ralph leapt across and landed a hefty punch to his brother's guts that doubled him over with a groan. Adam pulled free and threw himself once more at Ralph.

This time both ambulance men set about wrenching Ralph away, but it wasn't until a third set of arms – Renton's, sod him – joined in that Ralph felt the odds turn against him. Even now, pushing him up against the wall wasn't sufficient. They had to clobber him to the floor and throw themselves on top of him.

'Get out, sir! Just get out!' yelled one of the ambulance men.

Ralph caught a glimpse of Adam wiping away sweat and smearing blood across his face, before he straightened himself and left.

Renton and the ambulance men eased their hold on him, only to find themselves hurtled aside the instant they dropped their guard. He sprang to his feet.

'Get off my premises!' he roared at the ambulance men. 'Go on – now! – if you know what's good for you.'

'We ought to make sure the patient–'

'Bugger the patient! Sod off!'

Ralph made a move towards them and they practically fell over their feet in their haste. He swung round to fix Renton with his hardest stare. He saw the moment when Renton realised that pitching in had been a godawful mistake.

His voice neutral, Ralph ordered, 'Back to work.'

Renton looked at him uncertainly, then nodded and turned away. Bloody fool, taking his eyes off the enemy. Ralph stepped forward and planted his heel squarely in the crook of Renton's knee, bringing him down with a squawk that was instantly cut off when Ralph grabbed him from behind in a vicious headlock.

'Turn against me, would you? Not a good idea.'

He shoved Renton's head forward and down in a sharp movement, cutting off his air supply. He held the position for a long moment, and then kept on holding it while Renton twitched in panic.

He bent his face close to Renton's ear. 'It would be so easy. Just one quick move and...'

He administered a hard push to the back of Renton's head, felt the neck bones crunch. Then he threw the hapless bugger aside and stepped over him, going to the stairs.

Sod waiting for the seven o'clock feed. He wanted Carrie and he was bloody well going to have her.

Chapter Thirty-One

After all this time it couldn't still be adrenaline sloshing through his bloodstream, but it felt like it. Adam was dimly aware of the ice packs and antiseptic he would have prescribed for anyone else, but for himself he couldn't be bothered. It was dark outside. The maid had been in to draw the curtains and make up the fire. Everyone was in the dining room, leaving a few on duty on the wards.

He reached for his pipe, set it down again. His mind was churning with images of Carrie and Ralph and the disaster the afternoon had degenerated into. It was his fault for taking it upon himself to fetch Mrs Jenkins home; but if he hadn't, when would it have happened? It obviously hadn't been top of Ralph's agenda; quite the reverse. He didn't want the poor woman under his roof, not that Carrie seemed aware of it. But it was in Mrs Jenkins' best interests, Carrie's too, and so Adam had done what needed doing, knowing that Ralph would be furious, but so what? He was pretty bloody angry with his brother for having banished the invalid in the first place.

Not that Ralph's fury had been just because of Mrs Jenkins. It was because of Carrie and Adam too. Well, because of Adam, anyway. Ralph already suspected Adam of harbouring feelings for Carrie; now he suspected Carrie of returning those feelings. Pain came on Adam, swift and sharp, at the thought of Carrie's being in danger of retribution. Was Ralph sure? Or did he merely suspect?

Come to that, was he sure himself? Had that moment truly happened? He scrubbed his face with his palms, then groaned as his hands aggravated the bruises and abrasions his brother had hammered into his face. Would Ralph – surely he wouldn't raise a hand to Carrie? Of course not. He worshipped her. Much as Ralph resented his own attraction to Carrie, he also enjoyed the hopelessness of Adam's position, relished being the one to possess Carrie.

And there was the operative word: possess.

The sitting room, which became more like an office the longer he occupied it, felt like a prison. Shrugging into his outdoor things, he ran downstairs and out into the chill of the evening.

'Everything all right, sir?'

'Oh, it's you, Geeson.' A good chap, the

269

groundsman, solid and dependable. Admirable too, when you considered how he had carved out this new life for himself. 'Yes, fine.'

Beneath the peak of his cap, one eyebrow lifted, shrewd and appraising. 'Heading somewhere, are you?'

'Not really.'

'Walking it off, eh?'

'S'pose so.'

'Cold night for heading nowhere, sir. I could offer you a hot toddy, if you'd rather.'

'Thanks, but no.'

'Smells like rain. Bruised and cold, and wet to boot; or bruised with summat to warm you through. I know which I'd choose.'

He set off. He made good headway, could cover the ground at a pace that Adam knew must have cost him a deal of pain to build up. He didn't look back and Adam liked him for it.

He followed, knocking as he opened the door to the cottage that went with the groundsman's job, stepping across a lobby and finding himself in a kitchen-cum-sitting room.

Geeson, stirring up the fire, had his back to him. 'Take a pew. Kettle's on.'

There was a row of pegs on the wall. He hung up his things and took one of the armchairs by the hearth, various aches and pains insisting he lower himself into it gingerly. He wondered how easy it would be to stand up again.

Geeson produced a bottle of Scotch. 'Courtesy of Jimmy Whitney's folks.'

He nodded. Jimmy Whitney was their youngest patient, little more than a boy.

'His dad's a gent. New money, of course, which is probably why he likes to flash it about. Not that I'm complaining.' Geeson flicked his fingernails against the bottle with a tinging sound. 'I helped out when his missus drove their new Bentley into a ditch and Mr Whitney slipped me this next time they came.'

'Decent of him.'

Geeson caught the kettle before it started to sing, poured a mix of hot water and Scotch into a couple of mugs, and offered one to Adam before setting down his own on a small table to free his hands to manoeuvre himself into the other arm-chair.

'I've some ointment that might help,' he remarked, using his mug to gesture at Adam's face.

'I'm all right, thanks.'

'Permission to speak freely, sir? It fair pisses me off to see someone deliberately hanging on to an injury they could see off in half the time with a bit of treatment. Look at you. A cold compress would work wonders, but will you bother? It's by way of an insult, sir, to them of us as have injuries we can't do owt about.'

Fair enough. 'I'll apply ice packs when I get back – although,' he added ruefully, 'I'm not sure where to start.'

'What happened? Walk into a door, did you? That's what my sister allus says when her husband belts her one. A bad bugger, he is. Pity the war didn't do for him. What about yourself, sir? Or tell me to mind my own business.'

Adam took a swig to buy himself a moment. He had a lot of time for Geeson. The man had intelli-

gence and compassion and Adam knew that anything said inside these four walls would stay here.

He indicated his face. 'My brother's handiwork.'

'The antiques bloke. Presumably not a punch-
up over something precious?'

'Something unspeakably precious. Carrie – his
wife.'

'You haven't–?'

'No.' He would never attempt to take advantage
of Carrie. Except that – there it was again, that
moment in her room when the rumpus in the flat
evaporated, leaving them together inside a vast
silence filled with astonishment and realisation.
They had shared a look, nothing more, yet that
look had connected them, made them understand
they were bound together. Carrie had felt it too,
hadn't she?

'But your brother knows?'

He drew a deep breath, realised what he was
about to do and quickly expelled it. He had no
business sighing like a lovesick fool. 'He guessed
a while back. Then today... Long story, but I did
something he should have done and it riled him.'

'So the fight was over that, not his missus?'

'I was about to say it was both, but the honest
answer is, it was over Carrie.'

'Another man's wife, son.'

He had gone from *sir* to *son*. Geeson had a few
years on him, but not that many. Fifteen, tops.

'Did she choose between you when she married
him?'

'She didn't know I was interested. And I had no
idea Ralph was.'

'Or that might have given you the kick up the

272

jacksy you needed?' Geeson swirled the dregs of his hot toddy round the bottom of his mug. 'Pretty poor excuse, if you ask me. If you couldn't be bothered on your own account...'

A flush of resentment made his bruises burn. 'Her mother was my patient.'

Levering himself up, Geeson took Adam's mug and put the kettle on again. 'You could have put her under Doctor Todd.'

'Ditch a patient to pursue her daughter? I'd never do something so crass.'

'Bet you wish now you had.'

'I thought I was doing the right thing – hell and damnation, it was the right thing. I was going to get Mrs Jenkins' treatment started and I also wanted to give Carrie time. I didn't want to take advantage.'

'So what did she see in your brother?' Geeson thrust the replenished mug into his hands.

'He must have laid siege to her. It happened quickly.'

'That might seem romantic to a girl.'

Adam shrugged. 'He married her by special licence. I wanted to rush round there and say, "Don't marry him. Marry me instead." Only, of course, I didn't.'

'Why not?'

He had expected sympathy, not a challenge. 'Well – decent chaps don't try to steal other blokes' girls, certainly not their own brother's girl.'

'Oh aye, and that would have stopped him, would it, if it had happened t'other way about?'

'No, I don't suppose it would.' He had paid for his decency over and over. Carrie was the first beat

273

of his heart when he awoke and the last before he slept. 'Mind you, if I had made a move at the time, he'd probably have broken every bone in my body.'

'Sounds a bad 'un. Does he hit her?'

'Christ, no. I'm sure he doesn't. Carrie's pretty transparent. You can see she's learnt to tread warily, but she trusts him. I imagine his strength was one of the reasons she liked him in the first place. She was in a vulnerable position. Do you know the story? It was in Carrie's mother's kitchen that my father died. Mrs Jenkins suffered a stroke and has been under me ever since. On top of that, Carrie's young man jilted her because her father had been revealed as a deserter. Don't spread that around – I mean, with Carrie being Miss Baxter's sister.'

'Wouldn't dream of it, sir.'

'Of course not. No offence intended. Miss Baxter is understandably sensitive on the subject.'

'Aye, there's an unhappy woman if ever I saw one.'

'Unhappy? I can think of various words I could apply to Miss Baxter–'

'Careful what you say next, son. I wouldn't wish to hear the lady spoken ill of.'

'I was going to say: but unhappy isn't one of them.' Adam knocked back a mouthful. 'General gallantry towards all women or special interest in this particular one?'

'Special interest, since you mention it.'

'You've chosen a tough nut to crack.'

'It's not a question of choice, though, is it? It just happens. Like you with your brother's wife. That's not a situation you'd have chosen, any

274

more than I'd have chosen a woman who won't give me the time of day.'

'You can't cross paths much.'

'Aye, her in the office, me outdoors. It doesn't bode well, does it? It's not even as though she'll be accompanying the lads outside, come the kinder weather.'

Adam pictured Evadne's frigid distaste for the patients. 'No.'

'Still, I do what I can. You'll know, of course, him being your brother, that she does evening work at the Lloyds. I keep an eye out and when she heads up that way, I make sure I'm there when she comes out, just to see her safely home.'

'That's a start. Women like to feel looked after.'

Geeson surprised him by giving a great laugh. 'You might suggest to Miss Baxter that she wants looking after. Then maybe I wouldn't have to skulk after her while she stalks along, quivering with disapproval.'

Adam grinned. 'You're right. It doesn't bode well.'

'One of these evenings, there'll be a bobby about and she'll have me arrested for following her, I shouldn't wonder. That 'ud raise a few eyebrows. I used to be a copper meself before the war – a sergeant.'

'Really? I didn't know.' Adam spent a moment considering the changes the war had brought to Ted Geeson's life. 'Not to worry. I'll post bail.'

The shared laughter made him feel unexpectedly light-hearted.

'Eh, love's a bugger, isn't it?' Geeson shook his head. 'Time for another?'

Chapter Thirty-Two

Evadne could tell the table was rosewood and she knew the decoration on top was properly referred to as inlay. At least that was a smidgeon of knowledge to show for the time she had spent in Mr Weston's company. Today she was with Alex in the home of Mrs Cox, who lived along the road from Grandfather. After Mrs Warburton, there had been Mr and Mrs Keene, who, in the depths of their grief for their three fallen sons, had lost most of their savings to a confidence trickster; the elderly Goudge sisters round the corner, whose inheritance, considerable in its day, was said to be dwindling; and now Mrs Cox.

Evadne knew the form. Alex would visit once, twice at the most, then she would make the final visit.

'Having their good neighbour Major Baxter's granddaughter making the last call removes any lingering unpleasantness,' Alex said. 'It leaves them remembering the social connection rather than the business side.'

She enjoyed it more each time. Alex always provided money for a taxi and supplied a few appropriate phrases about the relevant item for her to use in front of the client. When he told her how much to offer, he routinely specified a sum, to which she would respond, 'Guineas?' and he would say, 'Pounds.' It had come to be a little ritual and she liked that too.

One thing she had learnt, however, was that Alex wasn't reliable about making arrangements for her visits. When he had forgotten to make that first appointment with Mrs Bentley, she had thought nothing of it; but when the same oversight occurred the next time, she started making her own appointments, smiling to herself as she did so. Alex needed a wife to keep him in order.

'Is it worth anything?' Hovering as Alex scrutinised the table, Mrs Cox couldn't disguise her anxiety.

'I'm happy to tell you it is.'

'Oh, you can't imagine the relief,' Mrs Cox gushed. 'Things have been so hard. My husband survived the war, only to succumb to the influenza just when we thought our troubles were over. I've got myself a little office job, but...'

'There are many ladies in unfortunate situations these days. Widows, spinster sisters, elderly mothers, all left without their breadwinners.' Alex was smoothly sympathetic. 'I can offer you forty for the table.'

'Forty pounds?' She sounded as if she could scarcely believe it.

'Guineas,' said Alex, just as Evadne knew he would.

'My goodness! Why, a family could manage on that for weeks – months.'

As they drove away, Alex said, 'If – or I should say, when – Mrs Cox invites me back, I suggest that you go, just to give the appropriate finishing touch. No embarrassing questions from the neighbours about the man who called. That pair of vases on the mantelpiece: offer twenty-five.'

'Pounds?' she asked archly.

He quirked a smile at her. 'Naturally.'

It was a wonderful moment. Changing the ritual brought them closer. She pressed her hands to her sides, knowing that if she let them loose, they would clasp or, worse, she would hug herself.

Yet how much more wonderful would the moment be when, armed with everything she was learning from Mr Weston, she was able to suggest the price before Alex could say it. She hadn't undertaken this new form of education to impress him, but it would be a gratifying side effect.

Another side effect would be to draw them closer still.

Bed rest was over. Carrie couldn't wait to get into the fresh air and show her baby to the world. The final few days in bed had felt interminable, providing far too much time for thinking – and for guilt. After all these months of wishing she could love Ralph, she had fallen in love with his brother. She lived again that breathless moment when her eyes had tricked her, showing her what she expected to see, and her whole self had responded to the sight of the man she believed to be her husband before Ralph, the real Ralph, had come barging in, and after a moment of stupefaction, she had realised the truth.

Her immortal soul must be as black as tar by now with all the sins she had accumulated and never confessed. Fornication, deceit, lies, and now her feelings for another man. Those poky little confessional boxes were all very well, but you could forget about privacy. Father Kelly had sharp ears and made a point of using your name, just to let you know you hadn't got away with owt.

Worst of all was the fear of what had gone on between Ralph and Adam. She knew there had been a big bust-up. She had heard all that clattering and banging, though Ralph never referred to it. But a few days later, it wasn't Adam but a colleague of his, Doctor Todd, who had come to check on Mam, explaining he had taken over her case. Carrie had been desperate to know why. Had Ralph banned Adam from the flat? He was furious that Adam had taken the initiative over bringing Mam home. Or had Adam made the decision to stay away? That moment in the bedroom – it hadn't just been her, had it, that it had happened to? Perhaps he was keeping away for both their sakes. Or had Ralph banned him, not because of Mam, but because he had sensed what had happened between his brother and his wife? Her bowels turned to water.

When Doctor Todd had departed, Ralph came upstairs.

'What's the new quack like?'

'He said I was doing a good job, though it's disappointing not to have had some response yet.'

'Just so long as Joey doesn't miss out.' There had been a warning in his voice.

'He won't.' It would have been unnatural if she didn't ask, so she forced herself to frame the question. 'Doctor Todd said he'd be coming instead of Adam. Was that your decision?'

'I'm sick and tired of Adam traipsing in and out like he owns the place. That business of bringing your mother home was the final straw.'

Now, at last, after a dinner she was almost too excited to eat, Carrie was taking Joey out for the first time. It was a beautiful day, chilly but fine, though she wouldn't have cared if it had been chucking it down. It was wonderful to be outdoors and she felt proud to be pushing such a smart perambulator with a jointed hood to put up if it rained and wheels that made a soft tick-tick-tick sound as they went round. All her life, her ambition had been to have a family and here she was with her first baby. It was a moment to be treasured.

Ralph had made her promise not to be out too long in case she tired, but she felt she could walk for miles. It was Saturday and she had always liked Saturdays because the children were out and about. She had her shopping list and Ralph had told her to arrange to have her hair cut. The bob had grown out in the latter stages of her pregnancy.

'Long hair these days is for old biddies and the working class,' he said.

The jibe had set memories rolling of the gossipy and judgemental but stout-hearted folk of Wilton Lane, who had pitched in to help when Mam was in dire need. Mrs Clancy and the rest would love to see Joey and would be disappointed and affronted if all they got was a glimpse after Mass. And what must Letty's mam be thinking, or had she given up on Carrie now? She felt her cheeks blotch with shame. How long was it since she had sat in the Hardacres' kitchen, supping tea and shelling peas and teaching their

Joanie lazy daisy stitch?

A man was running towards her.

'Carrie! Carrie!'

Billy. Her mind stumbled. She hadn't seen him since last summer, had dreaded bumping into him, though she had gradually realised she wasn't likely to. His work took him to town five and a half days a week and they had never attended the same Mass.

Now here he was in front of her. His nose was different, sort of pushed over sideways, and his front teeth were crooked. He was dressed in his suit. Her heart used to expand with pride and desire at seeing him togged up for work. She felt nothing now. The love had been blanked out a long time ago.

'Hello, Carrie. How are you?'

'Fine, thanks.' How normal she sounded. 'Yourself?'

'Aye. This must be Joey.' He leant over to look.

She felt annoyed. 'Where did you hear his name?'

'Letty.'

'Oh.'

Their glances met and fell away.

'I must get on,' she said.

'No, wait. I'm glad to bump into you. I saw you from the tram and jumped off.' Digging into his pocket, Billy pulled out a florin and thrust it at her. 'Here – buy summat for't little lad.'

She didn't want it, but didn't know how to refuse. 'You jumped off the tram to give the baby a present?'

'I ... I've been wanting to talk to you.'

'What about?' She shouldn't have asked. 'This isn't right. We shouldn't be seen together.'

'We're only talking.'

'I'm a married woman.'

'Let's go somewhere.'

'Billy!'

'Please. I need to speak to you. Five minutes – please.'

'All right. Cross over and stop outside Quarmby's. But if I see anyone I know, I'll go straight inside and when I come out, I shan't expect you to be anywhere in sight.'

They crossed the road separately and met up outside the stationer's, Carrie doing her best to look as if the window display was of consuming interest.

'The thing is,' Billy began, then stopped. 'Well, Letty said as how you'd had a bad time – you know, with the baby.'

'Billy!' she hissed. 'Don't be personal.'

'Sorry,' he mumbled. 'But it set me thinking and – and will you come back to me?'

Her head whipped round so fast her neck twanged. 'You what?'

'I were a fool, Carrie. I should never have let you go.'

'Let me go? Tossed me aside, more like. Tossed me on the muck-heap.'

'Aw, it weren't like that. There was the shock of your dad an' everything. My mam took that to heart.'

'So did mine. Mine wouldn't set foot outside her own front door, she were that ashamed. You should have stood by us, Billy.' If he blamed it on his mam, she would crown him.

'Aye, I should, and I can't tell you how many times I've regretted it. He were a good bloke, your dad.'

She softened. Pa would have loved being a grandad.

'I keep thinking about this time last year,' Billy coaxed, 'when everything were all right. Can't get it out of my head.'

This time last year. She felt a pang. She hadn't turned eighteen, hadn't been pregnant; had been mad about Billy, was dying for June so she could marry him.

'I've got it all planned.' He leant closer. 'I can work out my notice, then we can up sticks and go wherever you like. I've got my savings and I'll get a good reference. We can start again, the three of us – you, me and Joey. I'll not let you down again, I swear. You can call yourself Mrs Shipton and no one'll be any the wiser.'

Carrie couldn't believe what she was hearing. She waited for him to go all awkward and take the words back, but he didn't.

'You mean it, don't you?'

'Course I do. Look, I lied when I said I saw you from the tram. I've been stood over the road from your shop for the best part of an hour, hoping and praying for you to come out. When you appeared, I waited while you walked off and then...'

'You followed me?' It made her feel all prickly. She had been tricked.

'How else were I to see you? I could hardly come up to you right outside Armstrong's, could I? What do you say, Carrie? We're meant to be together, you and me. I'm sorry for what I did and I promise I'll spend the rest of my life making it up to you.'

'No, Billy.'

'Look, love, you're not giving me a chance. I know this is a shock. How about I meet you same time next week, eh, when you've had a chance to think it over?'

'I said no. You and me – that's long gone.'

'You allus said as how marrying me was the most important thing you would ever do.'

'Aye, well, that were then. I'm wed to someone else now.'

'But you only married him cos of ... you know, the baby.'

'Keep your voice down, will you? I'm married, and decent women don't run away from their husbands.'

Billy's eyes hardened. 'Aye, and decent girls don't whip their drawers off before they're wed, but that didn't stop you, did it?'

'Billy Shipton!' She grasped the perambulator handle and made to move, but Billy blocked her way.

'I'm sorry, Carrie, I didn't mean it. Only it's sort of true – I mean, it showed how much you loved me.'

'Aye, for all the good it did me.'

'You're never going to let me forget it, are you? I made a mistake, a bad one, and I'm sorry. I wish I'd stuck by your family. I wish I could turn back the clock, but I can't. Now, will you please put it behind you and let's start up again.'

'I don't want to start up again. I have a different

life now, a good life.'

'A better one than I can give you, you mean? That's a brand-new baby carriage, if I'm not mistaken, and your coat and hat never came off no market stall.'

Heat stained her cheeks. 'Are you saying I married Ralph for his money?'

'Well, you can't deny you've done well. Oh, I'm getting this all wrong. I can't bear to think of you with someone else when you're meant to be with me. All I want is to have you back. We can live anywhere you want. I won't ever have as much money as Ralph Armstrong, but I'll do my best for you. That was all you wanted not so long ago: me and half a dozen nippers. We can still have it, Carrie. I'll buy you a ring an' everything.'

'How many times must I say it? The answer's no.'

'You hate me, don't you?'

'I don't hate you, Billy.'

To her horror, his eyes filled with tears. 'I'd best cut along then, I suppose.'

Relief spewed through her, weakening her muscles. 'I must get on an' all. Please go, Billy.'

'Wait. You won't – you won't tell Letty, will you?'

Discretion vanished. She stared openly. 'You mean you're going to carry on walking out with her? You should have ended it the minute you decided to speak to me.'

'Anyroad, you'll not tell her?'

'I most certainly will. She's my best friend.'

'You breathe one word and I'll tell her about you an' me. You know what I mean. I never said owt before because – well, because I never. But I swear to God I will, if you tell Letty about this.'

'You wouldn't,' she breathed.

'I'll tell her about this conversation an' all and say it were your idea.'

'You wouldn't.'

Billy shrugged. 'It's only reasonable that you'd want to be with your son's dad.'

A terrible coldness poured through Carrie. Then it turned to a controlled fire. Digging in her handbag, she retrieved the florin Billy had pressed on her and shoved it into his hand. When his fingers refused to close around it, she let go, snatching her hand away. The coin clinked to the ground and rolled away.

She grasped the perambulator handle so fiercely her fingers burnt. 'Joey's not your son. Your baby was due in January. Joey didn't come along until February and that's because he's not yours.'

'You're lying.'

She shrugged. 'You're the town hall clerk. Do the sums. I was two months along when we were meant to get wed.'

Billy glanced at his fingers, his lips moving through the names of the months. She forced herself to fix her gaze on his face, because everyone knew a liar couldn't look you in the eye. Then he looked up and when she saw his narrowed eyes, her heartbeats roared in her ears.

'Nah.' Derision lengthened the word into a drawl. 'You told me you were due towards the end of January. So yon lad were born a bit into February – so what? You got your dates wrong or else the baby came late, one or t'other.'

'At least you're finally admitting responsibility,' she flung at him. 'You can't denounce me without showing yourself up.'

'Oh aye? I'll have you know that Father Kelly is my witness that I couldn't be sure I were the father.'

The moment was broken by an excited cry.

'Grandad – look what I found!'

'Oy!' said Billy. 'That's mine.'

'It were just lying there, mister. Finders keepers. Tell 'im, Grandad.'

Carrie swung the perambulator round and marched away.

Chapter Thirty-Three

The moment Evadne set eyes on the black marble clock belonging to Mr Browning and his sister, who lived along the road from Grandfather in the house with the monkey puzzle tree in the front garden, she gave a small gasp of delight. There was a similar clock on the mantelpiece in one of the rooms at Brookburn. Only yesterday Mr Weston had told her about it, pointing out various details; he had even suggested its value.

Hence Evadne was able to murmur a few pertinent comments, tactfully phrased as questions. 'The engraving, is it gilt? And is the mount bronze?' She glanced at Alex, delighted to receive his nod.

'Quite so. But this isn't what you want to show

us, is it, Mr Browning? I believe you have some china that belonged to your mother?'

The china was examined and paid for.

Driving away, Alex remarked, 'One more visit to the Brownings, I think, if you'd be so kind? Perhaps you'd like to offer for that clock that caught your eye.'

The price was on her lips. Dared she say it? She didn't want to look foolish.

Alex said, 'You might offer twenty.'

'Oh.'

'You sound surprised.'

'Not at all.'

'Aren't you going to ask, pounds or guineas?'

'Pounds, I assume.'

'Are you sure you're all right?'

She pulled herself together. 'Yes, thank you.'

What a good thing she had kept her mouth shut. Her valuation would have been way over and she would have undone the good impression she had made with her accurate remarks. The thought made her feel fluttery; she couldn't bear to appear less than perfect. She must be careful in future. The Brookburn clock was bigger, with more engraving, and Mr Weston had said the bronze was Florentine. No wonder the Brownings' clock was worth so much less.

Let that be a lesson to her. She stopped dwelling on it and enjoyed the day.

She had invested in a new coat and was wearing it for the first time. Having gone to Affleck and Brown's with a picture in her mind of cream wool flannel, she had caught sight of a fabulously stylish ankle-length coat in crushed velvet of deepest damson with generous fur trim at the collar, wrist and hem. From that instant, no other garment would do. The appreciation in Alex's eyes when he picked her up had been most gratifying.

Best of all, when he drove her back to Brookburn, he not only came round to open the door for her as always, but also escorted her up the steps to the front door, which he hadn't done before. He took her hand and it seemed he would raise it to his lips, but he simply bowed over it, then walked back to the motor.

Watching him go, Evadne noticed Geeson, trundling a wheelbarrow along. He stopped and seemed to be looking at Alex. Then he looked straight at her. She turned and went indoors. Trust Geeson to ruin the moment.

He was apparently intent upon ruining considerably more than that, however. First thing Monday morning, there was a tap on her office door. Others might work with their doors open, but not Evadne. She happened to be standing at the filing cabinet close by, so she opened the door herself.

There stood Geeson. With his burly figure wrapped in his greatcoat and those big gloved hands, he looked at odds with the precise neatness of these surroundings, but instead of his seeming uncomfortable, it was Evadne who felt a twinge of discomfort. She hadn't seen him indoors before. She was aware of the quiet strength of the man, a strength that she suddenly fancied lay in his heart and his spirit as much as in his muscles. She wanted him to twist his cap self-consciously, but he appeared composed, his weathered face grave.

'What can I do for you?' The words, politely spoken, nevertheless expressed her surprise, not to mention her displeasure. She was mistress of the cool put-down.

'Might I step inside? Only this is a bit awkward, like.'

'No, you may not. I can't imagine what you have to say to me, but kindly say it and leave.'

Geeson breathed in deeply; his wide chest expanded. 'Very well, Miss Baxter. I couldn't help noticing your companion on Saturday.'

'How dare you!'

'The thing is, I know Captain Larter–'

'I doubt that very much. The likes of you can hardly claim to know a gentleman like that.' Geeson's eyes narrowed as her barb hit home. Good.

'I mean to say, miss,' he continued doggedly, 'he was my commanding officer and I think you should be told that–'

She swung the door shut in his face.

No wonder they called it heartbreak. It was a physical pain, lodged deep inside his chest. Ralph had met enough men who had had bullets dug out of them, bloody great lumps of shrapnel in some cases, but there was nothing to be done about this injury. He felt as if he couldn't breathe out.

He battled with a mad urge to ask her outright. Suppose he did. Suppose he said, 'Are you in love with my brother?' But he would never humiliate himself like that. Besides, how could he bear to hear her answer? The bugger of it was that if she said yes, he would believe her, but if she denied it – what would she think then? He was tormented by the memory of bursting into the bedroom, furious with Adam for bringing that damn waxwork home, and seeing the starry bewilderment in Carrie's eyes as she gazed at his brother. She had never looked at him like that.

She was his perfect girl and she had never looked at him like that.

Oh, he had known all along she wasn't in love with him, and it hadn't mattered. She needed him. She was tied to him. That she didn't love him added a keen edge to his possession of her. Making love to her, knowing she didn't love him, endowed the act with a strong sense of ravishment, which, combined with the great passion he felt for her, made him think he would go mad with desire.

And now she loved someone else. His own bloody brother, of all people.

It was Molly all over again. She had been his girl until she clapped eyes on Adam. Adam hadn't wanted her, but Ralph had never forgiven him all the same. But Adam did want Carrie. Ralph had known it for some time and he had enjoyed it. It gave him a feeling of power. He might have lost Molly to Adam, who didn't even want her, but Carrie was his and Adam could never have her. That was how it should be.

Except that Carrie now wanted Adam.

Christ Almighty, he longed to pound his sodding brother to a pulp, then scrape him up and start all over again. He had shoved Billy Shipton up an entry and given him the pasting of his life, but he knew there was no damage he could inflict on his brother that would assuage his anger and jealousy.

And what of Carrie? Bloody bitch. He had given her everything and she had betrayed him. He loved her, he wanted her, he needed her. He would never stop loving her and he would never stop pretending he didn't know of her attraction to another man, to his bloody brother. She had no idea he knew. He had used Adam's high-handed interference in the waxwork's return to explain why he had banned Adam from his home and, in her innocence, she had believed him.

Yes, her innocence. Strange how he had never for one moment doubted her basic lack of guile, for all that she had foisted another bloke's bastard on to him and had now fallen head over heels for his brother. She was a bloody bitch like all women, but she was a decent, uncomplicated girl at heart and he knew she would never give Adam the smallest encouragement.

Not that she would get the chance.

And not that her fundamental goodness would save her from suffering as she deserved. His perfect girl.

Bloody bitch. Perfect girl. Bloody bitch.

Letty nestled Mam's hand inside both her own. It was Wednesday afternoon and here she was, same as every alternate Wednesday. No, not the same. There was something brittle about her that Carrie couldn't fathom.

Finally Letty said, 'I've got summat to tell you. I hope you'll be pleased.'

'Course I will, if it's summat good.' What could it be? Not a new job; Letty was happy at Trimble's.

'It's me and Billy. We're engaged.' Letty looked

away, as if holding Carrie's gaze was too much for her. 'What do you think, Mrs Jenkins? Are you pleased for me? I know it must feel strange after all the time Billy and your Carrie were together, but it's funny how things turn out, isn't it?'

He asked me to run off with him. Should she say it? Could she? And if she did, what might Billy say in revenge?

'Spit it out, Carrie,' Letty challenged.

'It's just that – well, you know he dumped me when things got difficult.'

'And that were right unkind, but it was his mam more than him, and it's not as though you didn't fall on your feet. He's a good chap, is Billy. You know that, don't you, Mrs Jenkins, or you'd never have let Carrie get engaged to him in the first place.'

Carrie's heart yearned towards her friend. What should she do?

Letty pushed away from the bed, her chair scraping on the floor. 'If you've nowt to say, I may as well go.'

Carrie reached out a hand. 'I'm sorry. It's like you say; it's a surprise.'

Letty waited. It was a test. If Carrie didn't say it, she would up and leave. But how could she say it, knowing what she knew? Yet how could she not say it, loving Letty as she did?

'All I want is your happiness.'

'And this makes me happy. So go on. Say it.' Letty's lip curled. 'You can't, can you? You can't bring yourself to congratulate me. What's the matter, Carrie? Were Billy meant to spend the rest of his life pining over you? Would you have been nowty no matter who he took up with, or is it because it's me?'

'It's only that–'

'–it's a surprise. Aye, so you've said. What was you expecting, eh? I told you Billy and me were walking out. What did you think would happen?'

'I never thought.'

'Then let me tell you. Folks do their courting, then they get wed. Next news, there's a baby. You don't know what it's like, Carrie. You set your sights on Billy when you were a lass and when he jilted you, you went straight off with Ralph.'

'I did not–'

'Some of us have never had a chap, and with so many dead in the war, lots of us–' Letty's voice dropped to a whisper. 'They're talking about sur-plus women – a whole generation of girls who'll never get married and have families, because there aren't enough men to go round.'

'Oh, Letty.'

'I don't want to be a surplus woman. I want to be a wife. I want children.'

'Of course you do.'

'When you're a little lass dreaming of getting married, you say, "I'll marry a handsome man and we'll have four children and a house of us own." You don't say, "I want to marry a jilt." You dont say, "I want to marry the man who ditched my best mate." But that's how it's turned out for me. I don't want to stop at home for ever. I want to get wed. I want a proper life. Billy can give me that. He's changed, Carrie. He's grown up. He knows what he wants and so do I.'

She made a last-ditch attempt. 'I understand

about getting married, but are you sure he's right for you? Only him and me were together a long time.' Her heart dipped into her belly as Letty's eyes narrowed. 'Are you sure he's not on the rebound?'

'You're a fine one to talk. You're the one what got wed on the rebound, if anyone did – hardly waited five minutes, you didn't. And did I say one word against you? No, I never. In fact, I stuck up for you when folks tattled behind your back. At least Billy had the common decency to wait before he went courting again.'

Carrie bit her lip. She couldn't bear the thought of her beloved Letty marrying someone who didn't love her with all his heart, but she didn't dare put Billy's threat to the test. 'I wish you all the best, love.' Scared of sounding resigned and sparking Letty off again, she forced a smile. 'Billy's jolly lucky and you can tell him I said so.'

What a far cry from the squeals and hugs that had erupted when she announced her own engagement to Billy. Perhaps Letty remembered too, because she reached for her handbag.

'I'll be off. I just came to tell you the news. I'll see myself out.'

Did Letty hesitate in the doorway? Just for a smidgeon? But Carrie's thoughts were so heavy her body couldn't move. She wanted to slink away and hide.

Billy would get to see the orchid corset after all.

Chapter Thirty-Four

God, but he found Renton irritating sometimes. Sometimes? All the bloody time, ever since the slimy toerag had ganged up on him with those ambulance men to prevent him from jamming Adam's brains into the cracks between the floorboards. It was galling to have to keep him in the shop, but he couldn't sack the bastard. Renton was one of the team and much as Ralph would have relished the opportunity to knock his teeth out of his stupid head and stick them up his arse, he couldn't do it. His mouth twisted into a sneer. Renton tried not to be obvious, but Ralph had noticed how he sidled away so a piece of furniture stood between them. Probably pissing himself with nerves.

Look at him now, explaining the finer points of a satinwood china cabinet to a possible buyer. Ralph wanted to get Renton out of the auction room and back to the shop. Renton could get by convincingly there. When there were just the two of them, Ralph lectured him at length about various items on display and Renton had proved to have a good memory.

'Never pretend to know something you don't,' he had instructed him on his first day and, give him his due, he never had.

'Let me double-check that for you,' he would say when faced by a tricky question and Ralph would put on his most urbane manner and step in.

But Renton didn't have the knowledge necessary for the auction room, where potential customers of all kinds, including fellow dealers, came early to view the pieces. Any question could be asked and an expert would soon spot Renton for the fraud he was. Ralph made his way around the room. The moment the punter moved on, he quietly dismissed Renton.

There was a hum of anticipation in the atmosphere. Ralph looked about, pleased; alert too. Monthly auctions had started back in September and he had worked hard to procure suitable items, at the same time as keeping the shop supplied with stock. It had meant increasing the amount of time spent going out buying, sometimes on private valuations, other times at sales and auctions, and that had meant leaving Renton in charge of the shop, something he hadn't found easy, but he had no option. There were times when he loathed this organisation he was part of. He didn't like working with others, trusted no one but himself, and being told what to do made his blood boil; but under no circumstances would he drop out. Not that they would have let him. Jonty Fellowes had wanted out and look what happened to him.

Anyway, after lying low all this time, the rewards were about to start rolling in.

Ostensibly, there was no difference between today and any previous auction day. Since September, auctions had been held monthly on Wednesday afternoons. From eleven, the auction room was open for viewing and people walked around, clutching Evadne's typed lists and feigning lack of interest in whatever caught their eye. The Lloyds set aside a smart room where a light luncheon was served and the proceedings opened promptly at two. Ralph acted as auctioneer and he would never have admitted to anyone how much he loved it. He glanced round the room, gratified by the quality and variety of items available. He had to admit that Larter had pulled his weight, bringing in a significant number of pieces, though why he bothered taking Evadne on his valuations remained a mystery.

All Larter would say was, 'The delectable Miss Baxter is generously providing us with an insurance policy. Let's hope for her sake we never need to use it.'

Come to think of it, Ralph hadn't seen Evadne. She was supposed to have arranged to have the day off from Brookburn. A table stood ready for her beside the small platform where his desk was. She had to record the sales; and before they started, she had to list the names and addresses of everyone who wanted to bid and allocate a number to each of them. Where the flaming hell was she?

Larter approached him. 'Problem?'

'Evadne's not here. It's a bit rich, her being late when she was the one who mithered Carrie to put in a word for her.'

'Miss Baxter is otherwise engaged today.'

He couldn't believe his ears. 'Doing what?'

'Providing us with insurance.'

'What are you talking about?'

'I've told you before. Leave Miss Baxter to me. She won't appear today and,' Larter added, an edge sliding across his voice, 'you won't say a word to her about it.'

'You're bloody joking! She goes off without a by-your-leave and I'm meant to swallow it? No one who works for me—'

'But no one does work for you, do they?' Larter cut in, quiet and menacing. 'Renton and Miss Baxter work for the same people as you, albeit Miss Baxter is blissfully ignorant of her involvement.' He held Ralph's angry glare through the thudding of several heartbeats. 'I repeat, you will make no mention of Miss Baxter's absence. We'll need Renton here to do her job. I think you'll find he's as quick at working out commission as he is with a flick knife. One more thing,' he added when Ralph would have left him standing there. 'As far as your brother is concerned, he released Miss Baxter from her duties today for her to come here. Don't disabuse him of that.'

'What game are you playing with her?'

'Let's say I'm playing a different game to the one the lady is playing. That fellow by the window,' he went on, deliberately fixing his eyes elsewhere, 'the one looking at the bookcase, he's a dealer, in case you haven't seen him before.'

Ralph bridled. Bastard, talking to him as if he didn't know. 'There are several dealers, but mostly these are private individuals.'

'That's what we need, plenty of private individuals who don't know any better, to buy our ... special items.'

God, he sounded smug, but then Ralph was feeling more than a little satisfied himself. In fact, everyone in their group was probably feeling

299

pretty bloody pleased today.

'Our man is the one by the grandmother clock. His name's Kemp. If a dealer looks like outbidding a private buyer on any of our special items, give Kemp a glance and he'll up the bidding until the dealer is forced out.'

'You don't need to tell me.' Ralph spoke through gritted teeth. 'It was my idea in the first place to have a plant in the room.'

In fact, the whole bally set-up had been his idea. Back in France, when the group discussed plundering the cellars of the fancy chateaux and making off with the family treasures locked away for the duration, he had been the one to devise the sophisticated plan of eventually selling the pieces through their own auction room. First, wait a couple of years, during which time the auction room would be established as a legitimate concern; then filter the stolen items into the sales, ensuring that each piece ended up in private hands, there to remain for many years to come, preferably for ever.

Of course, the auction room hadn't had a couple of years of above-board work because Ralph hadn't acquired the business immediately after the war, the way he had expected, and that was unfortunate, but did that really matter?

It was about to begin.

Entering the auction room in Chester, Evadne paused, inviting eyes to turn her way. She felt like a queen. She was wearing her coat of crushed velvet and knew how stylish she looked, the more so since, after Alex made his request, she had gone straight to a milliner's on Deansgate, where she had chosen an elegant hat with a dramatic upswept brim.

'Not everyone can wear a hat like this,' the milliner had murmured, looking over Evadne's shoulder into the oval mirror. Evadne had recognised this as truth, not flattery. Most women preferred their brims wide and flat, as if they wanted to overshadow their imperfections; but with her fine bones and flawless skin, she had no qualms about revealing her face to the world.

Better yet, the edge of the brim was trimmed with tiny silk flowers in a lilac that complemented the damson of her coat. The milliner produced a length of wide ribbon in the same lilac and suggested a bow.

Evadne was horrified. 'I don't want to look as if I'm wearing a chocolate box.'

For answer, the milliner snipped off a length, performed a few deft movements with her fingers and created a large, crisp bow that she held against the hat, trying it in a few positions before bringing it to rest to one side of the front. To her own amazement, Evadne was won over.

'A touch of flair,' observed the milliner. 'I can have it attached in such a way that madam's maid can remove it when it is time for a fresh look.'

So here she was now in her heavenly coat and hat, looking forward to a highly enjoyable experience, thanks to Alex.

He had appeared at her office door one evening while she was clattering away on the typewriter.

'Those pieces you purchased,' he remarked. 'How would you feel about seeing them through the auction process?'

'Well, I will, won't I? I'll be there to see to the administration.'

'I'm not talking about Armstrong's. You won't learn anything tied to a desk. I'm thinking of sending you to Foster and Wainwright's in Chester, a long-established house. I thought if we sent your items there, you might like to go along and see what becomes of them. I've made sure the things you purchased have been stored separately here.' He hesitated. 'Stop me if I'm taking too much for granted, only you seem so interested...'

'I am.'

'Good. What I have in mind is this. I won't accompany you. They know me there and they'd realise you're a professional person and they're rather stuffed shirts about women working, even these days; but they'll make a fuss of you if they think you're a lady of means. Spin them a bit of a yarn, if you like, or remain a lady of mystery. Just don't let on you're in the business. You'll need to get in touch with them in advance to arrange to have your things entered in their auction. It so happens they're holding an auction of pieces of general interest on the same day as Armstrong's next sale. Don't worry, I'll square it with your brother-in-law. Your items will have to be sent to Chester in advance. Would you mind seeing to that? Then, on the day, you can travel to Chester – first class, of course. Naturally, all your expenses will be covered in advance.' Again he hesitated. 'Assuming you're willing, that is.'

Willing? Before he finished speaking, she had decided to put through a telephone call to Foster and Wainwright's rather than to write. Tempting as it was to imagine putting *Brookburn House* as her address, she knew that conversation would offer greater opportunity to convey the right idea. Spoken hints were so much more tasteful than the written lie.

When she arrived, a top-hatted, gold-braided doorman admitted her and she was approached in the foyer by a well-spoken young man, who had ushered her here into the auction room – and what a room. The floor was richly carpeted and chandeliers twinkled above furniture of such quality that she couldn't be sure whether it was for sitting on or for sale. The young man darted away and reappeared with an impeccably dressed, silver-haired gentleman, who was none other than Mr Wainwright himself.

Alex was right. They made a fuss of her in a discreet way that made her sigh softly in appreciation. Tea was served in exquisite bone china, after which Mr Wainwright offered to show her round. The room with the chandeliers and the gracious seating was the auction room, while the items for sale were displayed in rooms leading off. Completely different to Ralph's arrangement, where one room served both purposes. She smiled to herself at the thought of Ralph's pride in his precious auction room – 'room' being the operative word – not an auction house, like this.

Viewing the items on display, she felt a flutter each time she saw one of 'her' pieces.

'So unfortunate, the way many of our old families are obliged to part with their precious things these days,' Mr Wainwright remarked.

'Indeed,' she murmured.

At the end of the morning, Mr Wainwright directed her to Willett's, a small hotel round the corner.

'A most respectable establishment, where it is quite in order for a lady to enter the dining room unaccompanied. I have taken the liberty of reserving a table for you.'

After a delicious meal, made more enjoyable by the courtesy of the staff, she returned for the auction. Remembering Alex's words to Mrs Bentley, she was expecting a ten guinea or so profit on each of her pieces, but every time the hammer came down, it confirmed a far greater amount and she found herself sitting up straighter. It must be because this was Chester and there was more money here, not to mention this being Foster and Wainwright's.

Afterwards, she was ushered into an office that looked more like a sitting room and again had tea with Mr Wainwright. A quiet tap at the door heralded the arrival of a plump, balding clerk, who gave Mr Wainwright a slip of paper and then withdrew a couple of steps. Mr Wainwright glanced at the paper, then offered it to her.

'The first figure shows the total value at auction of your pieces. Underneath is our commission; and the figure at the bottom is the sum due to you.'

She had to stifle a gasp. Deducting what Alex had paid, the profit was over three hundred pounds. She had seen for herself that her pieces were performing better than she had expected, but even so.

'To whom should the cheque be payable?' asked Mr Wainwright.

'Miss E. J. Baxter,' she said and, at a nod from Mr Wainwright, the clerk left the room. A few minutes later, she was holding the cheque in her hands, feeling rather breathless at the sight of her name above such a huge sum. It had been Alex's idea to have the cheque in her name.

'Simpler,' he had said. 'We can't have them realising at the last moment that you're not what they thought, can we? Not if we want you to go again with more of your treasures.'

'You've done very well today, Miss Baxter, if I may say so,' Mr Wainwright observed. 'I trust you are pleased?'

He escorted her to the front door, bowing over her hand before she went down the steps to the taxi the doorman had summoned. All the way home, she hugged to herself the picture of Alex's delight. It was a shame she wouldn't see him until Saturday.

'Bank the cheque as soon as you can,' he had instructed. 'That way it's safe. In fact, you should open a new savings account and put it in there, just to keep your business dealings open and above board. And remember – not a word to Armstrong. We don't want to rub his nose in it, do we?'

Chapter Thirty-Five

Carrie parked Joey's pram outside Trimble's, twitching the brake with her foot. Opening the door, she breathed in the familiar smell of wooden floorboards and soap. The Trimbles were behind the counter, each serving a shawl-clad woman, while an old man waited his turn.

'Eh, look who it is,' said Mrs Trimble. 'It's been a long while since you've shown your face.'

Everyone looked and heat flooded Carrie's cheeks. It hadn't been her choice to stop shopping here, but they weren't to know that. She knew the customers and when the two women left the counter, she made a point of saying how do and asking after their families. When all three customers had gone, she turned to her old employers.

'What brings you here?' asked Mr Trimble.

She wished she had brought her shopping basket. 'I've got my little lad to show you. Shall I fetch him in?'

The Trimbles were delighted and Carrie remembered Mam saying that nothing broke the ice like a baby.

'Can I hold him?' Mrs Trimble came round the counter. 'Eh, Letty said he were a bonny lad and she were right.'

'Where is she?' asked Carrie.

'Brewing up.'

'Can I go through? Only me and her had a bit

of a falling out and I want to mek up.'

'You and Letty have fell out? Well I never! That's not summat that would have happened in th'old days.'

She pushed aside the bead curtain and found Letty pouring three mugs of tea from the same old teapot, its spout stained where it dribbled.

'Look what the cat dragged in,' said Letty. 'What brings you here?'

'I want to wish you every happiness. You're my best mate and you know I do. Billy an' all.'

She had pictured a hug at this point. She and Letty had always been great huggers. Instead, Letty stared at her thoughtfully, her lips twisted into a crinkly line.

'There's summat I've got to ask first. I've been wondering for a while and last night my mam said I had to ask. Are you sorry you married Ralph?'

Carrie felt a chill slithering through her insides, trickling into every corner.

'Oh my goodness,' Letty exclaimed, clasping a hand to the bib of her apron. 'You are, aren't you? That's why you're stood there saying nowt.'

'No! I'm shocked rigid, that's all. I'm not sorry and you can tell your mam I said so. How could you think such a thing?'

Letty shrugged. 'You're the one what claims to be surprised every time I mention summat about me and Billy, and why would it bother you if you was happy with what you've got?'

The chill turned to ice. 'Is it just your mam you've talked to about this? Oh no,' Carrie groaned, 'please tell me you've not talked to Billy.'

'And why shouldn't I?' Letty demanded, but

she looked guilty. 'He's my intended. There's no secrets between us. Yes, since you ask, he were there when me and Mam were talking and, if you really want to know, it were his idea to ask you. He said it would clear the air. He doesn't want us falling out over him.'

What a louse, getting Letty to do his dirty work. Was he hoping she would confess to making the worst mistake of her life, so he could come skulking round again with his seedy suggestion, no doubt whilst keeping Letty dangling on a string in case it got him nowhere?

'Oh, Letty.' Carrie thought her heart would break for her friend. Was this the moment to speak of Billy's duplicity? But she had too much to lose. Much as she loved Letty, her first and greatest duty was to Joey. 'Let's get this straight once and for all. I count myself unbelievably lucky. Just when I thought my world had ended, Ralph came along. He fell in love with me and I returned his feelings. You have to believe that.'

Hopelessness washed through her. She must make Letty believe this lie ... and then she would stand by and permit Letty to marry her own lie.

Letty heaved a deep breath. There were tears in her eyes. 'Eh, I'm that sorry, love, but I had to ask. You can see that, can't you?'

'Aye,' she said, but she couldn't, not really. But if it convinced Billy she was unattainable and made him concentrate on being a good husband to Letty, then it would be worth it. 'So – am I forgiven for being shocked yesterday?' She rolled her eyes, poking fun at herself. 'Do you believe me when I wish you everything you wish yourself?'

'Of course, love. Come here.' Letty held out her arms, but, as Carrie walked into them, Letty danced back a fraction. 'Careful, I'm a bit floury. Don't want to mek a mess of your coat.'

They stepped back from one another, clasping fingers.

'I feel better now,' sighed Carrie.

'Better enough to agree to be my bridesmaid? We always promised to be each other's bridesmaids, only I remember someone what sneaked off to the registry office last year. But you'll be my bridesmaid, won't you? Matron of honour, I should say.'

'I need to ask Ralph.'

'What for? You don't need permission to be a bridesmaid. Oh, I get it. It's because of him not liking me, in't it?'

'He's never stopped me seeing you.'

'I notice you don't bother denying what he thinks of me.'

'Oh, Letty. What are you trying to make me say?'

'Some loyalty would be nice. How long have me and you been mates? Billy has far more reason not to like us being close, but he doesn't mind. Ralph has no reason at all – apart from thinking I'm not good enough.'

Carrie was heartily sick of swallowing Letty's barbs while being forced to keep her mouth clamped shut against spilling out what Billy had done. For one heated moment, she thought: Why not? She deserves it. Then the heat dissipated. Letty didn't deserve any of it, not Billy's disloyalty, nor Ralph's scorn.

'Ralph has never said owt to me about you not

being good enough.' Not out loud. He had never needed to.

'Right, then,' said Letty with a look in her eye that Carrie knew of old. 'Prove it. It weren't just being bridesmaids that we promised each other, if you recall.'

'What?' Ralph's voice was loaded with contempt. 'I hope for your sake this isn't a serious request.'

Carrie's heart sank, but she sat up straight in the armchair by the fireside. She kept her voice clear and confident.

'I told you. We promised one another–'

'I'm not obliged to stand by your ridiculous childhood promises, Carrie. When will you get it into your thick skull? You don't live in Wilton Lane any more. Any other female would be grateful to leave all that behind, but not Carrie Armstrong. It doesn't matter how much I've given you, how much better your life is, how good a start in life your son has, you can't part company with Wilton Lane.'

'Letty's my best friend.'

'And I've let you continue the association and look where it's got me. Backstreet Letty – godmother to an Armstrong? Over my dead body.'

'Don't call her that.'

Ralph's eyebrows climbed up his forehead. 'I beg your pardon?'

Carrie's palms went clammy; she wiped them together. 'I'm grateful for everything you've done for me, but that doesn't mean I've forgotten where I came from.'

'You'll forget it if I tell you to. What else have

you two been plotting behind my back?'

'Nowt – honest to God. And we didn't plot this. It dates back years to when we was young lasses sat on a doorstep, dreaming about our futures.'

'We was sat?' Ralph repeated contemptuously. 'We was sat? What sort of English is that? The Wilton Lane variety, and I have to tell you, I'm tired of it.'

'But you've never minded.'

'I mind now. I have a flourishing business and excellent prospects. I have a position to maintain and your slovenly English shows me in a poor light.'

'Oh, Ralph. It's only a way of speaking. But I do know how to speak proper–'

'Properly.'

'Properly. I'll remember in future. I don't want to let you down.' In the bedroom, Joey began to cry and she started to rise.

'Not yet,' Ralph ordered.

'He's crying.'

'And we're talking. I think your husband comes first, don't you? I want to know what else you and Letty have been planning.'

'Nowt – nothing. Ralph, he's hungry. It's past his feeding time.'

Ralph got up from his armchair. He stepped across and leant forward, one hand on each arm of her chair, trapping her. He bent right over, forcing her to shrink into the back of the chair. Dislodged, the antimacassar flopped against her hair.

'Tell me.' His voice was quiet, almost tender, but his eyes were cold and insistent. His breath settled on her face, warming it and bringing a trace of the

311

mulligatawny that had seen off the end of Sunday's mutton. 'I can see it in your face, so tell me.'

She fought a desperate urge to wriggle. 'Letty's asked me to be her bridesmaid – her matron of honour.'

Ralph swung upright. 'And you didn't tell me before because...? Come on, Carrie, don't gawp. That's part of your Wilton Lane vocabulary, isn't it – gawp? I know about women and weddings. You should have been babbling about it even before you brought my slippers. Hasn't she done well for herself? Is that it? It's one thing for you to be friends with an unmarried girl from Wilton Lane; I can just about tolerate that. But if her husband isn't up to snuff, that's the end of it.'

Carrie's heart gave a dull thump. 'It's Billy Shipton.'

'Billy Shipton?'

'The one I–'

Ralph crashed his fist down onto the chenille-covered table so hard that water slopped over the top of the vase of daffodils in the middle. 'I know who Billy Shipton is, thank you!' All at once he was leaning over her again, speaking right into her face, making her blink. 'How long have they been engaged?'

She was too alarmed and confused to remember and didn't know whether she could have told the truth anyroad. 'Not long.'

'How long is not long? And you didn't see fit to mention it? Dear God.' He flung himself away from her, scrubbing his face with his hands. 'To think I've been agonising over–' He swung round to face her. 'And all along Billy flaming Shipton

312

has been hovering in the background.'

'It wasn't like that. You mek it sound like–' And she had to stop because hadn't Billy done his best to turn it into precisely what Ralph was making it sound like? 'He's Letty's fiancé now. Him and me – that's long over. You know that.'

'You still kept it secret, though, didn't you?'

'I didn't know how to tell you. I knew you wouldn't like it. I don't like it either. I don't want my best friend marrying my old fiancé. It's an odd thing to happen.'

'It can be as odd as it likes from now on, because that's an end to it between you and Letty.'

'Oh, Ralph, me and Letty have been friends all us lives.'

'*Letty and I,*' he corrected remorselessly, 'and *all our lives.*' He sighed darkly. 'I'm not having my wife hobnobbing with some female whose husband isn't fit to associate with me.'

'Billy's a town hall clerk.'

He clicked his tongue. 'He could be the Lord Mayor of Manchester for all I care. I'm not having you being friends with the wife of your old fancy man. Do I make myself clear?'

Not to see Letty again? Not to be friends? It was unthinkable. Yet what had she expected, once Ralph knew about Letty and Billy? She hadn't let herself think about it. Coward.

A louder cry with a distinct element of surprise – Joey wasn't accustomed to being kept waiting, and that was something else that was her fault – made Carrie glance round, every nerve end jumpy with the need to tend her baby.

'Oh no, you don't,' said Ralph. 'I think you

313

need reminding of your duty.'

He reached out for her and when she uttered a protest, cuffed both her wrists inside one strong hand, and proceeded to flick her buttons open. Her heart sank. She made an attempt to wriggle free, but he held her fast. She didn't want this, not this way, not on the floor, with the baby bawling in the background, not – not with this man. Bile rose in her throat. Not with this man.

She had accepted his advances and his love-making all these months because he was her husband and she was grateful and he was entitled. And he was still her husband and he was still entitled – but her ability to accept had crumbled to dust. She loved Adam and nothing was going to change that. She couldn't bear the thought of Ralph shoving his way into her, his relentless thrustings leaving her sore and burning.

She tried to pull back. 'Please, Ralph, no–'

'No?' His eyes gleamed. 'Are you saying no to me, Carrie Armstrong?'

She swallowed. That was the one thing she must never say. He must never know she had tricked him into marriage, never know Joey wasn't his. He must never know she loved someone else. And he must never know that man's identity.

'Are you saying no to me?'

His voice was low and rough and Carrie had the oddest feeling that he wanted to be provoked. She willed all her senses into a state of dullness and prayed for the strength to keep the tears from gushing from her eyes, as, with no pretence of pleasuring her, he proceeded to take what he was entitled to.

Chapter Thirty-Six

Evadne accompanied Alex to town, where he had reserved a table in the elegant dining room at the Midland Hotel. She held herself proudly, feeling trim and fashionable, aware of what a handsome couple they made. Over drinks, she regaled him with the tale of her visit to Chester. When she expressed surprise at how well their items had performed, he dismissed it.

'That's Foster and Wainwright's for you. We'd never have made those prices at Armstrong's.'

She reached for her handbag. 'I must write you a cheque.'

'Wait.'

When she looked at him in surprise, he gave a little shrug and looked – goodness, she would never have expected it – vulnerable. Her heart skittered.

'Use some of the money to treat yourself – please don't be offended. You've given a lot of time to the business, far beyond what Armstrong pays you to do, and it's only fair that you be rewarded. You've become an unofficial partner, as it were, and the last thing I want to do is take advantage of your good nature. Besides...' He looked at her, as if assessing whether to continue; she felt a frisson of anticipation. 'May I speak plainly? You're a lady of quality and I know your current circumstances are unfortunate. I hold the major entirely to blame. My dear Miss Baxter – Evadne – I would take it as a compliment if you'd use some of the funds from Foster and Wainwright's for your own purposes. You're a beautiful woman and you deserve the best. I wouldn't want you to feel yourself at a disadvantage if you were to be introduced to – that is to say, my mother will be passing through on her way to the Lakes...'

His tact and understanding, combined with the uncharacteristic stumbling, not to mention the forthcoming introduction, were all it took to sweep aside her reluctance. Here was the real reason why he had wanted her to go to Chester – so that she would end up with a substantial sum in her bank account so she could kit herself out for maternal inspection. It was all she could do not to weep for joy.

It was Monday before Ralph let Carrie out alone. After the business about Letty on Thursday evening, he had informed her at the breakfast table on Friday that she wouldn't be leaving the flat again until he said so.

She wasn't sure she had heard properly. 'What do you mean?'

'Precisely what I say. The woman can do the shopping.'

The woman – that was how he referred to Mrs Porter. And Letty was Backstreet Letty. His rudeness, his callousness about those further down the pecking order, especially women, took her breath away. Was this what Joey would learn to do?

She hadn't been allowed to attend Mass yesterday.

'But I have to or it's a sin.'

'You go to Mass because I say you can. You're Catholic because I permit it. And if being Catholic means you answer me back, then I won't want a Catholic wife any more. Think on. I'm the one you obey, Carrie.'

To her surprise, they had gone on to have a pleasant day. Ralph had played with Joey and praised her cooking and in the afternoon they went for a walk. The days were lengthening; the air was milder and buds were shooting. Before they set off, he wedged a bag into a corner of the pram, refusing to say what it contained.

They walked to Chorlton Green. Stopping in front of the memorial flowers, he withdrew from the bag a blue vase and a bunch of daffodils.

'For your dad. It's about time he had a proper vase. Here, let me.' Crouching, he tipped a little water from other jars and vases into the blue vase. 'Where shall we put it?'

Carrie's throat was so full she could barely speak. 'Wherever there's room.'

He settled the vase and handed her the daffs. 'You put them in.'

She looked at Pa's flowers through damp lashes. 'Thank you.'

'I'm surprised you never thought of it before. I give you enough pin money.'

'I don't like to fritter it. Spending when you don't need to is swanky.'

'That's Wilton Lane talking.' For once his voice held no sneer. 'You mustn't think that way any more.'

When they arrived home, he said, 'Fetch my

slippers and put the kettle on; then why don't you spend half an hour with Mrs Jenkins?'

It was the first time he had ever suggested it and Carrie, accustomed to sliding off to see Mam virtually in secret, felt herself sag with gratitude.

Later, Ralph watched her bath the baby, then they played cards.

'You see how life can be when you're a good wife,' said Ralph.

At the breakfast table this morning, he had said, 'You may start going out again.'

He made it sound so reasonable, as if keeping her in was any old common or garden thing to do.

As she went round the shops, Carrie made plans. Sunday had shown her how good a life she and Joey could have with Ralph. If things weren't always as good as that, was she to blame? She had entered into this marriage with her eyes open. But was it sufficient just to appreciate the material things? Was she guilty of not making an effort in other respects?

She couldn't have it both ways. She couldn't be Carrie Jenkins from Wilton Lane and Mrs Ralph Armstrong. Ralph was entitled to expect her to pull her socks up when he married her. She must be a better wife. She must stop talking broad, for one thing, and stop harking back to Wilton Lane, for another. Moreover, much as it hurt, she must be gracious about losing Letty. She couldn't be friends with the wife of her old fiancé. She couldn't expect Ralph to put up with that; and much as it would hurt to lose Letty, it would be a relief to sever that link with Billy.

If she did these things, that would make her a

better wife; and then there would be more days like yesterday, and that would be good for all of them, especially Joey. He was more important than anything.

For Joey. She would do it for Joey.

As she was about to cross the road to the shop, something made her glance round, and there was Adam coming round the corner. He saw her at the same moment. Expecting to feel confused and panicky, she instead felt strangely unruffled. She felt warm and safe and thrilled. Her body, dry and dead to her husband's touch, flooded with need. She longed to reach out her arms to him and feel his arms wrap round her.

She wanted him to be Joey's father.

What was she thinking? Moments ago she had vowed to be a better wife. Now, with one look at Adam, all that was forgotten. But this was a basic truth of her life. It wasn't simply that she had fallen in love. She had provided her son with the wrong father. What sort of childhood would Joey have, growing up under the glare of Ralph's uncertain temper? Adam would make a wonderful father, loving, attentive and trustworthy. If her child could grow up to be like him, she'd be more than happy. What sort of son would Ralph raise?

'Morning, Carrie.'

Adam tipped his hat to her. A simple gesture: she could have been anyone. But she wasn't anyone. His face was a polite mask, but there was no disguising the emotion and vulnerability in his eyes. Her throat went dry; she gave him a nod. Could he see in her what was so obvious to her in him?

'How is Mrs Jenkins?'

'No change, but Doctor Todd is pleased her muscles aren't wasting away.'

'That's thanks to you and your hard work.'

It was too much. She didn't want his praise – well, she did, but she wanted so much more. She glanced away.

Adam took the hint or perhaps he felt the same. 'I won't keep you.'

Touching his hat to her, he walked on. She knew she mustn't watch him go, but she couldnt help herself; then she saw Ralph standing at the shop window.

As she crossed the road, the door was flung open.

'What did he want?'

'Nowt – nothing.'

'Come on, Carrie. He spoke to you. I saw him.'

'He asked after Mam.'

'And?'

'Nothing else.'

'When I say my brother isn't welcome under my roof, that means you don't have anything to do with him elsewhere, either. You'd know that if you weren't so stupid. Get inside.'

Evadne had worked out precisely when to 'discover' the papers that she had, with remarkable sleight of hand, removed from Doctor Armstrong's notes before he and Doctor Todd set off for the conference in town. She disappeared upstairs to change from the smart skirt and blouse she wore for the office into her caramel wool, concealing the dress beneath her damson coat;

then she hastened downstairs, waving the important papers and calling over her shoulder where she was going.

Half an hour later, having delivered the papers, she headed purposefully for the shops, her heart singing. How wonderful it felt to have money to spend. She wished she knew the sort of occasion at which she would meet Alex's mother. Did she require a new day dress for a smart luncheon or something beaded for evening? An evening dress would call for an evening coat or wrap – and matching shoes and long gloves – and an evening bag. All that would set her back a pretty penny. She could invest in that and rely on her caramel and damson to see her through a daytime meeting.

But – there was no getting away from it – the caramel and damson, individually so lovely, together made the most frightful clash. She had known it before she splashed out on the coat, but it hadn't stopped her. The coat had been irresistible.

To be sure of appearing at her best for Alex's mother, what she really needed was a new dress to complement her coat, something in cream or lilac, worn with a cameo brooch she could pass off as her grandmother's – since Grandfather had never handed over Grandmother's jewellery – and matching gloves in kid, and a handbag, perhaps in cream silk with lilac embroidery, or vice versa.

Which, though? An evening ensemble or something divine for day? Alex had given no indication and it would have felt crass to ask. The fact was – she gave a sharp little gasp of bliss – she ought to have both. It was the only way to be sure.

After that, it wasn't such a large step to thinking that her caramel dress deserved a toning jacket to do it justice. Something hip-length, with wide turned-back cuffs and decorative top-stitching ... and would it be impossibly extravagant to indulge in matching accessories? No point leaving the job half-done.

This was her life the way it should be lived.

Carrie peeled the potatoes and carrots, leaving them in water, and checked the meat. Then she fed Joey, delighted by his insistent tugging at her breast. Everything he needed, he got from her. The knowledge rendered her weak with love – weak and strong at the same time. With a final snuffle, he finished. She adjusted her clothing and laid him against her shoulder, making gentle circles on his back until he emitted a little chirrup of a belch that made his tummy twitch against her.

'Good boy,' she cooed. 'What a little lamb.'

She ought to put him down. She would spoil him summat rotten if she didn't. She could hear the admonishment in her head, as if spoken by Mam, but, oh, he was so warm and cuddly and she loved the smell of him, the soap and milk and powder that invaded her senses and made him hers.

She settled back in the armchair, feeling the bobbly French knots in the embroidery on the antimacassar against the back of her head, and snuggled Joey to her chest, her favourite way for him to sleep. Her eyelids began to droop. She made a token effort to pull herself back from the brink, then gave in. The topside didn't need any help from her to finish braising. With a happy sigh that made Joey's body rise and fall with her chest, she dozed off.

She woke, lifting a hand to secure Joey in place, her heart anticipating his murmur of response. Gently, she pushed one finger into his tiny palm for his hand to wrap around in slumber.

Nothing happened.

The beat of her heart turned to water. With the fingers of one hand splayed across Joey's back to hold him in position, she sat up, her other hand supporting his head. She lifted him from her chest and settled him on her lap. There was no movement, no flutter, no gurgle, just the tiniest sensation of – flopping.

Shock walloped her. It hummed through her bones. She couldn't move, couldn't think, didn't want to think. Then she was on her feet, Joey in her arms, and she was running along the landing and down to the shop, her throat swollen with words she couldn't possibly say.

She burst in upon a scene so ordinary it beggared belief. There was the furniture, same as always, the tables and cupboards and chairs, a circular table, its top deep enough to house shallow drawers, a dainty dressing table borne on slender legs that put you in mind of a wobbly newborn fawn. Winter light, grey with a sharp edge of dazzle, filled the windows, striking the hanging lustres on a cut-glass candlestick.

Ralph swung round, surprise and displeasure in his face, brows drawn close; then his face changed, muscles reworking into sharp concern.

He came towards her, curving his way around a marble-topped washstand, a display of blue-and-gold china, a dining table of honey-coloured wood, its legs twisted like barley sugar. How restful it would be to dust those legs, to wipe the cloth round and round, round and round.

Ralph was moving quickly and agonisingly slowly at the same time. Carrie had the sensation of being underwater. Sounds were hollow and misshapen. The air swelled around her. Her mouth went rubbery. She could feel it working, or trying to, but she couldn't follow her own babbling.

Ralph seized Joey. Her hands snaked after her baby, scrabbling against empty air. She was cold all over – freezing cold and clammy. A distant buzzing built inside her head. Her knees buckled–

Chapter Thirty-Seven

Carrie opened her eyes. She was stretched out on the bed. The candlewick bedspread was smooth-tufty-smooth-tufty beneath her fingertips. With a gasp, she sat up and would have scrambled off the bed, but firm hands stopped her – Ralph.

'Where's Joey?' she cried.

'He's not here.'

Shock lurched in her stomach.

'You've taken him, haven't you? You always take him ... when I ... when I – but I haven't done anything. Where is he? I want him.'

She dived off the bed and went streaming along the landing, throwing doors open. Joey needed her. Something was wrong. He was ill. He needed her. He needed his mummy. She was the one who loved him more than anyone else in the whole wide world and Ralph had no right – he had no *right*–

A hand clamped round her arm and swung her about-face. Ralph. Always Ralph. What sort of father separated a baby from his mother?

'The undertaker has him.'

Cold and sickness swooped through her. Her fingers carved through her hair.

The undertaker, the undertaker. She knew what it meant, but it couldn't mean that, because that would mean ... and it couldn't mean that. It was impossible. There was some terrible mistake.

She steadied. A mistake. That was it, a mistake. She could cope with that. Joey was all right. She could cope with a mistake.

But Ralph's face – Ralph's face, white and fixed, eyes so dark. No mistake, no mistake.

He had taken Joey away, he must have. He had removed Joey before, taken her baby from her. It was what he did. He was a bully. She had married a bully. A bully who took her baby from her when he thought she deserved it, but she didn't deserve it; she never deserved it. No mother deserved it.

And this, today, now, this was the next step. Not just taking Joey from her and plonking him with Mrs Porter, but putting him somewhere where she didn't know where he was, hiding him away, and telling her – saying–

'Listen to me, Carrie. Joey's not here. The

undertaker has taken him. He's gone to the Chapel of Rest.'

Jesus, Mary and Joseph, they thought he was dead. They were going to bury her baby, her precious baby boy. They were going to bury him alive – because he was alive, he definitely was alive, he couldn't not be, and she had to stop them. She had to get him back.

Deliberately she relaxed, letting her gaze fall away. She felt cunning and shrewd. The moment Ralph's grip loosened, she tore free and dashed pell-mell down the stairs to their front door. She spilt out onto the pavement, spinning round to look in all directions. The world swooped around her, buildings, road, the sky an astonishing blue. No one could die on a day like today, under a sky that blue.

'Come back, Carrie. He's gone.'

With hands that brooked no argument, Ralph propelled her indoors and up the stairs. She resisted, but he was adamant. She knew what was up there. The flat, the place where they lived, well-appointed and comfortably furnished, smartly furnished. Ralph and his father had seen to that. But not their home, not her home, not now, not any more, never again. How could it be a home without ... without–

With Ralph's hand on the small of her back, she popped out of the enclosed staircase onto the landing, where there were doors to rooms, rooms where she lived, rooms she couldn't enter ever again, because how could she, how could she, when they were so hideously and permanently empty?

My fault, my fault.

My fault, my fault.

Joey had been sleeping on her chest, his body snuggled trustingly on hers. The one place where he should have been safe – the one person who should have done anything to protect him.

And she hadn't even woken up.

My fault, my fault.

Had he wriggled? Suffered? Felt any pain? Did he – oh, God in heaven – did he cry out, a cry cut short, a cry unheard by her, his mother, his so-called protector? For all she knew, she had been snoring like a pig. She had let him down, her beautiful baby boy, she had let him down. All she had needed to do was be awake. Nothing more. Just be awake.

My fault, my fault.

'It should have been your mother,' said Ralph. 'It should have been her, not Joey. I'll send her to hospital. You don't want to be looking after her at a time like this.'

She stared at him, struggling to focus. 'No, don't,' she managed at last, forcing out the words through the fog in her head. Her mouth was rubbery, as if it was unused to speaking. Her mind was crammed with words, with blame, with remorse, but it was hard to speak. As if losing Joey wasn't bad enough, now she had to protect Mam as well. She wanted to scream at Ralph, scream at him for being so bloody stupid, so bloody wrong, but what was the point? It wouldn't bring Joey back.

My fault, my fault.

She sat. She stood. She walked round the flat, unable to settle. She sat again. She couldn't think. She was thinking all the time. My fault, my fault.

Dimly, she heard voices. Letty charged in, white-faced, then Mrs Hardacre and their Joanie.

'Oh, Carrie, we've just heard,' Letty cried. 'You poor love. Your poor little boy.'

'Carrie, I'm that sorry,' Mrs Hardacre said. She looked like she might try to take her in her arms, but Carrie didn't move, couldn't, and Mrs Hardacre drew back. 'I felt sick when I were told.'

'Ralph said you were doing the dinner,' Letty said, 'and when you looked in on Joey...'

Tears poured down Letty's face; her mother clutched Letty's hands and kissed her knuckles. Joanie was weeping too. The three of them perched on the sofa, huddled together. Carrie imagined going over to them, kneeling on the floor in front of them, their arms drawing her close, making her part of their knot. All she had to do was get up and move. Go on. Do it. Get up and move. Shift yourself.

She stayed put.

My fault, my fault.

'Sweetheart, you should cry,' Mrs Hardacre said. 'Let it out.'

They thought she should be weeping. She thought so too. She didn't know why she wasn't. It wasn't that she didn't need to. Her throat was clogged with gigantic unspent sobs. It felt like a wodge of food had got stuck in her gullet. She struck her chest to make the sensation go down, but it didn't budge.

'Did it help, seeing Letty?' Ralph asked later.

Stupid question. As if anything would help. 'I needn't have let her come, let alone bring those other females trailing after her.'

Those other females. Couldn't he set his scorn aside for one moment? But so what if he didn't? What did it matter?

My fault, my fault.

Ralph organised the funeral without telling her. 'You're in no fit state,' he said when she realised. She slumped. After the enormity of letting her beloved baby die, helping to organise a funeral was such a piffling thing. She ought to have done it. Yet, if she had, wouldn't her involvement have sullied it – the neglectful mother making a show of her grief?

The ceremony was held at St Clement's. Jesus, Mary and Joseph, he was having a Protestant burial. Was that her fault too, for not paying attention when arrangements were made? Ralph carried the coffin himself. A tiny white box in those strong hands. Ralph was a big man. A blokey bloke, Pa would have said. It was a good thing she didn't love him or the sight would have shredded her heart. Joey was laid to rest with the grandfather after whom he had been named. Funny how that was meant to bring comfort, putting the dead from the same family into the same hole in the ground. Except that Joey and Joseph Armstrong weren't the same family.

Adam was at the funeral. Carrie barely spared him a glance. She turned away, rejecting him, rejecting the feeling she had wasted on him when she should have been concentrating on the child who depended on her for everything.

Evadne was there too. Carrie had received a letter from her, short and awkward but oddly poignant.

I am sorry I didn't spend more time with you and Joey. I never held him and I wish I had.

Carrie had never known she wanted to. She glimpsed a cord of loss and anguish that tied her to her sister, then she shut her eyes to it. She couldn't face anyone else's grief. On top of her own, it was too much to bear. It would crush her.

Evadne squeezed her hand, or tried to. Carrie pulled away. Adam had written a letter too, but she couldn't bring herself to read it.

The day after the funeral, she wandered round the flat. She felt stunned. It was over. Joey was gone. What was she supposed to do? Joey had died and he had gone. She had died too, but she was still here.

The door opened. Mrs Porter shuffled awkwardly, then Father Kelly walked in, black rosary beads dangling from his fingers, *click-click-click*. He wasn't going to pray, was he? Joey's little knitted jumper, white with a blue line around the neck and cuffs, was her rosary now. She clung to it, folding it, stroking it, spreading it out on her lap and smoothing it, pressing it to her face and breathing it in, breathing in Joey, baby and milk and powder, Joey's smell, for as long as it lasted. How long would it last?

'A Protestant burial, is it? What were you thinking, Carrie Jenkins-as-was? A Protestant burial

330

on top of not being baptised.'

Pain swelled in her chest. Her little lad hadn't even lived long enough to be baptised.

'A decent Catholic burial, and at least you'd have had the comfort of knowing your babby was in limbo.'

'How cruel, leaving unbaptised babies in limbo. How can God want to do that to innocent babies? Punish me by all means, but don't punish my baby.'

'God moves in mysterious ways.'

'God can take a running jump.'

It hurt to lie in the bath. Her backbone was knobbly, sticking out because so much flesh had dropped off her.

'You must eat,' said Doctor Todd, but she was eating; Ralph wouldn't let her leave the table until she had emptied her plate. Yet the plumpness she had carried following Joey's birth had vanished, and more flesh besides. She was thin as a stick and her clothes hung off her.

Ralph dragged her into the bedroom and stood her in front of the mirror.

'Look at yourself. You have to take better care.'

The anguished gash where her mouth used to be, the despair in her eyes. She wasn't complete any more. Joey had made her complete when she hadn't even known she lacked anything. He had filled her life and her heart to the point where it had been impossible to imagine her life, her very self, without him.

Here she was – without him.

Except at night. In her dreams, Joey was fine and

bonny and they were together. In her dreams, his little toes scrunched up when she touched them and she could feel her face shining with love. She would wake and curl herself into a tight ball, her eyes dry and sore and unbelieving, as she clutched his jumper between desperate fingers. She kept it under her pillow at night and drew it out while Ralph slept, squeezing and smoothing and inhaling, trying to absorb it into herself.

Then one day, in the middle of peeling the potatoes, she started to cry. She nicked her thumb with the peeler and drew blood. It was nothing, certainly not enough to cause tears, and yet here she was, tears streaming out. She was appalled to find herself howling over this when she hadn't shed a tear for Joey; then she realised that she wasn't crying over a cut thumb; she was crying for Joey, she really was crying for Joey. A great shudder knocked her knees from under her and she sank to the floor. The sobs that had been locked inside gave a great lurch and began to heave themselves with agonising slowness, one by one, out of her throat, like Mrs Clancy's cat bringing up a furball. Her torso convulsed and her ribs ached. She was drowning.

Arms slipped around her, thin and strong. 'There now,' came Mrs Porter's voice. 'There now.' She made big circles on Carrie's back with the flat of her hand, pressing her withered cheek into Carrie's hair.

When Carrie was exhausted, Mrs Porter drew back, a slow movement that allowed Carrie time to gather her balance and sit up. She brushed a hand across her swollen face and blinked, trying to ease the soreness around her eyes. She fished for her handkerchief, only to have it twitched from her fingers by Mrs Porter, who got up stiffly, dampened it and plumped herself down again, her lined features concerned as she gently dabbed at Carrie's tender flesh.

'The trick is to keep busy. Otherwise you'll fetch up barmy. Too much thinking time never helped no one.'

Fear grasped Carrie's heart. 'Have you...?'

'Aye, chuck. Three, all told.'

She could feel herself about to collapse beneath this fresh horror, then something inside her threw up a wall, protecting her from this other person's pain.

'I would say to get thee a job, only himself would throw forty fits. But that's how I managed.'

Carrie sat silently while Mrs Porter rattled on about, not her lost children, but the jobs she had held down.

At last she said, 'Best get up now, eh? Himself will go spare if he comes in and catches us sat on't kitchen floor.'

Carrie thought about Mrs Porter's words. Keep busy. It made sense. Wasn't that how she had come to terms with her marriage in the early days? Just get on with it. And it had worked. But how could she compare this situation to that one? She had had everything to look forward to in those days, but now she must keep herself busy and occupied as never before. Like Mrs Porter said, it was that or go barmy.

'I need something to do,' she told Ralph. 'A job, a proper job. Looking after the flat and doing the shopping and cooking isn't enough. I've got to keep busy. Mam's arms and legs will drop off if I do any more exercises on her. And don't say there's the dusting in the shop, because that's not enough.'

'I'm not having my wife working.'

'Then you'll have your wife going mad.'

Ralph raised an eyebrow. 'Are you answering back?'

'Oh, Ralph. I need summat to do. Please. I'm trying so hard, but I need more. I know I can't get a job outside the home, because that would reflect on you. The only other thing I can think of is ... well, I know about Mam's exercises, so perhaps I could be useful at Brookburn. Even if they didn't want me for that, I could ... well, I wouldn't mind what I did.'

'No!' He huffed an exasperated breath. 'You could do the auction work. It would keep you respectably occupied and it wouldn't interfere with your domestic duties.'

'You mean Evadne's job?'

'Why not? She's off gadding with Larter half the time; and she annoys the hell out of me when she is there. Besides, it will keep you close to me. I like the thought of that.'

So, with a strong sense of unreality, she found herself installed in the office over the road, learning the ins and outs of the auction process.

Evadne took the change surprisingly well.

'It's served its purpose,' she said cryptically. 'Here's my set of keys. I'll just keep this one.' She slipped it from the ring. 'It's to that cupboard in the corner. You needn't worry about what's in there. I'll sort it out.'

Carrie pored over auction lists and struggled with the typewriter, spent ages adding up lists of figures on paper that Ralph would then glance at and work out in his head. He was a ruthless boss, making her do her work again and again until she got it right, but she didn't care. It filled the time, even if it didn't fill her mind the way she had hoped. But nothing could do that.

Her first auction day was approaching. She ought to feel nervous, but she didn't have any feelings left except those concerned with Joey. It was Doctor Todd's day for visiting Mam, but Adam came.

'Todd's away. Family illness. How's Mrs Jenkins getting on?'

She remembered loving him. Was Joey's death her punishment? Adam's presence was just another bloody thing to cope with. Ralph would be livid when he heard and she would have to appease him.

Adam went through the usual rigmarole, then asked softly, 'And you, Carrie, how are you?'

'What are you doing here?' Ralph bullied his way into the room. 'I told you to keep away. Get out,' he ordered, cutting across Adam's explanation.

'And you,' Ralph added, jabbing a finger at Carrie, 'you let him in. You – let – him – in.'

'Don't take it out on Carrie,' said Adam.

'Don't tell me how to treat my wife. Get out!'

With a final glance, Adam left the bedroom. Ralph kicked the door shut after him.

'I'm sorry,' Carrie whispered.

Ralph glared at her, then wrenched open the

335

door and marched out, leaving her to sink onto the bed. She caught Mam's hand and held it to her cheek, her eyes filling.

'I'm sorry, Mam.' Her body rocked to and fro of its own accord. 'I'm so sorry.'

She thought Ralph might keep her at home instead of letting her attend the auction, but he didn't. Afterwards, he told her she had acquitted herself well enough.

The following day, as she came downstairs with her shopping basket, the second post was sitting on the mat. She picked up the letters and popped into the shop. Ralph liked to have his mail immediately.

'Here,' he said, sifting through the envelopes. 'This one's for you. What are you doing receiving letters?'

She looked in surprise at the typewritten envelope. She tore it open. Inside was a single sheet, folded in half. She unfolded it and her heart gave an almighty lurch that cut off her breathing. On the paper were two words, each cut from a newspaper headline. She wanted to utter a great cry of shock and protest, but all that happened was that the paper fluttered from her fingers and twirled slowly to the floor. Even then, it didn't land face down but lay with the words upwards:

BABY KILLER

She broke out in a sweat. Dizziness swooshed through her and she was aware of Ralph springing forward to catch her.

Chapter Thirty-Eight

November 1921

Carrie looked in the mirror. It wasn't like looking at herself. Locked somewhere inside she had a picture of another Carrie, plump following pregnancy, breasts full and aching to be suckled, eyes bright with love and pride, hair a bit of a mess because Joey had cried the moment she started brushing it. That was the real Carrie. This person gazing solemnly at her was someone else, a stranger who had stepped into her life and taken it over.

The girl in the mirror was thin. Her face was narrow, the cheekbones sharply defined beneath huge blue eyes that held an expression of reserve, which suggested she had a story to tell – or to keep to herself. A crisp bob framed features that looked both vulnerable and impassive. She was well dressed in a way Carrie, the old Carrie, had never been, Ralph's generosity notwithstanding. Well, it had been difficult to do justice to smart clobber when you were as big as a tram and your swollen feet, squeezed into shiny new shoes, were desperate for the roomy comfort of a pair of clogs.

The mirror-girl's appearance was distinctly tailored. Her costume had a high Cossack neck and buttoned cuffs. A line of buttons added a severely stylish trim down the front of the narrow skirt, which fell to mid calf, a good three inches shorter than anything the old Carrie had ever worn, and her Wilton-Lane-bred heart found it flighty but didn't care.

These were her auction clothes. Deep down Carrie was aware she would rather be at Brookburn, doing whatever they asked of her, however menial; but that was what the old Carrie would have wanted, and she wasn't the old Carrie now so it didn't matter. The old Carrie had died along with Joey, and quite right too. What sort of mother could sleep peacefully while her baby died in her arms?

She drew in a breath, but stopped herself before she could sigh it out. Sighing wasn't allowed. Sighing smacked of self-pity. Carrie Jenkins didn't deserve pity. She didn't deserve compassion or sympathy or kindness. Carrie Jenkins was a liar. She had tricked her husband into marriage and fatherhood and then been unfaithful to him by falling in love with his brother. Carrie Jenkins had spent her whole life dreaming of being a wonderful mother. And a bloody great lie that had turned out to be.

The only thing that wasn't a lie was the poppy she wore on her lapel. They had sold paper poppies this year in memory of the hundreds of thousands of men who had died in the war. Ralph had told her about it and, seeing a poppy seller going into the Lloyds, she had marched across the road and thrust a week's housekeeping into the collecting tin in return for two poppies, one for herself and one which she pinned to Mam's pillow.

But that Sunday, when she accompanied Ralph to St Clement's, she had felt prickles of awareness. People were noticing, watching, murmuring, nudging one another, and she knew what they were saying. She hung her head. Her heart caved in, but she didn't remove her poppy.

Now she fetched her outdoor things to go to the auction room. She crossed the road. What would it be like to be hit by a motor car and die in the gutter? Entering the auction room, she experienced her usual sinking feeling. She wasn't suited to the work. Sometimes she wondered why Evadne had liked being a glorified clerk; but Evadne would have enjoyed rubbing shoulders with the well-to-do, here to purchase beautiful and costly pieces. Carrie didn't want to rub shoulders with anyone.

Soon she was ready to start. This was the part she hated. She scanned the room for buyers she recognised. They were easier to approach than strangers. Her eye fell on Mr Kemp. The success of the monthly auctions meant that Ralph had been holding fortnightly sales since May and Mr Kemp attended every time. He always took a bidding number, but Carrie had never seen him bid. Not that that meant anything. Some people bid so discreetly that it amazed her that Ralph apparently never missed one.

She had to list all the prospective buyers and issue them with numbers before viewing finished. After that, she went home, leaving everyone else to enjoy the hotel's hospitality. Ralph didn't think it appropriate for her to stay for lunch and she didn't want to. She made sure she returned in good time.

Better to wait around than slink in late.

The auction began. Ralph kept things moving at a smart pace. Halfway down the list was a desk with a drop front, or a bureau as Ralph would call it. Mr Bennett, a private gentleman who was one of their regulars, was in competition with a dealer called Hathaway. Just as Mr Bennett shook his head and dropped out, Ralph evidently detected another bidder – Mr Kemp. When, two minutes later, the bureau fell to him, Carrie was pleased he had purchased something at last.

The auction ended. She waited for permission to leave, trying to look busy while Ralph and Mr Larter worked their way round the room, shaking hands, commiserating with the unsuccessful, congratulating the buyers and discussing delivery. Carrie knew that on the other side of the door behind her, Charlie Harris and Tom Perry, who made the deliveries in the motor van Ralph was so proud of, would be hovering, crates and sacking at the ready. Arthur would be there too, ready to assist.

Presently, Ralph helped her into her coat and she left.

Letting herself in through their private front door, she started up the stairs, only to hear the smart click of the letter box behind her. Her knees turned to water. Would there be one today? That first letter had come as the most appalling shock, but it had never occurred to her that it might be followed by another. The second hadn't come until June, the gap of so many weeks lending it an impact as great as that of the first. Since then she hadn't felt safe, and the sound of the letter box was enough to turn her skin slick with fear.

BABY KILLER. That had been the first message. The second had said MOTHER KILLS CHILD, its words, like those of its predecessor, snipped from newspaper headlines and gummed to blank paper. The stark accusation had plunged her into a frenzy of sobbing that all but cracked her ribs. Then, just two days later, while shock and distress were still dragging her down, a third letter had come. The arrival of the second had taught her that a third might follow, but there had been such a long gap between the first two...

She had stared at the third envelope, its typewritten name and address taunting her. Something cold and sour had uncurled in her stomach and she knew that, whatever she did, she mustn't open it. It had trembled between her fingertips. She knew the sender was right. Had Joey twitched, stirred, whimpered? Her slumber had been untroubled. Some mother she was.

She had opened the third letter. Of course she had, despite Ralph's instructions.

'If another comes,' he said after the second letter, 'bring it straight to me.'

Trembling with determination, she had disobeyed. She didn't want Ralph to know there had been another letter. Not to protect him – well, yes, to protect him; but she wasn't shielding him from her distress. She was protecting him from this vile opinion of her, fearing that exposure to these messages might turn him against her. He was being so kind. Raw with anguish, she clung to his strength.

'You mustn't blame yourself,' he had said a hundred times; and a hundred times she had felt herself take another tottering step closer to the abyss.

She forced herself to go downstairs. Blood rushed to her head as she stooped to retrieve the letters. Three of them – and all for Ralph.

She propped herself against the wall. All for Ralph.

After fetching Ralph's slippers and comfortable jacket, Carrie dished up, then paused before starting her own meal to watch him tucking in. It was meant to give you satisfaction, wasn't it, seeing your husband enjoying what you had cooked for him?

He glanced up. 'What are you waiting for?'

She began to eat. He never let her leave so much as a smear of gravy, yet she remained as thin as a twig.

'Were you pleased with the auction? I'm glad Mr Kemp got that desk.'

'What d'you mean?'

'I mean, the bureau.' It was faintly embarrassing to use fancy words, but Ralph preferred it.

'I didn't mean that. I meant, why would you notice?'

'He's never bought anything before, at least not since I've been there.'

Had she somehow vexed him? Perhaps if he was annoyed, he might leave her alone tonight. But no. She knew that annoyance was the last thing to make him turn his back on her in bed. Quite the contrary.

Ralph was eager for another child and was hammering away at her on a regular basis while she lay crushed beneath his sweating bulk. She desperately did not want another baby – not yet. It was far too soon. She wasn't ready. Would she ever be ready?

Everyone wanted her to have another baby – everyone – even women she had never done more than pass the time of day with in the queue at the grocer's. No sooner had Joey died than they started on at her.

'Eh, love, I'm that sorry. Have another one, that's the best cure.'

Cure? She didn't want to be cured of Joey. She had stopped going shopping, sending Mrs Porter while she stayed indoors, spring-cleaning non-stop.

The women from Wilton Lane had been no better. The day she ventured back to church, they clustered round her. For the first time since her hasty marriage and social elevation, they had accepted her again. What a way to be accepted.

Then Mrs Clancy had made the fatal remark about having another and there were several echoing murmurs, and the next she knew, she was boiling with rage. She wanted to lash out and scream and shout until they understood what sheer bloody nonsense they were talking and how appallingly mistaken and cruel and thoughtless they were. But she didn't. She just stood there. When they went into church, she hung back, then trailed home. She hadn't been back since.

Ralph was pleased. He had taken to attending St Clement's every Sunday, requiring her to accompany him. She didn't care one way or the other. After the service, they would walk down the road to the old graveyard to visit Joey, and that was all that mattered. Joey's grave was her only destination these days unless Ralph took her for a walk.

She hadn't seen Letty in ages. Letty had cut herself off more effectively than Ralph could ever have achieved, by not attending Joey's funeral. Carrie couldn't forgive her. A few women from Wilton Lane had been there, Letty and her mother and their Joanie included, lurking on the other side of the wall, not daring to set foot on Protestant land, but that hadn't impressed Carrie. This was Joey's funeral, the last thing they would ever do for him, and if Letty couldn't be arsed to walk inside and pay her respects to the little boy whose godmother she had wanted to be, then Carrie couldn't be doing with her any more.

Letty and Billy were wed now. An invitation had come, but Ralph had refused it. He hadn't mentioned it until several weeks later. Carrie had known a moment of – sorrow? Regret? A twinge of conscience? But it was gone in a moment, leaving her alone in the bleak landscape of her heart.

The next auction day rolled round. Carrie listed the prospective bidders, then slipped home for a bite to eat. As usual, she was the first to return. While others filtered in, she examined some furniture. She had always enjoyed the handsome pieces Ralph sold. There was a warm glow to the wood of a cabinet, beside which the brass drawer handles gleamed on a desk that she knew from the list was called a secretaire. What the difference was between a secretaire and a bureau, she had no idea.

There were more dealers than usual today and competition was fierce. She could see Ralph relishing every moment. The secretaire generated a lot of interest. Finally, three bidders were left, then two, both of them dealers. When one dropped out, she had her pen poised to record the winner's number and the final price, only to realise a new bidder had joined in, causing a frisson of excitement to run round the room.

The new bidder was Mr Kemp – but he had bought that bureau just two weeks ago. Why buy another desk? When he outbid the dealer and the hammer fell, it took a quiet but meaningful, 'When you're ready,' from Ralph to prompt her to put pen to paper.

Towards the end of the auction, as bidding hotted up over a dinner service with twelve place settings, she noticed the doors opening at the other end of the room. Two men wearing over-coats walked in and stood looking round. Mr Larter was by the window and Carrie watched him thread his way towards them. Quiet words were exchanged, then Mr Larter ushered them out, following and closing the doors.

When the auction ended, Mr Larter returned and had a word with Ralph, who nodded and moved away. Carrie watched as Mr Larter talked to some of the customers. Not wanting him to catch her looking, she turned and saw that Ralph had let in Charlie, Tom and Arthur, who were already moving things out through the rear doors. Normally, that didn't happen until all the customers had left.

Maybe she looked startled because Ralph said,

'We need to get going. It was a bigger sale than usual.'

She was still awaiting permission to leave when she noticed the two strangers enter the room again. Mr Larter and Ralph joined them and there was a discussion, which ended with all four of them making their way the length of the room to where Charlie and Tom were about to lift a chest and Arthur was wrapping a clock in sacking.

Ralph said, 'Only a couple of pieces have been removed. The chaps can easily bring them back.'

'No need,' one of the strangers, a narrow-faced individual, replied.

'We can go through and look,' added his companion.

But Tom and Charlie had already gone, returning moments later manoeuvring a bookcase between them. They couldn't have been more efficient if they had been expecting the instruction, Carrie thought, impressed.

'Perhaps you'd like to start down the other end,' suggested Mr Larter, leading the strangers away while the other things were brought back.

'Who are they?' Carrie whispered. The strangers were eyeing up the various pieces, muttering to one another, occasionally shaking their heads.

'No one for you to worry about,' Ralph answered. 'Is that everything?' he asked Tom.

'Yes, guv. Bookcase, china cabinet, desk.'

Carrie glanced at the items as Tom named them. The cabinet was the one she had been looking at earlier and the desk was the secretaire Mr Kemp had bought, except that–

'You can go home,' Ralph said.

'Ralph,' she said, 'that desk–'

'I said, go home.'

She fetched her things. She felt a frown tugging at her brow. The desk now standing in the auction room had wooden knobs on the drawers and hadn't Mr Kemp's secretaire had brass handles? She was sure it had – well, almost sure. How could one desk have been taken out of the room and then a different one be brought back in? One thing was certain: she wasn't going to say anything, for fear of making herself look stupid.

On her way home from visiting Joey, Carrie looked through the shop window. A policeman was inside, talking to Ralph. Wondering if the bobby had information concerning Miss Deacon's tragic death, she pushed open the shop door. The bell bounced and tinkled.

'Go upstairs, Carrie,' Ralph ordered.

Times were when she would have resented being spoken to like that. Now she didn't care.

Upstairs, she couldn't settle to anything, which in itself felt odd, after all her months of resolute activity. She went to brush out Mam's hair and re-braid it, automatically reaching to pick up the brush from the top of the cupboard, only to glance round as her questing fingers found nothing but empty space. The brush was on the bedside table. Mrs Porter must have made a start on Mam's hair, though she didn't normally do things like that.

Poor Mam, her hair was thinner than it used to be and calling it salt-and-pepper was being polite. Most of it was iron grey. Carrie brushed it through, lifting her head to get at the back, then deftly plaited it. First Adam and then Doctor Todd had suggested cutting the plait off, but she wouldn't hear of it.

'I have a new magazine,' she remembered. 'I'll fetch it.'

Passing the window, she stopped. Going into the Lloyds were two uniformed policemen and two men in overcoats and hats, one of whom, yes, was the narrow-faced stranger from the auction. What was going on? She hovered at the window. At last, one of the policemen emerged and crossed the road. Carrie pressed her cheek against the pane in an effort to watch him enter the shop. Presently, he went back over the road, accompanied by Ralph.

Later, Ralph came upstairs. He looked sombre, and she hoped nothing dreadful had happened concerning his beloved auction room. 'Come and sit down,' he said. 'This is important.'

She took a seat in one of the armchairs in the sitting room. She sat forwards, ready to be sympathetic and attentive, the dutiful wife ready to offer her support.

'It's Evadne. The police are on their way to Brookburn. Your snooty sister is no better than a common thief.'

Chapter Thirty-Nine

Evadne was at her desk, tapping away on her typewriter. She had nearly finished and then she would heft the typewriter onto the table beside the wall, where it stood when not in use. She didn't like picking it up, but she preferred it to be out of the way. Without it, the desk made her look important. Typewriter meant clerk; but a handsome desk with a smart inlay of green morocco leather and a cut-crystal inkstand with compartments for blue and black, and grooves for pencils and pens, marked her out as a person of consequence.

She paused to glance over the letter in the machine, then looked down at the notes beside her to see what came next. When she had finished, she read it through before using the knob on the side to turn the cylinder and feed the letter into her waiting hand. With the tips of her fingers, she removed the carbon paper and put the letter and copy in the tray on the cabinet behind her. Then she lifted the typewriter onto its table and resumed her seat, taking some paperwork out of one of the drawers and laying it before her.

She breathed a small sigh to ease herself into the moment. She liked to – oh, it was so silly and she had to laugh at herself, but honestly, it was such a pleasure. When she had paperwork in front of her, she liked to pretend this desk graced the home of Mr and Mrs Alexander Larter; the supplies inventory was actually a seating plan for one of her famous dinner parties ('Do get yourself invited to the Larters', if you possibly can. The food is *divine.')*; the staff rota was really a guest list for an elegant supper and dance at which she was going to appear in a new black velvet evening gown of devastating simplicity from Mademoiselle Antoinette's in St Ann's Square.

There was a knock at the door. Before she could respond, Adam Armstrong appeared. He stepped inside and shut the door behind him.

'The police are here. They want to speak to you. I've put them in the common room. Would you like me to come with you?'

'Of course not.'

She smoothed her perfect appearance and went to the common room, and common was the operative word. Other parts of the house retained some of the original furnishings, but the common room contained a mishmash of sofas and armchairs, tables and shelves, for the use of the staff during their breaks from work.

There were two men, neither in uniform. One, an older man with a Bolton accent, introduced himself as Inspector Woods and his colleague simply as Drummond. Drummond was younger, narrow-faced. He stood to one side.

At Inspector Woods' request, Evadne explained about the dealings she and Alex had had with Mrs Bentley, Miss Kent and others the inspector named.

'Mrs Bentley understood that when you visited her on your own, you were buying on behalf of Armstrong's,' Inspector Woods remarked.

As she started to explain about Foster and Wainwright's, Drummond left the room. How rude! Inspector Woods kept her talking and she found herself admitting to letting Mr Wainwright and his colleagues believe she was a lady of consequence.

'So you lied.'

'A harmless deception. It wouldn't have done to let them know I'm in the business.'

Drummond returned. He slipped a folded sheet of foolscap onto the table in front of Inspector Woods and melted into the background. Woods unfolded the paper and glanced over it. His mouth pulled downwards into a thoughtful expression.

'While we've been talking, Drummond put through a telephone call to the police in Chester, and they visited Foster and Wainwright's for us. This is a list of the things Foster and Wainwright's have auctioned on your behalf.' He tapped the sheet. 'There's more here than you admitted to.'

'Admitted to? There would be things I purchased from other clients.'

'Things you neglected to mention before.'

'Had you enquired about other clients, I'd have told you.'

'I'm enquiring now. Shall we start with names and addresses, and then we'll match those up with what's on this list.' A few minutes later, he observed, 'These addresses are all in Parrs Wood, several in the same road.'

'My grandfather's neighbours.'

'Have you bought anything from your grandfather?'

'He isn't in reduced circumstances.'

'So you just pick on folk in reduced circumstances?'

'I don't pick on anyone. These people were happy to do business with Mr Larter and myself.'

'Ah yes, Mr Larter. Tell me, Miss Baxter, you said Mrs Bentley provided the introduction to Miss' – he glanced at his notes – 'Kent, and then she had a sister, and that was how you got into these houses. I hope you don't expect me to believe this chain of introductions led all the way to Parrs Wood.'

'Of course not. I provided Mr Larter with those introductions. I don't know what irregularity you imagine you've discovered, Inspector, but I'm sure Mr Larter, the Honourable Mr Larter, will support everything I've told you.'

Woods frowned over his notes. 'You say you bought a canteen of silver cutlery from the Goudge ladies, but that doesn't appear on Foster and Wainwright's list.'

'It's still at the Lloyds. I have a store cupboard there.'

'Is it locked? The key, if you please.'

And Woods and Drummond set off for the Lloyds. Evadne sat still, realising how startled she felt. What was going on? Inspector Woods hadn't given her the chance to ask any questions.

She went to the door, only to find a young constable in the corridor.

'May I ask where you're going, miss?'

'Outside. I require some fresh air. Not that it's any of your business.'

'Better stop indoors, if you don't mind.'

'I do mind.'

'Inspector Woods, miss.'

'What of him?'

'He'd rather you stopped inside.'

'Well, really!'

She went storming to her office, but when the young constable followed and stood outside, she marched back in high dudgeon to the common room, where he would be less conspicuous. She prowled the room. One shelf carried packs of cards, a draughts set and even a compendium of games – how childish! On another stood a line of books while the window seat was evidently the favoured place for stowing bags of knitting. Copies of *Woman's Weekly* and *Vera's Voice* were dotted around. She picked up one or two and flicked through the pages, but couldn't settle and soon threw them aside, every tick of the clock on the mantelpiece adding to her annoyance. She planned exactly what to say to the men for keeping her waiting like this.

Eventually, they returned.

'So, Miss Baxter,' said the inspector, before she could complain, 'you accompanied Mr Larter on visits to Mrs Bentley and others when he bought items for auction at Armstrong's. Subsequent to each visit, you made your own appointment and bought a small but valuable piece you could take away with you. The customers believed you were employed by Armstrong's. You then introduced Mr Larter to your grandfather's cash-strapped neighbours and the same thing happened. Mr Larter made purchases for Armstrong's that were later collected, after which you returned and bought small things you could carry away. You got in touch with Foster and Wainwright's, introducing yourself as a member of an old family embarrassed for the want of a bit of cash, and they auctioned your purchases for sums considerably in excess of what you'd paid.'

'That's the point of an auction,' she sniffed.

'Indeed. You then opened a savings account and deposited the profits.'

'That's what Mr Larter told me to do.'

'So you say. The fact is, Miss Baxter, you've been fleecing innocent citizens. You learnt about old things from this Weston chap you mentioned, who's now being brought in for questioning, and you used your association with Messrs Armstrong and Larter to buy things ostensibly for auction at Armstrong's.'

'That's preposterous.'

'You offered low prices for what you bought.'

'I offered what I was told to offer by Mr Larter.'

'Ye-e-s.' Woods stretched the word. 'I've heard a lot about Mr Larter recently, having called on Mrs Bentley and others. I gather he always paid in guineas – the sign of a real gent, according to more than one person. But you paid in pounds, I believe.'

'Well ... yes–'

'A small mistake, Miss Baxter, but a telling one, and not very many pounds at that. Mr Wainwright informed my colleagues in Chester that the sums raised on your items were' – he glanced down at the foolscap – "pleasing, though not excessive". But you made a huge profit, didn't you, because you paid paltry sums in the first place. But as you say, Miss Baxter, that's the point of an auction, isn't it?'

'Inspector, I don't know what this is about–'

'What it's about, Miss Baxter, is placing you under arrest.'

Carrie swung round as Ralph appeared in the sitting-room doorway. She had spent all this time telling herself there was nothing to worry about. Evadne, a thief? Utter rot.

But instead of saying, 'It was all a stupid mistake,' he said, 'She's been arrested. They've taken her to the police station on Beech Road.'

And it wasn't just what he said, it was the way he said it, that complacent quirk of the lips, that slightly raised eyebrow. Carrie clenched her fists.

The moment he went back downstairs to the shop, she threw on her things, ran down to their private front door and hurried to the police station. She had to stand by her sister. She would stake her life on Evadne's honesty.

'No visitors,' she was told by a young bobby, who looked like power had gone to his head.

'Then, please can I leave a message?'

'No visitors, no messages.'

'But it's important. Say Mrs Armstrong came – just that. I'm her sister.'

'I don't see the harm in it,' said another voice – an older policeman.

'Thank you.'

'There's nowt more you can do, so off you go.'

On her way out, she almost bumped into someone on the steps. The heavy door swung shut behind her, nudging her forward, and she lost her footing. Hands steadied her and she found herself looking into Adam's face, closer than she had ever seen it before, close enough to see the crow's feet that promised humour and kindness, the vertical lines between his eyebrows that showed dedication and careful thought, the surprise in his eyes that transformed into warmth and something deeper than warmth.

Around the two of them, Beech Road slid out of focus and they were encapsulated in their own moment. She had avoided thinking of Adam all this time, dreading in the depths of her heart that it was loving him that had distracted her from her role as a mother, leading her to neglect her baby at the vital moment. Loving him had turned her into a bad mother.

She pushed free so hard that he stepped backwards onto the pavement. She glared at him, but really she was glaring at herself for ever having loved him. How had she managed to live this long without Joey, without her precious baby boy?

'I've just heard,' said Adam. 'They told me when I finished my afternoon rounds.'

'You can't see her, if that's why you've come.'

'Isn't Ralph here?'

'He's in the shop.'

'He should shut the blasted shop. Sorry, Carrie, but he ought to be with you.'

She shut her eyes. Did he think she was stupid? Did he imagine she didn't know that?

'I'd best go.'

She had nothing to say to him. Head down, avoiding his gaze, she hurried away, thoughts careering between Evadne and Adam while, underneath, a horrified shame began to bubble.

She wasn't meant to do this. She wasn't meant to pay attention to other matters. She wasn't meant to care about other things – and yet she cared what happened to Evadne.

'Please can we go to court tomorrow?' Carrie asked. Never mind the stew and the apple fritters she had originally planned for their tea. She had shamelessly substituted them for toad-in-the-hole and baked custard, two of Ralph's favourites, intent upon buttering him up.

'It's not appropriate. An employer might be expected to turn up to see a thieving employee being dealt with, but Evadne's your sister. Our presence in court would be ambivalent, to say the least.'

So much for baked custard. 'She didn't do anything.'

He gave her a look. 'Are you defending her?'

'She's my sister.'

'Don't pretend you like her. She looks down on you.'

It was like having cold water dashed in her face. Whatever differences her and Evadne's starts in life had created, she entertained strong family feeling. You didn't have to live in your sibling's pocket to feel loyal to them. Ralph should know that, having a brother of his own. Except that he didn't know it, did he, because that instinct was missing in him.

'I know Evadne. She'd never do anything against the law.'

'The police have proof.' His eyes glittered and Carrie's insides shrivelled in anticipation of an outburst, but he merely shook his head. 'I'm disappointed in you, Carrie. You've tried hard to be a better wife – and you've succeeded. You don't talk in that common way any more; you've stopped hobnobbing with riff-raff; your appearance is smarter. At last I have a wife to be proud of – or so I thought. Look at you now, taking sides against me.' He gave a bitter laugh. 'This is how you repay me. After everything I've given you, all the comforts and advantages, this is how you repay me. Never for one moment have I held you accountable for Joey's death, and this is how you repay me. Shame on you.'

Battling to remain calm, Evadne sat on a wooden chair at a table in a small, windowless room deep in the bowels of the magistrates' court. At least it was an improvement on the grubby cell in which she had spent a sleepless night. She made a point of sitting correctly. Honest people sat up straight.

The door opened and in marched Grandfather. She came to her feet and was on the point of flinging herself into his arms when she realised they weren't open to receive her. She sank down again, belatedly noticing that another man had entered. She formed an impression of ruddy cheeks and pinstripes before Grandfather introduced him as his solicitor, Mr Denton.

'First things first,' Grandfather barked. 'When they ask your name, say Jenkins. Don't want the Baxter name dragged through the courts.'

Evadne was taken aback. She had expected something kinder, more supportive, but the Baxter name mattered deeply to him – four generations of men serving their country and all that – so maybe it was understandable.

She appealed to Mr Denton. 'You have to make the police speak to Mr Larter. They can't have done that yet, or I wouldn't be here.'

'With luck, you'll be out this morning,' Grandfather was saying in a loud voice as if he were addressing the troops. 'You're up before Hyland. Decent cove, known him for years. I'll have a word before things get going.'

But all this achieved was to make Mr Hyland withdraw from the case, leaving Evadne waiting to be referred to another magistrate, something that took most of the morning.

In court at last, she stared into every corner, desperate for the sight of Carrie. Carrie's attempt to visit her yesterday had meant the world to her, unleashing a primal need that only flesh and blood could fulfil, which was ridiculous, because Grandfather was flesh and blood and he was here. But he wasn't enough; he wasn't the right person. She wanted Carrie, her little sister, the infant she had adored when she was a child. Back then she had known what flesh and blood felt like. She had known what it was to feel connected to another person. A wave of need swept over her. She wanted her sister.

But Carrie wasn't present. Her spirits sagged but then steadied; she knew whom to blame for that.

Adam Armstrong was here, though. Her glance scraped across him without stopping. She wouldn't give him the satisfaction.

The magistrate entered. A gentleman with a lined face and a weary air, he had a long nose and appeared inclined to look down it at her, which made her stand taller. He consulted his papers and nodded to the clerk.

'Stand, please,' ordered the clerk. 'You are Evadne Josephine Baxter, currently residing at Brookburn House, Chorlton-cum-Hardy?'

'Jenkins. Evadne Jenkins.'

'Not Baxter?'

'Are you sure?' The magistrate's expression suggested a low opinion of female intelligence.

As if she wouldn't know her own name. Evadne gave him a disdainful look, but the complacency was soon knocked out of her in the ensuing confusion.

'A criminal alias, perhaps?'

She had no idea who uttered the words, but they sent panic swarming through her. Afterwards, that was the detail Grandfather seemed to consider the most important. Never mind that she had been placed on remand. Never mind that she was to spend tonight in prison. All he could go on about was how the fiasco over Baxter and Jenkins would render her far more interesting to the press than Baxter alone would have done. He glared at her as if it was her fault.

After Grandfather and Mr Denton took their leave, she perched on the wooden chair, fingers locked in her lap. A tray sat on the table. Perhaps she should make an effort. 'You must keep your strength up,' Mr Denton had advised. It was the most useful thing he had said all day. He certainly hadn't been much help when she was up before the bench.

Up before the bench – Evadne's blood ran cold

360

with shame. Oddly, it was Grandfather who had made her feel ashamed. Grandfather – the person she had relied on all these years.

With the day plodding closer to the dreaded moment when she would be bundled into a prison van and taken away to face God knows what, she sat in stunned silence, hands clasped until they grew so clammy she had to untangle them. She was too exhausted and upset to remember where Alex was. Had the police spoken to him? He would clear everything up.

Please let them speak to him before the prison van arrived.

The door banged open and she jumped.

A policeman stood there. 'A gent to see you.'

'Alex!' she exclaimed. Her muscles melted with relief.

Ted Geeson swung in.

Chapter Forty

It was a day for hogging the fire, but Carrie sat by the window all morning. She knew in her bones that Adam would have gone to court. She had known from the moment he first spoke to Mam in their bedroom in Wilton Lane that he could be trusted. Beneath the spikes of her anxiety for Evadne lay a solid core of certainty, because she knew he would do this for her; he would attend court and be her eyes and ears, knowing that Ralph wouldn't bother.

361

When she spied him coming along Wilbraham Road, recognising the length of his stride and the set of his shoulders in the distance, she raced downstairs; not the shop stairs – Ralph was in the shop – but the private stairs, flinging open the door and pelting along the pavement in her slippers to meet him, and bugger what Ralph would say if he saw. Ralph could go and boil his head.

She could tell the moment Adam saw her because he, too, broke into a run. They slowed as they approached, Carrie deliberately keeping several feet away. She didn't want to be close to him. She didn't want to be close to anyone, except just now Evadne. She had been separate from the world all this time. It had been just her and Joey, her and her grief, her and her guilt, her and the blame. And now, of all people, the person who had broken through her solitariness was Evadne.

'I'm sorry, Carrie–'

Her heart pounded. Was she out of breath? No, it was hatred, sheer hatred, that was making her heart beat so hard. How dare Evadne do this to her? How dare she land herself in such a serious predicament when all attention should be focused on Joey's memory? No, it wasn't Evadne she hated. It was herself for being wrenched out of her darkest grief. She felt wide awake in a startling, sharp-edged world that battered her senses. She wasn't prepared for this. It was too much. She couldn't face it, couldn't do it, couldn't breathe.

She swung away, leaving Adam standing there.

'Carrie–'

She breathed in deeply through her nose, clenching all her muscles and shutting her ears.

She wanted to shut out everything and go back to centring her existence around Joey, but she couldn't. There was too much to do. How was she to tell Mam? She had held off doing so, because what was the point when Evadne was going to be cleared? But now she must be told. It was almost enough to make you wish she couldn't hear.

Arriving back in the flat with her slippers damp and stretched, so preoccupied was she with breaking the news to Mam that when Mrs Porter handed her the afternoon post, she took it without a thought.

Her gaze landed on the familiar envelope with its typewritten address. A swoop of fear was followed by an inner stillness edged with sick misery. She deserved this. She had allowed herself to be wrenched away from Joey. She deserved it.

The cry erupted from deep inside, almost tearing her in two.

'I – don't – need – telling!'

Evadne stared at Ted Geeson. Somehow, after the trail of bizarre events since yesterday, she still had room to be astonished. In the cramped, impersonal room, he was big and broad and capable.

'What are you doing here? You can't stay. I'm expecting someone.'

'Your friend Mr Larter?'

'What business is that of yours?'

'It's very much my business, Miss Baxter, since I'm more of a friend to you than he'll ever be.'

She sprang up, nearly overturning the wooden chair. 'That's enough! Get out!'

For answer, he threw his cap and gloves on the

table and shrugged out of his greatcoat, hanging it over the back of a chair. He was dressed in a jacket and tie, and it jolted her to behold him so decently turned out. He was a burly man, but the smart clothes sat well on him.

Lips pursed, she resumed her seat. She couldn't pull off indifference, but she managed a brief shake of the head and a sharp sigh to make it clear he wasn't welcome.

'May I?' Geeson pulled out a chair. 'He isn't coming.'

'If you're referring to Mr Larter, the police haven't located him yet.'

'They spoke to him yesterday. Did you imagine they would arrest you without interviewing him? He's dropped you right in it.'

An old, scorned Wilton Lane word popped into her head. She was gawping. She snapped her mouth shut.

'I have it on good authority,' Geeson said softly. 'I used to be a copper, so I called in a few favours, asked some questions, got in here to see you.'

'You've been misinformed. If the police have already spoken to Mr Larter, why wasn't he in court? Why wasn't his name even mentioned?'

'Because he's out of the top drawer and the magistrate chose to keep his name out of it.' He rested his arms on the table and leant forward. 'I'm here to help you. I need to hear everything Larter said and did. Or,' he added, 'we could sit in silence and wait for the prison van.'

She flung him a dark look. What he was suggesting was monstrous. Yet why would he come here to tell lies? In a voice cracking with reluctance, she embarked on her tale.

'So whenever you visited a customer alone, it was because they'd sought another appointment with Larter?'

'Yes. My visit was always the final one.' Evadne lifted her chin. 'There! If Mr Larter has turned against me, which I don't believe for one moment, all the police need do is confirm with any client that he or she got in touch with Mr Larter and that I duly made an appointment. That proves he knew of my visits.'

Geeson shook his head. 'He's smarter than that. He might have let you believe your visit was the last, but he then made another – the real final visit – afterwards.'

'No, he didn't.'

'Thus enabling him to claim that the client invited him back and he duly went, and if you'd made a secret visit in between, how was he to know?' He permitted no time to let that sink in. 'Did he ever make arrangements for you? How about at that auction place?'

'I did everything.'

'Including telling a few whoppers about yourself, I gather.'

Oh, those delightful Chester trips. She had played her part to perfection.

'The customers believed you were buying for Armstrong's,' he pressed her.

'I was!'

'Yet the stuff you bought wasn't kept in the Armstrong's storerooms.'

'I had my own cupboard so my purchases could be kept separate, ready to go to Chester.'

'And your things didn't appear on any of the Armstrong's lists?'

'I told you. It was part of the Chester arrangement.'

'And you alone had a key to that cupboard.'

'Nonsense. Ralph has a huge ring of keys. He throws it on the table with a great crash so everyone knows how important he is.'

'He's never had a key to that cupboard, and the housekeeper's is missing. The police believe you swiped it. As for the money you made in Chester, you stashed it in a new savings account and went on a shopping spree.'

'Alex – Mr Larter told me to. He said... Never mind what he said.'

'Tell me.' Geeson spoke gently. 'I'll guess if I have to. Did he want you as his mistress?'

'Certainly not! As a matter of fact–' Her eyes were burning. God, she loathed this man.

'Were you expecting marriage?'

'He ... he wanted me to meet his mother.'

It was the closest she could come to admitting it. Geeson's hand stretched towards hers, but withdrew before she could snatch hers away.

'Larter lost his mother during the war. I know because I served under him.'

Recalling the disappointment with which Alex had explained that his mother's trip had been called off, Evadne closed her eyes. He had blamed it on the illness of his mother's oldest friend. 'So they're off to Switzerland together. Fresh mountain air and all that.' She had smiled bravely, even pretending a polite wish for the friend's recovery, all the while cursing the unknown invalid for coming between her and her heart's desire.

Now, her heart slumped in defeat. 'I can't believe it.'

With a sharpness that rattled through her, Geeson replied, 'You'd better start believing it, Miss Evadne Baxter, or you haven't a hope in hell.'

Careless of the damp, Carrie knelt beside Joey's grave, arranging the flowers she had brought. They would undoubtedly be blasted by frost overnight, but she couldn't bear Joey not to have flowers, even though it made her feel cruel to expose the blooms to harsh night-time temperatures. She had rushed here this morning, pulled by an agonising urgency that demanded capitulation. It happened this way sometimes. She could be in the middle of something, anything, changing the bed or paring rind to make lemonade, and suddenly she would feel herself drowning in the need to be close to her baby.

Sinking back on her heels, she pulled off her gloves and trailed her fingers down the headstone. How it had wounded her the first time she saw the fresh addition to the carved inscription. Here, Joey was *Joseph Ralph Armstrong,* which sounded like someone else, not at all like her baby boy, her Joey.

As for herself – *son of Ralph and Caroline.*

Caroline. *Who the hell is Caroline?* she had screamed inside her head the first time she saw it, before she slumped into dull acceptance. After neglecting her son and letting him die, she didn't deserve her own name.

'Carrie.'

367

She looked up. 'Adam.' A flare of resentment – how dare he intrude on her private moment?

'I have a message from your sister.'

Her breath caught. 'You've seen her?' She came to her feet, taking a step closer.

'The message comes via someone else. She says thank you for coming to the police station.'

'I'm just sorry I've done nothing else.'

'Perhaps you can do something. Will you come to Brookburn – now? I've gone to a lot of trouble to catch you today. I know you hardly set foot outside these days except to visit Joey. There's been a lad stationed by the cabbies' hut outside the Lloyds since breakfast, with orders to stay put until you appeared. Come with me. There's someone I need you to meet.'

'Really, I–'

'It could help Miss Baxter.'

That decided her.

They walked up the path between the old gravestones and out beneath the lychgate, then round the corner of the wall and alongside it down the sloping road. The pavement was narrow, just wide enough for two to walk abreast, but Carrie had no wish to be so close and walked ahead.

The morning was cold and overcast. As they passed the pub with its bowling green behind it, Adam slipped neatly into step behind her. He made an attempt at conversation, but Carrie cut him off. She wasn't here to talk. She wasn't going to play at conversation, at real life, at happy families. She was here to help Evadne, nothing more.

When they reached Brookburn's fancy gateway with the stone pillar to either side and the tall wrought-iron gates standing open, Carrie's step quickened. Her heart was thudding with hope. Adam led her, not up the gravel drive, but across the damp grass and through the trees towards a house in a fenced-off garden.

'The groundsman's cottage,' he said.

'That's never a cottage. You could stow a family of six in there and still have room for Grandma.'

He opened the door and she stepped through a lobby with boots standing beneath a bench and waterproofs hanging up, and found herself in a spacious kitchen-cum-sitting room. Immediately, she felt at home. Living in the kitchen was how she had grown up, one of the many things Ralph despised about Wilton Lane.

A man in shirtsleeves and waistcoat was lifting a singing kettle off the heat. Her diffidence melted at the sight of the kind smile in the serious, weather-beaten face. As he came forward, hand outstretched, Carrie realised he had an artificial leg and forced herself not to look down. Her hand disappeared inside his as Adam introduced them.

'This is Ted Geeson. He looks after the grounds. Geeson, this is my sister-in-law, Mrs Armstrong.'

'Miss Baxter's sister,' said Ted Geeson, as if this made it right.

'Take a pew, Mrs Armstrong. I'm about to warm the pot.'

She had to know immediately. 'Was it you who saw Evadne?'

'Aye, lass. She's frightened and confused, as you'd expect, and as innocent as a May morning, if I'm any judge.'

With that, Carrie gave him her heart. She and

Adam sat down while he set about brewing the tea. Carrie marvelled that a big man like that could make tea for a woman without being a figure of fun. As much as Ralph loved her, he wouldn't have poured her a glass of water if she had been choking.

She turned to Adam. 'You said I could help Evadne.' A look passed between the two men and her senses sharpened.

'We don't know for certain,' said Ted Geeson. 'It's only a maybe.'

'I don't care,' she said. 'I'll do anything.'

'Do you know why she was arrested?' asked Adam.

'Ralph told me. The police think she was pretending to buy for Armstrong's when really she was working for herself, but Evadne would never do that. I don't care what anyone says.'

'What does Ralph say?'

'That the police can prove it. It's not as though he knows her like I do,' she added, trying to hide her deep hurt. She squared her shoulders. 'Tell me what to do.'

'We need you to go through all the records you can lay your hands on,' said Adam, 'for the shop as well as the auction room. Ledgers, lists of acquisitions, anything.'

'What am I looking for?'

'Anything that catches your eye.'

'Such as?'

'For example, a seller or buyer who lives unusually far afield.'

'Like – Knutsford, you mean?'

'Or a piece of stock that arrives at the last min-

370

ute and is auctioned without delay,' said Adam. 'I'm sorry, Carrie. I'd tell you exactly what to look for, if I could.'

'Ralph wouldn't let me.'

'He mustn't know about it,' Ted Geeson said gravely.

'You want me to go behind his back?'

'It's the only way.'

Didn't they know what they were asking? Didn't Adam know what Ralph was like, how furious he would be if he found out? Ralph, the husband who refused to let her out of the flat when he was angry with her over Letty; Ralph, the father who used to take her baby away from her to ensure her quiet obedience. Well, he couldn't do that to her any more, could he? She could do anything now, because no punishment he meted out could possibly matter.

She looked at Adam. 'Why the secret? So what if Ralph doesn't like Evadne? So what if he believes the police? If you told him what to look for–'

'No.' Adam hesitated before asking, 'Do you know Alex Larter?'

'I've met him.'

'What's his connection to your husband's business?' Ted Geeson asked.

'Ralph calls him an associate, whatever that means. I know he finds stock, because he takes Evadne with him. Why?' When both men hesitated, she said sharply, 'I've a right to know.'

Adam said, 'We think Larter got Evadne into this mess.'

'On purpose? Why?'

371

'Listen, lass,' Ted Geeson stepped in. 'If Larter has done the dirty on Miss Baxter, who is Armstrong going to believe? The sister-in-law he doesn't know that well, and what he does know he doesn't like, or the man he trusts to work alongside him?'

'You mean, Ralph had to choose between them?' Carrie nodded. At least Ralph hadn't taken against Evadne out of blind prejudice. That was something. 'All right. I'll try. It's not just the police who need convincing. Ralph does too.' The clock on the mantelpiece pinged the half-hour. 'I must go. I have to get the dinner on.'

The men rose, Ted Geeson skilfully pushing himself to his feet.

She held out her hand to him. She wanted to give him both hands. 'Thank you for believing in Evadne. I'm that grateful.'

'Don't mention it, lass.'

Her glance landed on Adam and slid away. She couldn't meet his eyes, let alone offer her hand. She made a fuss of fastening her coat and smoothing her gloves. 'Mind, I don't know what use I'll be. I don't even know what I'm looking for.'

'Let's hope you recognise it when you see it,' Ted Geeson said sombrely.

'I'll walk you to the road,' Adam offered.

'No need.' Carrie made a dash for the door.

Chapter Forty-One

Standing by the window as Carrie hurried away, Adam's chest squeezed as his heart reached out to follow her. Grief had torn the flesh from her bones, giving her a vulnerability that made his throat ache with words that were forced to remain unspoken. Gone was the lovely young mother, so radiantly happy, replaced by a desperately slender creature with a pixie-pointed chin and haunted eyes.

There was nothing he could do for her. Even if he could, she wouldn't want it. The girl from Wilton Lane, whose gentle, generous spirit and quiet strength he so deeply admired and respected, and whom he loved with more capacity than he had known he possessed, had built a barrier around herself to hold the world at bay. He suspected that where he was concerned, the barrier was double-thick. He had lost her. He would have been her friend, her brother, anything if only he could give her comfort and support as she struggled to cope with the loss that still overwhelmed her.

That hurt, but what hurt more was knowing that she didn't seem to have anyone else either. As far as he knew, she had not turned to anyone. That she was carrying her burden alone tore into him. She deserved a better husband than Ralph.

Behind him, a door opened and he turned to see Woods, Drummond and their colleague

Parsons come in. With five men inside, the room seemed to shrink.

'I'm not happy about this,' said Woods.

'Believe me,' said Drummond, 'if there were any other way...'

'You shouldn't have told Mrs Armstrong that Larter was the one to drop her sister in the soup,' Parsons rebuked Adam.

He bridled. 'I said what needed saying. Carrie isn't stupid. She wasn't going to look through the paperwork just because we asked her. She needed an explanation and I happen to think she's entitled to one. Besides, it's better she blames Larter than that she realises the truth about Ralph's part in the arrest.'

'She should have worked out that bit for herself,' Parsons muttered.

'If you ask me,' said Adam, 'it's preferable that she doesn't know it was Ralph who had Evadne arrested for fraudulently using the Armstrong's name.'

'She certainly didn't twig that her husband could be involved with Larter's shenanigans,' said Inspector Woods.

'We don't know for certain Ralph is involved,' Adam pointed out, flushing as the others turned stony eyes on him. It was hard to believe it of his own brother; or was he being naïve? He liked to think he harboured no illusions about Ralph, was well acquainted with the aggression and cynicism, was aware too of the extremes of his brother's nature. How could passion and heartlessness co-exist? But – criminal? That was what the others believed, what he himself was struggling with.

374

Could Ralph be part of a gang that had stolen from their wartime allies and was now flogging the loot?

'You'll be glad to hear Weston's in the clear,' said Woods. 'He taught Miss Baxter a certain amount, but that's as far as it goes. It would look suspicious were he still employed in the shop, but he retired before Larter came along.'

'Retired?' said Adam. 'Is that what he told you? The old boy's trying to save face. My brother sacked him and brought in Renton who, unless I'm mistaken, knows as much about fine things as I do, which is to say I can probably sound quite knowledgeable but, if an expert tackled me, I couldn't stand up to the questioning.' He stopped. It didn't look good for Ralph.

'I still don't understand,' said Geeson, 'why Larter went to such lengths to make Miss Baxter appear a criminal.'

'I think I can answer that,' said Drummond. 'He did it to muddy the waters. Think about it: Parsons and I turn up at an auction to examine the goods and next thing you know, a complaint is made against Miss Baxter; so, yes, there's a problem at Armstrong's, but guess what, it's nothing to do with where the stock came from.'

'Who complained?' Adam asked. 'Larter?'

'Nothing so obvious,' said Parsons. 'It was a lady customer Miss Baxter had bought from. She claimed she'd been fleeced by someone purporting to represent Armstrong's.'

Geeson frowned. 'But that's just coincidence, surely, this complaint happening at the same time as you started investigating Larter?'

'No such thing as coincidence,' said Drummond, 'but I admit we can't find a connection between Larter and this Mrs Bentley.'

'Bentley?' Geeson exclaimed. 'He was one of Larter's men. He copped it shortly before the armistice. This must be his widow. What more proof do you need of Miss Baxter's innocence? You've got to get her released.'

'She's probably safer where she is for now,' said Parsons.

Adam saw the pain that flitted across Geeson's face at that.

When the others left, he and Geeson looked at one another.

'He's a bad bugger, that Larter,' Geeson said grimly.

'And a clever one.'

'You don't know the half of it. He's responsible for this.' Geeson slapped his artificial leg. 'No proof, mind, but,' he tapped his forehead, 'I've all the proof I need in here.'

'Christ. What happened?'

At first, Geeson said nothing. When he began to talk, his eyes narrowed and Adam guessed he was looking into the past.

'We were pinned down in a deserted farm. Larter was there – Captain Larter, he was then. Bentley, Renton, chap called Kemp, me.'

'Not Ralph?'

'No. Can't say I ever met him.'

Adam released a quiet breath. Whatever story Geeson was about to tell, and he had no doubt it wasn't going to be pretty, at least Ralph wasn't involved.

'Like I say, we were pinned down and had to get out quick. It was one of those now-or-never situations. The plan was that I'd set fire to the barn, then we'd get the hell out of there. It was dangerous because Jerry was nearly on the barn, but it had a small back door and I slipped across and got in that way.' He broke off, shook his head. 'It's odd, remembering the way I used to move. I dream about it, you know. I dream of running.' He huffed a breath. 'I started several fires, all the while hearing gunshots. Then Jerry appeared in the barn doorway, the big main doorway, that is, with his gun at the ready. The fires were well alight by then and he was nobbut a silhouette. I flung myself behind some crates and at the same time I heard two shots. Jerry went down and I took the other shot in the thigh. I managed to pull myself as far as the back door. I could hardly breathe by then and my eyes were streaming, the place was that thick with smoke. I had to shoot the lock off to get out. I dragged myself as far as I could, then rolled into a ditch and passed out. A couple of our lads found me two or three days later and carried me on a door to a field hospital. Walked miles with me, they did, and ended up with blisters as big as baccy tins on their hands. By then, my leg had took bad ways. Blood poisoning had set in. The doctor said, "It's your leg or your life," and set to with the saw.'

Adam nodded heavily. 'Why blame Larter?'

'The two shots in the barn: who d'you suppose fired them?'

'Jerry shot you and one of your men shot him from the back door.'

'No, both shots came from behind me. Who-ever killed Jerry shot me an' all and then I was locked in. Why else d'you think I needed to shoot the lock off to get out? I was shot from behind by one of my comrades, then locked in to burn to death if the bullet didn't kill me.'

'Bloody hell. Why, though? Why would Larter do that, or give those orders? Come to that, why would anyone follow those orders?'

'To get rid of me. Larter had been sounding me out. Knowing what I know now, I realise he was thinking of recruiting me for his looting gang. There were some strange conversations, not just with him, but with Renton and one or two others. It's hard to describe because it was done so subtly, but I had a bad feeling about it, so I made a point of saying I was a police sergeant before the war and had every intention of resuming my post after-wards. Two days later, I was shot and locked in a burning barn.' He heaved a sigh. 'I can't tell you what a shock it was, the day I saw Larter driving up to Brookburn with Miss Baxter beside him.'

All Adam could think of was Carrie. In seeking her help, had he placed her in danger?

Carrie's feet took her back to Joey's grave. She needed to see it; she had the oddest feeling that something would be different. She walked down the flagged path between the headstones, her eyes fixed on the bonny yellow of Joey's chrysanths, like a beacon in the grey morning. But when she stopped at his grave, nothing had changed.

What had she expected? Joey was still gone and nothing would bring him back. He was still lying in the ground – a damp, miserable ground today. Why had she felt so certain of change? Nothing had altered, not in the smallest detail.

Yes, it had.

But the difference wasn't here with Joey, with her grief, her guilt, her loss.

The change was in her. She had woken up. She had been made to think about something else and she couldn't pretend it hadn't happened.

She stood there for a long time. She had always felt lousy about letting Joey be laid to rest with the grandfather who was no grandfather at all; but now she remembered that Joseph Armstrong hadn't been a stranger to her. She had known her mother's unwanted but persistent admirer only slightly, but she remembered the bright eyes, the gruff good humour and the hearty chuckle. To tell the truth, she had rather liked him, only she never said so, because Mam would have had her guts for garters. Joseph Armstrong was what Pa would have called a decent bloke.

'Your grandad will look after you for now,' she whispered to Joey. 'Just for now, love. I have to see to Auntie Evadne.'

Carrie brimmed with energy, itching to be busy. It wasn't the same need she had had since Joey's death. That had simply been a matter of going through the motions, something to keep her from toppling over the edge. This new urge was different. Was this how she used to be?

She braced herself for the onslaught of guilt, but nothing happened. Something inside her recognised that she was no longer curled up somewhere in the dark halls of her mind. The time had come to find a new way of living with her loss and guilt, because her mind, for so long paralysed by anguish, was awake and alert, still in pain but ready to think of other things.

She kicked herself for neglecting Mam. Oh, she had tended her, kept her clean and free from bed sores, mushed up her meals and patiently fed her, never missed her exercises; but there had been no intimacy, no chatting, nothing interesting for Mam to listen to, to hang on to and feel herself still to be a person.

Well, that was one thing she could put right. She made tea and went to sit with Mam, holding her hand.

'D'you remember how we always had a cuppa together of an evening back at home? You'd have my tea on the table the minute I came in from Trimble's, and afterwards we'd pull the armchairs up to the fire and get our feet all toasty warm and spend ages nattering over a cup of tea. Well, here I am with my tea now, looking forward to us doing that again. I'll never give up and I know you won't either. I want ... I want you to come with me to see Joey's grave.'

Something blocked her throat – she had to work her jaw to disperse it – and was it her imagination or was there the smallest pressure on her fingers? The feeling was so slight it took her a moment to register it.

'Mam? Did you squeeze my hand? Do it again or I'll think I was dreaming.'

She focused all her energy into the moment. Please do it again, please do it again. She pressed

Mam's hand, showing her what to do, but nothing happened. Had she imagined it? No, definitely not. She had no choice but to leave it for now – but only for now.

'Listen, Mam. I have to tell you about Evadne.' She repeated everything that had been said in Ted Geeson's house. 'What I'm meant to look for, I've no idea, but I'll do my best. I don't want Evadne stopping in that place a minute longer than she has to. Ralph's done a big evaluation in Withington, a whole houseful. The owner died and the son wants rid of the lot and Ralph had first pick. It's being delivered over the road on Monday, so I'll have a reason to be there for a day or two. And maybe I'll have a chance to see some paperwork. Well, there's no maybe about it. I have to, though how, and also how I'm going to look at the shop books, I've no idea, but Evadne's relying on me and I won't let her down.'

She gave Mam's hand a final hopeful squeeze. Would it prompt a response? Nothing happened. She tried not to be disappointed.

'Tomorrow's Saturday and I'm going to visit Mr Weston. I've not been round in ages, not since... Anyroad, I'm going to bake a cake and while it's in the oven, perhaps you'd like to have a wash?'

She bustled about for the rest of the day. That evening, she told Ralph of her planned visit.

'I thought you'd stopped going.'

'I'd like to start again. I want to do my own shopping again too.'

'I don't like the sound of this. You've been a much better wife since you started sticking to the home. I won't have you gadding about, bumping

381

into women you used to know and picking up that slovenly way of speaking, or starting to dress down because they think you've turned posh. It's taken a lot to get you up to scratch and I'm not having you slumping back into your old ways.'

She winced. She had forgotten how hard it was to listen to Ralph slagging off Wilton Lane. Had he always been such a bully? How had she stood it? How different it would be if he said in a kind voice, 'I'm proud of how you've improved, but I'm worried you might slip back.'

She fixed a pleasant expression on her face. 'I want to go out again, that's all.'

'Aye, well, we'll see.'

'So can I go tomorrow?'

'May I, not can I,' he corrected her. 'You see how easily it happens?' He made her wait. 'Very well.'

'Thank you.' She made a point of smiling. She didn't want to appear humble or grateful – just polite.

'Straight there and straight back.'

'Yes, Ralph.'

The morning's fog had lifted, leaving a chill penetrating damp, and Carrie pulled her scarf higher as she stepped onto the pavement. The familiar aching emptiness washed through her and she hovered indecisively. Here she was, about to do something different and interesting and it felt like the most hideous betrayal. She might even enjoy it. Deep inside she shuddered, the tremor working its way inexorably outward until her whole body shook. The mother who had slept through her baby's death had no business looking forward to something and deriving pleasure from it.

The voice of guilt was insistent, the need to dash back inside compelling; but she knew Ralph would declare her unfit to be out and about and would insist on keeping her indoors, so she forced her feet to start moving, though her heart was bumping and her skin felt slick with guilt. Strangely, though, once she had forced her way through the powerful reservations, they subsided into a background ache that she knew she would be living with for a long time to come, possibly always.

She walked down Wilbraham Road, marvelling at how long it had been since she last came this way. The crossroads with Barlow Moor Road made the hair lift on her arms. It was so big, so wide, and there was traffic, even a tram clanking along. How was she to reach the other side? A businessman, pinstriped, bowler-hatted and umbrella'd, paused at the kerb beside her before starting across and she pattered beside him.

Passing the bank on the corner, she started along by the shops. It was exciting to be out and about. She glanced over the road – Letty and Billy – shock, dismay, embarrassment, but most of all a great rush of regret and nostalgia and love for the dearest friend she had ever had. How could she have turned her back on Letty? She wanted to run across and hug her old friend and have a good cry and start setting things to rights.

But Ralph had declared the friendship over.

And Billy was there.

She hurried on. A flash of memory: Mrs Jackson and Mrs Tilbury crossing the road to avoid her, pretending not to see her. But this was different. Wasn't it?

Not far now. Just the other side of the railway bridge.

Her heart was beating hard when Mr Weston opened the door. The sight of his dear face calmed and gladdened her.

His face brightened into kind lines. 'My dear Mrs Armstrong, what an unexpected pleasure.'

He drew her in and wouldn't be dissuaded from putting on extra coal that she feared he could ill afford. Was it her imagination or was he thinner? There hadn't been much of him to start with. They fell into their old comfortable ways, as if she had seen him last week instead of not for months.

She tried to apologise, but he waved her words aside.

'You've been in my prayers, you and your little boy.'

As her tears welled up, he distracted her by asking after Evadne.

'But at least you're not under suspicion now,' she finished.

When it was time to leave, she longed to hug him, but a warm handshake had to suffice, together with a promise to return next week.

As she walked away, glad she had made the effort to come, Billy – Billy! – appeared from round a corner.

'Carrie – I need a word.'

She ducked her head and tried to get past, but he blocked her way.

'It'll tek nobbut a minute, I promise.'

'I remember the last time you wanted to speak to me and the answer's no.'

'That's why I want to see you – to tek back everything I said last time. I'm a happily married man now. It's for the best that I ended up with Letty and you're to forget I ever said owt different.'

'That'd be a darned sight easier if you didn't spring out at me from round corners.'

'Happen I won't need to, not after today.'

'Not to mention the fact that you've followed me – again. Where's Letty?'

'She never saw you. I told her to finish the shopping on her own.'

'Then get home and wait for her.'

'Not until I've said my piece. I want you to know there's nowt left between you and me, not on my side anyroad. I'm going to be a dad.'

She gasped. He looked thrilled and proud and important, as if it had never happened to him before. He hadn't looked like that when she fell pregnant. It had taken him a while to get used to it.

'Things have worked out for the best from where I'm standing. I'm wed with a baby on the way. I had no idea things could be this good. I've got the right wife an' all. There's nowt iffy about my Letty or her folks. I liked your dad and he's the last bloke I'd have thought – well, you know what I mean. And now there's your Evadne inside. It's like I said last summer – blood will out.'

'Pa wasn't Evadne's dad.'

'He fetched her up, didn't he? Same difference.'

'You're twisting it to suit yourself.'

385

'I don't need to twist anything. You're to forget I ever came anywhere near you back whenever it was. If there's any feelings left, they're not on my side.'

'You can't believe–'

'I'm just saying, that's all. Righto, I'd best head home.' He turned to go, then stopped. 'Don't tek this the wrong way, Carrie love, but with your little lad gone, this one me and Letty are having, well, it's like it's my first, my first proper one, cos it's not as though I ever had owt to do with Joey, is it? It's made me feel reet sorry for you, losing him. This child what's coming, it's made me see everything differently. His first child is important to a man.'

Don't tek this the wrong way? Carrie thought she would swoon with the pain. Billy tipped his cap and walked away, shoulders back, step jaunty, every inch the proud father-to-be. The world tilted. Carrie wanted to drag herself under a hedge to curl up and wait for death like a sick cat.

But Ralph would be expecting his three o'clock tea tray.

Chapter Forty-Two

Beneath the caking of dried tears, Carrie's skin felt tight and hot. She dabbed cream on and gingerly smoothed it in, before going to the kitchen to warm the pot.

MOTHER WITH NO MERCY

It was her own fault for opening it. The moment she saw the letter on the mat, she had known this was another bitter accusation, and hadn't there been a voice inside her suggesting that here was her punishment for striving to pull her life back together? Coming on top of her meeting with Billy, it had left her wanting to wrap her arms over her head and hide from the world, but she must make herself presentable for three o'clock. As she carried the tray down, she plastered on a smile and tried not to meet Ralph's sharp eyes.

There was no avoiding him that evening, though, when he asked, 'How's old Weston?'

'Fine, thank you. He sends his best.'

'And you got there and back all right? Or was it ... difficult?'

Don't tek this the wrong way.

'It was good to be out.'

'You didn't look well when you got back. You looked like you'd been crying.'

'I had a bit of a weep, I must admit.'

'It was too much for you. You're best off being a homebody.'

'No, Ralph, honest.'

He lifted his eyebrows, silencing her. But she refused to be silenced.

'It's not what you think. The tears weren't because of going out. They – they were tears of joy. I was thinking about Mam squeezing my hand, only slightly, but I'm sure I didn't imagine it.'

'Mrs Jenkins squeezed your hand? When?'

'Yesterday. Isn't it wonderful?'

Later, when Carrie went in to kiss Mam good-night, she was surprised to find Ralph sitting at the bedside, leaning forward as if speaking into Mam's ear. As Carrie came in, he sat back. Mam's hand lay inside his. He held it up.

'No squeezing,' he remarked, getting up to leave the room. 'Don't be long.'

She stepped aside to let him pass. She had never seen him in here before and her surprise melted into gratitude. She knew he found Mam's condition disturbing. The good news, however, had apparently made him perceive her differently, making her more acceptable to him. Carrie fetched a deep sigh. There was no Joey and that would hurt her for ever, but at least she and Ralph and Mam might have the chance to be a proper family.

Carrie woke, not knowing what had disturbed her, only knowing something had. The only sound was Ralph's breathing. Then she heard something, a brief sound, indistinct, unidentifiable. She shook Ralph's shoulder.

'Wake up. I heard something.'

Before she could blink, he had pulled on a jumper and thrust his feet into a pair of shoes.

'Stay here,' he murmured and was gone.

She slid from the bed and bundled herself into her dressing gown, before opening the bedroom door a crack to listen. She couldn't hear anything. She thought of Mam, defenceless, so she flitted along the landing, sliding into the front bedroom, whispering, 'It's only me. Nowt to worry about.'

That was where Ralph found her a few minutes

later. 'False alarm, but you did the right thing, waking me. The flat's secure; so is the shop. Why are you in here? I told you to stay put.'

'I had to be with Mam. Supposing there had been someone.'

'Not worth putting yourself at risk for. Bed, Carrie.'

'I'll stop here a while with Mam.'

'Bed, Carrie.'

What Adam had asked her to do wasn't going to be easy, with Ralph keeping everything under lock and key. Carrie had Evadne's old set of keys for the Lloyds, including those to the small drawers in the office desk, but not to its deep drawers. Somehow she must get hold of those keys when the goods from the Withington house arrived and she had reason to be across the road. She was fearful and determined both at the same time.

On Monday, however, when she had hurried through her domestic tasks so as to be available for an afternoon in the office, Ralph said she wouldn't be wanted until tomorrow at the earliest.

'I'll be at the Lloyds all evening,' he said. 'I want to take a good look at the Withington haul.'

Her heart bumped. Here was her chance.

When Ralph left, she flew into Mam's room and peeked through the curtains, watching him cross the road and walk up the steps. Then she ran down to the shop and into the office, shutting the door before she reached up to the brass gas bracket. There was a soft *pop* and she regulated the flame.

Taking the heavy delivery book from the shelf, she sat behind the desk and opened it. It was a large volume, dating back several years, but if all she had to do was discredit Mr Larter, then it was only the newest entries that mattered. He had arrived on the scene at the same time as Ralph was starting up the auction room. It opened for business in September last year and Ralph had spent all that summer preparing by buying suitable stock; she knocked off another couple of months for good measure and flicked back to April 1920, where she found a bold, scrawly script that must have belonged to Joseph Armstrong. No – she had gone back too far. The auction room preparations hadn't started until after his death. She turned the pages until his writing disappeared, her eyes lingering on his final entry. He had written it with no idea it was his last one.

Concentrate, concentrate. Each entry contained date, name and address, price and a description of the article. She applied herself to her task, reading aloud in a soft murmur to help her remain focused, trying not to be distracted by the frustration of not knowing what she was looking for. It was all very well for Ted Geeson to say she might recognise it when she saw it, but he wasn't the one poring over these lists.

A sound: her shoulders went rigid. The shop bell jingled; the door closed. She shut the book, sprang up, lunged for the gas bracket, then threw herself beneath the desk, banging her elbow. Pain darted up her arm, but she ignored it, curling tightly inside the knee-space and not a moment too soon. The door opened. A couple of footsteps, then a pause followed by the soft *pop* as the gas caught and the darkness gave way to a glow of light. She pulled her knees closer to her chest.

Ralph came over to the desk, his trouser legs and highly polished shoes appearing in front of the knee-space. Carrie pressed herself against the wooden panel that covered the back of the space. What if he sat down? Then he stopped moving. Damn! She had left the delivery book on the desk. Ralph was meticulous about putting things away; she could practically hear him thinking he hadn't left it there. Please let him blame Mr Renton. Thank goodness she had at least shut the book. He started moving again. She detected sounds, the book being returned to its shelf, the jingling of keys, then a clatter as the key ring fell to the floor, landing just inside the knee-space.

Horrified, her insides turning to water, she watched Ralph's hand and arm swoop down, but fortunately his face remained above the level of the knee-space. The next moment, a drawer slid open and she heard papers rustling, then the drawer shut and the key clicked in the lock. A few more moments and the light went out; the door closed.

She didn't dare make a sound. She waited as long as she could bear it before crawling out of her hidey-hole. Pressing her ear to the door, she listened, but all she could hear was the rushing of her blood.

Slowly, she turned the handle. The door didn't budge.

Evadne jolted awake. She had dozed off sitting

391

bolt upright on the nasty little bed, waiting to be locked in, longing to be locked in, because being locked in was the only way of being safe. She was cold and stiff and her neck hurt. She was frightened too. She had been frightened ever since she arrived here, though she had tried her hardest not to let it show, knowing instinctively that it would be the worst mistake she could make.

The women here were ... she shuddered. She had never come across such hardness before, that knowing glint in the eye, that half-smirk that said you had better watch out. The women who weren't like that were timid shadows, desperate not to draw attention, watching the intimidation and cruelty and thanking their stars they weren't on the receiving end this time.

Her educated voice and air of gentility, her elegant carriage and smooth hands, had instantly marked her out as different, and here of all places it wasn't good to be different. Hoity-toity was the least unpleasant thing she had been called, and some of the words used against her had been so offensive that her skin had ended up a blotchy mess of outraged white and distraught puce. In her first desperate twenty-four hours, she had feared that the verbal abuse might destroy her. Yet just a day or so later she was immune to it, because the physical threat was worse.

She had been pushed and slapped and tripped. Yesterday, when she was at the top of the stairs, a pair of meaty hands landed on her shoulder blades, delivering an almighty shove that would have sent her downstairs head first, causing untold damage, except that she had managed to grab the banister and jerk herself to a halt, practically wrenching her arm from its socket in the process.

Later, she had made one of her dreaded visits to the water closet. Half a dozen cubicles lined a damp, stinking room. The doors had no locks and Evadne had quickly perfected the art of securing the door with an outstretched foot. But someone had climbed up inside the adjoining cubicle and poured a chamber pot all over her, transforming her into a shrieking, flapping madwoman. Far from taking her side, the wardresses had curled their lips in disgust and made her strip to the skin to be hosed down with freezing water.

Did Alex have any idea what he had condemned her to? Why had he done it? Grandfather hadn't been near her, hadn't written, hadn't visited. He had probably left the country to escape the scandal. Funny how she had pinned her hopes on him all these years, clinging to the belief that he would do the decent thing. No matter how many times it had failed to happen, she had never stopped believing. Well, she had stopped now.

The only person who had attempted to visit was Ted Geeson, but she had refused to see him, felt too ashamed. She recalled how he had insisted on escorting her back to Brookburn from the Lloyds. She remembered slamming the door in his face, refusing to hear a word against Alex. And she recalled him swinging into that poky room in the magistrates' building and declaring himself her friend.

The person she wanted to see was Carrie. For years, she had thought Carrie didn't matter to her, but now she remembered a young Carrie, her face glowing with adoration as she gazed at the big sister she worshipped; she remembered, too, an older Carrie, growing away from her.

All her fault. Carrie had a loving heart. She would have adored Evadne to this day if Evadne had provided her with half a reason. If she had been less absorbed by her own dire situation and paid Carrie some attention, they could have been friends.

Why hadn't Carrie visited? She hoped with all her heart it was because Ralph had forbidden it. She couldn't bear to think that Carrie had abandoned her.

A scuffling sound in the corridor made the hairs on her arms stand on end. Someone was there. What did they have in store for her now?

Carrie stood transfixed, almost light-headed with disbelief. She was locked in. She had to get out before Ralph came home. A fresh thought turned her cold all over. Suppose he had already finished at the Lloyds; suppose right this minute he was looking for her upstairs. How could she explain getting locked in the office?

She fought down panic. Think, think. Feeling her way across the darkened room, she found the window, fumbled with the catches, but they were stuck. Her fingers turned clammy with effort and skidded off the frame. Heat seared through her hand as a fingernail ripped, but she wouldn't give up. Taking Ralph's heavy glass paperweight from the desk, she used it to tap the catch. It started to give. She tapped harder and it slid back. She felt a surge of desperate relief and set to with a will on the other catch, forcing it to give.

She wiped the paperweight on her skirt and put it back, before applying her fingers to the window frame to throw up the sash. Her muscles clenched and strained; the wood squeaked; there was the tiniest movement. Her vision blurred and her hands felt as though they were going to snap off at the wrist, but with a jolt that vibrated up her arms, the frame started moving and she managed to raise it in small, painful jerks.

Massaging her wrists with fingers that felt like rubber, she realised she would need to stand on a chair to climb out, so even if she could heave the sash shut behind her, she would still be leaving evidence behind. Tomorrow, while Ralph was shaving, she would have to filch his keys and sneak downstairs and set the office to rights.

Placing the chair beneath the window, she climbed out in the cold darkness and jumped down. Pain twanged through her ankle as she landed in the yard. Stretching, she yanked on the sash and pulled it down as best she could.

Inching her way across the yard, she felt her way around the delivery van, stubbing her slippered toes against a crate. Her hands found the wooden planks of the gate and the smooth weight of the padlock. There was nothing for it but to put her meagre weight behind the nearest crate, wiggling her back into position and heaving with all her strength. The crate scraped across to the wall and she clambered up, sitting astride the wall before letting herself down the other side.

She still had to get back indoors. The air nipped her flesh and her feet were starting to freeze.

Hugging herself, she scurried round to the front of the shop. Well, she couldn't just stand here, awaiting Ralph's return, so that left one choice. She ran over the road to the Lloyds, plunging straight through the door that led to the back part of the hotel, where Ralph would be working.

He looked up from a table crowded with items in silver, brass and cut glass. 'What are you doing here? You look frozen.'

She pretended to laugh. 'I didn't think I'd need a coat. I came to see how long you'll be.'

'Miss me, did you?'

'I wondered if you'd like some supper. I came in such a hurry I forgot my key and I've locked myself out.'

'Eager to see me, eh?'

Her cardigan was fastened, but she pulled the edges closer together. 'Will you want supper?'

'A bit of sustenance is always welcome, especially when it's provided by the wife who couldn't face an evening without me. That's the best kind of fare there is. Come here.'

'Ralph, no.'

'I've told you before. You don't say no to me. Look, there's a dining table over here. How appropriate for a spot of ... sustenance.' He swept the matching chairs aside, caught her wrist, pulled her to him. 'I remember another table where you made yourself very amenable, Carrie Armstrong.'

Chapter Forty-Three

'Good morning, Mrs Armstrong,' said a smooth voice, and Carrie's pulse skittered. So much for keeping an eye on the office door while she searched. She thrust the ledger into the deep drawer at the bottom of the desk, guilt flaming in her cheeks.

'Good morning, Mr Larter.' How long had he been standing there?

'Are you looking for something?'

'No. That is, I just found it. Thank you, anyway.'

His eyes never left her face. 'That drawer contains business information. You don't require access to that.'

'No, I... Ralph lent me his keys because I needed fresh paper and I looked in here by mistake.'

'But you said you'd found what you were looking for, and you won't find paper in there.'

'Is there a problem?' And there was Ralph in the doorway, his presence causing Mr Larter to take a step inside, making Carrie feel hemmed in.

'I discovered Mrs Armstrong delving in a drawer she had no business opening in the first place,' said Mr Larter, 'and then she lied about it.'

'Don't be ridiculous, man,' Ralph said impatiently. 'She's in a tizzy, that's all. You make her nervous.'

Mr Larter lifted a single eyebrow. Then he strode from the room, obliging Ralph to clear out of his way.

After that, Carrie tried to concentrate on her work, but it wasn't easy after nearly being caught by the very person she was hoping to incriminate. She didn't even have the consolation of having discovered anything useful. Or she might have seen umpteen pieces of relevant information, but how on earth was she supposed to recognise them? You'll know it when you see it, my foot!

It was time to get the dinner on. She fastened her coat and put on her hat and gloves. Would the fog have lifted? First thing this morning, she hadn't been able to see across the road to the Lloyds. Now she emerged into a depressing mist that sucked the colour from everything, leaving the world uniformly grey, but at least she could see over the road.

Something caught her eye at Mam's window. A movement? A figure? It was gone before she could look properly. Carrie knew Mrs Randall would have played merry hell and docked her pay for gazing out of the window. Should she confront Mrs Porter? It had taken her a long time to get used to giving instructions to the char, but she would never be able to reprimand her. She mustn't say a word to Ralph, because he would expect her to lay the law down.

'Mrs Armstrong.'

She spun round. Mr Larter was right behind her, standing a shade too close, fingers of mists curling around him. The chill seemed to have deepened the indentation of his scar.

'I apologise for upsetting you and making you lie on the spur of the moment. Good thing Armstrong was there to explain away your confusion, wouldn't you say?'

'Well ... yes.'

'So pleasant chatting to you, Mrs Armstrong. I trust there won't be any repeat of the ... confusion.'

He raised his hat and walked away, leaving her staring after him as the mist blurred and then swallowed his tall, aristocratic figure. What did he mean? Did he suspect her of ... something?

She must talk to Adam. When Ralph came home, Carrie dished up beef stew and dumplings, making sure, as any decent wife would, that the bulk of the meat ended up on her husband's plate.

'I thought I'd visit Joey this afternoon, if you don't need me over the road.'

'Fine. I'll be in the shop. I don't like to have a whole day away from it.'

When the shop reopened, she set off. Mist clung like the regrets of the bereaved to Chorlton Green as she passed the makeshift memorial, which appeared heartbreakingly grey and thin through the winter months. The sooner there was a proper memorial the better.

She hurried on past the graveyard and the pub, presently turning in through Brookburn's gates. Was it her imagination or did the mist hang lower here, close by the brook? She drew her coat more snugly round her as she paced up the drive. Brookburn House was grand and she knew in her bones that a nobody from Wilton Lane ought to knock at the back door.

'Eh, lass, it's good to see you again. Doctor Armstrong expecting you? No, well, not to worry. Let's get you inside, that's the main thing on a day like today.'

The next thing she knew, she was up the steps, through the front door and standing in a spacious hallway with a splendid staircase; Ted Geeson was beside her, seeming bigger than ever wrapped inside a greatcoat, removing his cap as he spoke to a passing nurse, before ushering her along the hall into a room furnished with items that even her untrained eye knew Ralph would kill to get his hands on.

'Here, sit by the fire.'

'Thank you.' She unfastened her coat.

'Have you seen Miss Baxter?'

'I'm afraid not.'

'Your old man won't let you, eh? Shame, that. I thought she might agree to see you. Now, me, I have permission from Doctor Armstrong to go every day, only she won't see me.'

Carrie realised with a thrill of surprise that this man cared for her sister, but her initial pleasure was quenched by the certainty that Evadne would never look twice in his direction. Poor Mr Geeson.

Adam walked in and she felt a deep pang of yearning intermingled so powerfully with sorrow that her heart swelled and she couldn't breathe. She mustn't have feelings for this man. But not only was her mind reawakening from its darkest torment, it seemed that her heart too was making room for something besides misery. She pressed a hand to her chest. She didn't want this.

She came to the point. 'I haven't found anything. I've tried the shop delivery book and the auction room ledger.'

'There is somewhere else you might try: the safe,' said Adam. 'You know the airing cupboard inside the chimney breast in the sitting room?'

'I barely use it. Our washing goes to the laundry.'

'The safe is inside it, set into the wall. Its door looks like part of the wall, but if you know it's there, you can feel for the keyhole. Dad used to keep the key in a desk drawer with a false back.'

Such secrets in her own sitting room – a safe, a drawer with a hidden compartment.

'There's a row of small drawers beneath the pigeonholes. If you open the second one from the left and feel the back, you'll find a narrow dent. Press hard and the back will pivot. There's a space behind it where the key is. Well, that's where Dad kept it.'

She wanted to object, to tell him she had already been locked in the office, not to mention almost being caught by Mr Larter, but she couldn't, not without letting Evadne down and she wasn't about to do that. There was something she didn't understand, though.

'I don't see why you can't tell Ralph.' Seeing the men exchange glances, she felt a flash of vexation. 'There's something you're not telling me.'

Ted Geeson turned to Adam. 'Perhaps Mrs Armstrong should drop out now.'

'Don't talk about me as if I'm not here,' Carrie objected.

Adam turned to her and she could have sworn he was about to reach out his hand, but he

401

didn't. Inside her sleeve, her skin glowed where he would have touched her.

'Geeson's right,' Adam said. 'You mustn't do any more. Forget the safe. Asking you to help was a long shot. There are others who'll take over now.'

'No! You can't seek my help and then cast me aside. Ralph could lay his hands on what you need in an instant. If you won't tell him, I will, and never mind that tripe about him choosing between Evadne and Mr Larter. I'll make him listen.'

'No!' both men exclaimed vehemently.

Adam sighed. 'All right. I'll tell you what Larter's involved in, on condition you swear not to breathe a word. I'm only telling you so you can appreciate how serious this is. It isn't just to do with Evadne. Alex Larter is involved – or rather, is strongly suspected of being involved – with a gang who, while serving in France, stole precious goods – furniture, paintings, ornaments – and now they're feeding them into the home market in such a way as makes them virtually untraceable, by selling to private individuals who will put the table or vase in their front room and there it'll stay for years to come.'

'And Mr Larter might be using the auction room to do this? Adam, you must tell Ralph.'

'No. There are men who are investigating this, who, incidentally, would have my hide if they knew I'd told you. Say one word and you'll damage their investigation.'

Carrie pressed her lips together. Was she supposed to be content with that?

'I'll see you home,' Ted Geeson offered, nodding at the window.

She saw threads of mist clagging together and reforming into ropes of fog.

'No need. I'll be fine if I leave now.'

She stood up and fastened her coat, looking at the buttons because she knew Adam was looking at her. Bidding the men a brisk farewell, she hurried away, her mind brimming.

Adam was right: she mustn't tell Ralph. If he knew what Mr Larter was suspected of, he wouldn't bother with proof. He would grab his business associate by the throat and throttle him for daring to use Ralph's beloved business for such despicable purposes.

When she arrived home, she entered through the shop to tell Ralph she had returned safely.

'Good. I'm about to shut up shop. We'll get no more business with this fog setting in. I've sent Renton home and I'll be over the road, pricing the Withington goods.'

Carrie slipped behind the counter and went through the back hall and upstairs, where the first thing she did was send Mrs Porter home. Typical Ralph: he hadn't given the woman a thought.

In the sitting room, she looked at the chimney breast, her eye going to the small door in the side; then she looked at the roll-top desk. But Adam wanted her to leave well alone and, anyroad, she had her own jobs to attend to. She went to stir up Mam's fire and make sure she was warm enough. Then she settled down to talk, taking her hand.

'Eh, Mam, you'll never guess what I found out today about that Mr Larter.' She repeated everything Adam had said, including his mention of the safe. 'Only he doesn't want me looking in there after all.' She fetched a sigh. 'I wish I'd found something to help Evadne, but there was nothing. Wait – there was something. Not in the books, but something that happened in the auction room. Mr Kemp bought a bureau and two weeks later he bought that secretaire. That's two words for desk, Mam. Who wants two desks? Oh yes, and the secretaire was taken out at the end, but then it was brought back so those men could see it, only it was a different piece that was brought back. I knew it all along, but I told myself I'd made a mistake because it didn't make sense. D'you suppose it means something? Oh, Mam, do you think it could help Evadne?'

She went to the window to draw the curtains. The fog was stodgier than when she had walked home.

'Not today, though.' She took Mam's hand again. 'The fog's getting worse and I'd never get back in time to do the tea.' She was fidgety, anxious to do something useful. 'I'll search the safe, see if there's anything in there.'

Starting to rise, she gasped when Mam's hand clutched hers.

'Mam!' She dropped back onto her chair. Drawing Mam's knuckles to her lips, she smothered them with kisses, then stopped as the grip faded. 'It's a good sign. It means you're on the mend. Wait till I tell Ralph.'

Mam's hand went slack. Carrie laid it down, her heart in a whirl. She felt torn in two. Part of her wanted to fling back the bedclothes and exercise Mam's limbs for all she was worth, but this might be her only chance to try the safe.

'I shan't be long.'

Finding the dent in the back of the drawer, she administered a sharp push and felt a moment's childish delight when the back of the drawer pivoted, revealing a small compartment. There was the key. Opening the airing cupboard, she closed her eyes as warmth poured over her; then she reached inside, her fingertips travelling over the wall time and again before she detected the tiniest difference in the surface. Not daring to remove her fingers, she reached in with her other hand to fiddle with the key and the next moment the door swung open. Goodness, she had done it.

It was too shadowy to see properly, but there were two shelves. Carrie withdrew a sturdy tin box – locked. She replaced it. Next came some books. Glancing inside, she saw lists of items together with columns of money. She put the books on the table behind her. On the other shelf was another book, some fat documents tied with string and a large envelope. She took everything out. Dare she untie the string? The envelope was unsealed. Reaching inside, she felt some pieces of paper, small and flimsy. She pulled them out.

Her guts turned to water. All she could do was stare at the bits of paper in her hand. Small pieces snipped from newspaper. DEAD... NEGLECT... KILLER... CHILD... WOMAN... MOTHER... She gave a great gasp and shook her hand free, watching the words flutter to the floor. Nausea swooped through her and she sank into a chair.

Presently, eventually, however long it took, she lurched to her feet and staggered along the landing. In Mam's room, she stood beside her mam, for once not taking her hand.

'I have...' She cleared her throat and started again. 'There's something I never told you. I've been getting poison pen letters, accusing me of ... of killing Joey. I've just found ... in the safe... It was Ralph. Ralph sent them.' A terrible fear washed through her. What an appalling thing to say about her husband. Suppose she was wrong. But she knew she wasn't. 'I have to go out. Adam will...' Adam would what? She hoped he would have some idea what to do, because she hadn't a clue. She only knew she had to get away. 'I'll come back for you, I promise.'

She returned to the sitting room. It was an effort to move, to think. The newspaper cuttings lay on the carpet. Should she take them? She remembered how she had dreaded picking letters off the mat, how her stomach had lurched as she looked through them.

It had been Ralph all along.

A sound made her swing round, goosebumps scattering up and down her arms.

Ralph called, 'I've come for my notebook. I thought I'd left it in the shop, but– Carrie? What's wrong?' He was in the doorway. Then he saw what was behind her and Carrie retreated a step as his expression darkened. 'What the bloody hell's going on? Did you do this?'

She swallowed. She glanced at the bits of paper, saw his eyes flick towards them, felt a shudder run through her as he lifted his gaze to hers. There was no sorrow, no remorse, no shame.

'It was you,' she whispered. 'You sent them. You

said over and over that I mustn't blame myself, yet you were sending the letters. You said I mustn't blame myself and every time you said it, I blamed myself more. Did you know that? Did you do it on purpose? Were you ... were you punishing me?'

'Not for Joey, no. His death was regrettable, but it turned you into a better wife. But you're right, the letters were a punishment. My God, when I think of everything I've done for you! Haven't I been a good provider? Haven't I given you status? Not that you ever wanted it, you with your Wilton Lane obsession. I let you have your mother – who, let's face it, is nothing more than a dummy – live under my roof. I even– God Almighty, Carrie, I even took on another man's baby and never let on.'

'You knew?'

'Yes, I knew, but I never held it against you, did I? You'd never have guessed if I hadn't just told you and I'd never have punished you for it. But yes, you're right, the letters were a punishment. The question is, are you going to stand there playing the innocent and pretending you don't know what for?'

'But ... if not Joey...'

'The thing is this, Carrie. At what point does infidelity begin? The first time you go at it with one another like a pair of rutting animals? I imagine that's what most people think. I know I did until a few months back. Or does it start the moment you realise you have feelings for someone else? Even if you never act on those feelings, doesn't the simple fact of having them mean you've broken faith? Can you answer the question, Carrie? I'm not sure I can. I'm not sure I could bear to. But even if you can't answer, you can see, can't you, why you had to be punished?'

He knew. She had tried so hard to hide it, but he knew.

'Well, Carrie,' Ralph said, softly, 'do you deserve it?'

Transfixed, she gave the faintest nod. She felt and heard a great crack as the back of Ralph's hand connected hard with the side of her face and she went flying. The other side of her face crunched against the armchair as she landed. She didn't know which side of her face to hold. From somewhere inside came the idea that she mustn't cradle both sides or it would look like a bid for sympathy.

Ralph yanked her to her feet. Her head was humming. Instinct took over and the moment he let go, Carrie darted away. She barely made it to the door before his hand landed on her shoulder so hard her knees buckled. Her arms flailed, grabbing at thin air for balance, as Ralph swung her about to face the open cupboard, the books on the table, the documents tied with string.

'What about all this, eh?' He was close behind her, head bent, his breath scalding her cheek.

She squirmed round to face him. 'Ralph, I swear this is for the best.'

'The best? There's only one way you can have found out about the safe. You've seen him, haven't you? *Haven't you?*'

'Please, it's not what you think. He wants to help – oh!' Ralph shook her so hard her teeth clicked.

408

'What's going on?' he demanded. 'What's he said?'

He snatched her wrists, cuffing them so hard she thought they would snap.

'Ralph – don't – you're hurting me–'

'What did he say?'

'It's Mr Larter. He's using the business to...' She had the oddest impression of movement in the background behind Ralph, but that must be the combination of tears and the black spots of pain swarming before her eyes.

'To what?'

Ralph squeezed harder. Carrie couldn't believe the strength in his fingers. She couldn't believe his desire to hurt her. She could feel every tiny piece of bone and gristle inside each wrist vibrating beneath the imminent danger of shattering beyond repair.

'What did Adam say?' Ralph's face was white with fury, his voice loud and clipped. Then he uttered a sound somewhere between a gasp and a grunt, his eyes flickered and he slumped to the floor, taking her with him.

Carrie lay pinned beneath him, too winded to move, too astonished to try, one leg doubled agonisingly beneath her. Had Ralph fainted? His body was a dead weight. She panicked, wriggling furiously until she wrenched her way out from underneath, her legs still trapped but her upper body free. She sucked in a great breath, but before she could haul her legs out, something drew her eye to the door, where–

Disbelief all but scooped her heart from her chest. Mam was there, leaning against the door frame, slowly sinking down it, a poker lying at her feet. Carrie stared. Mam looked haggard and ill and exhausted and surprisingly tall, but perhaps that was because Carrie was on the floor. She shook herself; of all the stupid things to think.

Next thing she knew, she was out from underneath Ralph and walking, dreamlike, across to Mam. She felt as though her legs were about to give way, but she mustn't let them because if she collapsed in a heap, who would pick Mam up when she sagged all the way to the carpet?

'Mam?'

Carrie stopped short, not quite close enough for touching. Mam's face turned and their eyes met.

'Oh, Mam, oh my goodness!'

She tried to gather Mam into her arms, taken aback by how awkward it was with Mam propped against the door frame, her body not doing anything to cooperate. After a moment Carrie felt the merest whisper of a touch on her back and her heart swelled. She wanted to hug Mam to her, but she was frightened of damaging her.

'G ... go...'

The word was so quiet that Carrie barely heard it, but the hand that had tried to pat her was now making little flapping attempts to push her chest. Carrie took a step back.

'G ... go. R ... un.'

'Mam, you can walk, you can move. Why have you never–?'

'Go n ... ow. N ... not ... safe.'

Carrie looked at the figure on the floor. Her wrists hummed, promising bruises to come. 'I'm

410

not leaving you.'

'M ... ust.' Mam's gaze flickered towards Ralph. 'Nev ... er s ... saw me.' Her eyelids fluttered and she sank further down the door frame. 'A... A...'

'Adam. Yes, I'll go to Adam. But first, let's get you back to bed. Ralph never saw you, so you'll be safe.'

Carrie part supported, part dragged Mam's sagging body along the landing, aware that her dear brave mam was doing her best with rapidly depleting strength. In the bedroom, Carrie gave up the struggle and they both collapsed across the bed, breathing raggedly. After a minute, Carrie got up and began manoeuvring Mam beneath the covers, taking care to lie her the same as usual.

'G ... go.'

Carrie couldn't bear the thought of leaving. Mam's skin was pasty-white and she couldn't keep her eyes open. Carrie bent and kissed her, then froze, her face an inch away.

'Armstrong! What the devil's taking you so long?'

Mr Larter. Carrie's instincts screamed at her to hide, but that would be pointless once Mr Larter found Ralph. Heat coursed through her veins. She had to stop Mr Larter finding Ralph, not to mention the open safe.

She raced along the landing, pulling the sitting-room door to, just as Mr Larter appeared.

'Ah – Mrs Armstrong. Sorry to barge in.' He walked along the landing, making a nonsense of the apology. 'Is Armstrong here? We're meant to be looking at the stock over the road and he's kept me waiting.'

'He was here a minute ago. You must have

411

missed one another crossing the road in the fog.'

Carrie could have sworn something rippled beneath the puckered flesh of his scar. 'I think not.' His voice was silky smooth. 'We came across the road together and I've been waiting in the shop.' He took a step closer. 'Why are you lying to me ... again?'

She swallowed. A sound – a groan, cut off, followed by another longer groan – made them both swing round. As Mr Larter covered the distance to the sitting room in two strides, Carrie backed away, trying to creep downstairs at a run. Would he be all concern for Ralph or would the open cupboard catch his eye, leading him to the safe?

Her answer came a moment later.

'You bitch, what have you found?'

Carrie fled.

Chapter Forty-Four

Wrenching the door open, sending the bell jingling madly, Carrie ran into a world of yellowy-grey cotton wool. She stopped and the air enveloped her, gluey and stale. Careful not to move her feet, because they were pointing in the right direction, she looked over her shoulder. Already, from just a few steps away, the shop had been swallowed by the fog. Edging forward, sliding her feet along the ground, she found the kerb and stepped into the road.

She heard Mr Larter come bursting out of the

shop – footfalls – an exclamation. He had evidently found the kerb the hard way. She hurried forward, trying to hold a straight line. It was like walking through cake mixture. Stubbing her toe on the opposite kerb, she winced but smothered a gasp.

'Mrs Armstrong? I know you're here. Come back inside. This deuced fog is dangerous.'

From somewhere over to her left came a thump. Had he bumped into the cabbies' hut? With one foot on the kerb and the other in the gutter, she headed for the corner. Behind her, muffled by great lumps of fog, she heard voices, men's voices, begging one another's pardon. Carrie strained her ears, realising Mr Larter had found the front steps of the Lloyds. Please let him search for her inside. She followed the curve of the corner and headed down the gently sloping road. From somewhere – impossible to tell how far away – came the voice of a woman reassuring a child.

By the time the kerb turned at the next corner, her teeth were chattering. She rubbed her hands briskly up and down her arms, for all the good it did. Stretching her hands out again, she watched them disappear into the pulp before she braved the road, anxious for the moment when she would stub her toes and be safe from being run over. Then she would use the kerb to guide her as far as the Green and that was more than halfway to Brookburn.

An obstacle – she cried out ... stumbled ... felt herself pulled up. Then she and the man – his face loomed out of the blur – did an awkward little dance as they righted themselves.

'Sorry, love. Are you all right?'

'Yes, yes. Let go. I'm in a hurry.'

'Oh, hey, I were only trying to help.'

'Have you got my wife there?' Mr Larter! 'Hold on to her, there's a good chap.'

'Righto,' the stranger agreed cheerfully.

Carrie tried to pull away. 'Let me go!'

'Now then, love.' The man's voice was reassuring, but the strength of his grip filled Carrie with panic. She wriggled like a mad thing and kicked out. 'Hey there! Well, bugger me–'

She wrenched herself free and darted into the blankness, then stopped. Through the clotted air came men's voices.

'Why did you let her go? I specifically said–'

'I'm surprised you want her back, mate, a vixen like that.'

She edged away, though in this curdled atmosphere it was hard to tell where they were and that brought her to a standstill. With a collapsing heart, she accepted she had lost her bearings. Footsteps crunched – she whirled round, but no one grabbed her. Think, think. She couldn't have run back into the road or she would have come a cropper on the kerb; and she wasn't on the cinder path of the pavement; so she must be on the plot of ground where Father Kelly wanted to build the new church.

'Spare a minute to help me find her. She's terrified of the fog, poor thing.'

'Well, just a minute, guv, then I must get on.'

Think, think. This plot occupied one entire end of the block, bordered on one side by fences and on the other three by pavement and road. At the far end of the block lay Chorlton Green, so all she need do was find a kerb and follow it.

Her flesh prickled, covering her in pinpricks of dread. The dense mass in front of her seemed to shift, like a curtain about to be pulled back to reveal – Carrie dodged away, then tripped and squealed as she measured her length on the ground. She didn't waste time getting up, just scrambled away on all fours, hoping she was leaving the exclamations of 'Over here!' behind her.

Pulling herself to her feet, she walked blindly into grey treacle. When her hands found the fence, she clung to it. Should she climb over and knock at one of the cottages? Impossible to do so in silence and if Mr Larter caught up, no one would believe her over a gentleman like him, especially if he had the other fellow in tow, blathering on about this daft female reduced to hysterics by the fog.

Find Adam. It was the only way.

Hugging the fence, knowing she had to trust it and not care about the grey scum she was plunging into, Carrie hurried as best she could to the far end, then slid her feet until she found the kerb, whereupon she resumed her awkward one foot up, one foot down gait, panting her way down the road to the Green.

At the corner, she halted. The muscles in her calves and thighs were screaming. Hovering at the kerb was like being on the edge of a precipice. The kerb had kept her safe, told her where she was. Now she must plunge into the gunk and pray to keep a straight line.

She knew when she had reached the Green, because her feet sank into cold soggy grass and she uttered a soft 'Uff!' as her fingers scraped on tree bark. Holding on to the tree, she moved around it; she must keep her straight line. Arms outstretched, she slid onwards, gasping as her knees banged into something and she nearly pitched forwards.

Grasping blindly, she made out a bench. She edged past and continued. Was there another bench? She couldn't remember. She walked with one hand stretched out at normal height, the other waving around lower down. Even so, her knee found the bench first. She barely had time to register the sharp pain in her kneecap before her hand landed on something at once firm and soft – something that moved.

A hand seized her arm and she screamed.

'Eh now, don't fret, lass,' came a woman's voice.

'Sorry, sorry.'

'I'm just resting me bunions before I get on home. It's a reet so-and-so, in't it, this blessed fog?'

Carrie didn't answer, just stumbled away, and not a moment too soon. An indignant squawk behind her almost made her swing round, but she caught herself in time. Straight line. She must keep to her straight line.

'Oy! What d'you think you're up to, laying hands on me?'

'I beg your pardon. I thought you were someone else.'

'Oh aye, and she doesn't mind being made free with, I tek it?'

Heart thumping, Carrie stumbled on through the murk.

'I know you're here. Stand still. I only want to talk to you.'

The wet ground sucked at her slippers as she pressed on. She could hear him behind her – no, over to the side. Then something – sound, instinct – told her he was close, and perhaps that same something told him she was too, because as she hurled herself sideways, there was a surge of movement in the gloom, followed by a clatter and a yell. What on earth–? The memorial. Oh Pa, please help me.

A hand snaked out just above ground level and all but ensnared her ankle, only she stamped and wriggled and hauled herself away, taking off at a run. One foot landing on the cinder path gave her the half-second's warning that saved her from turning her ankle on the kerb. She sprinted across the road, tripped over the kerb and slammed into a wall. A chest-high wall – otherwise she would have mashed her face into it. The graveyard.

Around the wall she went, clinging to it, grazes tearing palms and fingers, creating a background stinging sensation. Her wet slippers slop-slopped. At the far end of the wall, she kept going, hands out in front, knowing that she might or might not walk bang into the Bowling Green pub. If she did, should she knock on the door, on the windows, yell for help? Pointless question, since she must by now have walked right past it.

Brookburn next. She had to find the wall. She veered left, arms outstretched, hands lost in the clammy depths. The wall would lead her to the gates, then there was the crunchy drive, and then Adam and safety. Her hands hit the wall. She staggered along, hugging so close to it that with every step she scraped and bumped herself.

When the wall ended, she patted her way to the gate's tall metal bars. Thank goodness the gates were standing open. Another step and the familiar crunch underfoot made her freeze. She couldn't afford to make even the tiniest sound, but if she left the drive, she might blunder around in circles for hours in the grounds. No, she must keep to the drive.

The gravel felt like needles pricking through the soles of her slippers as she edged forwards, working her way hand over hand along the bars of the gate. When her fingers found the wide bar at the end, she instinctively braced herself to step out with nothing to hang on to. She let go, took a step, then was seized from behind by swift, silent hands, her scream cut off by a hand snapping down to cover her mouth, giving her a taste of leather glove. The arm encircling her waist jerked, expelling the breath from her body in a single expert move. She sagged, but he hauled her upright.

'Keep still,' Mr Larter hissed. 'You've saved me some trouble. If I hadn't gone careering into that memorial, I'd have throttled you on the Green and then had to carry you here to throw you in the brook. As it is, all I need do is snap your neck and in you go. A tragic accident, such a pity, but these things happen in the fog.'

He released her mouth and Carrie said in the most determined voice she could muster, 'Adam will know it's no accident. He told me all about you.'

His hand moved to her neck and throat. This

was really happening. He was going to kill her.

She wrapped chilled hands round his fingers and tugged with all her might, appalled by his strength. She sucked in a breath, her stomach executing a somersault at the bilge-water of the fog, but her attempt at a cry for help was cut off by a vicious shake that reduced it to a gurgle.

'Carrie! Carrie!'

Ralph! Mr Larter's fingers, instead of releasing her, were locking into position, selecting particular bones in her neck, pressing into her throat, shutting off her windpipe. With one final effort, she flung out her arm and banged the gate, catching her funny bone and gasping as pain jangled up and down her arm. It took her a moment to separate the pain from the clattering sound that was oddly hollow and short-lived in the fog.

'Carrie! Is that you? I knew you'd come here.'

The crunch of footsteps, another dull clatter, and Ralph loomed out of the murk. He looked ghastly. Carrie thought it was the fog leeching the colour from his face, then she saw his skin was grey, his eyes blurred and slow. It took him a moment to react to Mr Larter's presence.

'Larter! Why are you here? Good grief, man, what are you doing?'

'Dealing with the immediate problem.'

'You can't mean – my God, you wouldn't. Let her go.'

Carrie sensed Ralph's lunge before it happened and then found herself on the ground, gravel biting her hands and knees, as Mr Larter hurled her aside to block Ralph's assault. She scrambled away, stopping only when she reached grass.

Behind her, instead of the sounds of a punch-up, she heard Mr Larter's voice.

'Don't be a fool, Armstrong. You're in no fit state. I'm surprised you're on your feet after that bashing you took.'

Carrie waited. Then Ralph spoke, slurring a little. 'My head ... is pounding, I must admit. Feel rather woozy. I've thrown up a couple of times.'

'Charming. That'll be concussion. She fetched you one hell of a crack.'

Another pause. 'She?'

'Your wife.'

Carrie clutched at the grass. Don't let him realise.

'No ... no, it wasn't Carrie.'

'You aren't thinking straight. Face it: the little woman has taken sides against you, which is why we have to find her.'

'It wasn't Carrie, I tell you. She was right in front of me when – Christ, who could it have been?'

'Your brother?'

'*Adam?* Are you crazy?'

'Well, who else knows about the safe?'

'Christ!' Then came a small sound, part grunt, part sigh, as if the exclamation had hurt his head.

'First things first. We've got to find her and stop her.'

'If you lay one finger–'

'And when I've stopped her, I'll stop you too, if needs be. I don't intend to lose everything, up to and including life and liberty, just because you baulk at what needs doing.'

Muffled sounds squeezed through the gummy layers of fog. A momentary scuffle – a dull clang

– a groan.

'Carrie!' Ralph's voice sounded choked. 'Run!'

She stumbled a few steps, then picked up pace.

Get on the drive and go hell for leather to the house. Don't think. Just do it.

With one toe, she found the gravel. She stepped onto it and ran through the mushy air. But the crunching ceased beneath her feet and she skidded to a halt. She had run the wrong way. Instead of heading up the drive to the house, she had run back to the road. Instinctively, she twisted round but tripped and fell hard, the impact singing through her.

No time to recover. As she got to her feet, her knees wobbled and she had to scoop herself up before she fell again, but in so doing, she turned partway round. Which way was she now facing? Towards Brookburn? Or in the other direction, towards Ees House, the posh place where the Kimbers lived?

Indistinct sounds came weaving through the fog. She screwed up her face, trying to hear. She couldn't risk another go at Brookburn's drive, not with both men roaming the grounds. But if she could find the gates, they would be her starting point for heading back the way she had come. She only had to get to the pub and hammer on the doors.

Waving her hands about in front of her like a child playing at ghosts, she plunged into the fog. When her feet found the gravel again, she turned and almost immediately banged into a gate. She turned to her left and struck out along the road, her right hand trailing along the wall, picking up grazes. When the wall ended and she had nothing to guide her, she took heart, knowing the pub lay ahead; but she couldn't find it.

Clamping down hard on a surge of panic, she veered sharply right, hands lost to sight as they groped in the murk until – not a wall, but a fence. A fence? Yes, and bushes. Her mouth went dry. The gate she had found hadn't been one of Brookburn's. It had been one of the Ees House gates opposite ... and that meant she was heading the wrong way.

This fence belonged to Brookburn Farm. Go back or go on? A faint noise put her on the alert. She clutched the fence.

'I know you're there,' said Mr Larter. 'I've been following the sounds. Do you imagine you're safe if you stand still?'

Loosely clasping the top of the fence, she rushed on, nearly falling over her feet when the fence turned the corner. She stumbled to a halt. Was she skirting a field or had she found the track to the farmhouse? She stepped away from the fence with its narrow verge of overgrown grass. Beneath her feet, the ground was compacted earth and her heart pitter-pattered in relief. This must be the way to the farmhouse.

She pressed on through the fumey blankness, stumbling as she found a pothole. Except that it wasn't a pothole, she realised, it was the track sloping downwards, and it was nothing to do with the farm. It was the beginning of the lane leading on to the meadows.

Carrie stood still. She couldn't go back and she couldn't leave the lane, so she must go forwards towards – yes, she could be at Jackson's Boat in minutes, and over the other side was the Bridge pub.

The lane shrank to a slender path, one-person-wide, overhung here and there by trees and bushes, their leafy branches slapping her face and draping damply over her arms.

At last, the path widened and she groped about. If she was where she thought she was, then the path would divide and close by would be the steps up to Jackson's Boat. She cast her hands about, but it was her foot that found one of the rocks near the steps.

A hand grabbed her arm and yanked her back, making her cry out, a cry that was cut off by a clout across her face. Coming on top of where Ralph had landed her one, it was almost enough to make her swoon, but knowing that just a step or two away were the rocks, she pulled forwards. The instant her leg grazed rock, she sidestepped. Mr Larter stumbled against the rock and staggered, letting go. She tried to run, then collapsed as he flung himself on top of her. She lay flattened by his weight, then he shifted, but instead of dragging her up, he pinned her down with one knee in her back and felt for her neck.

A thud. The knee vanished from her spine as Mr Larter went flying, followed by the heavy weight of another body that ended up sprawled across her, winding her all over again. Mr Larter hauled Ralph up, one of them stepping on her.

'You bloody fool,' growled Mr Larter.

'Leave ... my wife ... alone.'

She heard the thud of a fist, followed by grunts

and pummelling. She heaved herself to her feet, tottering on the sloping riverbank. With a yell, the punch-up burst out of the fog, clipping her and sending her spinning down the bank. At the bottom of this slope was a sharp descent into the river and, a lesson drummed into her years ago by Pa, she dropped to the ground to stop herself tumbling further.

Rising unsteadily, leaning into the slope, she began a careful ascent, trying to veer away from the sounds of the blows as the two men slogged it out. Ralph was bigger and heavier, but he had that head wound. Everything went quiet. Carrie's insides turned slushy. She chanced a couple of steps, then a couple more, then fell over Ralph's prone form. She gasped in horror, not because of Ralph, but because she sensed the presence out of sight.

Mr Larter grabbed her, but they both slid and stumbled on the wet slope. The grass felt greasy. She tried dropping to the ground, but Mr Larter jerked her to her feet. There was a gut-churning moment when they swayed and tottered on the brink. Then they went over.

Hitting the water, she was consumed by terror as she went under, but Mr Larter still had hold of her and he dragged her to the surface. She burst out of the water, gasping, then Mr Larter clapped his hand on top of her head and thrust her back under. She struggled, but he was too strong. Just before her lungs exploded, there was a disturbance in the water beside her and a great flailing and lunging began, in the midst of which Carrie bobbed up to the surface in time to see Ralph erupt from the water like a monster from the deep, before plunging down on top of his adversary.

Sick and dizzy, she floundered away. Even here, close to the bank, she could feel the insistent plucking of the current. If she didn't climb out soon, it would tug her into the middle and sweep her away.

Making a desperate effort, she bumped into the bank only for gratitude to turn to a silent howl of despair as she realised the impossibility of climbing up. Yes, there were dents and outcroppings that might do for hand- and footholds, but not in her state of cold and exhaustion. Beneath Jackson's Boat, the banks sloped right down to the water, so she must pull herself as far as the bridge – if her strength would last that long.

She found the slope and dragged herself out of the water, too exhausted to be grateful or relieved or anything. She lay there, stunned with fear and fatigue, unable to move, not even wanting to. What she wanted most was to go to sleep. She shook her head, trying to snap herself awake, but she had no energy left. She wondered vaguely how it was possible to feel utterly numb and yet ache from head to foot at the same time.

What was that? She forced herself to sit up and listen, but the buzzing of tiredness inside her head was louder than any other sound. She inched away, found the bridge's foundations and tucked herself behind the ironwork. A sloshing noise told her that someone was emerging from the river. She felt rather than heard him slump to the ground, then she caught heavy breathing and a few muttered words. At last, he blew out a great long breath, then squelched up the slope and disappeared.

She didn't dare move. Ralph – or Mr Larter? And what had become of the other one? She must have dozed off, because suddenly she was awake again, her muscles spiralling with cramp. With the cold and the pain, she could barely move. She managed to rub one calf to ease it a little. She needed to wriggle her toes, but she couldn't feel them. Feeling ill, she grasped the edge of the bridge and struggled to her feet, only to fall over, toppling head first down the slope and landing practically on top of a body.

She rolled away, heart pumping.

'C ... Carrie?' His voice was barely a croak.

'Ralph?'

'You're ... here. Alive.'

'Mr Larter's gone.'

'I know... I couldn't ... fight any more. My head... I stayed under ... as long as I could ... so he'd think ... I'd drowned.'

'Did he think I'd drowned too?'

'Maybe ... or gave up. He'll be ... on his way. Listen, Carrie... Die of ... 'sposure out here. Go.'

'I'll fetch help.'

She struggled up, her muscles screaming for mercy. She clambered up the slope to the bridge and hauled herself across it. At the far side she half-tumbled down the steps and collapsed onto the ground. She wanted to curl into a ball and sleep for ever. Waves of nausea swooping through her, she staggered to her feet. She tottered down the slope, finding the pub by walking into the wall.

426

She felt her way round, tapping bricks until she found herself tapping on glass. She could see light through a chink in the curtain. The curtain twitched aside, making her stumble backwards in alarm even though this was what she wanted. She had the oddest impression that the fog had found its way inside her head and then all thought was blotted out.

Chapter Forty-Five

Carrie opened her eyes. She ached all over, inside and out. Even the mattress and the pillows seemed to ache. Her eyes shifted into focus and she frowned, not recognising where she was. Memories deluged her, the fear, the fog, so many images all at once. She had an obscure memory of weird, frightening dreams; she remembered struggling to waken. There had been another dream too, a topsy-turvy dream where, instead of her sitting at Mam's bedside, it was the other way round, with Mam watching over her.

Sensing movement, she glanced round and there was Mam in an armchair, bundled up in blankets. Her face shifted into a lopsided smile. So that bit wasn't a dream. She toppled back into slumber.

Carrie awoke, no longer exhausted. The aching had subsided to a dull roar. The first thing she did was look to see if Mam was still there. She was.

Carrie lifted her hand. Mam reached, missed, then seized it.

'I'll fetch Doctor Armstrong,' said a quiet voice, and Carrie glimpsed a nurse's uniform before the door shut.

'Mam.' She didn't know where to start. 'Why did you never...?'

'Hush, love. All in ... good time. You're at Brook ... burn. This is Ev ... adne's bedroom. I'm in an ... other room ... along the landing.'

'Except you aren't there, Mrs Jenkins,' came Adam's voice, 'because you insist on spending every moment at your daughter's bedside.'

Carrie's throat ached at the smile in his voice. She didn't dare look at him. She thought of the punishment she had endured at Ralph's hands and quaked.

'Where's...?' Her voice vanished and she had to try again. 'How is Ralph?' He must be in a bad way if he had let himself be brought to Brookburn.

Adam said, 'I'm sorry. He died.'

Her heart surged as if to deliver an almighty clang, but instead seemed to hang in mid-air, leaving a strange, empty feeling that made it difficult to breathe.

'He lay a long time in the bitter cold,' said Adam. 'He'd obviously been in a brutal fight. In particular, there was a nasty injury to the back of his head.'

'Mr Larter said he had concussion,' Carrie remembered. She froze, clutching Mam's hand secretly. 'Was it the head injury that...?'

'No. He died of exposure.'

428

Exposure. The very word Ralph had used. 'I went for help, only...'

'You collapsed,' said Adam, 'and no wonder.'

'But if I'd–'

'You mustn't blame yourself.'

'Don't tell me what to think,' she snapped, startling herself as well as him. 'Sorry,' she whispered. 'Sorry.'

'The police want to speak to you.'

A memory swam into her mind: Ralph keeping the police at bay after poor Miss Deacon died. She had been in bed then too. Joey.

'You'll be up and about in no time,' Adam said, 'so we must get the story straight now – to protect Mrs Jenkins, for one. We don't want the world to know she attacked Ralph with the poker. And to protect you, for another. Those letters Ralph sent...'

She shuddered. No, she didn't want anyone knowing. How did Adam know?

'Here and now,' said Adam, 'we speak the truth. We'll worry later about what to tell the police.' He looked from her to Mam. 'Shall I start? There was a telephone call yesterday morning from the pub the other side of Jackson's Boat.'

She waved a hand to stop him. 'Yesterday ... was Tuesday.' And the nightmare hadn't started until Tuesday evening.

'Yester ... day was We'n's. .. day.'

'It's Thursday now, ten o'clock in the morning,' said Adam. 'You've been out for the count, with a little help from a sedative.' He let her think about that for a moment. 'On Tuesday evening, the landlord took you in, soaked through and covered

429

in bruises. His wife put you to bed and sat up with you. Apparently, you kept almost coming round, but she couldn't make out what you were saying, not until early Wednesday morning when she caught something about Brookburn. Hence the telephone call. Ted Geeson and I and a couple of orderlies took the ambulance to the top of the lane down to the meadows, then walked to Jackson's Boat and stretchered you back.'

'Did you...? Is that when you found Ralph?'

Adam's eyes clouded. 'We must have passed within feet of him.' He looked away. 'I didn't know until later that he was missing. The police found him yesterday evening.'

Carrie closed her eyes.

'I went to the flat,' Adam continued, 'because I knew Mrs Jenkins would need looking after. Fortunately, I arrived before your cleaning woman. The shop was unlocked. I went upstairs and found – well, you know what I found – the poker, the contents of the safe...' He hesitated. 'Bits of newspaper on the floor.'

'I had ... lain there all ... night,' said Mam, 'too exhausted to ... move. I kept ... trying to get up, but ... all my strength was ... gone.'

'Mrs Jenkins told me what had happened,' said Adam. 'I brought her here, then informed the police that Ralph had been missing all night.'

After that, it was Mam's turn. Carrie listened in mounting horror.

'...Ralph k-killed ... his father.'

'No!' Carrie exclaimed. Ralph – a murderer? Had she been married to a murderer?

'Killed him?' said Adam. 'What – on purpose?'

430

'Saw it ... with my own eyes. Threw ... him down de-de...'

'Deliberately?' said Adam.

'It was m-m–'

'Murder?'

Mam's eyes flashed. 'D-don't ... speak ... for ... me.'

Carrie reached for her hand. 'Take your time.'

After witnessing Joseph Armstrong's death, Mam had collapsed, only to waken inside a body over which she had no power, her heart breaking as her jilted daughter fell under the murderer's spell and became his wife. All the time that Carrie had been caring for her so tenderly and determinedly, Ralph had been slipping into her room now and then.

'But he never went near you!' Carrie protested.

'He would ... ask if I ... could hear and then he ... said things.'

'What things?'

But Mam wouldn't say.

'I was ... frightened. I knew he would ... k-kill me if I showed signs of ... 'covery. To start, I ... really couldn't ... move. Terrified ... awake inside ... paralysed body. Wished ... he'd killed me when he killed ... his father. Then I started ... get better, but had to ... make my ... self a ... dead weight when you did the ... exercises on me...'

'Oh, Mam,' Carrie wanted to jump up and pace the room, but she had to stay still and calm, for Mam's sake.

'Can't tell you how ... much I wanted to give ... a sign. You ... so dedicated. But I knew ... only hope was to recover ... enough to dress, sneak

431

down … stairs… get to Wilton Lane. It felt … taking for ever… Exercised every night … arms and legs … just like…'

'Just like I did for you,' Carrie said, fighting to hold back the tears.

'I was … so weak. My body… All my strength was in my head, in my … thoughts. Eventually started … levering my … self out of bed … trying to … to walk… So tiring. No … stamina.'

'But you didn't give up. You're so brave.'

'Worried about you after … you lost Joey. Spurred … me on. But … mistakes. One time … brushed my hair, but left … brush … wrong place.'

'I remember that. I thought it was Mrs Porter.'

But that was nothing compared to the mistake that followed. She slowly explained how, when Carrie, after months of not chatting, had opened up again, and especially when she had spoken of visiting Joey, she had been overwhelmed by emotion and squeezed Carrie's hand.

'When you told … Ralph, he came and … stood over me. Thought he w … would throttle me. Got … careless. Pushed myself too … hard. Fell over during that night … woke you up. Only just … back to bed in … time. But when … you saw me at … window on Mon … day, thought the … game was up.'

'I thought it was Mrs Porter skiving.'

'Then you said … open the safe. Had to mek you realise … if evidence in safe … had to mean … Ralph criminal.'

'That's why you squeezed my hand again.'

'Wanted … stop you.'

'And later you heard me and Ralph, and you

432

dragged yourself to my rescue.'

'You're a remarkable woman, Mrs Jenkins,' said Adam.

'Not ... really. Were all I could do to ... carry that ... poker and after I'd ... bashed him, I were neither use ... nor orn'ment.'

'Oh, Mam,' Carrie said again, half-laughing, half-crying. Sitting up in bed, she leant over and hugged Mam, her arms tightening as she thought of all Mam had suffered.

Adam surrendered his handkerchief and Carrie mopped her face. Then it was her turn and she described the blundering chase through the fog.

'Ralph wanted to save me. The concussion was bad, but he wouldn't give up.'

When she ran out of steam, there was a sober silence before Adam said, 'He loved you.'

'Then why ... poison pen letters?' Laboured speech or not, Mam sounded acerbic.

Carrie didn't want to answer, but felt obliged to. 'Punishment.'

'For Joey?' Adam asked.

Well, of course he would think that, having read the words scattered on the floor. It would be so easy to say yes. No, it wouldn't. It was impossible. She wouldn't attach this lie to Joey.

'No,' she whispered. 'It was ... something else.'

She saw understanding in Adam's eyes and looked away.

Evadne's hands trembled so much she could barely fasten the buttons on her blouse. She was wearing her own clothes again. She had been taken to see the governor, who had looked up from his work long enough to inform her that the charges against her had been dropped and she was to be released. No information, no details. Then his gaze returned to the papers in front of him and she stood there like an imbecile, not daring to feel relieved in case she had misheard, until the wardress plucked at her arm and she was led away.

But not back to her cell, thank God. She was taken to – she hadn't the faintest idea where she was taken, because now relief and hope and gratitude were breaking through and it was all she could do to walk in a straight line.

'Your things are over there.'

But she lurched at a chair instead, plonking down before her knees buckled.

'You're going home.'

It was safe to believe it. It wasn't the words that made her certain. It was the absence of her surname. 'Do this, Baxter. Do that, Baxter' and 'Posh bitch, aren't you, Baxter?' had been the refrain since she was dumped here; and the lack of that *Baxter* was what told her the nightmare had come to an end.

She dressed. Oh, the feel of fine-quality underwear, the soft yielding cotton of her blouse, its starch long since gone, the sheer smartness of her elegant skirt and matching jacket! Her throat thickened with emotion.

'There's a gent come to fetch you.'

Grandfather. But she had learnt various things during her time in this godforsaken hole, one of which was that when you were set free – if you were ever set free – you were taken to a small door set inside a pair of massive doors and you stepped through onto the cobbles, where a loved one might or might not be waiting for you. Oh, the shame of stepping outside like any common thief or – or woman of the night. Grandfather would not be there to share the shame. He might send Mr Denton, but he wouldn't set foot within a mile.

'He's waiting along the corridor. The governor allowed it, under the circumstances.'

Grandfather! That was good. It was perfect – wasn't it?

She didn't want her grandfather. She wanted ... but would he be described as a gentleman? Well, why not? He might not be, socially or financially, but in his person and his character he most certainly was, and that was what mattered.

With an unaccustomed flutter in her belly, Evadne followed the wardress down the corridor. The woman waved her into a room and she walked in to see – please let it be – Adam Armstrong.

Oh. She stood tall, smoothing her features, keeping her secret.

'Congratulations on your release,' he said. 'I'm here to take you home.'

'Thank you.'

'This way.' He ushered her back down the corridor and towards a staircase. 'I should warn you, there are reporters outside, but not to worry. The governor owes me a favour: I saved his godson's life during the war. Plus, the circumstances of your case are now known to certain people and that's another reason for him to let us creep out of a back entrance. I've a motor waiting.'

'I don't understand why the press is interested,' she said, as they started down the stairs. 'It's not as though I was found guilty of anything.'

'My dear girl, that's precisely why they're interested. Most of what's happened has been kept quiet while the investigation proceeds, but there's nothing hush-hush about your part in it, which we believe is what Larter intended. Throw your beauty into the mix and you've got yourself a story. We've even had the odd reporter sniffing round at Brookburn; Geeson's had to padlock the gates.'

In the most casual voice possible, she asked, 'How is he?'

'Fine.' He pushed open a door on to a grim yard with a phalanx of evil-smelling dustbins. A motor stood waiting. 'Now, where should I take you? Carrie and Mrs Jenkins have been at Brookburn for a couple of days, but now they're back over the shop. I could take you there or to your grandfather's.'

'The shop, please.'

He smiled. 'I'm glad you said that. It saves me having to rush round the front of the building to deliver a change of plan to Geeson.' He cranked the starting handle and jumped in, steering the motor carefully out of the shadowy yard. 'He's passing the time of day with the reporters and if he happens to drop the name of the road where Major Baxter lives, well, it isn't his fault if the press acts on information received, is it?'

So he had come for her. Her heart swayed under the impact.

'Do the reporters know about the flat over the shop?' she asked.

'If they don't, they'll soon find out. You'll have to lie low for a while. Don't worry, you'll have plenty to keep you busy. Your mother's going to need a lot of help.'

She listened in amazement, shaking her head in disbelief. Mother's recovery – Ralph's part in the crime ring – the danger that had stalked Carrie through the fog. Astonishment upon astonishment; and also resentment. She had thought herself to be the one in dire need – the *one*. Her breath hitched as shame engulfed her. She was a better person than that. She hadn't always been, but she was now.

Yes, she was bruised, both physically and emotionally. Comfort would be lavished upon her by Carrie, that great looker-afterer, and Mother, however incapacitated, would be filled with concern for her suffering. But as well as receiving their comfort, she would give comfort in return. Her sister and mother had suffered too and she wanted to support them.

And when Evadne Baxter wanted something, she went all out to achieve it.

Chapter Forty-Six

Carrie placed the pot of snowdrops on Joey's grave and gazed at his inscription, laying a hand against her breastbone. How could Ralph have known her darling little boy wasn't his? How had he found out? How? Her mind raced, seeking answers – and finding none.

All along, she had thought herself the clever one for providing a decent home for her child and her mam, yet Ralph had known all along. She was the one who had been manipulated. Was she hypocritical to feel wronged, duped – tricked? She had tied herself in knots trying to make good her deception of Ralph. How hard she had tried to please him, to be the best wife she could, to make up for not loving him. Had he ever felt the need to make up for his own deception? Had he tried harder to please her, to be the best husband he could?

No. He had felt no such impulse. If he had wanted to do the decent thing, he would have admitted to knowing her secret. But he hadn't wanted to do the decent thing. He had wanted to manipulate her. He had been skilled at controlling her, she saw that now, right from the early days of their marriage when she had been so eager to be a suitable wife. From the first, she had let him rule her, because she had so much to be grateful for. But if she was honest, wasn't it more than that?

Hadn't fear come into it? Ralph was a bully boy and she had learnt to walk on eggshells.

And the ultimate form of control had been those vile letters, which had urged her deeper into grief and self-recrimination, deeper under his control.

The more she thought about it, the more she realised not just how cruel he had been but also how clever. His timing had been faultless. There was the letter that arrived the day following Evadne's arrest, which had served the dual purpose of distracting her from perhaps finding out that he had been a party to the arrest and also injuring her just as she was emerging from the seclusion that, now she thought about it, had given him power over her every limited move. And that time she had ventured out to see Mr Weston, she had returned to another letter – punishment and sabotage rolled into one, for her attempt to rebuild her life.

In the couple of days she and Mam had spent at Brookburn, they and Adam had agreed on their public story. Blackening Ralph's name would tarnish – further tarnish – the reputation of his surviving family. She and Mam had clutched one another's hands. They were already a deserter's family. But to be a murderer's family to boot? It was too much. So the murder of Joseph Armstrong must never be spoken of.

All Carrie had told the police was that she had walked in on a row between Ralph and Alex Larter, whereupon Mr Larter, believing her to have overheard and understood something that she hadn't overheard and therefore couldn't possibly repeat now, had turned on her. She had escaped into the fog, pursued by Mr Larter, himself pursued by Ralph. No mention was made of the safe, the poison pen letters or the poker; and Mam's actions remained a secret.

Carrie, clasping Mam's hand throughout the police questioning, had felt Mam tremble and held on tighter.

'It's all right,' she whispered reassuringly.

But the eyes that had swung round on her snapped with resentment. Mam's mouth worked before she was able to squeeze out the words. 'Not scared, not up ... set. *Angry.*'

Who could blame her? Ralph the murderer, of whom she had lived in such fear during her secret recovery, had got away with it in death just as he had in life.

And then there were Ralph's criminal acts. Carrie shuddered with shame to think she had been married to a thief, and not just any old thief, but one who had stolen from their wartime allies.

Murderer. Thief. Liar. Tormentor. It might be a sin to be glad someone was dead, but honestly, the world was a better place without Ralph Armstrong in it. She had had him buried in Southern Cemetery, which was where everyone was buried these days.

'I have examined the grave papers and there is still space in the old family grave in Chorlton,' the undertaker had said.

She went cold, but kept her voice steady. 'My late husband told me that before his father was buried there, there were two more spaces – now occupied by his father and my son.'

Ah, well, Mrs Armstrong, the little boy was so tiny, d'you see? It's always possible to...'

'No!' What? Make Joey budge up to make room for Ralph Armstrong? Not flaming likely. Carrie's hands balled into fists. She wouldn't make Joseph Armstrong lie with his murderer, either. 'I should like my husband to go to Southern Cemetery, please.'

And he did, more or less the moment the coroner released his body. It was a small, private ceremony, attended by just her and Adam, the widow and the brother, both of them already armed with suitable phrases about letting press interest die down, should anyone ask.

If ever anyone deserved to have their misdemeanours paraded for all the world to see, that person, that criminal, that cruel, conniving so-and-so was Ralph Armstrong. He deserved to have his name reviled, but, oh no, this was something else he was going to get away with.

A quiet burial ... and they had buried the truth with him.

Adam had arranged for Carrie to meet Mr Drummond, one of the investigators. He had offered to bring him to the flat, but Carrie preferred Brookburn, wanting to protect Mam as far as possible – though she knew what Mam would say to that.

Adam came out to meet her as she climbed Brookburn's front steps. She saw the concern in his eyes, the warmth, the... She looked away.

'The most private place for this is my sitting room upstairs,' said Adam, 'or I can bring Drummond down here if you prefer.'

'Upstairs.'

Adam's sitting room looked like it was trying to be an office. Didn't he have anywhere else to put all his papers and files?

A man stood by the window. He looked round.

'I remember you,' she said, before Adam could perform introductions. 'You came to the auction room to see pieces that had been sold. Later that day, my sister was arrested.' She gave him a challenging look, making it clear she knew he had been instrumental in the arrest.

Mr Drummond asked a great many questions. Finally, she was fed up with it.

'I'm not answering any more until you do some explaining.'

Mr Drummond raised his eyebrows at her. She raised hers back at him.

'The stolen items are discreetly being traced to their new owners. Renton, Kemp and others around the country have been arrested, including your deliverymen.'

'Charlie and Tom? Nonsense! Wait – I remember now. The day you and your colleague came to the auction, there was a secretaire with brass handles that Tom and Charlie were meant to bring for you to see, but they brought a different one. They must have hidden the first one because it was stolen. That was the one Mr Kemp bought, even though he had bought a bureau only two weeks earlier. I thought it strange that he wanted two.'

Mr Drummond made rapid notes. 'Kemp's job was to buy any stolen piece that might otherwise be knocked down to a dealer. They couldn't risk these articles being sold on the open market. The trouble is, all the evidence points to other people, and not one scrap of it to Alex Larter.'

'I'm not surprised. Look how he manipulated my sister.'

To cap it all, Alex Larter had disappeared. So, it seemed, had Mrs Bentley.

'Oh,' said Carrie. 'Poor Evadne.'

'May I ask more questions now?' Mr Drummond asked wryly.

His skilful probing made more memories surface.

'The silver salver!' Carrie repeated the snatch of conversation she had overheard, remembering how Ralph had made her distrust her own ears. 'But of course, that doesn't mean it was stolen.'

Then she remembered how the salver later vanished from Miss Deacon's house when the dear old lady was brutally killed. Ralph again? She clamped her lips shut so as not to blurt it out. Letting a murderer get away with it went against everything she believed ... yet here she was, doing it.

He was still manipulating her.

Adam had brought Mr Weston back to Armstrong's to hold the fort while Carrie, Mam and Evadne recuperated. While Mam's journey back to health would take rather longer, Carrie felt better once she had had a good rest.

'The shop is yours now,' Adam told her. 'You must decide what to do with it.'

'Mine?' She hadn't given it a thought. Good heavens. 'But I don't know anything about antiques.'

'What shall you do? Silly question. You need time to think.'

'No, I don't. I know exactly what to do.' She almost bounced on her toes in her eagerness. 'I'm keeping it, and the first thing I must do is ask Mr Weston to take back his old job permanently. We can't manage without him.'

When he was asked, Mr Weston wasn't ashamed to shed a tear. 'My dear Mrs Armstrong, it would be a pleasure and a privilege.'

'Only you would have such a lovely way of saying yes.' Carrie had to knuckle the corner of her eye to deal with her own tears.

Now she and Mam were on a crusade to feed up Mr Weston. Carrie insisted that when the shop shut for dinner, he must come upstairs and share their meal. Hearty stews, savoury pies and indulgent puddings were the order of the day.

But Mr Weston's permanent return was only part of Carrie's plan. She had an idea she hadn't shared with anyone.

Today was the day. The four of them ate a creamy vegetable ragout with hunks of crusty bread, followed by rice pudding, which was one of Mr Weston's favourites.

'Evadne, I need to show you something downstairs,' said Carrie. 'Mr Weston, you'll stop and have a cup of tea with Mam, won't you? We shan't be long.'

Evadne allowed herself to be led into the shop. 'Has something come in that you want me to see?'

'No, I want a private word.' Carrie huffed a breath. She couldn't quite believe that she,

Carrie Jenkins-as-was, former shop girl, ordinary daughter of an ordinary man, was about to say these words to her socially superior, educated sister, the Beautiful Baxter. 'I want to offer you a job here in the shop. I know you like antiques and you started learning from Mr Weston; and it's no secret that you never wanted to be a teacher or work in the office at Brookburn; but I thought – hoped – that you might like this.'

Evadne's hand flew to her chest. 'Do you mean it? Are you sure?'

'Of course.'

'Oh, Carrie, I'd love to. Thank you.'

'You shan't be free to visit Major Baxter every Saturday,' Carrie warned her.

Evadne glanced away, then changed her mind and looked straight into Carrie's eyes. 'That isn't the hardship it would once have been. I've spent a long time trying to ingratiate myself with Grandfather in the hope he would take me in, but he never did. It's time for me to back away.' She shrugged. 'I don't suppose he'll mind.'

'Sweetheart...' Carrie wanted to hug her, but Evadne was strictly a hands-to-yourself person.

'I ... I made rather an idiot of myself over Alex Larter. I really thought he was interested in me.'

'I thought as much.'

Evadne's eyebrows lifted. 'How? I never said anything.'

'Evadne, you might have had the posh education, but I'm not as green as I am cabbage-looking.'

'That's one of Pa's sayings.'

'I know.'

'I've made mistakes over the years. I loved Pa's admiration, but I rather despised Mother for marrying down, and I always had my sights set on the glory that is Parrs Wood.' Sarcasm curled her lips. 'When Alex came along, I was ripe for the plucking. What a twerp he must have thought me. I believed in him until the last possible moment, when Ted Geeson made me face the truth. I've certainly found out who my friends are.'

Aha! A chance to put in a word for Ted Geeson? 'Mr Geeson is a good sort. I like him.'

'Doctor Armstrong has shown himself a good friend. He wanted to support me through that first police interview, though I wouldn't have it; but he attended the court hearing, and then he was the one who drove me home. Pa would say he's a proper gent.'

'Yes,' Carrie said briskly. She wasn't about to be drawn into a conversation about Adam. 'Anyroad, I'm delighted you want to work here. Let's go and tell Mam and Mr Weston.'

Evadne could barely believe how much she was enjoying herself. She had a job that made her glad to get up in the morning. Through her years of teaching and her time at Brookburn, all she had wanted was to get married and leave. It had never occurred to her that in the right job, she might feel satisfied and fulfilled, and now here she was in just such a job.

The auction room had been shut down, its remaining pieces removed for examination, only to be returned as being nothing to do with the stolen goods.

'What will we do?' Evadne wailed. 'We haven't got room.'

'The smaller pieces can come into the shop or we can store them,' said Mr Weston, 'and we can ask a dealer to look at the bigger things. Actually, the furniture Mr Ralph listed as the Withington collection could do well at auction.'

Evadne's heart gave a sickening lurch, but she refused to evade the matter. 'Would it be worth shipping it to Chester?'

'Foster and Wainwright's? Undoubtedly. They should get us a magnificent price. Would you wish to be present?'

Part of her wanted to return to Chester with her head held high, as befitted the innocent party; but it was more important not to revive memories of how she had been duped by Alex. She wanted to put all that behind her.

Anyway, she had more important things to do these days – like learning all she could about fine things and reading to the chaps at Brookburn and helping Mother with her sewing, which meant for every three good stitches unpicking a clumsy one, as Mother battled to restore her dexterity. She was learning to gauge her mother's moods. Sometimes quiet encouragement was needed, other times mock exasperation in an atmosphere of shared laughter.

'Once I'm prop'ly better, I'll offer my ... services at Brook ... burn,' Mother announced. 'No need for ... you two to be the only ... ones.'

Remembering her former distaste for the stricken soldiers made Evadne squirm. She tried to make up for it by spending two evenings a week and one afternoon reading to them – and Ted Geeson's usually being around to walk her home afterwards genuinely wasn't part of her plan, though his company was the cherry on the cake.

'It's an improvement on when I used to see you home from the Lloyds,' he said with a grin. 'At least these days we're side by side and talking.'

'You're a good friend. I'm only sorry it took me so long to see it.'

She risked a quick sideways glance. Would he take the hint? Would he respond? Oh, please. But he didn't. In the evenings, he dropped her off outside the private front door, but in the afternoons, he left her at the shop door and she watched him through the window as he walked away, admiring his broad manly figure and the confidence of his uneven gait. He managed so well with his artificial leg. You couldn't possibly pity him, because you were too busy respecting him.

She held one elbow and tapped her knuckles against her lips. Had she put him off? She was sure – well, as sure as she could be – that he used to like her. Had she rejected him once too often? She had treated him sharply, dismissively; she had shut a door in his face once, the memory of which made her want to crumple with shame now. But even after all that, he had come to see her after her court appearance and had tried to visit her in prison, only she had refused to see him; he had helped bring her home.

She had thought – she had hoped … but maybe she was wrong. Maybe he had done these things purely out of a sense of justice, because he knew she had been wrongly accused. After all, he had once been a police sergeant. Maybe ... maybe supporting her through her ordeal had been as close a return to police work as he could get. Maybe it was his last hurrah as a copper and he would have done it for anyone.

Certainly, he hadn't made any advances since her release from prison. Walking her home didn't count. She wanted it to count – oh, how she wanted it to count – but it didn't, because he hadn't used those occasions to further their relationship.

Relationship? Ha!

Carrie appeared at her side. 'He walked you home again.'

She tore her eyes away. 'He's that sort of fellow.'

'I bet he walks on the outside of the pavement and keeps his sword-arm free an' all.'

'Very funny.' But actually he was precisely that sort.

'What did you talk about?'

Was she fishing for information?

'This and that. Friendship. We talked about friendship.'

At least she had. She had told him what a good friend he was – and he had failed to take the hint.

'Speaking of which.' She needed to divert Carrie. 'What about you and Letty? She sent that kind letter of condolence. Why not go and see her? You've been friends since you could walk and talk.'

'It won't be the same,' said Carrie.

'Nothing's the same.' Should she say it? 'I've never had a best friend. You should hang on to Letty with both hands.'

'Oh, Evadne.'

'Don't look at me like that. I don't want your pity. I know I need to make friends.'

But the one she wanted most was Ted Geeson, and it wasn't friendship she had in mind.

Chapter Forty-Seven

The gramophone in the corner was playing 'Don't Dilly Dally on the Way', and Adam's toes tapped along as he paused by each bed on his afternoon rounds. He wasn't the only one. The chaps were nodding in time to the music or tapping their fingers. A couple were croaking along, encouraged by Nurse Edwards, who had a surprisingly pretty voice, quite at odds with her battleaxe appearance.

'It's a grey old day out there, Manning,' he told Stanley Manning, as he replaced the notes he had been scanning. 'Still, it'll soon be Christmas. We'll have Nurse Edwards warbling "Hark the Herald Angels" before you know it – isn't that right, Nurse?'

But he didn't catch her reply, because outside, coming up the drive, was Carrie. Well, both sisters, together with Mr Weston, to be precise; but – Carrie.

He leant towards the window, drinking in the sight of her. Her sister was taller, elegant, beautiful, and not a patch on her. He wanted to run downstairs and throw open the door to draw her in, to help her out of her overcoat ... to slip his arms around her and hold her close, to utter the promises that filled his heart to the brim.

Not that he ever managed to see her on her own. At the shop or in the flat, there was always Mrs Jenkins, Miss Baxter, Mr Weston. Here, there were patients, staff.

But if he went down now, just as the three of them separated, he could quite naturally accompany Carrie to whichever ward she was going to, and ask her to spare him some time before she went home.

'Give me a few minutes, Nurse,' he said. 'I'll be back directly.'

He left the room, followed by the strains of 'If You Were the Only Girl in the World', which made him picture himself down on one knee with Carrie sitting on his thigh, her arm looped round his neck. What a fool.

He found the visitors emerging from the corridor where the cloakroom was.

'I saw you arriving with a pretty girl on each arm, Weston,' he said cheerfully.

'Setting a good example to you younger men.' Mr Weston looked more than a little pleased with himself.

'Half-day closing today,' said Miss Baxter, 'so you've got all three of us. Mr Weston is reading and I'll offer to write letters, and what about you, Carrie?'

'I said I'd help sort out the linen.'

'Excellent!' said Adam, and it was. Mr Weston and Miss Baxter would head off in one direction while Carrie went in the other. 'I'm going that way.'

It would give them a minute together, but that was more than he had had since he couldn't recall when.

The office door opened and Sister Wicks appeared.

'Miss Baxter – thank goodness. Could I trouble you to assist with a little paperwork?'

'Haven't you replaced me yet? I thought you held interviews last week.'

'We did, but there were no suitable candidates. Most disappointing.'

Miss Baxter went into the office. Adam tried to usher Carrie away, but her eyes were fixed on the office.

'Excuse me, Sister. If you aren't suited yet, I wonder ... my friend's sister. The Hardacres are decent people and their Joanie was always bright. She didn't go to high school, but her parents let her sit the scholarship so she'd always be able to prove she was clever enough, even if they couldn't afford to send her. What do you think, Evadne?'

'I don't know her. She's much younger than I am. But if she's clever like you say, and willing...'

'You could train her,' said Carrie.

They both looked at Sister Wicks, who looked across at him.

'Worth a try?' she enquired.

Adam sighed, accepting the inevitable. 'Doctor Todd should have a say. I'll fetch him.'

How had it happened? The private conversation he had hoped for had expanded into a general discussion of Miss Baxter's successor. Would he never get Carrie on her own?

Mr Weston fell in step beside him. 'Are you

452

heading upstairs? I'll walk with you. You look rather down in the dumps, if I may say so.'

'Things on my mind.'

'Such as Mrs Armstrong?'

Adam looked at him, couldn't help it. He didn't say anything, but merely looking had been answer enough.

'Tell me to mind my own business if you wish, but I've known you all your life and I've got eyes in my head.'

At the top of the stairs, Adam drew Mr Weston into an empty room and shut the door.

'She won't give me the time of day.'

'She has been through a lot. Maybe she needs time.'

'Then all she has to do is ask for it – if she has any interest in me. But she's made it clear that my ... interest is unwelcome.' Interest! His lasting love reduced to such a piffling word. 'So I'm thinking of moving on. I've been offered a post at a place on the south coast. It's a big hospital with links to a nearby lunatic asylum. Doctors are starting to accept that some of the soldiers who were locked away because of so-called madness are actually suffering from the same sort of debilitating mental condition that we see here at Brookburn. The idea is to combine as many different kinds of treatment as possible so that every man is treated according to his needs.'

'It sounds like admirable work and I'm sure it would suit you.'

'But?'

'But are you sure it is what you want?'

No, he wasn't sure. That is, yes, it sounded like

a fascinating and important opportunity, but he wasn't ready just yet to give up on Carrie. Which brought him back to where he had started.

Was he never going to get her on her own?

There wasn't a drop of moisture in Carrie's mouth. Should her tongue touch the roof of her mouth, it would stick there for ever. Her heart marked the occasion with deep, solemn beats. Could she do this?

The door opened before she reached it and Mrs Hardacre drew her inside. She gave Carrie a brief hug, placing her cheek close to hers to whisper, 'Good girl,' and give her a kiss. Carrie's mind swirled. Next news – and she had no idea how she got there – she was approaching Letty's bed and there was Letty, sitting up against a mountain of pillows, hair loose, face shining.

Her own face had once shone like that.

There was a flutter in front of her and her hands lifted instinctively as Mrs Hardacre popped the baby into her arms. Icy water sloshed inside her. She was holding a baby and it wasn't Joey. How could she? How could they expect it of her?

Her treacherous arms remembered exactly how to hold a baby. The smell of infant and powder and milk streamed through her. The floor opened beneath her feet and she fell back through time all the way to last year when she had had Joey to love. Longing, anguish, regret, remorse, she was going to die of it, right here on Billy and Letty's bedroom floor.

Her vision blurred.

And cleared.

The baby didn't feel the same as Joey, didn't look like him. Letty's baby, Letty's little girl. The baby snuffled and waved a tiny fist. Not Joey. And not a fake Joey. A little person in her own right.

Adorable. She was a baby, so how could she be anything else? Carrie's heart opened. Her face was wet. She raised her eyes to meet Letty's, saw her friend's anxiety and blessed her for understanding, for knowing, for caring.

'She's beautiful,' she whispered. 'What's her name?'

'Dorothy, known as Dolly.'

'Little Dolly Shipton.'

'I know we allus said we'd name us eldest girls after one another,' said Letty, 'but, well, you know.'

Carrie had no intention of discussing it. 'Dolly is just right. She's so small and perfect, with big blue eyes like a doll.'

It hadn't been easy to start with, getting back with Letty, but of one thing Carrie was certain: it was worth persevering. Getting their Joanie that job at Brookburn had gone a long way towards restoring the old warmth, not just with Letty but with Mr and Mrs Hardacre. Visiting their house, it was almost possible to forget that Billy was anything to do with them. Almost.

When she saw Letty, it was while Billy was at work, and that was best all round. Now he knew what it was to hold his child in his arms, did he regret how casually, clumsily cruel he had been that time? *Don't tek this the wrong way.* By all accounts, he was besotted with his beautiful daughter and couldn't wait for the next one.

'If you know what I mean!' Letty said, with a

naughty gleam in her eye, and the two of them hooted with laughter in a moment of uninhibited familiarity. Letty leant forward, dropping her voice. 'It was that pink corset what done it, the one you gave me.'

The back of Carrie's neck went cold. 'The orchid corset.'

'Orchid – aye, that's right. Billy loves it. He likes easy access to his titties, does my Billy.'

And there it was, their friendship summed up in one crude sentence. Carrie was glad to have Letty back, and Letty would always be special, but they could never be the best friends they had once been.

'Thank you for making me get back with Letty,' she said to Evadne as they walked to Brookburn one evening. 'It was the right thing to do.'

'I'm glad.'

'Friends are important.'

Might she and Evadne become friends? No, she was being silly. She wasn't the right person for her educated, well-spoken sister. You only had to see them at Brookburn to know that. Evadne read to the patients or helped them write letters; and on Wednesday afternoons, she supervised Joanie as she learnt her way round the office. Compare that with Carrie. She much preferred housekeeping jobs. Should Evadne be looking for a friend, she certainly wouldn't want her younger sister.

As they entered Brookburn, hurrying in from the cold, Carrie stuck like glue to Evadne as they stowed their outdoor things. You never knew when Adam would pop up and she didn't want to be alone with him. The only time Carrie ventured here on her own was one afternoon a week; she and Evadne each took an afternoon off from the shop to volunteer here, as well as coming here together on Wednesday afternoons.

But coming with Evadne presented its own difficulty, because Carrie didn't want to play gooseberry if Ted Geeson walked Evadne home. Carrie liked him enormously, though Evadne seldom mentioned his name. Carrie could only hope that Evadne would come to see his worth. Or maybe, having been made a fool of by Mr Larter, she wanted to keep herself to herself. Carrie longed to ask – but Evadne might then start asking questions about Adam, and she couldn't face that.

Carrie had done it again – slipped off early from Brookburn while Evadne was in the middle of helping a fellow write a letter. Mind you, if she had stayed, then Evadne wouldn't have the chance of walking home alone with Ted Geeson. Goodness, she was grinning like an idiot. She pulled her mouth into a semblance of demureness. Would he appear this evening? Would he accompany her? She moved so as to turn her back to the door. Otherwise, she would be looking more at the doorway than at the letter in front of her.

'What else can I say, miss?' asked the lad.

'Well, you're writing to your friend, so why not mention something you used to do together?'

He heaved a sigh. 'I'm not sure he'll still want to be my mate.'

'Maybe he won't, but you must give him a chance.'

'All right, then. Well, we used to tie a rope to a branch over the river, and there was this one time when…'

Maybe he won't, but you must give him the chance.

So easy to say. Much harder to do. She was trying hard to make herself acceptable to the female staff at Brookburn in the hope they would see her as something other than the stuck-up so-and-so she used to be. Was that how Ted Geeson still viewed her?

That evening saw a little breakthrough, which she gladly shared with him on the way home.

'Sister Wicks had a cup of tea with me this evening. It doesn't sound much, but it's a step forward. I've made a point of being pleasant to everyone, but they've been pretty starchy.'

'Give it time. They'll come round.'

'I hope so. I would dearly like to have a friend. May I tell you a secret? What I really want is a best friend. Carrie's got one and you can't imagine how I envy her.' She did too. Her ribs tightened when she thought of Carrie and Letty together. 'Then I think how lucky I am to have a job I love and think perhaps I'm being greedy.'

What would it take to make him regard her in a warmer light? Was she wrong to imagine he had once liked her? Could he like her again? What could she say to show his advances wouldn't be spurned?

'Actually, I do have a best friend. It's you. You put up with me at my worst; you kept trying to visit me in prison; and here you are still, taking an interest and just … being here. You've even put up with me droning on about wanting a friend when

458

you're the dearest, truest friend anyone ever had.'

Please respond, please respond. But, far from taking his cue, he was if anything even quieter for the rest of the journey. Had she offended him? Had she put him off totally?

What could she say next time to retrieve the situation? But any ideas she had were neither here nor there, because the next time she went to Brookburn, there was no sign of him and she walked home alone.

Chapter Forty-Eight

Carrie loved Armstrong's. Her own shop! Who would have thought? Carrie Jenkins-as-was, the girl from Wilton Lane, had her very own business, and a fine establishment at that. Having Evadne in the shop was going well – surprisingly well, some might say. Evadne wasn't lording it over her, which was how it would have been in the old days. But not now. These days, Evadne was a kinder person, and even though she knew something about antiques, she wasn't snooty about it. Nevertheless, Carrie felt her own lack of knowledge deeply. Compared to Evadne and Mr Weston, she was fit for nothing but the dusting.

'I can teach you too,' Mr Weston offered.

Times were when she would have back-pedalled like mad at that point, knowing she wasn't anything like as capable as her educated sister. But not these days. After everything she had gone through, everything she had had to face, she believed in herself.

'If Evadne can learn, so can I.' Saying it felt good. She wanted to tilt back her head and laugh for joy.

Later, she admitted to Mam, 'It's the first time I've ever seen myself as Evadne's equal.'

'It wasn't easy ... having girls with different back ... grounds. And Evadne clung so hard to ... her status.' Mam's smile was firmer these days. 'Pa thought she was marv'lous. Almost as marvellous as Evad ... ne thought she was!'

'Mam!'

They burst out laughing, but there was no malice in it, just warm acceptance.

'I asked Mr Weston to tea tonight,' said Carrie.

'It's only p-poached eggs, but we've got plenty.'

'Now he's offered to teach me, it seemed like a nice gesture. We couldn't manage without him. You don't mind that I invited him without asking you first, do you?'

'It's your ... shop, love, your flat.'

'I don't want you thinking I'm going all bossy.'

'You? Never.'

'It's your home, Mam. For ever. I want you with me.'

'I know, chick. All those ... months you fought to make me ... better.'

'Am I interrupting?'

There was Evadne in the doorway, looking like her old cool self. Before either of them could reply, she made herself scarce. Carrie looked at Mam, then followed her sister to her room at the back of the building, which Adam said had been

460

Ralph's boyhood room.

Evadne was fussing with the trinket boxes on her pretty dressing table. She glanced round.

'Sorry. Didn't mean to barge in on something private.'

'It wasn't.'

'It's all right. You and Mother have always been close. I know that.'

'Perhaps you'd like to be close to us too.'

'You don't have to say that. I'm not a child in need of pacifying.'

Go on, say it. 'Evadne, do you think we could be friends? I was best mates with Letty for years, but not now. And I really would like a best friend. I wouldn't expect you and me to be best friends. I expect you'd like someone more educated–'

'You want us to be friends?'

'Why not? We had different starts in life, but I think things have evened up recently. Anyroad, the offer's there, if you want it.'

'If I want it?'

Oh, cripes. She was going to say no. She was offended. 'I'd love us to be friends,' said Evadne.

Carrie huffed out a huge breath and hugged her. After a moment, Evadne hugged her back.

'I can't remember the last time you hugged me,' said Carrie.

'I can. You were tiny and Grandmother told me off.'

Carrie found herself being hugged even more tightly.

'He looks fuller in the face, don't you think?' Evadne whispered and Carrie nodded.

461

Working at Armstrong's and occupying an essential role clearly suited Mr Weston, as did the home cooking he was enjoying, though he never took it for granted. He ate with the family when the shop shut for dinner and once or twice a week he stayed for tea in the evening, repaying this additional hospitality by bringing boxes of Cadbury's chocolates.

Today was Wednesday, half-day closing, and after a dinner of chops followed by apple charlotte, Evadne got ready to go out, feeling an unaccustomed pleasure. Had Grandfather ever invited her before? He had never had the chance; she had been too quick to invite herself. But now he had written a postcard, asking her to come and see him.

Had he missed her? She had been so busy in recent weeks, what with the shop and Brookburn – and enjoying being with her family. That would surprise him. Would she mention it? His displeasure, his criticism, used to crush her and leave her scrambling to make amends; but if he sneered at her new-found closeness to Mother and Carrie, she would call him a pompous old snob, and let him put that in his pipe and smoke it.

Not that she wanted any argument or ill feeling, even if he had let her down when she needed him most. She had never referred to the matter and neither had he, which had felt odd to start with, but then she shrugged it off. She couldn't have it both ways. She had no business claiming she wanted to put it all behind her if she was secretly hankering after apology and explanation.

And the fact was they were rubbing along better than she could remember. Because she was no longer haunting Parrs Wood? Because he was no longer bombarded by hints and sighs and complaints? What a trial she must have been.

It was a beautiful day of snowdrops and sparkling winter sunshine. Evadne thought cheerfully of the bottle of home-made all-year-round chutney in her bag that, no matter how tangy it was, would make Grandfather rumble with discontent that his granddaughter had sunk so low in the world as to mince her own onions and apples.

Descending from the tram, she set off for Grandfather's, keeping her eyes firmly to the fore as she passed the homes of the unfortunate neighbours who had been part of Alex's scheme. They hadn't been swindled, but they must know, the whole world must know, that Miss Evadne Baxter had been involved in ... something, albeit unwittingly. Being seen as honest mattered, but it hurt to be thought of as honest but stupid.

She could enter Grandfather's house these days without being overpowered by yearning. She slipped off her outdoor things and went into the sitting room, dropping a kiss on Grandfather's whiskers before holding out her hands to the fire.

'How are you, Evadne? Still at that shop? Pretty poor show for a Baxter, working in a shop.'

'You make it sound like a corner shop that sells paraffin and cough drops until ten o'clock at night.' She took a seat. 'Working at Armstrong's suits me.'

'For how long, that's what I want to know.'

'Did you invite me here to scold me?'

'I've a proposition for you. Mrs Hanbury has

463

given notice. She and her sister are going to pool their resources and open a boarding house in Rhyl, so I need you to live here and run things for me. That's what you've always wanted, isn't it? Well, now it's yours.'

The beginning of February. A year ago Joey hadn't been born. A year ago she had been thanking heaven and all the angels that he was overdue. Carrie stood in front of the chest of drawers. It was a handsome piece, its elegant bow front housing eight drawers, two wide ones at the bottom and two half-sized pairs above. Joey's things were in one of the smaller drawers. She had disposed of Ralph's things without a second thought, couldn't get rid of them fast enough, but Joey's remained, a little bit of him left behind, a part of herself that would never be still.

Her hand reached out, but didn't touch. The drawers had slender brass handles, two each for the large drawers, one each for the smaller. They lay flat against the wood until you lifted them to pull a drawer open; and when you let go, they dropped back with a soft sound like a teeny-tiny letter-box flap.

Her hand stayed in mid-air, yearning towards Joey's drawer. Her heart was hot and swollen. You were supposed to be reunited with your loved ones in heaven, but she didn't really believe in heaven any more. Besides, what was the point of going there when Joey was in limbo? Unbaptised and a Protestant burial. It didn't get much worse than that. Yes, it did. Not living long enough to fill one of the large drawers.

Her hand dropped to her side, fingers brushing the warm wool of her skirt. Jilted, widowed and childless, and not yet twenty. It wasn't much to show for a life. She wouldn't have minded the other two if the third could be different.

Not much to show? She had nothing to show. Just a wedding ring she kept on for form's sake and a half-sized drawer she couldn't bring herself to open.

Stop wallowing!

It wasn't wallowing. Just let anyone dare call it wallowing. It was bereavement; it was mother love. It was hopeless endless yearning that sometimes pounded her into the ground like a runaway horse.

And she did have something to show for her life. She had the shop. Owning it remained a source of pride and amazement in equal measure. She hadn't worked for it; she hadn't achieved it; but, by heck, she had earned it, brick by brick, jingle after jingle of the brass bell over the door. Every day she had been married to Ralph, she had earned a bit more.

And she had her family, Mam and Evadne, the three of them close now as never before. But her family would be for ever incomplete. My fault, my fault.

Carrie Armstrong, bad mother, plastered a smile on her face and went to have breakfast. Not that she actually ate anything, unless a single bite of toast and Marmite that lodged in her throat and took two cups of tea to swill it down counted as eating.

She went downstairs to the shop. She wanted to

465

disappear into the office, sit at the desk, fold her arms on top of it and put her head down, like the babies' class used to at school after dinner.

'There's so much to learn,' she said in an undertone to Evadne as Mr Weston discussed the merits of decorated glass with a customer. 'Not just about furniture and fine china, but running the business. It's too much to think about.'

'I'm happy to take on the administration. I'm good at that kind of thing.'

'No. Sorry, I don't mean to be abrupt. But I wouldn't be much of a shopkeeper if I couldn't do the books.'

'A matter of pride.'

'Common sense.'

'Both,' said Evadne. She glanced at Mr Weston and the customer, then indicated with a small jerk of her head that Carrie should join her in the office. 'You aren't yourself today. If you tell me why, I can help.'

'Big sister laying the law down?'

'Or a friend expressing concern.'

Carrie tugged at her cuffs. 'It's Joey. He's never far away, but today he feels very close.'

Evadne squeezed her shoulder, then let her hand fall away when Carrie didn't respond. 'What do you need?'

'Need? I need Joey to be alive. That's what I *need*.'

She glared at Evadne. Go on. You're supposed to be so clever. Say the right thing.

Evadne gave her a long, assessing look. 'Well, I fear for the stock if you stay here.'

'What?'

'You heard. You're … boiling over. I'm meant to go to Brookburn this afternoon. Why don't you go instead?'

Was she insane? 'To read to the men?'

'No, do something else, preferably something that involves banging and crashing. Let your feelings out, before you explode. I shan't insult you by saying I understand how you feel, but I remember how it felt to be desperate to escape my old life and live with Grandfather. I'd get so angry and frustrated and frightened that I hardly knew what to do with myself. Then I discovered that if I borrowed Miss Martindale's bicycle and rode as hard as I could, it relieved some of my feelings. It didn't change anything, but it took the edge off the unhappiness for the time being. So do as you're told. Go to Brookburn. Strip all the beds, vacuum-clean all the carpets: I don't care what you do, but don't come back here until you've worn yourself out. Big sister laying down the law.'

Evadne could be right. Physical activity might help, and the more mindless and strenuous the better. And because today wasn't her regular day, Adam wouldn't be on the lookout. She could slip inside, get a job allocated and get on with it, without having to keep one eye open for him.

She didn't want to think about Adam. She wished he would clear off and leave her alone, then maybe her feelings for him would die away. If she didn't see him, her heart would beat normally instead of giving that absurd little jump. If she didn't see him, her skin would be smooth and cool instead of warm and tingly.

If she didn't see him, she might loathe herself less.

Entering Brookburn via a side door, she headed for the housekeeper's room. Rounding a corner – someone there – she danced sideways.

'Sorry – oh! It's you.'

'There's no need to sound quite so thrilled,' said Adam, with a forced smile.

It was as if her thoughts had conjured him up. And yes, her heart did give that absurd little bump. And her skin did feel warm and tingly.

'I didn't know you were coming today,' he said.

Or you'd have been on watch. 'Neither did I until a while ago.'

'I'm pleased to see you.'

He was, too. It was there in his expression. The hope in his eyes, the softening of a frown into a look of–

She didn't want this. 'Excuse me. I–'

'I need to talk to you, Carrie.'

'I must get on–'

'Stop avoiding me!'

There was an edge of desperation in his tone that ripped into her. She almost – almost – reached out a hand, but restrained the impulse. She couldn't let herself respond.

'Adam, leave me alone. If you're going to hound me, I'll stop coming. Brookburn is important to me and I don't want to give it up, but I will if you don't leave me alone.'

He stared. She wanted to look away, but she couldn't. He looked dazed, then he stiffened, standing taller.

'Very well. I apologise for ... hounding you.'

She winced. 'Adam–'

His hand moved, silencing her. 'Actually, you've helped me make a decision. I won't trouble you again.'

A chill shimmered through her. 'What decision?'

But he was already walking away.

Chapter Forty-Nine

Evadne felt fidgety. She had done the right thing in giving up her Brookburn slot, because Carrie obviously needed to work off her turmoil, poor girl. Imagine suffering like that, suffering that would never end, even if it dulled over time.

Joey. She had barely known her little nephew. She bitterly regretted that now. She had been so busy, rushing round making a twit of herself over Alex, when what really mattered had been right under her snooty nose – her family and the possibility of friendship and maybe more than that with a good man, a solid, dependable, honest man who would never lie to her or let her down. She had rebuffed Ted Geeson countless times without putting him off. Now that she had changed, now she knew his true worth, was it too late? Had she rejected him one time too many? Had he given up?

Hence the fidgets. It was so unlike her. She was self-possessed, elegant, sophisticated. She had all the social graces. She was a lady.

It wasn't elegant to tap-tap-tap-tap-tap the end of her pencil against the ledger. It didn't show poise to rearrange the display of figurines for the dozenth time when there had been nothing wrong with it in the first place. It wasn't good manners to be so lost in thought that Mr Weston kept having to repeat himself.

'I beg your pardon,' she said – again. 'I do apologise. My mind is elsewhere this afternoon.'

He nodded. 'Mrs Armstrong also appeared distracted, if I may say so. If this isn't a good day, perhaps I shouldn't join you for tea this evening.'

'You must come. I'm sorry if we've made you uncomfortable.'

'I wouldn't wish to intrude.'

'You won't, I promise. Please come. You'll be doing us a kindness. Carrie and I – well, we've had better days.'

He smiled and there was a twinkle in his eyes as he said, 'I do have some rather nice chocolate that would go to waste if I took it home.'

'That settles it. We can't do without our Cadbury's.'

'Actually, I've brought Fry's for a change. I hope you don't mind.'

'We'll try not to.'

And now she really must concentrate. But it was hard. She had been anxious to get to Brookburn today because she wanted to seek out Ted Geeson, even if she had to search every inch of the grounds and take the woodpile to pieces, so she could tell him about Grandfather's offer. Surely that would give him the prod he needed.

She didn't want to be mistress of Grandfather's house. Amazing. It was what she had craved since she was a girl. Live with Grandfather, meet a suitable man, get married. Over the years, her craving had matured, or possibly degenerated, into heart-twitching desperation as the post-war dearth of men hit home.

But now, she didn't want it. Not that she planned to tell Ted Geeson that. No, she was going to tell him of Grandfather's offer and watch his face as he realised he couldn't bear to let her go. Her pulse quickened, hope, fear and excitement merging into one tight knot.

And now, after building herself up, the opportunity had vanished. No, not vanished. She had given it away willingly to ease Carrie's troubled heart. She felt a glow of love and concern. Carrie was worth putting first, even though it meant giving up the chance of seeing Ted, because Carrie was her sister and her friend and she loved her.

A memory. Pa's voice. 'Here, hold your baby sister.' A bundle being placed into her arms. The little face, eyes closed, the tiny rosebud mouth. Surprise at how small she was. Interest. Pride. And ... a sensation of opening, of release, as the loving began.

Carrie was worth it. She was worth anything. And seeing Ted Geeson was only postponed. She could wait.

No, she couldn't.

'Mr Weston, would you mind awfully if I went out for a while?'

'Not at all, Miss Baxter. During the war, when it was just myself and the late Mr Armstrong, I was often alone in the shop when he was out looking at new stock.'

She didn't need telling twice. Forget poised,

forget sedate: she flew upstairs for her coat. Putting on her hat, a gorgeous midnight-blue velvet toque embroidered with silver thread, in front of the dressing-table mirror – Carrie had insisted she choose one of the three pretty dressing tables that were in the shop when she moved in – she saw the flash of excited colour high on her cheekbones. She was going to see Ted!

Soon she was hurrying through the darkening streets, along the side of the Green and past the old graveyard. The road sloped downwards and the graveyard wall was correspondingly high, so she couldn't see over. Was Carrie in there, perhaps, beside Joey's grave? Ought she to double-back and see? No, Carrie had to find her own way through today, and whether that meant beating every carpet Brookburn possessed or crouching beside her son's headstone was up to her.

'Miss Baxter.'

'Oh – Mr Geeson. I'm on my way to Brookburn.'

'Then I'll turn round and walk with you, if you don't mind.'

'Not at all. I'd welcome your company, as long as I'm not keeping you from an important errand.'

'Nothing that won't wait.'

He fell in step beside her. Evadne walked on towards Brookburn, which was stupid, because she didn't want to go there, not if he was out here. She ought to stop and turn to him and talk face-to-face.

'Are you reading to the men this afternoon?' he asked.

Her mouth went dry. She swallowed. 'Actually,

I was hoping to see you.'

'Oh aye?'

'Yes. I've got news.'

'And you're sharing it with me? I'm honoured.'

'Of course I want to tell you. I like to think we're friends.'

Would he care? Would it matter to him? And if he responded the way she longed for, was the most romantic moment of her life really about to take place walking past the Bowling Green pub?

'My grandfather has invited me to live with him in Parrs Wood and take over the running of his house.'

Say something, say something.

He said nothing.

'Goodness, I've made myself sound like the housekeeper.' Where did that silly trilling laugh come from? She had never laughed like that in the whole of her life. 'Grandfather's frightfully keen. He says as mistress of the house, I can have carte blanche, do any redecorating, as long as I leave his den alone, and organise the house as I see fit as long as he gets his dinner on time.'

Say something, say something.

'Well,' he said.

Well, what? Well, I can't say I like it. Well, I'd rather you stopped here with me. Well, I'd rather you moved into my house. Will you marry me?

Say it, say it.

'It's no secret this isn't the life you were born into.'

Was that it? Was that all?

'What do you think?' she asked, forced into bluntness.

They had reached the gates of Brookburn. He stopped. Evadne turned to face him. His expression was sombre beneath the peak of his cap. If she kissed the corner of his mouth, would he smile? Would he smile before he pulled her into his arms and–?

He nodded, lips pursed. 'I can see how it would be right for you. I've not known you long, Miss Evadne Baxter, and I can't claim to know you closely, but I know this.'

That you're the only woman for me, the one I want to marry and spend my life with. Say it, say it.

'You want more from life than you've got at present. You were born into a certain station and here's your chance to return to it. I wish you well. Now I'd best get off before the ironmonger's closes.'

He touched his cap to her and walked away. She stared after him, tears freezing in her eyes. What should she do now? He hadn't said it. If she had no hope of a future with him, she couldn't carry on volunteering at Brookburn, where she might bump into him at any moment. In fact, wouldn't it be better to put her dashed hopes behind her and start again elsewhere? Grandfather had been astounded when she turned him down. Should she go back and say she had changed her mind?

The savoury aroma of beef and onions filled Carrie's nostrils as she walked into the flat, followed by Evadne and Mr Weston. Cottage pie today. Mustard tart yesterday. Toad-in-the-hole the day before that. Mam hadn't said a word, but she was

474

churning out all Carrie's favourites and Carrie knew it was because Joey's birthday was coming up.

'I've been thinking about this afternoon,' she said, as the four of them tucked in. 'Evadne, you should go on the evaluation visit with Mr Weston. I'll be fine on my own.'

'Are you sure?'

'I promise not to pretend to know something I don't.' This was Mr Weston's golden rule. 'If you go, you'll learn. That's more important than us holding one another's hands in the shop.'

'A wise decision, if I may say so,' observed Mr Weston.

So she spent much of the afternoon on her own. She had customers, but they were what Mr Weston called 'likers'. No specialist knowledge, but if they liked what they saw, they bought it. She smiled to herself. Her kind of customer! But one day she would be equipped to serve the knowledgeable ones too.

She said as much to Mam and Evadne when they settled down for the evening.

'My girls working in a place like Armstrong's,' said Mam, 'and one of them owning it. Who'd have thought? I can see how much Evadne is enjoying it, but what about you, our Carrie?'

'I've a lot to learn, but I don't mind that.'

'I know, love. You're a grafter like your dad. But that's not what I asked.'

'Leave her be, Mother, if she doesn't want to talk.'

Carrie looked from one to the other. 'Have you been discussing me behind my back?'

'Of course,' said Mam, unabashed. 'We love you and we're concerned for you.'

'There's no need.'

'There's every need,' said Evadne.

'If there's no need,' said Mam, 'answer my question.'

Carrie stilled. She was poised on the brink. Step back with an easy lie, which they would recognise as such – or step forward. Tell the truth. But that would open her up to – she didn't know what. 'Yes, I enjoy it. It keeps me busy and interested. But...'

'But?' asked Evadne.

'It doesn't fill me up.'

She could almost hear the clang of shock. Good God, what had she unleashed? She wished the words unspoken, but it was too late. She had had her chance to retreat from the brink and she hadn't taken it.

'Well, it wouldn't, would it?' Evadne said carefully. She licked her lips and Carrie felt a tingle beneath her flesh. 'You're never going to feel right again until you have another child.'

'Oh! Is this what you've been saying to one another? You're just like those stupid women who said I must have another, as if Joey didn't matter.'

'Of course he matters, but that doesn't mean you have to blot out the possibility of more children. And if you did have another, it would' – she drew a breath, as if steeling herself to utter the words – 'fill you up again. Your words, not mine.'

Carrie could scarcely believe her ears. How dare Evadne speak to her like this?

'What do you know about it? All you ever

wanted was a rich husband.'

'Carrie!' exclaimed Mam. 'There's no call for that.'

'It's all right, Mother. I've spoken frankly and Carrie's entitled to answer in kind.' Evadne's voice was steady, but her face was pale. 'You're right, Carrie. For a long time, that's all marriage meant to me – the right sort of man who could give me the right sort of life; and I never gave children a thought except in so far as I assumed I'd have them. I never dreamt about children, like you did. But I'll tell you something I learnt from Joey.'

Carrie felt giddy. Then Evadne was on her knees in front of her, clasping her hands, looking into her eyes, twisting her head, her neck, to stay locked on Carrie's eyes.

'The first time I saw Joey...'

Her words trailed off as if she hadn't the words to express herself. Carrie stilled. She returned the clasp of the hands, focusing with all her heart on this unlooked-for link to her son. No one spoke to her of him. She thought of him constantly, but no one else mentioned him. The chance to hear him spoken of snatched her heart and held it, ripped it in two and stuck it back together. At her core, she trembled with anticipation.

'I loved you when you were a baby,' said Evadne, 'but somehow I forgot it. I forgot how special babies are, but when I saw Joey, I experienced such ... wonderment. He taught me that a baby of my own would be delightful. That's what I learnt from Joey. That's what he means to me, what I'll always remember.'

Carrie parted her lips, but words wouldn't come. Joey's legacy could be a cousin he would never know. Might she find solace in that?

Evadne sat back on her heels. 'It grieves me to think you might not have another child.'

The only way to cope was to make light of it. 'In case you hadn't noticed, there's a serious obstacle in the way of what you're suggesting.'

'No, there isn't. I've seen the way Adam Armstrong looks at you. It's plain as anything how he feels.' Evadne met her eyes. 'I've seen you looking at him too.'

There were so many things she wanted to say, words that would have ensured Evadne never again dared venture into such deeply personal territory. She opened her mouth to set them pouring out and the only words that crawled out were, 'It's not possible.'

'Do you mean for legal reasons? They changed the law last year about men marrying their brothers' widows. They had to, after the war.'

Carrie's head filled with tears, her eyes, her sinuses, her throat. She couldn't move, didn't dare try, in case the floodgates crashed open. If that happened, she might never be able to force them shut again.

'Shall I tell you one of my biggest regrets?' said Mam. She looked at Evadne. 'It's to do with Daddy. The last time I saw him, I said all the things a soldier's wife says when it's time to part. Be careful, come home safe, all those things; but I didn't say I loved him. I didn't miss it out on purpose, but after he'd gone, I realised I hadn't said it. I said to myself: That's all right. I'll make

478

sure to say it next time.'

'But there wasn't a next time,' said Evadne.

'Did you say it to Pa before he went?' asked Carrie.

'Lord, yes. A dozen times. The last time, I stood on tiptoe and put my arms round his neck. I wanted to say it right into his ear, only I weren't tall enough. But I know he heard because of what he said back to me.' She pressed her lips together and shook her head. 'If there's something you should say to that young man, Carrie, say it. I didn't get a second chance with Evadne's dad.'

'You have to speak to him,' said Evadne, 'before it's too late.'

'Now you're being dramatic.'

'I'm not. Mr Weston told me this afternoon about a hospital down south that has offered him an important position. He's preparing to go to a conference there and – well, he might decide to go and work there.'

You've helped me make a decision. I won't trouble you again.

'I don't know what's keeping you apart from him, Carrie, but if you don't go and talk to him, I will.'

'No, you won't,' said Mam, and they both looked at her, 'because you'll be busy talking to your Mr Geeson.'

'He isn't *my* Mr Geeson. I've tried talking to him a dozen times and he isn't interested.'

'Ah, but did you say the right things? Goodness me, for someone so well educated, you can be remarkably stupid at times, Evadne. Listen to me, the pair of you. There's a cabbies' hut straight across the road. If there isn't a cab there now, there'll be one along soon. What are you waiting for? Get gone, and don't come back without a couple of sons-in-law.'

Chapter Fifty

Evadne climbed out of the cab at the bottom of the drive and felt a moment's fear; how dark it was. She should have waited until tomorrow – no, she shouldn't. This wanted doing, and it wanted doing now. She hoped she wasn't about to make a colossal ass of herself. No, actually, she didn't care if she did. She had to do this.

Through the trees was a glow of light. The groundsman's cottage. She headed towards it, the grass damp and chill. Her shoes would be ruined. She should have worn her ankle boots, but she had wanted to look her best for Ted.

She stopped outside the cottage door, fishing for a hanky. There was a nip in the air and her nose felt runny.

The door swung open.

'Who's there? Miss Baxter – what brings you here?'

Rats! She hadn't wiped her nose yet.

'Come in, lass. Is something wrong?'

She walked through a lobby into a large room that combined kitchen with sitting room and held her breath, half-expecting to feel let down. It was a long way from the kind of home she had dreamt of. But what she felt was interest. She looked round, assessing the place. It was spacious and well appointed, containing the necessary items, but lacking little comforts. It needed a woman's touch.

'Give me your coat and sit by the fire. I'll put the kettle on. We'll soon have you warmed up.'

She didn't want tea, but she did want him to turn away so she could wipe her nose. She whipped out her hanky and gave a discreet blow.

Ted put the kettle on the gas. Could she respect a man who made the tea? Yet why not? He was taking care of her and what could be better than that? Alex wouldn't have got her a drink unless he could pour it from a decanter.

How cosy it would be to be Mrs Ted Geeson!

'Leave the tea,' she said. 'I came to talk to you.'

'Oh aye?' He lowered himself into the other armchair. 'What about?'

'My grandfather's offer. Do you truly want me to accept it?'

'It's not for me to say.'

'Well, I don't want it. I used to, most dreadfully, but not now. In fact, when Grandfather invited me, I said no, thank you.'

'What will you do instead?'

'I'm already doing it. Working in the shop, living in the flat, volunteering here. This is what I want.'

'I'm glad for you.'

Heat flushed through her. 'Is that it? Are you really that dense? I've been dropping hints like bricks ever since I came home from prison and you haven't picked up a single one. Is it because–

is it because you don't like me?'

'I like you well enough. You should know that. You're always telling me what friends we are.'

'That's because I wanted you to know how deeply I appreciate everything you've done for me. I hoped it might ... encourage you.' She bit her lip. Her face scorched, but it was nothing to do with the crackling fire.

He grinned, his face creasing into lines of humour and ... something else that she didn't dare name. The prospect of being mistaken was too horrible to bear.

'A word of advice. Calling a man your best friend isn't encouraging. Quite the reverse, in fact.'

'But you are my best friend. Can't you think of anything more wonderful than your best friend also being the person you ... you...? Oh, must I say it? I've spent years chasing after other people, desperately trying to please them so that I could get what I wanted. Since I was at school, I've been trying to make Grandfather take me in, but he never would; then I thought I had a chance with Alex Larter, and look where that led. But in my own way, I was as bad as he was. I didn't love him. I just wanted his status and his wealth. But what I want now is the most important thing I've ever hoped for and ... and I want the way it happens to be different. I don't want to do the chasing. I want ... I want the other person to want me, to come to me and seek me out. Oh, goodness,' she said as tears began to flow.

Ted stood up as fluidly as any able-bodied man. He took the hands that were trying to smooth away the tears and drew her to her feet and into his arms. Her heart rampaged all over the place, then settled into the steady, contented beat of certainty and security.

'There now, I've got you. You're safe. Look at me. You shall be courted,' he promised. 'My dear love, you shall be courted.'

Evadne stood on tiptoe in shoes that were wet and tight, and slid her arms round his neck. She was tall enough to speak right into his ear so that there was no possibility of his not hearing, only her voice caught and broke, but she knew he had heard because of what he said back to her.

'I love you too, Miss Evadne Baxter, though it's a bit early in our formal courtship to say so.'

'No, it isn't, Ted Geeson. No, it isn't.'

When Sister Wicks said Doctor Armstrong was in his rooms, Carrie bolted upstairs. With a brief knock, she rushed straight in. Adam looked up in surprise from the settee, where he was relaxing with his pipe and a newspaper.

She scooted to a halt as he came to his feet. He was as tall as Ralph, but with a slimmer build, not the bulk of a bully boy; and his handsome features were kind and trustworthy, where Ralph's had been alert and dangerous. How could she ever have mistaken one of them for the other? She couldn't meet his eyes. Would he turn away from her in disgust when she ... if she...?

'I imagined you packing. Evadne says you're leaving.'

He balanced his pipe on the edge of the ashtray. The sharp, sweet aroma of his baccy hung in the air. 'I didn't want you to know about that yet.'

'Why not?'

'Have a seat and I'll tell you.'

She whisked away as if he had tried to force her into the armchair. 'I don't want to sit down. I want to know what's going on – and why you haven't told me.'

'Yet.'

'So when were you going to?'

'After Joey's birthday.'

The energy that had brought her here evaporated and the dull ache of loss that accompanied her everywhere ballooned into a huge spasm of anguish that stifled her pulse. She sank into a chair, sniffing great dollops of air to forestall the tears.

'Sorry,' she whispered. 'I wasn't expecting that.'

'I'm sorry. It was tactless.'

'So we're both sorry.' How easy it would be to leave, to walk out, to tell herself she shouldn't have come. She had to concentrate on why she was here. 'Tell me what's going on.'

Adam returned to the settee, sitting on the edge, leaning forward, elbows on knees, hands lightly clasped. He had slender, sensitive hands, what Mam would call a piano-player's fingers, though doctors must need clever hands too. Adam's hands looked kind as well as clever. Ralph's hands had never looked like that. Ralph's hands used to pluck Joey from her.

'I've been offered a post running the whole show in a place similar to this, only much bigger, but I haven't accepted yet. I'm going down there to give a lecture at a conference and I'll give them

484

my decision then.'

'Are you going to accept?'

'Looks like it.'

She couldn't bear it if he left. She had ignored him and avoided him, but it had been safe to, because he was always there, one of the constants in her life. She couldn't do without him. She had avoided him and ignored him, but she couldn't do without him.

'Why?'

'For pity's sake, Carrie, I don't want to, but I think I ought to. Don't you see, being here, seeing you ... it's too difficult. Since Ralph died, you've never given me the smallest indication of anything. I don't know what to think.'

She had to tell him. Yet how could she? How could she share her blackest secret?

Her throat closed. Her heart was going to explode with pain. She forced herself to meet his eyes, saw worry, confusion ... hope; but above all, kindness. Kind, kind, kind. That was what she had to concentrate on.

'It's ... it's because of Joey. He ... he died because...' The hair lifted on her arms and at the back of her neck. Her skin went clammy, '...because I wasn't a good mother.'

'Carrie, no! You were the best–'

Her hands waved in front of her. To interrupt him? Or to pull the words back inside, to snatch them out of the air and unspeak them?

'A good mother doesn't have feelings for another man. A good mother concentrates on her child. Her mind shouldn't be all over the place, teeming with ... other things.' Yanking off her

485

gloves, she clenched her fists, digging her nails into the palms of her hands. The pain was meant to steady her, but her voice emerged on a wail. 'All my life, the only thing I wanted was to get married and have a family, and when it happened I didn't do it right. I stopped – I stopped paying attention.'

He fell to his knees in front of her. 'Carrie, Carrie, listen to me.' He disentangled her fingers. 'What happened to Joey wasn't your fault.'

'It was!' Remorse and shame swamped her. Her shoulders curled over into her chest, then sprang back. She pulled her hands free, shaking him off. 'I didn't come back and find him dead. Everyone thought that, everyone assumed it, and I let them, I let them, because ... because what I did was so bad.'

'Carrie–'

My fault. My fault.

Dozing off, falling asleep ... while he died, he died, he died.

'I was with him. I was there every moment. I never left the room. I was holding him – *holding* him. He was lying on my chest and ... and I went to sleep and when I woke up, he was dead. He was lying on top of me and I never even felt him die. My own baby, and I didn't feel him die.'

Her anguish was too much to be contained. It burst out of her. She thrust her fingers under her hat, into her hair, clawing at her scalp, hurting herself, deserving to be hurt. Adam captured her hands, forced them to be still.

'Look at me, Carrie.'

She couldn't. She couldn't bear to see in his face

what she saw every day in the mirror-girl's eyes.

'Look at me.'

He pressed her hands between his own. He gave them a shake, but she wouldn't, couldn't look at him. He moved backwards, pulling her with him, toppling her off the armchair so that they were both kneeling on the rug, close together. The un-expectedness of it brought her eyes up to his and once there, his eyes locked hers in position.

'It sometimes happens to babies. The mother puts the baby down to sleep and when she comes back, he's dead. He's slipped away. We don't know why. I wish we did. If we did, maybe we could stop it happening. Would to God we could. Carrie, I swear it wasn't your fault. Oh, my love, Joey died; he died; he just ... died. It wasn't anything you did, or anything you didn't do. It just ... happened. I'm so sorry, Carrie. I'd do anything to bring him back to you. But even if I'd been there with you when it happened, there is nothing I could have done, nothing I as a doctor could have done. No doctor could. And if no doctor could, then please believe me, please believe me, neither could you.'

'But I'm his *mother.*'

'My sweet girl, you were the best mother he could have had. You did everything for him in his short life. No mother could have done more. He was loved and cherished. And he was with you as he died, nestled against you, kept warm by you, kept safe–'

'Safe? Safe you call it? He *died*. I didn't keep him safe. I might as well have left him in his per-ambulator outside the front door. I might as well have left Mrs Porter to keep an eye on him while

I nipped to the shops. What good did I do? I did nothing, absolutely bloody nothing. Don't you understand? I was *asleep.*'

'Carrie, nothing you could have done would have made any difference – nothing anyone did. And that being the case, isn't it better that he died in your arms?'

'*Oh!*' The cry was ripped from her.

'Listen to me.' He caught her shoulders, held her when she would have jerked away. 'What greater comfort could Joey have had than to share such closeness with you in his final moments? What greater comfort than to be with the mother who adored him? I know that doesn't make it easier for you, Carrie, but perhaps ... perhaps it made it easier for him.'

His words penetrated the darkness inside her and sank deep within. She waited for the darkness to spit the words out, as she knew it would. But they stayed put. They stayed inside her and a faint glimmer appeared in her heart.

'Is that what has kept us apart?' Adam's voice was soft. 'Now isn't the time for lovemaking, but give me a word, Carrie, just one word, and I will stay. I promise I will stay for ever.'

She couldn't speak. Her throat was packed solid.

But she could nod. Once. And then the tears flowed.

Chapter Fifty-One

The bell jingled and Carrie looked up eagerly. Mr Weston, holding his hat on, thanks to the mad March wind, entered the shop. Thank goodness! She and Evadne flew across the shop.

'We've been worried about you,' she said.

'You're never late,' said Evadne. 'We knew there'd be a good reason.'

Mr Weston's face was sombre. 'I apologise for my tardiness, Mrs Armstrong. As to the reason, I'm not sure that good is the correct word to describe it.'

'Why? What's happened?'

'May I suggest we close the shop and go upstairs? This concerns Mrs Jenkins as well.'

Someone walked over Carrie's grave. She turned the sign to CLOSED and led the way up to the flat. She looked into the kitchen, where Mam was humming to herself as she made pastry.

Carrie smiled, trying to hide her misgivings. 'Mam, could we borrow you for a minute? Mr Weston has something to tell us. Let's go in the sitting room.'

'What's going on?' Mam wiped her hands and followed.

Mrs Porter was standing on a wooden chair, buffing up the windowpanes with screwed-up newspaper. The tang of vinegar hung in the air, all the more pungent because the room was toasty-warm. Vinegar – the smell of shame. That same faint aroma had been lingering in their old kitchen the evening they heard the terrible truth about Pa.

'Mrs Porter, could you possibly leave that for now and do something else?' asked Carrie.

Mrs Porter looked over her shoulder at them. 'Right you are, love.' She climbed down and disappeared.

Mam sat on the sofa and Carrie sat beside her. She had the feeling that Mam might need her close by.

'What's this about, Mr Weston?'

'The war memorial that is going to be built. I was late this morning because I had the chance to find out the details. I took the liberty of enquiring as to whether...'

Man's hand snaked across and found Carrie's.

'Whether Pa's name will be included,' said Evadne. 'It won't, will it?'

'I'm afraid not.'

Carrie squeezed; Mam squeezed harder.

Evadne blew out a breath. 'Well, it was to be expected, but even so, it's a shock.' She pressed a hand to her chest, fingers spread out. 'I thought I was ready for it, but my heart is pounding.'

'You can't prepare for something like this,' said Mam. 'Thank you for finding out for us, Mr Weston. You've done us a kindness.'

'It was the least I could do, after all the hospitality and attention your family has shown me.'

'Is the memorial going to be in Southern Cemetery?' asked Mam. 'That's what everyone expected.'

'Yes.' He hesitated. 'Would you like to know

what form it will take?'

'We don't need to know,' Carrie said quickly.

Mam raised her chin. 'Yes, we do. We mustn't begrudge all those other families. The men who gave their lives deserve to be remembered.'

'It is to be a cross of sacrifice; and behind it, a panelled stone wall will be erected, on which will be engraved the names of the local men who made the ultimate sacrifice.'

But not Pa. Carrie felt hollow. This was sorrow and pain that would never end, the family shame immortalised by the absence of Pa's name. Other families would take their children to visit the memorial to show them Grandpa's name, Dad's name, Uncle's name, and explain to them the sacrifice their own family had made in the name of freedom. But she and Evadne would never be able to do that.

So great was the loss of life that every single place in the kingdom would have its own memorial, inscribed with the names of the fallen. Not just the big places, the towns and cities, but all the small places, the villages and hamlets, no matter how tiny or remote. Mr Weston had said that just one tiny village in the entire United Kingdom had escaped without loss. Just one. But everywhere else – every single place in the atlas of the British Isles that she had used at school – everywhere else would have its own memorial to the men who gave their lives.

But Pa wasn't one of the glorious dead. He wouldn't be remembered, except in shame. All those memorials, all those inscribed names, all those families bound together by loss and sacrifice. And she and Mam and Evadne were for ever excluded. After everything the country had been through, they weren't entitled to feel any share of the pride or sorrow. And it would be that way for the rest of their lives.

'Is there anything I can do?' Mr Weston asked.

'No,' Carrie began.

'Yes, there is,' said Evadne. 'We should stay here with Mother. We need some time together, just the three of us. But perhaps you could go to Brookburn and tell Ted.'

'Of course.'

'And Adam,' said Carrie. 'He travelled back overnight from his conference. He should be there by now.'

'I'll go immediately.'

Left alone, they looked at one another.

'Nothing's changed,' said Mam. 'We already knew Pa's name wouldn't be included. Nothing has changed.'

She was right. It hadn't.

And yet it had.

'We'll leave the shop shut for the rest of the day,' said Carrie. 'Even if I felt like opening up again, which I don't, it wouldn't be respectful, not on the day that folk are hearing about the memorial. It wouldn't look right.'

'I'll go down and draw the blind on the door,' said Evadne.

On the evening they heard about Pa, she had drawn the Wilton Lane curtains as a sign of shame. Now, Carrie was leaving her shop shut for the same reason. It was the best part of two years later and the shame was as keen now as on that first day. Would it never end? Would the world ever forgive them? Stupid questions.

When Evadne returned, there was a quiet bustle, extra footfalls. Carrie looked towards the door. Evadne walked in, followed by Mr Weston, Ted – and Adam. Oh, the relief, the gratitude. Carrie got up and walked straight into his arms. She slipped her arms around his waist and rested her temple against his chest. This man would never let her down. He would stand by her and support her, no matter what.

'Thank you for coming,' she said. 'You too, Ted.'

'We were on our way in any case,' said Adam, 'but we met Weston en route. He told us about the memorial. I'm sorry, Mrs Jenkins.'

'It was to be expected,' said Mam, in a tight voice.

'The reason we were coming here,' said Adam, 'is that I have something to tell you – the girls as well, but you in particular, Mrs Jenkins. It's to do with Mr Jenkins.'

'Pa?' Surprise snatched at Carrie's insides.

'I believe you know that he spent his last night in company with an army chaplain.' His gaze moved round, landing on each of them. 'I tracked him down.'

'Him!' snorted Mam. 'He started all this, him and his big mouth.'

'I left the conference early in order to spend a day with him.'

'How could you?' Evadne demanded. She swept across the room to sit beside Mam on the sofa, laying a hand over Mam's long elegant fingers

493

curling round knuckles that were white and rigid. 'Haven't we been through enough?' She glared at Ted. 'Did you know about this?'

'Let him speak.' Ted's voice was quiet. 'You should hear this.'

Carrie swivelled her head towards Adam. How could this possibly be something they needed to know? She moved nearer Mam, shoulders touching, linen brushing wool.

Adam sat in one of the armchairs, his face grave. 'The trenches where Mr Jenkins was stationed were under continuous shelling for seventy-two hours, with great destruction and loss of life up and down the line. When at last the whistle blew, telling the men to go over the top, Mr Jenkins stood there, just stood there, dazed, not responding to anything, neither to bellowing nor to shoving, while in no man's land his comrades died instantly if they were lucky, with agonising slowness if they weren't.'

'At least they died doing their duty,' Evadne said, and Carrie looked at her, remembering how she had spoken against Pa when they first heard the news; but Evadne wasn't criticising now. Her voice was sombre and she looked into the air, as if she couldn't meet anyone's eyes.

'The chaplain asked him what had been in his mind in those moments,' Adam continued, 'and Mr Jenkins said he hadn't been thinking anything, because his mind had been stolen from him. That was what he said. His mind had been stolen.'

'D'you mean he had gone mad?' asked Mam.

'No, not that, though God knows, after the way the men in the trenches suffered, it would be understandable if any of them had lost their minds. The horror, the slaughter...'

'It's come to something when you'd rather your husband was mad than ... than...'

'Mrs Jenkins, he wasn't mad, I can assure you of that. And whatever alternative you have in mind that you couldn't bring yourself to put into words, he wasn't that either. He wasn't bad or shallow or cowardly. He was an ordinary, decent man, trying to do his duty. A good man with a conscience and a stout heart and a sense of honour, and I'm sure that all he wanted, all he prayed for, was to survive the war and come home to his wife and daughters, the beloved family he left behind.'

'Then why did he run away?' Evadne challenged, a raw edge to her voice.

'He didn't.'

'Yes, he did. He deserted. God almighty, they shot him for it. The army shot him, his own side. They wouldn't do that unless he had done something *bad*.'

'Desertion meant many things, but it seldom meant running away.'

'Don't be ridiculous. That's exactly what desertion means.'

'More than three hundred of our men were executed for desertion, but I promise you not many of them actually deserted in the generally accepted understanding of the word. The war we've just lived through was unlike any other before it, and the effect it had on many of the men who served in it was catastrophic. The term shell shock is being used. At Brookburn, we call it mind-horror, and that's what overcame Mr

Jenkins. All his experiences combined to engulf him and render him unable to respond. I can't explain it any more clearly than that. No one can. We are just starting to learn about it.'

'So ... he didn't run away?' asked Carrie.

'No. I promise you.'

Everything seemed to slow down as Adam's words sank in. Did not running away make it any better? Had public opinion, public lack of understanding, done Pa a grave disservice?

'Is he going to be exonerated?' Carrie asked. She felt all fluttery inside. Oh, to have Pa's good name restored! He deserved it. It turned out he deserved it. He was a good man after all. He was dear, lovely Pa after all.

'I'm afraid not,' said Adam. 'We're just at the beginning of understanding this. There are still many people who don't believe in it, who regard shell shock – mind-horror – as lack of moral fibre. It will be many years before there is true acceptance.'

'Pa was a good man,' said Evadne. 'We've always known that.'

'A good man who was overwhelmed by bad things,' said Ted; and Evadne gave him a sad, grateful smile.

'I'd like to be alone, please,' said Mam, her voice thick with unspent tears. 'Please, just go,' she added as Carrie and Evadne turned to her. 'I've lived with fear and shame for so long, ever since I first found out. Now, I need time to think about what Adam has said.' She reached out a hand to him. 'Thank you from the bottom of my heart.'

He let her squeeze his hand. 'I hope I did the

right thing.'

'Oh, yes.' Her voice wobbled. 'More than I can say.'

'You young ones go for a walk,' said Mr Weston. 'I'll stay behind, if I may, and sit quietly with you, Mrs Jenkins. Your daughters will worry if they have to leave you alone. Why don't you all walk down to the memorial on Chorlton Green?'

'Yes,' said Carrie. 'That's the right thing to do.'

Chapter Fifty-Two

'This won't be here much longer now that the official memorial is being built,' said Carrie, as the four of them stood quietly in front of the display on the Green. The wind had dropped, leaving a bright day with a snap in the air that spoke of spring. How much longer would Pa have his vase? And once it was gone, there would be nothing to remember him by.

'A good man overwhelmed by bad things,' said Evadne. 'It makes it harder, in a way.'

'Harder?' Adam turned to look at her.

'I know. You'd think it would be easier. I used to try to imagine him being so frightened that he ran away. I tried to imagine how bad it would have to be before you would abandon your comrades and run the other way to save your own skin, while everyone else was doing their duty and serving their country. I wasn't trying to make excuses for him. I just wanted to understand how this decent

497

man, this thoroughly decent man, who brought me up and thought the world of me, could possibly have been such a coward. And at the same time, I couldn't bear to understand, because who could bear to understand something as disgraceful and disgusting as that?'

'Then shouldn't knowing what we know now make it easier?' asked Carrie.

'At least if he was a coward he would have made his own decision. Not that I want him to be a coward, but he would have made a choice and suffered the consequences. But he wasn't a coward. He was afflicted by this mind-horror. He was a good man. He didn't deserve to be overwhelmed like that. I hate to think of his losing control.'

'He had no power over what he did,' said Ted, 'but he still suffered the consequences.'

'That's another thing,' said Carrie. 'I've always found it hard to think of him leaving us to face a lifetime of shame. But he didn't. If I've understood correctly, he couldn't help it.'

'He didn't let you down,' said Adam, 'and he didn't let his country down, but unfortunately, it will be many years before that is widely accepted. You'll have to come to terms with that.'

'How many years?' She could manage a few, if she had to. Say, five. Ten, at a push.

'Many years, Carrie. You need to understand that. Possibly not in our lifetimes.'

'You're kidding!'

'No. I'm sorry.'

Unbelievable. Or maybe not.

'Come back to the cottage,' said Ted.

'In a minute,' said Carrie. 'I'd like to go and see Joey.'

'Would you like us to come too?' Evadne offered.

'Not today. You go on ahead.'

She watched Evadne and Ted walk away, arm in arm, Evadne tall and slender, Ted big and broad-shouldered. They made a fine couple. Carrie was so proud of her sister. She had learnt some hard lessons and grown in character. The old snooty Evadne was long gone, replaced by a considerate, selfless person with bags of common sense and a warm heart.

She would make a stunning bride, come June. Carrie was going to be her matron of honour. She felt a little shiver of pleasure every time she pictured it. Not a bridesmaid, but the matron of honour. She would herself have been married for two whole months by then. Two wonderful months. Evadne had invited Violet Wicks to be her bridesmaid. The three of them had become friendly after Evadne had got Violet's widowed sister the post of housekeeper to Major Baxter.

Carrie had already given Evadne her wedding present – a half-share in Armstrong's.

'I won't take no for an answer. We'll be working wives together, and when the children come along, we'll share looking after them.'

'If we can prise them away from their proud grandmother,' said Evadne, and then had to brush away a tear. 'Oh, Carrie, thank you a thousand times. To let me share the business is so generous of you. I shan't let you down.'

'I know.' And she did know. She and Evadne were dear friends as well as sisters and they

499

worked well together. Carrie's heart lifted whenever she pictured Armstrong's future.

'There was a time when I couldn't have said this, when I couldn't have even imagined it,' she told Adam, 'but I have things to look forward to and I can think about them without feeling guilty, without feeling I don't deserve them.'

'Personally, I'm looking forward to April, Mrs Adam Armstrong-to-be.'

Carrie leant closer to him. It felt important to marry in the spring. It was part of her new beginning. For the bouquets, she had chosen roses of buttercup yellow, interspersed with dainty white spring snowflakes, which closely resembled the snowdrops that represented the special time of year of Joey's short life.

Her left hand was tucked through Adam's right arm. Now he took her hand with his left hand so he could slide his arm around her and draw her to his side. The deserter's daughter in a public embrace – scandalous! She leant into him. This was where she belonged.

'I must find another best man now you've filched Ted,' said Adam.

'My need is greater. You've got any number of colleagues you can ask, but Ted is the only one I want as father of the bride.'

'I was thinking of asking Weston. He's known me man and boy, as they say.'

Pleasure warmed her. 'That would be perfect.'

'Especially if he plucks up the courage to make advances to the mother of the bride.'

'If he what?'

'Disgraceful, isn't it? Everyone knows the best

man is meant to set his sights on the bridesmaid, but, alas, she's got herself firmly attached to the father of the bride, so what's a fellow to do?'

Carrie was still boggling. 'Mr Weston – and Mam?'

'Why not? I'd say they both deserve some comfort. Why do you think he stopped bringing you Cadbury's and brought Fry's instead? It's your mother's favourite.'

'Well,' said Carrie, half-laughing, 'I know I said there were things to look forward to, but honestly...'

'You don't mind, do you?'

She wasn't sure what to think – no, wait, yes, she was. Mr Weston was a darling of a man, gentle and honest. After everything Mam had suffered, not just at Ralph's hands, but going right back to the fateful day she had received the damning letter about Pa, she deserved to find a safe harbour.

'Penny for them,' Adam offered.

'I was thinking wouldn't it be perfect if Mam and Mr Weston... I'm sure Evadne will think so, too.' Carrie laughed. Not an uncertain half-laugh, but a proper laugh, spilling over with warmth. 'Imagine – we might have three weddings this year.'

'You don't waste any time, do you? One thing at a time – one wedding at a time, my girl. Roll on, April the 15th, is what I say.' He removed his arm from her waist and looped her hand back into the safety of his elbow. 'Shall we go and see Joey now?'

They crossed the road, passing under the old lychgate. Carrie could come here these days without feeling that guilt was dragging her inexorably to Joey's grave. Her visits to him were poignant and tender, filled with sorrow and longing; but her terrible burden had eased. The guilt was still there and perhaps it always would be, but she was no longer tormented by it every waking moment. She now knew in her head that she wasn't to blame for Joey's death. And maybe one day her heart would accept it too.

She and Adam walked together down the flag-stoned path to Joey's grave. How many times had she stood here, knelt here, gazing at this stone, filled by an overwhelming emptiness because she needed her child, not a piece of York stone?

'It's a comfort to me that you knew him,' she said. 'It makes him a part of us, not just a part of me. That's important. And I want you to know that I do realise this is not just Joey's grave. I was never able to let that sink in until recently, but I'm going to stop hogging the grave to myself and thinking of it as his alone. Your dad's in here, and three more ancestors. I'll bring flowers for your dad as well as Joey.'

'He would have loved being a grandad.'

'So would Pa.'

'There is something we could do for your father,' said Adam. 'Joey was named after one grandfather, so we could name our first son after his other grandfather.'

'Do you mean that?' She pictured it, allowing the sweetness of the idea to fill her. But then she shook her head. 'People always ask where a name comes from and he'd never be able to say. Even though we know about the mind-horror, and we'll teach our children about it, no one else is going to know, not for years and years.'

'It's good to hear you talking about having children.'

She turned to him. 'I'm ready for my second child and it will be a child in its own right, not a replacement for Joey, but a brother or sister for him.' Her voice dropped to a hoarse whisper, but she ploughed on. 'I'm going to be so scared of something bad happening. I may well never sleep again for the rest of my life, but that's a price I'm willing to pay for the joy and privilege of being a mother.' She seized Adam's hand and raised it to her face, crushing the leather glove against her cheek. 'And I want you there when our child is born. Not delivering it like you delivered Joey, but at my side, holding my hand, just being there with me to welcome our child into the world.'

'Carrie, my dear love, my one and only love.'

She moved into his arms, there in the bright March sunshine, in an old disused graveyard, where her child lay and a part of her heart with him. It was time to move on now, to take her sadness with her and move into a hopeful future.

She stood on tiptoe and reached her arms round Adam's neck. She wasn't nearly tall enough, but he bent his head, probably expecting a kiss. She pushed her cheek against his so she could speak straight into his ear to be sure he heard every word. Her voice caught, thick with tears, but she knew he had heard because of what he said back to her.

'I love you, Carrie, and I will cherish you and our children for the rest of my days. We'll have a good life, my love. Whatever happens, we'll face it together.'

Carrie subsided onto her heels. She moved beside him and slid her arm through his.

'Let's go to Brookburn,' she said. 'Evadne will be waiting.'

Side by side, close together, they walked up the path.

Author's Note

With a few exceptions, notably Wilton Lane and Brookburn House, the places, roads and landmarks in *The Deserter's Daughter* are real, although local historians will see that, for the purposes of the story, I have opened Chorlton Park a few years early.

I should like to thank Mr William Lees-Jones of J. W. Lees & Co (Brewers) Ltd for his kind permission to use the name of the Lloyds.

The publishers hope that this book has given you enjoyable reading. Large Print Books are especially designed to be as easy to see and hold as possible. If you wish a complete list of our books please ask at your local library or write directly to:

Magna Large Print Books
Magna House, Long Preston,
Skipton, North Yorkshire.
BD23 4ND

This Large Print Book for the partially sighted, who cannot read normal print, is published under the auspices of

THE ULVERSCROFT FOUNDATION

THE ULVERSCROFT FOUNDATION

... we hope that you have enjoyed this Large Print Book. Please think for a moment about those people who have worse eyesight problems than you ... and are unable to even read or enjoy Large Print, without great difficulty.

You can help them by sending a donation, large or small to:

**The Ulverscroft Foundation,
1, The Green, Bradgate Road,
Anstey, Leicestershire, LE7 7FU,
England.**
or request a copy of our brochure for more details.

The Foundation will use all your help to assist those people who are handicapped by various sight problems and need special attention.

Thank you very much for your help.